THE WESTERN CAPTIVE AND OTHER INDIAN STORIES

broadview editions
series editor: Martin R. Boyne

E. Oakes Smith

Portrait of E. Oakes Smith. Frontispiece, Thomas Buchanan Read's *The Female Poets of America* (1849). Engraving by Joseph Ives Pease. From the collection of the Rochester Public Library, Local History & Genealogy Division.

THE WESTERN CAPTIVE AND OTHER INDIAN STORIES

Elizabeth Oakes Smith

edited by Caroline M. Woidat

broadview editions

Library and Archives Canada Cataloguing in Publication

Smith, Elizabeth Oakes Prince, 1806-1893
[Works. Selections]
      The western captive and other Indian stories / Elizabeth
Oakes Smith ; edited by Caroline M. Woidat.

(Broadview editions)
This edition recovers Elizabeth Oakes Smith's successful 1842 novel
      The Western Captive; or, The Times of Tecumseh with many of
      Oakes's Smith's other writings about Native Americans, including
      short stories, legends, autobiographical and biographical sketches.
      The primary texts are accompanied by selections from Oakes Smith's
      Woman and Her Needs and from her unpublished autobiography.
      Other captivity narratives, writings by Oakes Smith's colleagues Jane
      Johnston Schoolcraft and Henry Rowe Schoolcraft, and contemporary
      depictions of the Shawnee people are also included.
Includes bibliographical references.
ISBN 978-1-55481-120-5 (paperback)

      1. Indians in literature. 2. American literature. 3. American literature—
Women authors. I. Woidat, Caroline M., editor II. Title. III. Title: Times of
Tecumseh. IV. Series: Broadview editions

PS2859.S8A6 2015   813'.3   C2015-903807-3

Broadview Editions
The Broadview Editions series represents the ever-changing canon of literature by bringing together texts long regarded as classics with valuable lesser-known works.

Advisory editor for this volume: Michel W. Pharand

Broadview Press is an independent, international publishing house, incorporated in 1985.

We welcome comments and suggestions regarding any aspect of our publications—please feel free to contact us at the addresses below or at broadview@broadviewpress.com.

North America
PO Box 1243, Peterborough, Ontario K9J 7H5, Canada
555 Riverwalk Parkway, Tonawanda, NY 14150, USA
Tel: (705) 743-8990; Fax: (705) 743-8353
email: customerservice@broadviewpress.com

UK, Europe, Central Asia, Middle East, Africa, India, and Southeast Asia
Eurospan Group, 3 Henrietta St., London WC2E 8LU, United Kingdom
Tel: 44 (0) 1767 604972; Fax: 44 (0) 1767 601640
email: eurospan@turpin-distribution.com

Australia and New Zealand
Footprint Books
1/6a Prosperity Parade, Warriewood, NSW 2102, Australia
Tel: (61) 1300 260 090; Fax: (61) 02 9997 3185
email: info@footprint.com.au

www.broadviewpress.com

Broadview Press acknowledges the financial support of the Government of Canada through the Canada Book Fund for our publishing activities.

PRINTED IN CANADA

Contents

Acknowledgements

My work is indebted to a galaxy of scholars and editors dedicated to the recovery and study of American women writers. For their generous support, encouragement, and feedback, I would especially like to thank Ken Cooper, Rob Doggett, Teresa Goddu, Bill Harrison, Florence Howe, Maria Lima, Beth McCoy, Alice Rutkowski, Cecelia Tichi, and the editors at *Legacy* and Broadview. I am also grateful to students at SUNY Geneseo: Shannon Dennehy for her invaluable contributions to this project, members of my Plotting Women class for their incisive responses to *The Western Captive*, and Monica Wendel for assisting with the text of the novel.

Work on the edition first began with the support of New York State and United University Professions through their Drescher Leave Program, and a Roemer Summer Faculty Fellowship from the Geneseo Foundation provided time and travel necessary for its completion. At the New York Public Library, Philip C. Heslip was exceptionally helpful as I worked with the Elizabeth Oakes Prince Smith papers in the Manuscript and Archives Division, a collection essential to the preparation of this edition. My research was also aided by the staff at the University of Rochester's Rush Rhees Library, the staff at Geneseo's Milne Library, and the administrative expertise of Michele Feeley and Anne Baldwin.

Finally, I want to express my strong and enduring gratitude to my family—my husband, son, daughter, parents, and siblings—for the most fundamental sustenance of all.

Introduction

Elizabeth Oakes Smith's historical novel *The Western Captive;
or, The Times of Tecumseh* (1842) places the fictional Margaret
Durand, a transculturated white captive, at the side of the great
Shawnee leader Tecumseh (1768–1813) and in the midst of conflicts leading to the War of 1812. Tecumseh's rebellion occupied
America's cultural imagination as writers of Oakes Smith's era
strove to define their nation's identity and values, and her novel
participates in the historiography and myth-making surrounding a
figure who has inspired many works of literature and art. In con-
templating Tecumseh's legacy, Oakes Smith begins *The Western
Captive* with an argument that the inability to achieve his grand
vision of protecting Indian lands against white encroachment does
not diminish the importance of his heroic endeavors. She situates
the Shawnee leader among "patriots [who] have struggled and
fallen," who "were stricken in the race, that they might become
heralds and guide-marks for others. Such was the fate of Tecumseh—doomed, not to realize the high designs he had conceived,
but to add one more to the list of those who have labored for the
enfranchisement of a people, and to prove that, in every grade of
society, the yearnings of the heart are still for freedom" (p. 47).[1]
Oakes Smith herself was dedicated to the cause of women's rights
together with contemporary writers and activists including Margaret Fuller (1810–50), Elizabeth Cady Stanton (1815–1902), and
Susan B. Anthony (1820–1906). Published several years before
the Seneca Falls Convention in 1848 would advance the women's
rights movement in the United States, Oakes Smith's portrayal of
Tecumseh as a "herald" and "patriot" resonates today, when history shows that these early feminist activists would not live to see
woman suffrage achieved with the Nineteenth Amendment to the
US Constitution in 1920 and many other milestones in civil rights.
Tecumseh's fight to empower Native Americans is indeed but one
chapter in a continuing tradition of Indian resistance, activism,
and self-determination stretching from the colonial era into the

---

1   All quotations from the texts included in this volume will be cited by
    page number only.

present. In the aftermath of the Indian Removal Act signed into law by Andrew Jackson in 1830 and the forced relocation in 1838–39 known as "The Trail of Tears," Oakes Smith's reconstruction of American history in *The Western Captive* questions the moral imperatives of westward expansion. Her novel develops parallels between Tecumseh's efforts to defend individual liberty through collective action, an Anglo-American tradition of religious dissent and political revolution, and the development of feminist thought and activism. The linked fates of Tecumseh and Margaret in *The Western Captive* invite readers to rethink histories of American nation-building and social constructions of freedom, gender, race, moral duty, and heroism.

This volume contributes to the ongoing recovery of Oakes Smith's work and, more specifically, to her legacy as an author who wrote extensively about the land and indigenous peoples of North America throughout a long and prolific career. With the success of *The Western Captive*, a paperback that sold over 2,500 copies within four days, Oakes Smith would enjoy decades of critical acclaim before seeing her reputation wane in later years, when she would clip and save Susan E. Dickinson's 1885 article "Women Writers. A Chapter on Their Ephemeral Reputations. Hopes and Ambitions That Have Faded in Sad Disappointment." Dickinson somewhat wistfully imagines how few readers of her day recognize Oakes Smith's name despite a career spanning five decades and former renown as "one of America's most popular writers for a generation," an author associated with such writers as "Poe, Hawthorne, Bryant, Longfellow, Whittier, Irving, Willis, Thoreau, Frances Osgood, Margaret Fuller, and many another brilliant man and woman whose names will be suggested by theirs." Oakes Smith was indeed prolific, widely known, and well-connected: a frequent contributor to journals including *The Ladies' Companion*, *Godey's Lady's Book*, *The Southern Literary Messenger*, and *Graham's Magazine*, she also gave lectures on the lyceum circuit and published novels, short fiction, poetry, sketches, gift books, children's literature, and essays on women's issues. From this vast and varied canon of work dating from the 1830s to the 1880s, Oakes Smith's literary reputation was established largely by her long narrative poem "The Sinless Child," which received wide critical acclaim upon its publication in 1842, and by the series of essays she wrote on the topic of women's rights for Horace Greeley's *New York Tribune* between 1850 and 1851, collected in *Woman and Her Needs* (1851). While Dickinson observes shifts in the literary canon at the end of the nineteenth century, in recent decades Oakes Smith's importance as a writer, feminist, and reformer has become the subject of renewed critical attention.

Oakes Smith's *The Western Captive* and various other writings on Indians establish her place in literary history as a contemporary of novelists James Fenimore Cooper (1789–1851), Lydia Maria Child (1802–80), Catharine Maria Sedgwick (1789–1867), and Ann S. Stephens (1810–86), poets Lydia Huntley Sigourney (1791–1865) and Henry Wadsworth Longfellow (1807–82), and other nineteenth-century American writers who turned to Native American subject matter. Like her Ojibwe acquaintance Jane Johnston Schoolcraft (1800–42)—also named Bamewawagezhikaquay, Woman of the Sound the Stars Make Rushing Through the Sky— Oakes Smith published versions of Native American stories and songs. Henry Rowe Schoolcraft (1793–1864), Jane's husband and a prominent ethnologist of his day, included Oakes Smith's renditions of Indian legend and lullaby in *Oneóta, or Characteristics of the Red Race of America* (1845).[1] Oakes Smith's literary influence has been attributed to such writers as Longfellow, author of the epic poem *The Song of Hiawatha* (1855),[2] and her writing about the outdoors went hand in hand with a reputation for being "An Adventurous Lady" and, according to the *Bangor Courier*, the first white woman to summit two different mountains during her excursions into the

---

1 Published in different versions as *The Indian in His Wigwam, or Characteristics of the Red Race of America* (1848) and *The American Indians, Their History, Condition, and Prospects* (1851).

2 Wyman observes that Oakes Smith's characterization of Iagou, the storyteller, in *The Salamander* (1848) is echoed in Longfellow's *The Song of Hiawatha* (*Two Pioneers* 182–83). Although he does not write in reference to Indian subject matter, in a review for *The Broadway Journal*, Edgar Allan Poe accuses Longfellow of "bold" plagiarism, quoting stanzas from Oakes Smith's "The Water" and then comparing them to Longfellow's "Rain in Summer" (103). Longfellow cites Henry R. Schoolcraft's writings as 'the primary source' for *The Song of Hiawatha* in his notes to the poem (299–300), and Schoolcraft himself relied upon his wife as a key source (see p. 30).

woods of Maine.[1] In addition to the texts collected in this edition, Oakes Smith published literature about Native Americans even more widely, as in "Hokomok: A Legend of Maine" (1843), *Stories for Good Children* (1847), *The Salamander: A Legend for Christmas* (1848), her Beadle and Adams dime novels *Bald Eagle: or, The Last of the Ramapaughs* (1867) and *The Sagamore of Saco* (1868), and "The Crusade of the Bell" (1875). Echoing Henry Schoolcraft's praise of Oakes Smith, editor and critic Rufus W. Griswold's introduction to *The Prose Writers of America* (1847) situates her in the literary canon as "a woman of a most original and poetical mind, who has succeeded, perhaps better than any other person, in appreciating and developing the fitness of aboriginal tradition and mythology for the purposes of romantic fiction" (34). The "purposes" of white writers' romantic portrayals of Native Americans to which Griswold alludes are varied and complex, however, as are the tangled webs of source materials and collaboration among authors and editors—such as Oakes Smith and the Schoolcrafts—in the production of such texts. Beyond providing new contexts for understanding Oakes Smith's ideas and work, her writing about Indians also offers an opportunity to critically examine the genre of nineteenth-century "Indian" literature itself.

Reading *The Western Captive* together with diverse related texts—such as the short fiction, autobiography, history, reform literature, and ethnography included in this volume—exposes the blurry lines between genres in these representations of Native Americans and also reveals the lively cultural interchange of voices and perspectives in which Oakes Smith played an active part. In their effort to create a national literature distinct from English tradition, nineteenth-century white American writers often turned to colonial conflicts with Native Americans and the wilderness for subject matter and to historical records for their source material. While Oakes Smith likewise writes from a perspective shaped by history books and representations of Indians in popular culture, first-hand experiences including her up-bringing in Maine and her association with the Schoolcrafts contributed to the development of a nuanced understanding of Indian–white

---

1 "An Adventurous Lady" is the title of a clipping in Oakes Smith's scrapbook that reprints an item from the *Bangor Courier* without a source or date indicated. From the Elizabeth Oakes Collection, New York Public Library.

relations and the North American landscape. Although she did not take up the cause of Indian rights like activists such as Lydia Maria Child and Helen Hunt Jackson (1830–85), Oakes Smith's critical examination of American history links her to other writers seeking social transformation. With a consciousness of her own hybrid identity and the complicated interplay between French, English, and Indian cultures along the US-Canada border, Oakes Smith explores the dynamic space of a "middle ground" or "contact zone"—terms deployed respectively by scholars Richard White and Mary Louise Pratt to reconceptualize Frederick Jackson Turner's idea of the frontier as a line between civilization and savagery. In *The Western Captive* and other writings about Indians, Oakes Smith frequently turns to the syncretism of the middle ground as a vantage point for looking critically at rigid social, political, and religious hierarchies.

Autobiographical Connections: A Puritan Maiden and "Young Indian"

Oakes Smith's approach to American Indian subject matter draws upon her imaginative engagement with family ancestors, her native state of Maine, and her experiences with religion and marriage—all relationships fraught with tensions that cultivated her moral and political consciousness. Elizabeth Oakes Prince Smith was born on 12 August 1806, to David Prince and Sophia Blanchard Prince in what was then North Yarmouth, now Cumberland, Maine. Oakes Smith's autobiographical writings provide important contexts for reading her work, and the most extensive is her 600-page manuscript *A Human Life: Being the Autobiography of Elizabeth Oakes Smith* (c. 1885), held in the Manuscripts and Archives Division of the New York Public Library. A complete text of *A Human Life* has not been published, so readers have often turned to the expurgated version by Mary Alice Wyman, *Selections from the Autobiography of Elizabeth Oakes Smith* (1924),[1]

---

1   Wyman draws from published excerpts of the autobiography and blends in other autobiographical material, piecing together a text that condenses, rearranges, and alters Oakes Smith's own words and narrative forms. Because it is important to distinguish Wyman's heavy hand in crafting the narrative itself, *Selections from the Autobiography of Elizabeth Oakes Smith* appears in the bibliography under her name rather than Oakes Smith's.

which is less reliable than the unabridged text in Leigh Kirkland's unpublished dissertation, "'A Human Life: Being the Autobiography of Elizabeth Oakes Smith': A Critical Edition and Introduction" (1994). My edition relies upon the original manuscript, in which Oakes Smith pieces together a narrative of her life by inserting (and often editing) print clippings from previously published pieces into her handwritten pages, creating a series of sketches and reflections blending together her older and younger selves, her public and private personas. With this cutting and pasting technique, the autobiography draws from myriad sources, recycling and recombining oral and written stories— a composition process that bears some intriguing similarities to the form of Henry Schoolcraft's "miscellany," the term he uses to describe *Oneóta*, with its subtitle *"From Original Notes and Manuscripts."* Oakes Smith's writing is featured in Schoolcraft's miscellany, and her own autobiography resembles its structure in the way that it collects different materials: reminiscences of childhood, sketches of famous people, poems, letters, etc. The autobiography also reveals thematic connections between Oakes Smith's writings about Indians and her personal struggles, particularly in their common concern with the freedom and sacrifices of individual women who are caught in the throes of religious and political conflicts.

Oakes Smith's *A Human Life* draws a portrait of a divided self that emerges from a sense of bondage, creating strong parallels between her life story and her Indian captivity narratives. In writing about her childhood, Oakes Smith positions herself as a descendent of English Puritans on her father's side and French Huguenots on her mother's, a split lineage that immersed her from a very young age in Calvinist beliefs, traditions of religious dissent and persecution, and an awareness of larger historical events. She sees herself as thoroughly Puritan in her sense of duty and higher obligations, but her embrace of the spirit of dissent paradoxically enables her to reject the Calvinist principles inherited from her ancestors. Oakes Smith tells how as a young child she voiced objections to the doctrine of predestination with its concept of a God who separates the Elect from those who will burn in hell, shocking her classmates and elders, while in secret she tested her own spiritual endurance by self-inflicting physical pains. Influenced by a grandfather who she believed "might yet be burned at the stake" for his questioning of religious dogma and by literature such as John Fox's

Book of Martyrs,[1] Oakes Smith writes: "I had read enough of history to see that there had been tyrants in the world, but I saw that the great struggles of nations were different from the persecution of individuals, and then I felt that I was just in the condition to do as those martyrs did. I must hold on to what I believed, or die as they did, or, what was worse, give up my truth" (see Appendix A1, pp. 258–59).[2] This portrait of her young self compares to Oakes Smith's characterization of protagonists who confront martyrdom, notably Tecumseh and Margaret in *The Western Captive*, who both dedicate themselves to higher causes and personal visions while negotiating the complicated dynamics of the War of 1812, an event that also marked her childhood. Oakes Smith's stories frequently examine the sacrifices women make for others—as lovers, mothers, and wives, but also as victims of social codes based upon misguided religious and political beliefs. In "Indian Traits" (1840) and "Beloved of the Evening Star" (1847), the female protagonists' lives are threatened by warring nations and competing moral agendas, while Oakes Smith also associates martyrdom with the daily, common experiences of love, marriage, and motherhood that women share. She thus draws parallels between Indian and white societies rather than creating a binary distinction between the two, challenging the conceptual dichotomies based upon race ("civilization" vs. "savagery") or gender ("male" vs. "female" spheres) as narrow-minded and detrimental to both individual liberty and social progress.

In her poems and autobiography, Oakes Smith gives detailed attention to the topic of "maidenhood" and celebrates the time before marriage as a phase in which a young woman can consecrate herself to personal reflection, spiritual growth, and moral goodness—a transcendental state that is then brutally sacrificed at the altar with her wedding vows. The younger self Oakes Smith portrays in her autobiography resembles the character of Eva in her famous poem "The Sinless Child," given the connections to the natural world and

---

1   Commonly used spelling and title for editions of John Foxe's *Actes and Monuments of these Latter and Perillous Days, Touching Matters of the Church* ..., first published in English in 1563.
2   References to the excerpts from *A Human Life* included in Appendix A in this volume will be indicated by page number within parentheses. Portions of *A Human Life* not included in this volume will be cited by the abbreviation *HL* and page number within parentheses, referring to the manuscript edition of that work listed in the Select Bibliography.

ethereal spirituality that they both possess,[1] traits that are likewise shared by many of the heroines in her Indian stories. Her portraits of the besieged maiden compare to other narratives of forced assimilation: when Niskagah is taken into captivity by a warring tribe in "Indian Traits," the narrator reflects that "the separation from her kindred was little different from what it would probably have been, had this been her bridal excursion" (p. 207). Writing of her own marriage, at age 16 in 1823, to Seba Smith (1792–1868), Oakes Smith describes removal from her home and an assault upon her identity—a recurring theme not only in captivity narratives, but also in later accounts of Indian childhood and boarding schools like Zitkala-Sa's.[2] Learning "like a perfect little drudge" to perform the incessant household duties demanded of a wife, Oakes Smith writes, "transformed myself to an utterly different creature from what had been native to me" (see Appendix A1, p. 262). She describes her transition to married life as a disruptive, painful process rather than a natural course, an imposed change leaving her no choice but to adapt. Oakes Smith laments this as the loss of a realm she once inhabited: "Oh! the beautiful world that at once faded from my view! The world that seemed utterly destroyed—" (p. 262). In contrast to the confines of domesticity, she idealizes the freedom she experienced after suffering a mental breakdown at age six and temporarily losing the ability to read. Describing her convalescence, Oakes Smith writes that she "was allowed to be 'as wild as a young Indian,' as they phrased it," enjoying an existence and state of mind "in perfect accord with Nature" (p. 256). Her Indian fiction likewise explores women's relationships to nature, an aspect of American women's lives she foregrounds rather than subverting to marriage plots. As Annette Kolodny establishes in *The Land Before Her: Fantasy and Experience of the American Frontiers, 1630–1860* (1984), a tradition of women's literature about the American landscape reveals responses diverging from the masculinist approach to conquering wilderness, including Oakes Smith's contemporary Margaret Fuller (1810–50), who documented travels including a visit among Indians at Mackinaw Island in *Summer on the Lakes, in 1843* (1844).

---

1   "Eva" in fact became Oakes Smith's nickname among some friends.
2   Zitkala-Sa's "Impressions of an Indian Childhood" and "The School Days of an Indian Girl" first appeared in the *Atlantic Monthly* in 1900 and were republished in *American Indian Stories* (1921).

More specifically, Oakes Smith's stories of individuals who attain greater self-knowledge and moral consciousness through their experiences of nature connect her to American Romanticism and the Transcendentalist writers with whom she was acquainted, including Fuller, Ralph Waldo Emerson (1803–82), and Henry David Thoreau (1817–62). The struggles of fictional characters who follow their own visions and higher callings rather than conforming to the dictates of society—like Tecumseh and Margaret in *The Western Captive*—recall Oakes Smith's accounts of the spiritual and existential questioning she began to undertake even as a child, in particular during the time when she was compared to a "young Indian." In the section of her autobiography titled "Perfect Harmony with Nature," she explains the chain of reasoning that allows her to move from detailed observation of a snake's physical characteristics to reflection about the nature of God, with the following conclusion: "This sympathy with nature has been a marked feature of my life, and this, with my tendency at this early age to solitary speculations, was a natural sequence to the grave, earnest, secluded habits of my Pilgrim ancestors" (see Appendix A1, p. 257). Oakes Smith does not see herself as merely playing Indian, but rather adapting elements of Puritan tradition to her native surroundings, the same land that her ancestors purchased from Indians. The American landscape for her is a palimpsest with layers of American Indian and European-American stories: Oakes Smith blends Indian legend with personal adventure in "Kinneho" (1851), for example, and with Maine's colonial history in "The Sagamore of Saco" (1848) and "The Crusade of the Bell" (1875).

While portraying life in the woods *as* "Indian," Oakes Smith's fiction and autobiography also invoke a pastoral tradition dating to ancient Greece with her visions of the harmonious existence rural life offers. In *A Human Life*, she idealizes her parents' first "love home" as "a little cottage set like a pearl in emerald," at least a mile away from any neighbor in a "sequestered Arcadian spot, befitting of the times, but full of domestic happiness," and she longs for a similar life for her own family (*HL* 4–6). Oakes Smith was aware, however, that this dream of a peaceful life in an unspoiled wilderness was under threat: the deportation of the Acadians,[1] white en-

---

1   The French colony of Acadia included what are presently the Maritime provinces and eastern parts of Quebec and Maine. The Expulsion of the Acadians, also known as Le Grand Dérangement, took place during the French and Indian War, when the British forced Acadians into exile.

croachment upon Indian lands, and a volatile real estate market all loom large in her view of Canadian and American histories. Oakes Smith is appalled by the capitalists engaged in land speculation during the 1830s who bring about financial ruin for adventurers like her husband, and she urges him to try to preserve a homestead for their family by "squatting" upon it: "to leave all" and "go into the wilderness, build up a log cabin, and there live, educate, and bring up our four boys to manly toil and simple habits" (*HL* 362–63). She writes, "I was greatly in earnest in this, and as I look back I have not a doubt of the feasibility and excellence of the plan—It had an Arcadian beauty to me, and a sweetness of solitude that would ennoble me to study, which I so much desired" (*HL* 363). The whims of her husband's commercial ventures instead forced her family to move to Charleston, South Carolina, where first-hand observations of the South solidified her opposition to slavery, and then to relocate again to New York City after the cotton-cleaning machine in which Smith had invested proved too unwieldy and costly to be marketable. She is sensitive, then, to experiences of diaspora—that is, of populations dispersed from their original homelands—as a consequence of American settlement and expansion. Moreover, in contrast to Thoreau's self-imposed retreat to experiment with living as simply as possible in his cabin at Walden Pond, Oakes Smith shows at this juncture of her life the relative inaccessibility of such contemplative solitude and economic self-reliance to a married woman and mother of four surviving sons.[1]

The Path of a Reformer

This is not to say that Oakes Smith did not seek, argue for, and exemplify ideals of self-sufficiency and nonconformity through her writing, experiences in the woods, and progressive thought. Oakes Smith indeed entered a prolific period in her literary career following the move to New York in 1839, providing financial support for her family and establishing herself as a trail-blazer in the outdoors as well as on the lyceum circuit and in the publishing world. She hiked,

---

1   She gave birth to six sons, including two who did not survive childhood: Benjamin (1824), Rolvin (1825–32), Appleton (1828–87), Sidney (1830–69), Alvin (1832–1902), and Edward (1834–65). Oakes Smith had her sons' last names changed legally to Oaksmith.

camped, and climbed mountains in Maine, earning a reputation as the first white woman to reach the summit of Mount Katahdin in 1849 (three years after Thoreau made the ascent) and the top of Mount Kineo. "Heaven save the mark," she wrote in 1851 of the latter achievement, "The chances for fame are precarious, you know. Women who write now are not a few slatternly, odd, withered-looking bugbears; they make a little array of nice, dashing, elegant feminines, who are capable of anything that arrests their attention" ("Kinneho" p. 241). She became the first woman to lecture at the Concord Lyceum, notable for speakers such as Emerson and Thoreau, when she addressed the topic of "Womanhood" on 31 December 1851. Traveling widely on speaking tours across New England and cities farther west including Buffalo, Chicago, and St. Louis, Oakes Smith also regularly attended or otherwise participated in annual National Women's Rights Conventions beginning in 1850, the same year that she launched her series of essays for the *New York Tribune* entitled *Woman and Her Needs*. In an 1852 letter, Elizabeth Cady Stanton comments upon the difficulties Oakes Smith faced as an early advocate for feminist issues: "Mrs E.O.S. has yet to learn the great lesson of the true reform—to stand alone patiently & cheerfully & endure with an undisturbed spirit the jibes & jeers of the gaping crowd—'Let the weal & the woe of Humanity be everything to us, but their praise & their blame of no account.' The noble soul is not puffed up with praise or cast down with ridicule. But Dear E.O.S. will learn it all step by step—as prop after prop is swept away one learns self reliance."[1] Oakes Smith's ascension to the women's rights platform places her among the other historical figures who captured her own imagination for their active dedication to the cause of human rights despite the personal costs and risks—a type of individual she recognized across cultural divisions with her portrayals of characters like Tecumseh and Margaret in *The Western Captive*, and the Pawnee Chief in "Indian Traits."

As a reformer, Oakes Smith insists upon the importance of individual conscience and vision—exemplified in her writing by proph-

---

1   Stanton to Pauline Wright Davis, Seneca Falls, 6 December 1852 (*Selected Papers* I:214–16). The quotation is a motto that Stanton attributes to Hugues-Félicité Robert de Lamennais (1782–1854), a liberal French religious and political writer, and embraces for the women's rights movement (*History of Woman Suffrage* 2:324).

ets, martyrs, and seers—as both a means to social change and a main argument for women's rights. *Woman and Her Needs* locates a sense of higher duty at the center of human progress: "From the moment that an individual or a class of individuals, in any community, have become conscious of a series of grievances demanding redress, from that moment they are morally bound to make that commitment vital in action, and to do what in them lies to correct abuse" (see Appendix A2, p. 266). She details nineteenth-century women's particular needs but also links their cause to a larger history of human progress, making this declaration at a time when the Fugitive Slave Act of 1850 was intensifying the nation's conflict over slavery and the US was in the second interbellum of the Seminole Wars, engaged in ongoing clashes over Indian removal and land rights. Oakes Smith recognizes that each person possesses distinct traits and abilities, arguing that these should determine a woman's sphere rather than her gender—a principle that likewise opposes discrimination based upon race or class, informing her anti-slavery stance and advocacy of labor reform, as in *The Newsboy* (1854). If men are not held to one standard but can pursue various occupations including cooking and sewing, Oakes Smith argues, women should be treated as similarly diverse in their capabilities and vocations: "Our right to individuality is what I would most assert. Men seem resolved to have but one type in our sex" (p. 276). Oakes Smith's popular statement of this idea—featured in many collections of famous quotations—appears in her novel *Bertha and Lily: Or, the Parsonage of Beech Glen* (1854): "*The measure of capacity is the measure of sphere to either man or woman*" (83). Given the novel's arguments for a number of women's issues in its story of a fallen woman who becomes a religious leader, it is not surprising that Susan B. Anthony and other reformers greeted its publication enthusiastically. The complex character of Bertha, whose morals and ideas cause her to be viewed variously as a heretic and an angel, creates an argument for more openness to women's perspectives—to their understanding of both harsh material realities and a vast spiritual realm. Oakes Smith herself served in 1877 as pastor of the liberal, anti-sectarian Independent Church in Canastota, New York, and her autobiographical *Shadow Land; or, The Seer* (1852) draws upon her dreams and mystical experiences to lay claim to the importance of the spirit world, a belief central to the Spiritualist movement, which attracted abolitionists and suffragists and had many women leaders, mediums, and trance lecturers. Throughout her canon of literature, Oakes Smith critically examines patriarchal church dogma while presenting alternative forms of spirituality for readers to consider, and her writings about Indians fit this pattern of embracing other worldviews.

Oakes Smith enacted the principles articulated in *Woman and Her Needs* by extending the range of her literary endeavors and sphere of influence while asserting what she calls "womanmind"[1] as a powerful force that is not inferior to "masculine" thinking and writing. The development of Oakes Smith's public persona and authority is reflected in her literary signatures, which become increasingly assertive of an independent identity and political voice separate from her husband's. Whereas she began publishing anonymously in Seba Smith's Portland weekly *The Eastern Argus* and other periodicals, often over the signature "E.," her signature evolved to "Mrs. Seba Smith," used for her first two books *Riches Without Wings* (1838) and *The Western Captive,* and finally to the distinct name "Elizabeth Oakes Smith," as her name appears in *The Sinless Child, and Other Poems.* During the 1840s and 1850s she wrote under both her own name and a pseudonym, a strategy that critic Eliza Richards interprets as follows: "After *The Sinless Child* galvanized the author's feminine credentials, Oakes Smith began experimenting with masculine conventions of authorship under the name Ernest Helfenstein. [...] By writing as a man, Oakes Smith demonstrated the interdependence of gendered conventions rather than enforcing separate spheres of poetic discourse" (165). As a female public figure, her self-presentation was highly scrutinized: members of Oakes Smith's audiences at lectures commented upon her feminine appearance and speech at a time when women's rights activists were negatively stereotyped as mannish, aggressive, and quarrelsome, yet her dress was also allegedly criticized by women's rights activists at the Syracuse convention as too fashionable and revealing, causing them to deny Oakes Smith the presidency. A reviewer for *Sharpe's London Magazine* attacked her concern with dress reform in *Hints on Dress and Beauty* (1852) as "superficial" compared to Harriet Beecher Stowe's treatment of slavery in *Uncle Tom's Cabin* of the same year, overlooking Oakes Smith's support elsewhere for abolition in writings and lectures.[2]

---

1   See "Kinneho" (p. 241) and *Woman and Her Needs* (Appendix A2, p. 274).
2   "American Opinions," an unsigned review.

In "Performing Womanhood: the Lyceum Lectures of Elizabeth Oakes Smith," Angela G. Ray writes that Oakes Smith "found it necessary to navigate the dangerous waters of cultural expectations of gendered performance and to avoid female monstrosities while also generating reinterpretations of those same characters" (9). Richards's and Ray's studies of Oakes Smith's poetry and lectures open a critical conversation we might expand by likewise exploring the rhetorical strategies and hybrid forms of her prose writings about Indians, which draw from various traditions and genres that have been gendered as masculine or feminine: frontier literature, sentimental novels, ethnography, nature writing, historical fiction, and others.

Tecumseh, Tippecanoe, and Indian Rights

In addition to comparing *The Western Captive* to other novels of Indian captivity by women authors such as Child, Sedgwick, and Stephens, for example, we might read Oakes Smith's reconstruction of American history in the context of the many biographies of William Henry Harrison (1773–1841) to compare the political arguments created by their versions of the times of Tecumseh, as with the examples in this volume from James Hall's *A Memoir of the Public Services of William Henry Harrison, of Ohio* (1836) and Samuel Jones Burr's *The Life and Times of William Henry Harrison* (1840) (see Appendix C). Campaign biographies like these proliferated from the time of Harrison's first bid as a presidential candidate in 1836 until his election in 1840, and they portray Harrison as a national hero for his role in Indian negotiations and battles, including his dealings with Tecumseh and the Prophet, and especially for leading US forces to victory in the Battle of Tippecanoe in 1811. After winning the election with running mate John Tyler under the famous campaign song and slogan "Tippecanoe and Tyler Too," Harrison served the shortest presidency in American history, from 4 March 1841 until his death on 4 April 1841. His death generated additional literature in the form of biographies, sermons, eulogies, and orations, so there were numerous accounts of Harrison's encounters with Tecumseh circulating as Oakes Smith published *The Western Captive* in 1842. Authors borrowed freely from existing published accounts, which varied widely in their perspectives, and in particular concerning their interpretation of Tecumseh's character and speeches.

There are indeed so many histories and legends of Tecumseh that modern scholars like R. David Edmunds, Carl F. Klinck, and John Sugden have faced the challenge of sorting out fact from fiction while tracing the various interpretations of his legacy in different contexts and time periods. A military hero allied with British Canada against the Americans, a political leader who advocated a confederacy of Native nations, and a fierce opponent of treaties ceding Indian lands, Tecumseh earned a reputation in the US as a formidable obstacle to the nation's growth. At the same time, Tecumseh's efforts to build a Native confederacy that could resist US expansion resonated with Americans who, in the wake of his death in the Battle of the Thames in 1813 and subsequent decades of Indian removal, could romanticize his lost cause and the Indians themselves as a noble, vanishing race. For her part, Oakes Smith writes against this emergent nationalist narrative affirming the inevitability of Indian removal and Western settlement, exemplified by James Fenimore Cooper's series of novels, the *Leatherstocking Tales* (1827–41), in which the white hero advances westward as the last of the Mohicans disappear, and also by campaign biographies of Harrison celebrating his heroic defense of white settlers against dangerous but doomed Indians. Novelists and biographers alike relied upon secondary sources and fictional devices to tell their stories, and the selections from Hall and Burr in this edition illustrate the widespread dramatization of Harrison's meetings with the Shawnee using "translated" Indian speeches.

Hall rightly points out that the interactions between Tecumseh and Harrison at Vincennes "have been much misrepresented," but the claim that his own biography is "an accurate account" oversimplifies the line between fiction and fact (p. 300). Because he was not speaking in English, Tecumseh's words had to be translated and transcribed, and thus many free—and fictionalized—renderings of his speeches abounded. Henry Schoolcraft addresses the complexities of translation from the perspective of an ethnographer in this era, lamenting the culturally insensitive portrayals of Indians in American fiction (see Appendix D4)—a problem that we can see extends to renderings of Indian oral literature in other genres, including histories and biographies. Scholars continue to debate questions surrounding the authenticity of "texts" of Indian oratory and to explore ways that Native American discourse might be reinterpreted and better understood. In his study of the various, often inconsistent versions of Tecumseh's famous speech at Vincennes, Robert Yagelski argues that "Tecumseh's rhetoric represents a point of contact between two cultures in conflict and that his rhetoric both shaped and was shaped by that conflict" (65). Hall's biography, however, tends to distort the complexity of Tecumseh's rhetoric: he criticizes popular versions of Tecumseh's speeches as false ones arising from "a love for the romantic and the marvelous," but his own account of Tecumseh's conduct as distinguished "by violence, not by eloquence" is itself colored by the political aims of the campaign biography (p. 300). In contrast to Oakes Smith's noble portrait of Tecumseh, Hall's biography paints the Shawnee leader as an immoral and unreasonable opponent of treaties—a haughty, violent, impulsive leader "surrounded by a lawless band, composed of desperate renegadoes from various tribes, by the young and hot, the dissolute and dishonest" (p. 295). Hall was himself a fiction writer known for the sensational violence in his story "The Indian Hater" (1828), and his biography relies heavily upon secondary sources including Moses Dawson's 1824 biography of Harrison and Robert McAfee's 1816 history of the War of 1812. In his later campaign biography, Burr cites his own reliance upon Dawson, McAfee, and Hall, and he also acknowledges borrowing from Benjamin Bussey Thatcher's *Indian Biography* (1832) in recounting an old Shawnee chief's story of the "The Master of Life." This "retelling" of the Shawnee tradition resembles legends published by Schoolcraft and calls to mind Oakes Smith's "Machinito," but Burr uses the story's stated threat to white Americans—the "Long Knives"—to support Harrison as a candidate who has successfully defeated Indians characterized by both deep-rooted and "new fangled doctrine" at odds with US interests and progress (p. 300).

Oakes Smith similarly negotiated materials presenting inconsistent details and interpretations to create her own characterizations of Tecumseh and Harrison within a vast body of literature on the subject, documented by Kenneth R. Stevens in *William Henry Harrison: A Bibliography* (1998). It is significant that the historian Stevens locates *The Western Captive* in this literary tradition, which arguably demonstrates Oakes Smith's engagement in debates over the legacies of Tecumseh and Harrison, and her entrance into a genre of writing dominated by male writers and subjects. Not only does she assert her own voice as a historiographer, but Oakes Smith also places women characters at the center rather than the margins of US history and politics with stories that create space for the heroism of both women and Indians. The Indian captivity narrative serves this purpose well given that it is, according to critic Kathryn Zabelle Derounian-Stodola, "arguably the first American literary form dominated by women's experiences," one that some critics see functioning "as *the* archetype of American culture," and a genre that "is all about power and powerlessness" (xi–xii). While there are many variations of the captivity narrative to explore, this edition focuses upon white captives who encountered the Shawnee with selections from the popular narratives of Mary Jemison (1743–1833), John Dunn Hunter (c. 1797–1827), and John Tanner (c. 1780–c. 1846) (see Appendices B1–B3). Transculturated captives such as Jemison offer a model for characters such as Oakes Smith's Margaret, and they also complicate the neat binaries of white-Indian conflict that inform the type of nationalist discourse surrounding Harrison's campaign for presidency.

The Western Captive is not dominated by the exploits of American frontiersmen, soldiers, and patriarchs, but rather celebrates Tecumseh and Margaret as figures embodying an enduring spirit of resistance. In a popular legend that John Sugden suggests may have been inspired by *The Western Captive*,[1] Tecumseh once proposed marriage to Rebecca Galloway, a white woman who refused because she did not want to live among Indians (see Appendix B4). In Oakes Smith's more radical imagining of Tecumseh's relationship to a white woman, Margaret returns his love and embraces life apart from white society. Oakes Smith sets her novel in the Indiana Territory shortly before the Battle of Tippecanoe in 1811, a time when Tecumseh traveled among Indian nations in the Midwest and the Southeast while his brother Tenskwatawa (1775–1836), known as the Prophet, presided as the leader of a religious revival in the multitribal community of Prophetstown. Tecumseh and Margaret defy prevailing assumptions about white-Indian relations, as their spiritual union transcends the cultural clashes around them and points to syncretism—that is, a merging of different beliefs and traditions—as an alternative to nativism (advocated by the Prophet with his rejection of white society), conversion (idealized in representations of Pocahontas), and assimilation (later

---

1 See *Tecumseh, A Life*, p. 397.

enforced through the Indian boarding school system). Moreover, Margaret paradoxically possesses more power in captivity, where she is known as the Swaying Reed, and her ability to develop progressive ideas alongside Tecumseh works to challenge the notion that a government of white men can provide freedom for all Americans.

Of the many reform movements Oakes Smith famously supported, however, she is not known for dedicating herself to popular Native American causes or making political appeals on their behalf. Her writing about Indians took many forms, but in contrast to nineteenth-century reformers like Lydia Maria Child and Helen Hunt Jackson, Oakes Smith did not directly engage government officials to pursue changes in Indian policies. More than four decades after Child's historical novel *Hobomok* (1824) treated the subject of inter-marriage between Indians and whites, she responded to the Report of the Indian Peace Commission with the pamphlet *An Appeal for the Indians* (1868), a plea for action that contributed to reforms instituted the following year by Ulysses S. Grant. Appalled by ongoing systemic injustices, Helen Hunt Jackson documented the US government's wrongs against Native Americans in *A Century of Dishonor* (1881) and presented copies of the book to members of Congress. Jackson then wrote a report on the Mission Indians of California for the Department of the Interior before shifting course to follow Stowe's example by attempting to sway public opinion with a novel: her romance *Ramona* (1884) features a part-Indian heroine and a plot exposing the need for legislative reform. Oakes Smith's approach to reform seems to share the spirit of Transcendentalists who sought change through the individual enlightenment of American citizens, as she does not take up the institutional issues that absorbed Child, Jackson, and the Women's National Indian Association, an organization formed in 1879. Although Oakes Smith's name is among those petitioning the Senate to extend suffrage to women and in attendance at women's rights conventions, she writes in *Woman and Her Needs* of some ambivalence toward this political process, stating that she "may not sympathize with a Convention" or "feel *that* the best mode of arriving at truth." She continues: "I reverence their search in their own way, the many converging lights of many minds all bent upon the same point, even although I myself peer about with my solitary lantern" (see Appendix A2, p. 267). Her writing about Indian issues is consistent with this sentiment, as she idealizes Tecumseh, Margaret, and other characters in short stories as "solitary" visionaries negotiating a capricious political landscape.

Oakes Smith and the Schoolcrafts

Oakes Smith's experimentation with literary forms in writing about Native Americans also coincides with the work of contemporary ethnologists, placing her at the center of various, ongoing critical debates surrounding "Indian" literature. White women writing about Native Americans faced criticism not only as reformers who were charged with sentimentalism, as in the case of Helen Hunt Jackson, but also by literary critics skeptical of their ability to produce so-called "authentic" portrayals of Indians. Despite and even due to nineteenth-century American women writers' immense popularity, critics often associated their work with the domestic sphere, excessive sentimentality, and "melodramas of beset womanhood" in disparaging terms that feminist scholars such as Nina Baym, Jane Tompkins, and Annette Kolodny would reevaluate and contest in the 1980s, an era when literary theory energized canon debates and revision, and critical editions by scholars like Carolyn Karcher and Mary Kelley drew attention to women's writing about Indians. Such stereotypes are indeed problematic given the existence of a body of literature by women treating the complexity of frontier conflicts, and the double standard applied to "domestic" women writers when it was not uncommon for literary men to write about Indians at their desks without having ventured out among them. Women did inhabit the contact zones created by American colonization and nation-building, as the genre of the captivity narrative makes palpably clear with numerous accounts of white women among Indians, including women like Eunice Williams[1] and Mary Jemison who did not return to white society. Beyond her knowledge of Maine's history, Oakes Smith's friendship

---

1   Eunice Williams, also known as Marguerite Kanenstenhawi Arosen (1696–1785), was taken captive in 1704 during a French and Mohawk raid on the English colony of Deerfield, Massachusetts. She married and lived among the Mohawk throughout her life despite the efforts of her father, the Puritan minister John Williams (1664–1729), to bring about her return (see John Demos, *The Unredeemed Captive: A Family Story from Early America* [1994]). Oakes Smith tells a story of the raid on Deerfield in "The Crusade of the Bell" (1875).

with the Schoolcrafts, a white and Ojibwe family with roots in the Great Lakes region, also familiarized her with places and histories in which French, English, American, Canadian, and Indian cultures interrelate. Oakes Smith's writing about Indians thus can be traced to her experiences with a middle ground in which various cultural perspectives intersect and literary forms transform one another. As a colleague of Jane Johnston Schoolcraft and the prominent ethnologist Henry Rowe Schoolcraft, she occupied an important intellectual circle dedicated to studying and writing about American Indians—their histories, cultures, languages, and literature.

Their relationship shows how writers specializing in such genres as ethnology, fiction, poetry, memoir, and Ojibwe oral tradition worked together, experimenting with both literary form and collaborative authorship to produce a vast body of "Indian" literature. It also points to problems surrounding the creation of such work, however, given Henry Schoolcraft's own cultural biases and his dependence upon his Ojibwe wife as he wrote about Indians for a white audience. To critics of the day, Henry was, as Griswold argues, "the standard and chief authority respecting the Algic tribes," and his writings the essential source for all American fiction writers lacking their own observations of Native peoples (300). Whites with such first-hand knowledge were respected at the time as authorities on Indians, and there was a high demand for their observations in the literary marketplace. It is not surprising, then, that Oakes Smith claims a special affinity with Native Americans in her own writing: she portrays herself as a transcultural woman—similar to white Indian women like Williams, Jemison, or the fictional Margaret in *The Western Captive*, although not transculturated to the same extent—by recounting dialogue in which Indians such as Jane Schoolcraft grant her the distinction of possessing an "Indian soul." Oakes Smith thus shares in prevailing notions that white writers could not only provide "accuracy" in their stories about Indians, but could also possess an "Indian" spirit.

Jane Schoolcraft seems to have inspired Oakes Smith as a muse of sorts, providing not only material for Indian stories, but also a model of the type of culturally complex identity that we find in many of Oakes Smith's characters. Jane, her Ojibwe mother, Irish-born father, and siblings lived in a world that the scholar Robert Dale Parker describes as "not so much half-and-half or bicultural as it was its own evolving and mobile space in the cultural landscape" (4). Parker's depiction of Sault Ste. Marie, on the upper peninsula of Michigan, during Schoolcraft's lifetime calls to mind the type of changing landscape in which Oakes Smith set her first Indian novel: "the Johnston family saw their world shift not only from Ojibwe and French-Canadian cultural dominance to the dominance of the encroaching United States, but also from British rule to US federal rule, with the accompanying changes in language and religion as well as shifts in the sense of centering cultural identity" (4). In *The Western Captive*, Oakes Smith turns to a place and time in which characters must similarly negotiate tangled and shifting religious, political, and social alliances leading to the War of 1812. Her particular interest in the roles that women play in these dynamic exchanges—and, by extension, in the historical process—is reflected in Oakes Smith's many stories of inter-cultural relationships, both in her fiction and in a personal account of the Schoolcrafts published in 1874, well after both of their deaths.

Oakes Smith remembers the Schoolcrafts among "the celebrities of New York" in a biographical sketch of both writers that is nonetheless entitled "Mrs. Henry R. Schoolcraft," a move that underscores the Ojibwe author's importance to American literary history and to Oakes Smith herself (see Appendix D5). The sketch describes an educated woman who "spoke the Algonquin, French and English languages fluently, and read Latin, Greek and Hebrew," was a skilled piano player and conversationalist, and dressed "much in the prevailing fashion, varied with admirable skill, just enough to present a *soupçon* of the Indian wild wood, if by nothing more than a belt of wampum" (pp. 315–16). Oakes Smith's admiration for Jane Schoolcraft's intellectual and social accomplishments is balanced with detailed observations of her physical characteristics that identify certain attractive features as Indian—her feet, her mouth, and even her voice, described as "a musical sigh, a something like an echo dying out" (p. 316). Her portrait at times draws upon romantic images of Indians, as this language conjures up the idea that they are a "vanishing" race, and Oakes Smith invokes the popular stereotype of an Indian princess with the suggestion that Schoolcraft's mother was a "Mohawk Queen." In the account, however, we also see how Schoolcraft herself shaped this public image and performed her Indian identity by "playfully" lapsing into Algonquin when telling Indian tales, or even the Lord's Prayer, to captivate listeners with the mere sound of the language. If Oakes

Smith idealizes Schoolcraft, she also presents a more nuanced sketch of the ways that her Indian acquaintances manipulated stereotypes of Indians to powerful effect and even to their own amusement, captivating white audiences by speaking in a native tongue or issuing a spine-tingling "war-whoop." The sketch's conclusion elevates Jane Johnston Schoolcraft's legacy by proclaiming that she deserves credit for her husband's renowned book: "She was, unquestionably, nearly, if not quite, the author of the *Algic Researches*" (p. 319). The question of authorship is indeed problematic in the case of Indian legends that are translated into English, given the dependency of ethnologists upon Native American storytellers. As Oakes Smith implies, readers often encounter an author's retelling or so-called "translation" of a Native American story, legend, chant, or poem without a context for understanding how it was created: this is likewise true of her own legend "Machinito," for example, which lacks an explanation of its source material.

With her nod to Jane Johnston Schoolcraft's authorship, Oakes Smith calls attention to the intricacy of literary collaborations not only between Indian and white authors, but also between husbands and wives. Jane Johnston married Henry Rowe Schoolcraft in 1823, the year after he arrived in Sault Ste. Marie as the area's first Indian agent, and she became an invaluable contributor to his studies of Ojibwe language and literature, and to his numerous ethnological publications. As Parker writes, "we will probably never know the degree and form of Henry's dependence on Jane, her mother, the other members of her family, and other Ojibwe people, except to say that he relied on them heavily" (61). While he sometimes attributed pieces to his wife's hand, Schoolcraft also published versions of her work without acknowledging her authorship, as in the case of "Moowis, The Indian Coquette" (see Appendix D1). The legend was first published in 1827 signed "Leelinau," Jane Schoolcraft's pen name, and then later revised and republished several times as the work of Henry Schoolcraft, beginning in 1844.

The Schoolcrafts' union was a literary one in which the lines of authorship could sometimes become blurred or effaced, which also happened in Elizabeth Oakes Smith's own marriage to Seba Smith. Both women published work variously under pen names and as "Mrs. Seba Smith" and "Mrs. H.R. Schoolcraft," appellations barely distinguishing them from their husbands to the extent that

The Western Captive has in some cases been erroneously attributed to Seba Smith. As married women, their literary careers were attached to those of their husbands, whose own professional and economic difficulties are what brought their families to New York City at the same time, after Seba Smith's failed investment in 1839 and Henry Schoolcraft's loss of his job as Indian agent in 1841. The paths of their lives crossed with these parallel circumstances, but only briefly before Jane Johnston Schoolcraft's unexpected death on 22 May 1842, at the age of 42. She and Oakes Smith are joined in literary history as co-contributors to *Oneóta, or The Red Race of America* (1845), the miscellany that includes Oakes Smith's "Machinito," a poem entitled "To a Bird, Seen Under My Window in the Garden" attributed to "the late Mrs. H.R. SCHOOLCRAFT, who was a grand daughter of the war chief WABOJEEG," and the unsigned "Moowis, or The Man Made Up of Rags and Dirt," presumably Henry's revised version of the legend penned by his wife. Within a few years of her death, Schoolcraft was already being remembered with this posthumous publication of her poem and Margaret Fuller's wistful remarks in *Summer on the Lakes, in 1843*: "By the premature death of Mrs. Schoolcraft was lost a mine of poesy, to which few had access" (201).

Fuller calls attention to the way that nineteenth-century literature circulated in manuscript form, a type of publication with a limited readership in which significant literary work was nonetheless produced, by Emily Dickinson as a famous example, but also by both Oakes Smith and Jane Schoolcraft. Oakes Smith, as discussed earlier, created a vast body of work in manuscript form; by comparison, Jane Schoolcraft published pieces in the manuscript magazine *The Muzze-ni-e-gun, or Literary Voyager* that circulated among intellectuals in Sault Ste. Marie, and she distributed many poems in private letters, notably to her husband. Correspondence between Jane Schoolcraft and Oakes Smith is representative of this practice, as Oakes Smith attached a poem to a letter she wrote to Jane in 1842, the year of *The Western Captive*'s publication (see Appendix D2). Oakes Smith's letter shows that she valued Schoolcraft as a fellow woman writer with whom she shared certain affinities, expressing her pleasure in "proof of interest and regard from one of her own sex, to one who has ever been emulous to merit them" (p. 305). Schoolcraft's opinion clearly matters to Oakes Smith, and the poem dedicated to Jane claims that they possess a particular sympathy and understanding as literary women: "Yes, Lady, thou hast read a heart, / That passive hears the voice of fame" (p. 306). These sentiments are consistent with Oakes Smith's description of an expanding community of women writers in "Kinneho": "Each lady writer understands the power of her sister author, and so far from disparaging her or it, and being eaten up with envy, as the uninitiated suppose, she is joyous and appreciating" (p. 241). While this appears a somewhat idealized vision of a completely harmonious and supportive sisterhood among women writers, Oakes Smith's writing to and about Schoolcraft does reveal a glimpse of the relationship that the two authors shared.

Whereas in this letter Oakes Smith writes of a mutual understanding of one another's "heart," she also portrays Jane Schoolcraft as recognizing in her a kindred "Indian" spirit based upon her enthusiasm for the outdoors and for Native American legends. In her sketch of the Schoolcrafts, Oakes Smith recounts this invitation from Jane to travel with them to Sault Ste. Marie: "You have an Indian soul, all that an Indian exults in would speak to your mind, you should go to the sources of the Mississippi, which my husband was the first to discover, and we would talk over those rare old mythologies, so little known and appreciated by white people" (p. 318). Oakes Smith also imagines that Dr. Peter Wilson, a Cayuga included in the sketch, thinks her "a very obliging white 'Squaw'" for inviting him to smoke a pipe in her presence, and in her story of climbing Mount Kinneho she describes this acknowledgment from her Indian guide: "'The white woman has an Indian soul,' he murmured; 'she can close her face over her heart'" (p. 246). Oakes Smith's "Indian" identity is thus a fiction of her own making: her portraits of Native American acquaintances create self-portraits in which she lays claim to like-mindedness with them and, in turn, to her own authority as a writer. Her relationship to the famed Schoolcrafts provided Oakes Smith with a form of validation as an author of Indian tales, given the preoccupation of readers and critics with the "authenticity" of literature representing Native Americans. While the question of what constitutes "authentic" Native American literature is a vexed one still subject to debate, Oakes Smith faced this kind of critical scrutiny and earned praise from Henry Schoolcraft for the "truthful" elements in her writing about Indians. As an ethnologist he is perhaps less concerned with Oakes Smith's so-called "Indian soul" than he is with her literary abilities, that is, with the craft she brings as a poet to the task of translating Indian literatures into English. When Oakes Smith writes that Henry Schoolcraft declared her rendering of a legend "truly Indian," she refers to his comments upon what he believes is the proper *style* for rendering Native American literature in English. His "Idea of an American Literature based on Indian Mythology" is a literary manifesto of sorts from an ethnologist concerned with the challenges of translation, and in it Schoolcraft celebrates the attempt to create American literature using Native American materials while lamenting what he sees as failed attempts that merely create "English figures, drest in moccasins, and holding a bow and arrows" (see Appendix D4, p. 312). Schoolcraft disparages the "verbosity and redundant description, false sentiment, and erroneous manners" in the Indian fiction published in American magazines, arguing that "the chief points of failure, in the mere literary execution of attempted Indian legends, consist in want of simplicity, conciseness and brevity" (p. 312). He lauds Oakes Smith's telling of the legend of Machinito for displaying "the appropriate simplicity of thought" and proclaims that the story "proceeds by the true modus operandi of the natives of telling the story" (p. 313). As an ethnologist, Schoolcraft would often provide both a "literal" and a "literary" translation in an effort to bridge the gap between Indian oral tradition and written English versions. With "Nursery and Cradle Songs of the Forest," he describes the tenderness of relationship between an Indian mother and her child as a context for the lullabies and then explains his reasons for entrusting Oakes Smith to create this type of literary translation from his literal one. Schoolcraft suggests that a woman writer is better suited for the task of rendering lullabies when he writes that "they were almost too frail of structure to be trusted, without a gentle hand, amidst his rougher materials," although he also credits her authority as "a refined enthusiast of the woods" in his appraisal of her "chaste and truthful pen" (see Appendix D3, p. 307). Given his renown as an expert ethnologist, Henry Schoolcraft's stamp of approval upon Oakes Smith's ability to render Indian songs and legends in an appropriate style bolstered her reputation as a writer of "Indian" literature, as evident in Griswold's assessment.

Oakes Smith's writings about Indians were thus judged favorably by the critics of her day and earned respect from two of the era's important ethnographers, Jane Johnston and Henry Rowe School-craft. Changes in critical perspectives since then have, of course, generated different approaches to Native American literature and to the work of nineteenth-century writers such as Oakes Smith and the Schoolcrafts. With the twentieth century's Native American literary renaissance, a term referring to the proliferation of literary publications by American Indian authors beginning with N. Scott Momaday's Pulitzer Prize-winning novel *House Made of Dawn* (1968), a body of criticism has also developed that complicates definitions of "Indian" literature and the questions of its "authenticity." Second-generation Native American authors and literary critics such as David Treuer (Ojibwe) and Craig Womack (Creek-Cherokee), for example, challenge dominant methods of analyzing Indian literature: Treuer objects to the treatment of Native American fiction "*as* culture" rather than "as *literature*" (3–5), and Womack calls for criticism connected to Native American communities—one that "attempts to find Native literature's place in Indian country, rather than Native literature's place in the canon" (11). In *Native American Fiction: A User's Manual* (2006), Treuer exposes the gaps between both Henry Schoolcraft's "literal" and "literary" translations of a chant and their Ojibwe source, and he goes further to consider how contemporary Native American fiction writers use various literary techniques to craft writing that appears Indian and seems to originate from a "culture" rather than being created by an author drawing upon various tools and traditions. Readers, writers, and critics tend to approach Indian fiction as *Native American* rather than as *literature*, Treuer argues, and are reluctant "to treat it as literature that exists within a field of other literatures" (196). In *Red on Red: Native American Literary Separatism* (1999), Womack uses the model of the Red Sticks, a faction of traditionalist Creeks allied with and influenced by Tecumseh, to argue for a Native American literary criticism that resists colonialism: "What they had to develop was a vision that was not simply reactionary but the application of tradition in radical new ways with attention given to analysis, criticism, and political reflection" (12). Womack's approach thus advocates the development of Native critical approaches to Native texts much in the same way that, according to Joel W. Martin, the Red Sticks "innovated on tradition and initiated new ways of life within the world created by contact."[1] Studies of the entangled literary productions of Oakes Smith and the Schoolcrafts have much to contribute to ongoing debates surrounding Native American literature, as their collaboration invites scrutiny of the relationship between ethnographic and literary writing in the nineteenth century, the influences of Native and European-American literary traditions upon one another, and what is at stake for both white and Native authors in their writing.

---

1   Joel W. Martin, *Sacred Revolt* (Boston: Beacon Press, 1991), 179. Quoted in Womack, 12.

Elizabeth Oakes Smith: A Brief Chronology

1806   Elizabeth Oakes Prince born 12 August, in North Yarmouth (now Cumberland), Maine, to David Cushing Prince and Sophia Blanchard Prince.

1809–13   Death of her father at sea, 26 March 1809. Moves to Cape Elizabeth, Maine, after her mother remarries, reads and attends school at a young age, suffers a breakdown at age six, and spends time with grandparents.

1812–15   War of 1812. Death of Tecumseh, 5 October 1813.

1814–22   Moves to Portland, Maine. Distinguishes herself as a student, teaches a Sunday school for blacks at age 12. Aspires to pursue a career as a schoolteacher, but her mother objects and insists that Elizabeth should marry.

1823   At age 16, marries editor and author Seba Smith (b. 14 September 1792), a man twice her age, on 6 March.

1824–34   Gives birth to six sons, mourns deaths of the first two, Benjamin (1824) and Rolvin (1825–32). Changes surname of sons to "Oaksmith." Assists her husband with newspaper editing and begins publishing her own work in periodicals.

1837   Panic of 1837. Family plunges into bankruptcy and is forced to live with relatives.

1838   Publishes *Riches Without Wings, or The Cleveland Family,* a tale of moral education for young people written about the panic.

1839   Moves to Charleston, South Carolina, when her husband invests in a cotton-cleaning machine; moves again to New York City when machine fails. Enters a vibrant literary circle (including Henry R. and Jane J. Schoolcraft) and begins a prolific period of publication and editorship, often co-editing with her husband.

1840   Publishes "Indian Traits: The Story of Niskagah." William Henry Harrison elected ninth President of the United States.

1841   Death of William Henry Harrison, 4 April.

1842   Publishes "The Sinless Child," in the *Southern Literary Messenger* (January-February, issues 1–2) and *The Western Captive* in Park Benjamin's *The New World* in a supplement edition (October, nos. 27–28), an early form of the paperback novel. Moves to Brooklyn.

1843　Publishes *The Sinless Child and Other Poems*, edited by John Keese, and "Hokomok: A Legend of Maine."

1845–47　Publishes "Machinito, The Evil Spirit; From the Legends of Iagou" in Henry Rowe Schoolcraft's miscellany *Oneóta, or Characteristics of the Red Race of America*, two collections of poetry (*The Poetical Writings of Elizabeth Oakes Smith* and *The Keepsake: A Wreath of Poems and Sonnets*), and three volumes in a series of children's books, "Stories, Not for Good Children, nor Bad Children, but for Real Children": *The True Child, The Dandelion*, and *The Moss Cup*. Publishes "Beloved of the Evening Star" and edits the gift book *The Mayflower for 1847*.

1848　Seneca Falls Convention. Publishes "The Sagamore of Saco: A Legend of Maine" and, as its "editor," the novel *The Salamander: A Legend for Christmas, Found Amongst The Papers of The Late Ernest Helfenstein* (Oakes Smith's pseudonym). Edits *The Mayflower for 1848*.

1850–51　First National Women's Rights Convention. Publishes series of ten articles entitled *Woman and Her Needs* in Horace Greely's *New York Tribune* (November 1850–June 1851), republished as a pamphlet in 1851. Production of her play *The Roman Tribute* at the Arch Street Theatre in Philadelphia. Makes first platform appearance at a National Women's Rights Convention, Worcester, Massachusetts. Begins to tour widely as a lecturer in various cities and delivers the first lecture by a woman at the Concord Lyceum in Massachusetts. Publishes "Kinneho: A Legend of Moosehead Lake."

1852　Addresses Third National Women's Rights Convention in Syracuse, New York, serves as a vice-president, and continues to attend conventions throughout her life. Argues in favor of a weekly paper supporting women's rights, with her own prospectus for one called *The Egeria*; contributes instead to Paulina Wright Davis's *The Una* (launched in 1853). Publishes *Hints on Dress and Beauty, Shadow Land; or, The Seer*, and *The Sanctity of Marriage*.

1853　Publishes *Old New York: or, Democracy in 1689. A Tragedy, in Five Acts* (also known as *Jacob Leisler*), produced at the Broadway Theatre in New York.

1854	Publishes *The Newsboy* and *Bertha and Lily; or, The Parsonage of Beech Glen, A Romance.*
1855	Moves back to New York City.
1860	Moves to Patchogue, New York, where the Smiths call their Long Island home "The Willows."
1861–65	American Civil War. Her son Appleton Oaksmith arrested for outfitting a ship for the slave trade in 1861, bringing infamy to family in the North. Oakes Smith works for years to obtain a Presidential pardon for Appleton, denied by Abraham Lincoln but finally issued by Ulysses S. Grant in 1872.
1865	Death of her son Edward (b. 1834).
1867	Publishes Beadle and Adams dime novel *Bald Eagle, or, The Last of the Ramapaughs: A Romance of Revolutionary Times.*
1868	Publishes a second dime novel, *The Sagamore of Saco.* Lydia Maria Child publishes *An Appeal for the Indians.*
1868	Death of Seba Smith, 28 July.
1869	Death of her son Sidney (b. 1830).
1874	Moves to Hollywood, North Carolina to live with her son Appleton. Publishes "Mrs. Henry R. Schoolcraft."
1875	Publishes "The Crusade of the Bell."
1877	Serves as pastor of the Independent Church in Canastota, New York.
1878	Attends and speaks at National Woman Suffrage Association's celebration of the 30th anniversary of the Seneca Falls Convention at conference in Rochester, New York.
1879	Attends and speaks at the National Association's Eleventh Washington Convention. Four of Appleton Oaksmith's daughters drowned in boating accident.
1885	Completes manuscript of *A Human Life: Being the Autobiography of Elizabeth Oakes Smith.*
1887	Death of her son Appleton (b. 1828), leaving only one surviving son, Alvin (1832–1902).
1893	Elizabeth Oakes Smith dies in North Carolina, 15 November, at age 87, and is buried next to her husband in Patchogue, New York.

A Note on the Texts

Elizabeth Oakes Smith's *The Western Captive; or, The Times of Tecumseh* was published as an original novel in *The New World*, a large, weekly newspaper edited by Park Benjamin and published by J. Winchester in New York. This fiction supplement was an early form of paperback novel. The text is reprinted from *The New World*, vol. 2, nos. 3–4 (October 1842) (Extra series nos. 27–28), pages 1–39.

Oakes Smith published "Machinito, The Evil Spirit; from the Legends of Iagou" in Henry Rowe Schoolcraft's miscellany *Oneóta, or Characteristics of the Red Race of America* (New York and London: Wiley and Putnam, 1845), the text I selected for this edition because of the importance of its original context, in which Schoolcraft praises her ability to write "Indian Mythology." The legend was republished without revisions in *The American Indians, Their History, Condition and Prospects* (1851) and in a slightly edited version in the gift book *The Mayflower for 1847* (1847).

An excerpt is included from "The Sagamore of Saco: A Legend of Maine" *Graham's Magazine* 33 (July 1848): 47–52, a story Oakes Smith significantly revised and expanded into the dime novel *The Sagamore of Saco* (1868), republished by Beadle and Adams in the new dime novel series in 1881.

The sources for Oakes Smith's other stories are as follows:

"Beloved of the Evening Star." *The Opal for 1847: A Pure Gift for the Holydays*. Ed. John Keese. New York: J.C. Riker, 1847. 45–59.
"Indian Traits: The Story of Niskagah." *The Ladies' Companion* 13 (July 1840): 141–44.
"Kinneho: A Legend of Moosehead Lake." *Godey's Magazine and Lady's Book* 42 (1851): 175–79.

I have retained Oakes Smith's notes and spellings, altering the texts only to amend inconsistencies and obvious errors.

THE WESTERN CAPTIVE AND OTHER INDIAN STORIES

THE NEW WORLD.

PARK BENJAMIN,
EDITOR.

J. WINCHESTER,
PUBLISHER.

"No pent-up Utica contracts our powers; for the whole boundless continent is ours."

EXTRA SERIES. OFFICE 30 ANN-STREET. NUMBERS 27, 28.

VOLUME II. NEW-YORK, OCTOBER, 1842. NUMBERS 3, 4.

Original American Novel.

Entered according to Act of Congress, in the year 1842,
BY PARK BENJAMIN,
In the Clerk's Office of the Southern District of New York.

THE WESTERN CAPTIVE;

OR,

THE TIMES OF TECUMSEH.

BY MRS. SEBA SMITH.

"Hearing oftentimes
The still, sad music of humanity."—Wordsworth.

TO THOSE OF HER SEX,

WHOM THE DESIRE FOR UTTERANCE, OR THE NECESSITIES OF LIFE, HAVE CALLED FROM THE SANCTITY OF WOMANLY SECLUSION, THESE PAGES ARE RESPECTFULLY INSCRIBED BY THE AUTHOR.

CHAPTER I.—Freedom.

"Thy birthright was not given by human hands :
Thou wert twin-born with man. In pleasant fields,
While yet our race was few, thou satt'st with him,
To tend the quiet flock and watch the stars." Bryant.

The greatness of an enterprise is to be tested, not by the splendor of its achievement, but by the magnitude of difficulties overcome in its conception. Patriots have struggled and fallen, having accomplished nothing, it may be, in their career, except to add one more impulsive throb to the great beating of the universal heart for freedom—yet time may fail to reveal how essential was that one throb to the high interests of humanity. We may deplore the fate of the individual, at the same time that we rejoice for man. History is full of illustration—slowly but surely is the race advancing to a goal where the chain shall of itself fall from the free limb ; and the eye, wandering backward through the long vista of despotism and revolution, shall behold how strong men were stricken in the race, that they might become heralds and guide-marks for others. Such was the fate of Tecumseh—doomed, not to realize the high designs he had conceived, but to add one more to the list of those who have labored for the enfranchisement of a people, and to prove that, in every grade of society, the yearnings of the heart are still for freedom ; and that the first and great principles of legislation have their elements in the mind itself ; and therefore, the untutored savage being nearer the threshold of truth, may be better able to expound her doctrines, than the statesman, enveloped by custom and the huge intricacies of government.

Tecumseh beheld with dismay the encroachment of the white man upon the soil of his people, and saw that their system of purchase, as it was called, would soon leave them scarce a place for burial, while the infusion of vice among a primitive people was rapidly sealing their destruction. Thence, his active and powerful mind conceived the vast plan of union and peace between those western tribes, occupying the great valley of the Mississippi. He proposed consolidating them into one grand confederation, one of the principle articles of which should be, the non-bartering of their lands. Vast as was the design, it scarcely exceeded the personal sacrifices and hazards necessary to put it in execution.

At the period of the Council of Fort Wayne, in which several of the tribes ceded their lands to our Government under the agency of General Harrison, Tecumseh was absent upon a mission to the southern tribes, that he might obtain their assent to the terms of the league, which had already been obtained from all their northern brethren.

The ceding of lands, therefore, at the Council of Wayne, was in violation of a solemn pledge, and was thence not binding in itself, but also exposed the recreant leaders to the vengeance of the remaining tribes. The followers of Tecumseh and of Eliskwatawa, "the open door," or, as he is most commonly called, " The Prophet," remained at their town upon the Tippecanoe, gloomy and inactive, waiting the return of the great chief from his southern crusade. They held little communication with the chiefs of the seceding tribes, regarding them as traitors to the common cause, and unworthy to partake of the high destiny reserved, even now, degenerate and weakened as they were, for the proud and independent children of the woods. They waited impatiently the return of that remarkable man, who united in his own person the bravery and skill of an accomplished warrior, the far-seeing and truth-discerning spirit of a reformer, with the power and persuasive eloquence of the orator. The chiefs of the several tribes had bound themselves by solemn vows and severe penalties, never to part with a foot of their land to the white man, to resume as far as possible the primitive habits of their people, and thus to throw off their yoke of dependence upon the white intruders. All the tribes bordering upon the great lakes of the north, those upon the Mississippi and its noble tributaries, even to the wilderness of the far west, had bound themselves by a like oath ; and now the eloquent warrior was preaching his crusade at the south, confident of returning with a like pledge from those distant and excitable people. Skilful were the weapons to be used, and persuasive the tongue which was to give utterance to the conceptions of a great mind, about to realize the hopes and expectations of a patriotism, pure and engrossing, as ever swayed the bosom of a Roman in the proudest days of her freedom. He could not fail of success, for he was a Shawanee, and endowed with even more than the ordinary share of the hardihood and talent belonging to that extraordinary people. He could bring up the traditions of their old men, when the Shawanee dwelt upon the beautiful savannas of the south, and hunted game where the wild grape hung in festoons upon the palmetto, and the moss waved solemnly in the wind, as if a gray

THE
WESTERN CAPTIVE;
OR,
THE TIMES OF TECUMSEH.

BY MRS. SEBA SMITH.

"Hearing oftentimes
The still, sad music of humanity".—WORDSWORTH.[1]

TO THOSE OF HER SEX,
WHOM THE DESIRE FOR UTTERANCE, OR THE
NECESSITIES OF LIFE,
HAVE CALLED FROM THE SANCTITY OF
WOMANLY SECLUSION,
THESE PAGES ARE RESPECTFULLY INCRIBED BY
THE AUTHOR.

---

1 William Wordsworth (1770–1850), "Lines Composed a Few Miles above Tintern Abbey, on Revisiting the Banks of the Wye during a Tour. July 13, 1798."

CHAPTER I.—FREEDOM.

"Thy birth-right was not given by human hands:
Thou wert twin-born with man. In pleasant fields,
While yet our race was few, thou satt'st with him,
To tend the quiet flock and watch the stars."—BRYANT.[1]

The greatness of an enterprise is to be tested, not by the splendor of its achievment, but by the magnitude of difficulties overcome in its conception. Patriots have struggled and fallen, having accomplished nothing, it may be, in their career, except to add one more impulsive throb to the great beating of the universal heart for freedom—yet time may fail to reveal how essential was that one throb to the high interests of humanity. We may deplore the fate of the individual, at the same time that we rejoice for man. History is full of illustration—slowly but surely is the race advancing to a goal where the chain shall of itself fall from the free limb; and the eye, wandering backward through the long vista of despotism and revolution, shall behold how strong men were stricken in the race, that they might become heralds and guide-marks for others. Such was the fate of Tecumseh—doomed, not to realize the high designs he had conceived, but to add one more to the list of those who have labored for the enfranchisement of a people, and to prove that, in every grade of society, the yearnings of the heart are still for freedom; and that the first and great principles of legislation have their elements in the mind itself; and therefore, the untutored savage being nearer the threshold of truth, may be better able to expound her doctrines, than the statesman, enveloped by custom and the huge intricacies of government.

Tecumseh beheld with dismay the encroachment of the white man upon the soil of his people, and saw that their system of purchase, as it was called, would soon leave them scarce a place for burial, while

---

1   William Cullen Bryant (1794–1878), "The Antiquity of Freedom."
Bryant, an American romantic poet, journalist, and editor, was a close literary acquaintance of Oakes Smith and her husband Seba Smith during their years in New York. Like Oakes Smith, Bryant was a defender of human rights, and his work includes poems about Indians such as "An Indian at the Burial-place of His Fathers," "An Indian Story," and "The Indian Girl's Lament."

the infusion of vice among a primitive people was rapidly sealing their destruction. Thence, his active and powerful mind conceived the vast plan of union and peace between those western tribes, occupying the great valley of the Mississippi. He proposed consolidating them into one grand confederation, one of the principle articles of which should be, the non-bartering of their lands. Vast as was the design, it scarcely exceeded the personal sacrifices and hazards necessary to put it in execution.[1]

At the period of the council of Fort Wayne, in which several of the tribes ceded their lands to our Government under the agency of General Harrison,[2] Tecumseh was absent upon a mission to the southern tribes, that he might obtain their assent to the terms of the league, which had already been obtained from all their northern brethren.

The ceding of lands, therefore, at the Council of Wayne, was in violation of a solemn pledge, and was thence not binding in itself, but also exposed the recreant leaders to the vengeance of the remaining tribes. The followers of Tecumseh and of Eliskwatawa, "the open door," or, as he is most commonly called, "The Prophet,"[3] remained at their town upon the Tippecanoe, gloomy and inactive, waiting the return of the great chief from his southern crusade. They held little communication with the chiefs of the

---

1   Tecumseh (1768–1813) was a Shawnee tribal leader who advocated a political alliance among Indians in the Midwest and also the Five Southern Tribes to resist United States territorial expansion. He and his brother, known as the Shawnee Prophet, worked to create this intertribal confederacy, urging Indians to oppose the sale of Indian land and to protect their communities against the encroachment of European ways, especially the use of alcohol. While his brother influenced a religious revitalization, Tecumseh emerged as a political and military leader. He collaborated with the British and attempted to negotiate with American officials (including William Henry Harrison), but these relationships were plagued by tensions.

2   The Treaty of Fort Wayne, also known as "The Ten O'clock Line Treaty," completed in September 1809, transferred approximately three million acres of Indian lands to the United States.

3   Eliskwatawa is a variant spelling of Elskatawa, or Tenskatawa, "the open door," the appellation by which the Prophet came to be known following his religious vision and awakening. Before this transformation, he was named Lalawethika, "the rattle" or "noisemaker," for his quarrelsome, boastful personality.

seceding tribes, regarding them as traitors to the common cause, and unworthy to partake of the high destiny reserved, even now, degenerate and weakened as they were, for the proud and independent children of the woods. They waited impatiently the return of that remarkable man, who united in his own person the bravery and skill of an accomplished warrior, the far-seeing and truth-discerning spirit of a reformer, with the power and persuasive eloquence of the orator. The chiefs of the several tribes had bound themselves by solemn vows and severe penalties, never to part with a foot of their land to the white man, to resume as far as possible the primitive habits of their people, and thus to throw off their yoke of dependence upon the white intruders. All the tribes bordering upon the great lakes of the north, those upon the Mississippi and its noble tributaries, even to the wilderness of the far west, had bound themselves by a like oath; and now the eloquent warrior was preaching his crusade at the south, confident of returning with a like pledge from those distant and excitable people. Skilful were the weapons to be used, and persuasive the tongue which was to give utterance to the conceptions of a great mind, about to realize the hopes and expectations of a patriotism, pure and engrossing, as ever swayed the bosom of a Roman in the proudest days of her freedom. He could not fail of success, for he was a Shawanee,[1] and endowed with even more than the ordinary share of the hardihood and talent belonging to the extraordinary people. He could bring up the traditions of their old men, when the Shawanee dwelt upon the beautiful savannas of the south, and hunted game where the wild grape hung in festoons upon the palmetto, and the moss waved solemnly in the wind, as if a gray pall were hung upon the forest, and the white magnolia perfumed the air with its blossoms. He could tell of his mother, who was a Cherokee, and of the wondrous circumstances of his own birth. How every night, when his mother lay down to rest, a manitou,[2] in the shape of massasauga,[3] glided to the cabin door and slept beside her skins; and how the manitou disappeared only when the young mother lay dead within her wigwam, and three sons in their helplessness beside her, thereby

---

1 Variant of Shawnee; also referred to as Shawanese.
2 A spirit or deity. Manitou are supernatural beings and forces, sometimes appearing to humans in the form of animals.
3 [Oakes Smith's note:] A rattlesnake.

pointing plainly to the great union of the tribes—the brotherhood of the north, the south, and the west.[1]

The boys grew, in their solitariness, strong and beautiful; "the sun their father, the earth their mother, and they reposed upon her bosom."[2] The Great Spirit talked with them in the strong wind that shook the forest, in the stillness of the midnight stars, and in the soft dews of the morning. He taught them to regard all the red men as brothers. The Great Spirit had, in his displeasure, permitted the whites to wrest from them a part of their land, but now he warned them to unite—to forget all animosities among themselves, and combine in one grand effort to keep the whites east of that high ridge which he had raised to guard the tributaries of the Mississippi. He would have the tribes become one, to guard sacredly the old hunting-grounds of their people, the graves of their fathers, and the ancient stones of their council-fires. He would crowd back the whites to the south and east of the Ohio, and the Alleghanies,[3] or the time would come when the retreating tribes would stand upon the shores of the great waters that receive the setting sun, and there fight only to perish in its bosom.

The tribes met in solemn council, and the pledge that was to bind in one great confederation all the tribes of the north, the south and the west, was given in the midst of solemn and mysterious rites; and

---

1 There are various accounts of Tecumseh's family history and his mother, Methoataske, including a story that she was Cherokee. Although there is some disagreement whether she was Creek or Shawnee, Methoataske lived and met her husband in the Creek communities in Alabama where the Shawnees found refuge. Two sons and two daughters preceded Tecumseh, who was born in Ohio, followed by another daughter and a set of male triplets from which two survived: Lalawethika (who would become Tenkswatawa, the Prophet) and Kumskaukau. Tecumseh's father, Puckeshinwa, died before the birth of the triplets in 1775; four years later his mother migrated with many other Shawnees, leaving her children behind in the care of those who remained in Ohio.

2 An allusion to a statement Tecumseh reportedly made when an interpreter told him that his "father" General William Harrison was offering him a chair in which to be seated at a meeting at Vincennes. Tecumseh's reply was widely circulated in various sources, including Schoolcraft: "the *Sun* is my father, and the *Earth* is my mother, and on *her* bosom I will repose" (*Travels in the Central Portions of the Mississippi Valley* 145). See Oakes Smith's depiction of the scene in Chapter X, p. 101.

3 The Allegheny Mountains, also spelled Alleghany.

from henceforth the Indian should dwell securely in his wigwam—should traverse the deep forest, bound over the wide prairie, and launch his canoe upon the noble stream of the west, and the white man no more should molest or make him afraid. The tomahawk should rest in the earth, or be dug up only to repel aggression. The white man should dwell in peace beyond the mountains, but only there—should his steps encroach upon the soil they were now pledged to defend, in whatsoever point, it should be common cause with the tribes; all holding themselves in readiness to resent the injury, to drive back the intruder, and preserve undivided the heritage of the tribes. They were now to be one. One in peace, one in war. Tribe should no more war with tribe, for they were all brethren.

The great mission was accomplished. Wherever the skilful orator appeared, his earnestness and address had won him the hearing and the assent of his people; for where was truth ever presented in its purity and sincerity, without hearts to respond to its utterance? They had listened to his teaching, as to the communications of an invisible spirit, whose eye beheld the past and the future. The long story of the wanderings of their people from land to land, led ever by the Great Spirit; their appearance in the mighty solitudes of the west, their divisions, their wars, their thousand suns of increase and prosperity, and the final scourge of the whites; all the past history of their nation, all the fears and hopes of the future, passed in vivid review before them. They seemed to stand with him upon a height, commanding a prospect of all the tribes, where the children sported by the threshold, and the white hairs of the aged floated in the air as they bowed themselves in the sunshine; fields of grain glanced in the light, and measureless hunting-grounds, full of game, swept away in the distance, swelling into hills or towering into mountain peaks; they heard the war of many waters, and the swaying of the old woods: they bent the ear to listen with hearts exulting in the goodly heritage of the red man. In sympathy with the fervid action of the speaker, tears rushed to their eyes—they started from their seats, and spread out their arms with him as if to embrace the whole tribes as one.

Such had been the eloquence of Tecumseh, such his success; and now he turned his steps northward, with many fears, but many hopes. He knew the nature of his people, their proneness to impulse, and reckless disregard of the future; yet it is the nature of elevated motives to inspire trust and hope, and there was that about himself that forbade despair.

The modern rail-road, that still preserves its directness in spite of hill, valley, or interposing river, is but a more thorough illustration of the mode of travelling practiced by the savage in his long and perilous journeys through the wilderness. The experienced eye of Tecumseh discerned every feature of the immense country through which he was passing, and with no guide but his own sure judgment and unerring instinct, he could preserve his direct route with scarce the variation of a mile, even from the council-fires of the southern-most Creeks, to the head waters of the Wabash. The solitary canoe was paddled up the then silent rivers, and on the shoulders of his followers was carried around falls and dangerous rapids. He knew where the branches of different streams approximated, making what they usually termed a "carrying place;" and there it was again borne across the country, to be launched once more upon a stream whose waters should mingle with the great Lakes, take the dizzy leap of Niagara, and find their way to the ocean through the St. Lawrence; and that too, while the bark still dripped with the waters that should mingle with the Ohio and the far-off Missouri, bearing its tribute from the Oregon mountains, the melted snow of their summits, to be sunned under the citron and cocoa, to glitter in the shadow of the palm-tree, and mingle its melody with birds of the tropics.

It was mid-day when Tecumseh reached the town of the Prophet upon the banks of the Tippecanoe. His step was firm and haughty, and there was an elevation in his look and mien betokening a man whose energies are swayed by great and noble principles, and who is on the verge of realizing all the proud dreams of his imagination. Unlike the few followers who attended him, he was unadorned with a single ornament. Leggins[1] of deerskin with a tunic of the same material, a belt of wampum, and upon his head a helmet with a tuft of the feathers of the war-eagle, indicating his rank as a warrior, and some curiously carved shells fastened upon one side, denoting the number of wounds he had received in battle, completed his costume. The followers of himself and the Prophet had thrown aside the blanket, as an innovation introduced by the whites. The appearance of Tecumseh contrasted powerfully with that of his brother, who had followed him in his southern campaign. While Eliskwatawa lived in the mysterious visions of the future, practising the greatest austerity,

---

1 Leggings.

and living apart from his fellows, as one called by the Almighty to reveal his will to his children; Tecumseh mingled so much with them as to preserve a degree of sympathy and companionship, devoting the best energies of his soul to the good of his country. Patriotism and glory were the idols of his heart, and he knelt at no meaner shrine. Unlike these, the third brother, Kumshaka, would gladly have thrown off the yoke which the loftier spirits of his brothers imposed upon him; and, disregarding the past history of the tribes, their present debasement, or future expectations; would gladly have sought the retirement of a green-wood lodge, and with some beautiful daughter of the forest, have found that peace which the dreams of ambition can never realize. But it could not be—the spell of his birth and the power of his brothers was upon him, and he followed in the path prescribed, powerless to turn aside. He was less in height and muscular development than Tecumseh, but possessed the same regularity of features, and even more of symmetrical beauty. The maidens, who could never win a smile from the one, were sure of the most approving glances of the other; and though Kumshaka's voice might be of little note in the council, where the sterner spirits of his brothers prevailed, yet in the green-wood bower, none could win greater favor from the dark-eyed daughters of the woods. He was a good hunter, and the scalps at his belt and plumes upon his helmet, betokened a warrior too. Yet Kumshaka, the admired of his people, could not submit to the stern simplicity that governed them. The gay belt, the ornamented moccasin, and deerskin robe, elaborately adorned with the quills of the porcupine, had been the labor of many fingers and were the reward of many smiles. Trinkets that Tecumseh regarded with contempt, were the envied perquisites of his brother.

They had reached the borders of the village, and Tecumseh, standing upon an elevation that commanded a prospect of the surrounding country—the wide-spread prairie, the undulating hill, dressed in verdure, the great Lakes, beaming like molten silver in the sunlight, the river, glittering like a string of gems, trailed in the solitudes of the great wilderness, and the far-off streams, giving tokens of their presence by their belt of mist rising in the distance—might have been taken for the Genius of the tribes, looking down benignly upon their heritage.

At a signal, the Prophet and his followers emerged from the village. Tecumseh's brow fell, as, file after file, a thousand warriors approached, each with his visage painted black, and arms depressed. Gloom and disaster were written upon every brow. The women and children remained in their cabins, while, solemnly and in silence, the chiefs assembled around him. Tecumseh moved not. Slowly the files opened, and the Prophet, bearing a belt before him, approached the chief. Raising it in the air, he wrenched it asunder, and flung the pieces from him.

Lightning seemed to dart from the eyes of the stern warrior, as this gesture of the Prophet revealed the breaking of the compact—the severing of the bonds of the confederation of the tribes.

"They shall die!" he exclaimed, vehemently. "Summon the chiefs who have drank of the strong-water of the white man, and let them die. The spirit of the red man is dead within them—let them die!"

Messengers were dispatched to the recreant tribes, calling upon them to appear in council at Tippecanoe, and answer for the crime of breaking the pledge that forbade the sale of Indian lands to the whites.

Whatever might have been the internal suffering of Tecumseh, thus to behold the thwarting of his great plans for the union and protection of his people, he showed no other emotion than what was requisite to decide upon their fate. His countenance resumed its tranquil and sad expression, for deep thought is sure to leave an impress of sadness—calm, beautiful sadness—that seems to look away from the present, far onward, into the unseen and eternal. When, therefore, Tecumseh led the way for his followers, they might have sought in vain any response to their own wild turbulence of passion. His calm, stately bearing awed them into submission, now as ever; and yet his was not the finesse of one willing to control, by practising the arts that are sure to impress the multitude; but the simple majesty imparted by purity and greatness of sentiment.

CHAPTER II.

That pale-face man came out alone
From the moaning wood's deep shade.—SEBA SMITH.[1]

When the day set apart for the meeting of the council arrived, instead of the gathering of dusky chiefs and the wise men of the several

---

1   Oakes Smith's husband Seba Smith (1792–1868), "Powhatan" (Canto Fifth).

tribes, a solitary youth was seen leisurely riding in from the prairie, habited in the simple uniform of the north-west,[1] being little more than a huntsman's frock, a low cap surmounted with a black feather, and a belt containing a knife, pistols and powder-horn. Henry Mansfield was a native of Vincennes, where his father had built the first log house of the opening. Mr. Mansfield, being of an open generous temper, and withal, fond of the adventurous life of the back-woods, had associated familiarly with the Indians, always ready to relieve their necessities, and often to share in their hunting expeditions. Henry, his only child, had lived a demi-savage life, roving for days with the natives in the wild woods, chasing with them the fleet deer to its covert, managing the light canoe, and practising with them feats of strength and agility; then returning to the log-cabin of his parents, to con with greater zest the treasures of his father's small library, and indulge in the ease which an abundance of the good things of life afforded. He was well known, and a favorite with the youth of the different tribes; and when General Harrison selected him to convey a message to the brothers at Tippecanoe, he could not have chosen one more acceptable. Tecumseh himself welcomed his young friend to the village, and, calling the principle warriors together, listened to the 'talk' of the white Father.

General Harrison desired the Prophet and Tecumseh to meet him at Vincennes, to make known their claims to the land sold by the Indians at the Council of Fort Wayne, and also desired that the chiefs engaged in that treaty might not be disturbed, till the white Father and Tecumseh should hold a council together: moreover, it was the will of General Harrison, that no more than forty warriors should attend the brothers at Vincennes. Further, he desired that the murderers engaged in the slaughter of the Durand family, should be delivered up to justice.

Tecumseh waved his hand impatiently. "The white Father, General Harrison, is a great chief—so is Tecumseh. The land sold upon

---

1   The Old Northwest, or Northwest Territory, is the area around the Great Lakes that now encompasses the states of Ohio, Indiana, Illinois, Michigan, Wisconsin, and part of Minnesota. The Northwest Ordinance passed by Congress in 1787 accelerated Westward expansion by opening the area for settlement and establishing a means for admitting new states to the nation. Tippecanoe, Vincennes, Fort Wayne, and the town of the Prophet (or Prophetstown) are located in what is now the state of Indiana. See map on p. 294.

the Wabash does not belong to the tribes who sold it, but every red man has a right therein. No one tribe can sell without the consent of all. I will meet the General in council. I do not desire war. The red man has buried his talons deep in his flesh: he may be handled like the cub of the panther, when it sports among our children. It is many suns since the Durand family were slaughtered. The murderers are not with us: they belong to the Crooked Path—Winnemac.[1] We will meet in council."

Low, guttural sounds of displeasure broke from one of the younger members of the council. Maveerah sprang from his seat:

"While we smoke the pipe at the council of the white man, the chiefs will be saying there is no union of the tribes—it is broken— and we dare not revenge it. We are weary of rest. Show us the smoke of their cabins, that we may put it out with their blood."

A thousand tomahawks glittered in the light, and the war-whoop burst from every lip.

Tecumseh stood unmoved till the tumult had ceased.

"Chiefs, they are our brethren. The Great Spirit hath stamped the same features upon his red children everywhere. I have been where our brothers hunt the bear amid the ice of the great lakes, the buffalo by the mountains of the setting sun, and where the alligator is dragged from the rivers of the burning sky. The red man is the same everywhere. The Great Spirit made him of the color of the land he hath given us to inherit. It is ours. The white man shall not wrest it from us. We will tell their great chief so, and he will restore it. The Great Spirit is angry with us, that we slay one another. Chiefs, hear me:

"The red fox and the gray fox were originally of the same stock. The red fox wandered away, and finding the country warm and abounding in game, he did not return to his old haunts. After many suns, the foxes increased so that they often met in pursuing game; and, as the red fox had grown very expert, a treaty was agreed upon, and they were henceforth to live in unity—to hunt together, and unite in repelling the wolf, who was growing every day more troublesome. At length it was discovered that the gray foxes were selling their game to get possession of some choice meat, which the wolf only could procure. The red foxes determined upon revenge. A great

---

1 Potawatomi leader who opposed Tecumseh.

battle took place. The woods were full of the slain foxes. The scent attracted their enemies, the wolves, and they poured in upon them, devouring all, without stopping to see whether they were red or gray: they were all foxes. It was too late for defence. The foxes have ever since been inferior to the wolves in power and numbers. But it taught them that cunning which has ever since distinguished them."

A smile mantled the visages of the chiefs as each one made the application, and Tecumseh slowly retired.

The tall figure of the Prophet next appeared. He bore in one hand a rude vessel of earthen, through the pores of which large drops of water were oozing, and hanging in heavy beads—looking deliciously cool in the hot atmosphere; in the other, he held two dry pieces of wood. A long deerskin robe, covered with numerous devices, swept upon the ground, confined at the waist by a belt of wampum. Hoofs of the wild deer depended in a long string from his neck, and the rattles of the massasauga fastened upon the sleeves of his robe, shook at every motion. An immense skin of the same animal, preserved with great skill—the fiery tongue still projecting, and the spiral tail borne aloft with its many rattles—was flung across one shoulder, and at the other hung the bow and quiver.

Passing slowly around the assembly, he sang in a monotonous tone: "A poison lurked in the veins of the red man, but it is passing away. It sapped the strength of our warriors, but their might shall return. Children were fading from our wigwams, and old men from the council hall. They shall sport once more at our thresholds, and the head of snow shall smoke the council-pipe."

Then raising the vessel of water aloft, he scattered its contents among the assembly.

"This was the drink of our fathers; it came leaping from the mountains, or was poured out from the hand of the Great Spirit. It made them strong. It was no burning serpent, to steal away their brains."

Rubbing the dry pieces of wood together, a flame burst forth, and he kindled a fire with the dry leaves at his feet:

"Thus did our fathers light the fire of our cabins. The musket of the white man, the flint and the steel, and the water of flame were unknown to them. Thus did they bring down the game to supply their wants."

He disengaged the bow from his shoulder, and an eagle, soaring like a speck in the thin atmosphere above, wavered in its flight, shivered its heavy wings, and fell to the ground. A cry burst from the assembly: "Let us do as our fathers did, that their strength may be ours."

Eliskwatawa stood, as the arrow had sprung from the bow, with foot advanced, his shoulders thrown back, the bow still elevated, his proud head raised to the sky; while his deep glittering eyes were fixed upon the group before him. The skin of the massasauga had slid from his shoulders, and lay like a living thing at this feet. Without changing his position, he continued in a deeper tone, with his teeth clenched in the strength of his emotion:

"Our fathers were strong men. Like the massasauga, they gave the alarm: but their blow was deadly."

His arm fell to his side, and, moving onward, he sang in the same low key with which he had commenced:

"The strong arm shall return, and the smoke of our cabins shall go up from every valley."

One after another the chiefs arose to depart, with arms folded upon their bosoms and head depressed; as men swayed by great purposes, and resolved to do all things for the furtherance of the vast scheme that was to restore the tribes to their primitive greatness and simplicity.

When Henry Mansfield retired from the council of the chiefs, the long shadows lay upon the grass, and the sun glittering through the leaves of the trees, fell upon the river as it rippled by, lighting it up as if a shower of gems were sparkling and heaving in the light. The old men had seated themselves at the doors of their wigwams, smoking, while the younger portion were disporting themselves into groups, practising games of hazard or feats of strength. Children were collected upon the area in front of the village, trying their skill with the bow, and their strength in poising the javelin. In the rear of the cabins might occasionally be seen a canoe in the progress of construction, while the women were busy in preserving beans, corn and other seeds for the winter stock, or spreading fish upon rude flakes to dry in the sun. Though the blankets and many other articles introduced by the whites had been thrown aside, and most of the males were clad in the primitive garments of the tribe, the women still retained many of the obnoxious articles, such as rings for the fingers and arms, and a profusion of colored beads; and in more than one instance might be seen, suspended upon the breast, a plate of silver rudely chased, and of the size of an ordinary saucer.

Mansfield had determined to await the marching of Tecumseh and his guard to Vincennes, and he sauntered leisurely through the village, recognizing old acquaintances, and remarking the progress of the several amusements, well pleased when the lofty chief, Tecumseh, left him to the more companionable Kumshaka. Adopting at once the Indian mode of locomotion, which consists in always preserving a direct line, stepping one foot upon the line of the other, with no turning out of the toe, as is the case with Europeans, he kept within the foot-paths of the natives, though no wider than the foot. These were always worn to the hardness of a rock, and intersecting each other in all directions, looked like serpents gliding through the green grass. Following his companion, they reached the banks of the river as the last ray of sunset glittered a moment upon a lofty pine, that towered up above the natives of the forest; its polished spires quivering like myriads of tiny spears, and then as the light receded, softly resuming their bright green hue, and fading away to the sombre shade of the dim woodland.

Scarcely had they seated themselves upon a point projecting into the river, when Kumshaka sprang to his feet, and sent a keen glance down the river. Mansfield followed the direction of his eye, but nothing was obvious to the senses. At length a faint plashing of the water fell upon the ear, but whether from the dip of an oar or the wing of a wild duck, he could not determine. The sounds approached, and he could distinguish the measured fall of a paddle, and soon a slight curve of the river revealed to him a canoe of diminutive dimensions, propelled by a single voyager. The youth sprang forward with eager surprise, as a moment more revealed the occupant to be a young girl of surprising beauty; her slight figure gently bent, as, with the least imaginable effort, the small paddle sent the canoe rippling over the water. Filled with her own sweet thoughts, her lips were slightly parted, and her head thrown back, revealing an outline that a sculptor might envy. Her deep, expressive eyes, were fixed upon the pile of gorgeous clouds that draped the pavillion of the setting sun, and occasionally a few notes of a wild song burst from her lips, as if she sang in the very idleness of delight. "It is the Swaying Reed," whispered Kumshaka.

A few strokes of the paddle brought the slight barque under the shadow of a tree, almost at the feet of the young men. Kumshaka leapt to her side, and took the canoe from the water to the green bank. A sweet, but haughty smile played for a moment over the face of the girl, and then a blush mantled her cheek and bosom as she perceived his companion. An instant her full eye rested upon his face, and then she passed on, her small slender fingers instinctively grasping the robe that shaded and yet revealed her bosom. Her dress was a mixture of the savage, with a tasteful reference to the civilized mode. It was composed of skins so delicate in their texture, and so admirably joined together, as to give the appearance of a continuous piece, the whole resembling the richest velvet. The robe reached but little below the knee, with a narrow border of the porcupine quills, richly colored. It was confined at the waist by a belt wrought in the same manner, while a like facing passed up the bust in front, leaving it partially open, and spreading off upon each shoulder, descended the arm upon both sides of the sleeve to the elbow; the two portions of which were joined together by a row of small white shells. In this way the neck and shoulders were left exposed, and the bust but partially concealed. Her hair was drawn to the back of the head, and fell in long braids below the waist; a string of the crimson seeds of the wild rose, encircling it like a coronal of rubies. She was rather above the ordinary height, delicately, and yet so justly proportioned, as to leave nothing to desire. There was a freedom and grace in her stately step, totally unlike the long trot of the natives. Mansfield was a young man, and familiar with classical allusion; and he thought, as might have been expected, of Diana and her nymphs, and the whole train of goddesses from Juno down; and concluded, by turning as if to follow in the direction of the maiden. Kumshaka arrested him.

"The Swaying Reed is a proud maiden, and fit for the councils of our people."

"Can it be, that she belongs to the tribes? I thought she must be some white girl from the settlement, who perhaps in sport had adopted your dress."

"A white girl!" retorted the chief, scornfully; "a white girl, with a step like the fawn in its stateliness or speed, an eye that can bring the eagle from the cloud, and a hand to paddle the birch canoe over the rapids, to the very verge of the cataract!"

"Surely, surely," said the other, "she can be no Indian maid with those soft features; and where the wind lifted the hair from her brow it was pure, as—as"—in his eagerness he was at a loss for a comparison, and the Indian laughed at his perplexity.

"She is beautiful," resumed Kumshaka, "for she hath lived in the freedom of wood and mountain. The spring-time blossom hath slept upon her cheek, and the red berry clustered about her mouth. The brown nut hath painted her hair, and the dusky sky looked into her eyes. The wind that swayeth the young woods hath lent her its motions, and the lily from the still lake made its home upon her bosom. But the Great Spirit hath given her a proud heart, and wisdom to mix in the councils of old men."

Mansfield did not press his inquiries, for he saw that his companion was adroit in evasion; and though inwardly resolved to fathom, if possible, the history of the fair girl whose appearance had so fired his imagination; this, his first essay, had taught him the necessity of caution in pursuing his inquiries. He threw himself upon his bed of skins and slept soundly until morning, for the fatigues and excitements of the day had so predisposed him to slumber, that even the image of the Swaying Reed, the last that dwelt upon his memory, was insufficient to drive the god from his pillow.

CHAPTER III.

When the hunter turned away from that scene,
Where the home of his fathers once had been,
And heard by the distant and measured stroke,
That the woodman hewed down the giant oak;
And burning thoughts flashed over his mind
Of the white man's faith, and love unkind.—LONGFELLOW.[1]

Leaving Mansfield and his companion at the verge of the river, the Swaying Reed passed onward to the tent of the Prophet, where Tecumseh, and some of the older chiefs were assembled. Pausing at the threshold with her fingers carelessly interlocked, and arms falling down before her, she said in a rich, low voice,

"The chiefs have left a woman to seek out the councils of their foes. Winnemac is too wary to be caught in the snare, or to be tracked home to the den." She pursued her way, leaving them to divine as best they might the meaning of what she had said.

It is impossible to say what vague reminiscences the appear-

---

1   Henry Wadsworth Longfellow (1807–82), "The Indian Hunter."

ance of Henry Mansfield had awakened in the bosom of the forest girl. When she sought the wigwam of Mother Minaree, she scarcely replied to the gratified welcome of the good woman, but throwing herself upon the skins, buried her face in her hands, and burst into tears. Minaree tried to console her, by applying the most endearing epithets of which her language was capable. "Tell me what shadow has fallen on the head of the Swaying Reed, and I will chase it away."

"Call me Margaret, dear Minaree," said the weeping girl.

Minaree sank on the skins beside her, and tears gathered in her aged eyes.

"Margaret is tired of her Indian mother. She longs to be with her own people."

"No, no, mother, but a weight is upon my breast, and the shadows of many years are crowding back upon me."

She raised herself up, and began to caress a snowy fawn that had laid its head upon her shoulder to attract her attention.

"I love you, Minaree, you have been a mother to me. I have none to love amongst my own people: I will listen to the singing of the night-bird, and my heart will be light again."

She threw a string of wampum over the neck of her favorite, and disappeared in the thick foliage that skirted the river.

The cabin of Minaree possessed many points to distinguish it from the others of the village. It stood upon the very outskirts, and a slight sweep of the stream brought the waters within a few paces of the threshold. Margaret had trained the wild rose, and the woodbine, and the delicate clematis, to the very roof, so that the dwelling could scarcely be distinguished from the surrounding shrubbery. Upon each side were patches of flowers, which she had sought in the woods and transplanted to embellish her dwelling. Where the green sloped to the river, a wild vine had draped the trees into a natural arbor, and Minaree had helped her foster-child to weave about it a lattice and seats of osier.

The interior of the cabin, likewise, combined an air of taste and comfort, which could only have been supplied by the recollections of Margaret. Minaree still spread her skins upon the floor, and seated herself upon them in a mode resembling the Turk upon his ottoman; but Margaret's couch was woven of osier, raised about a foot from the floor, and covered with skins of snowy whiteness. Small stools of the same construction occupied one side, and a bow and arrows, light paddles for a canoe, nets, strings of wampum, embroidered belts, moccasins, and rude ornaments, were suspended from the walls. A heavy skin of the buffalo concealed the entrance, which in the day time was turned upon one side, by means of a loop fastening it to a peg driven into one of the frame logs of the house.

Away from the sympathy and condolence of her foster-mother, Margaret abandoned herself to the luxury of weeping alone, in the secrecy of her own heart, with none to wonder thereat, and none to attempt the futile task of consolation, gathered, as it too often is, from the very sources that but aggravate the poignancy of grief. With instinctive gentleness of heart, she threw one arm over the neck of her favorite fawn, which looked mutely in her face, as if it sympathized in her sufferings. She bowed her head upon her hand, and wept freely; for the sight of one of her own people had awakened the deep echoes of other years, and brought back the voices of the dead, and the long-buried recollections of childhood. A new sense of solitude weighed heavily upon her, and she felt as one who had been severed from the loves and kindnesses of her race, and abandoned to the wild and strange destinies of another people. Her heart yearned for the voice of kindness, for the household tones of other days, for the holy observance of an enlightened faith, and the refinements and quietude of civilized life. She would once more have nestled in the lap of affection, with the security and confidence which only peace and love can bestow.

The thick clusterings of the vine were lifted up, and Tecumseh stood in the little bower. Margaret raised her head, and arose listlessly to her feet.

"The night-dew hath weighed the Swaying Reed to the earth— can Tecumseh brush it away?" and the voice of the chief was low and musical, as he bent his brow over the beautiful girl.

"Call me Margaret, chief; call me by the name of my childhood;" and the poor girl looked imploringly, and with an expression of utter wretchedness, into the face of the warrior. A sharp expression of pain came to the features of the chief, and he placed her upon the rude seat, while he laid himself upon the turf at her feet.

"The blossom pines for the soil in which it was first nurtured— for companionship like its own—for the long-remembered dew and sunshine of other skies. The will of the maiden is law with Tecumseh. She shall return to her people."

Margaret's hands were clasped, and her eyes fixed as one that sees, and yet regards not; and her utterance was as one that talks to himself, or murmurs in unquiet slumbering. "I behold a dwelling in the deep woods, with its vines and blossoms. I behold a stern man, wrestling in prayer; prayer to the true God, whom I have forgotten, or worship under the name of the Great Spirit. There is a sister with her bird-like voice, and brow of gentleness, and she folds me to her bosom, as the shadows of night gather around us. A pale, calm face is bending over us, with a sweet smile, but full of sadness, and she calls me child. Dreams, long—long dreams of sunshine, of peace and love are with me. There is the brook, where the gay fish leaped in the light—the bridge which my sister helped to build—the verge of the dark woods where the fox came out to bark—the pasture where we gathered the ripe berries. Hark!" and she sprang wildly from her seat, overcome with the vividness of the picture which her own fancy had brought before her; "hark! I hear yells and shrieks! The feeble woman is covered with her own blood, and the terrified eyes of the child meet mine, as it swings in the air to be dashed against the tree! The stern man is writhing and prostrate, and I am powerless!" She sank backward, pale and trembling, and the chief regarded her with that awe, with which all are inclined to listen to those suddenly bereft of reason; as if their speech were akin to inspiration—the spontaneous utterance of the divine soul.

A gush of tears came to her relief, and the chief, with native refinement, did not interrupt their flow. After a pause, in which she recovered her wonted composure, she remarked:

"The nest of the bird was riven, and scattered to the winds; but it sought a shelter in the bosom of Tecumseh."

For a moment, a melancholy smile played over the face of the girl, but it yielded to a quick expression of suffering, as painful memories had driven the blood back to her heart; and she replied with that apathy which misery alone can bring;

"A thankless boon, Tecumseh; life, only life, which we hold in common with the reptiles at our feet. A wretched boon. A breathing existence of solitude and misery."

The chief sprang to his feet, and a tomahawk glittered in the moonlight. Margaret, without life or motion, lay at his feet. He threw the tomahawk aside, and raised her gently in his arms, while he held back the thick vines, till the night-winds brought the color to her lips.

"Margaret, is life valueless? I did but jest with thee;" and then, in a deeper voice, as one whose holiest emotions have been stirred from their fountain, he went on. "Maiden, I will restore thee to thy people; I will give thee back to those who will speak thee fair, with hollow hearts, where kindness will be as water spilled upon the earth; and the poor Indian is but a beast of the woods, to be hunted down, and destroyed. Go—go, it will but take a beam of light from the eyes of Tecumseh."

Margaret bent her head as if listening to the tones of pleasant music, with her hands folded, and tears trembling upon her eye lids. Crowding back the tumultuous recollections of other days, she replied solemnly.

"No, Tecumseh, the Swaying Reed will return no more to her people. There is none left for her to love. I would this stranger had not appeared among us, for he brought back what I fain would have forgotten. It is past now, and I am again one of the red people. Their wrongs are mine: I will suffer with them—die with them."

The chief bowed his head, admiringly. "The tongue of the Swaying Reed is as the melody of a bird; it liveth on the ear, when the sound hath passed from the lips. Tecumseh has wept at the sorrows of the Swaying Reed, and her pale, proud beauty amid the dark maidens of his tribe, has always gone to his heart. She has been as a fawn deserted of its dam, and the red man has sheltered, and nourished her. In the long march he has saved her from toil, and returning from the hunt, he has laid his spoils at the door of her wigwam. She has been light, and beauty, and gladness to the heart of Tecumseh. He has wept, when the maiden wept, for her sorrows have been his own. He knoweth of the deadly vengeance of his people; that it can never slumber; but the white man first put blood upon his face. The innocent now suffer with the guilty, but the fault is his own. The Indian mother paddled her canoe upon the river; her infant slept upon her bosom, and her children dipped their fingers in the water, over its edge. The white man's rifle is sure, and deadly—the child swallowed blood for its milk, and the canoe floats idly down the stream. The old man, and the helpless maiden, are robbed, or murdered, in the wantonness of blood, and there is none to do them justice. There is no help for the poor Indian. Wrong and outrage are heaped upon him, and there is none to help. The Great Spirit hath cast a cloud of blackness about him. The stars tell of war and disaster, and the dreams of our old men are full of wo.[1] The strong water of the white man stealeth away the brains of his red brother, and he bartereth away the village, where his children have sported; the graves of his fathers, the old hunting-grounds and council-fires, and the ancient mounds, that tell our children of the battle-grounds of warriors, and the graves of great chiefs. There is no home for the red man. His fires have gone out in a thousand valleys, and the ploughshare of the white man passeth over his bones. Like the mist that saileth off over the big lakes, he is passing away; voices call him from the Spirit Land—the night wind bringeth the sound of warriors, as they pursue their game in the spirit land. The spirit-bird sitteth all night upon the roof of our cabins, and he singeth of the spirit land. The Indian must pass from the earth. He must be as a dream that is no more."

There was a tone of the deepest pathos in the utterance of the chief; and after his voice ceased, the melody of its tones seemed to linger upon the ear. He stood with his head inclined, the flexible lip parted, and his dark eye fixed in melancholy vacancy.

Margaret was about to reply, when a slight rattling and stirring of the vines arrested her. She clung to the arm of the chief, pale with terror.

"Fear it not, maiden. It is the good manitou of the Shawanee—a noble reptile; it telleth of its presence, and striketh only when molested. The Great Spirit hath sent it to speak hope to the heart of Tecumseh. But alas! the spirit of the red man hath departed. The Swaying Reed is wise and noble, like the manitou of the Shawanese. Did she seek out the councils of the Crooked Path?"

"Winnemac is with the white chief at Vincennes. All the chiefs that have taken of the strong water are with him."

Tecumseh's brow contracted sharply. "Said I not the spirit of the red man has departed?" He stood a moment wrapped in thought, and then taking the hand of Margaret, he led her from the arbor, passing the massasauga, as it lay coiled in the moonlight, its burnished folds gleaming and changing like a heap of gems piled on the green earth. It moved not as they went by, though Margaret could plainly see its strange, glittering eyes, motionless in their repose; and she felt, as all do on looking into the eyes of the brute creation,

---

1 An archaic spelling of *woe* that is used consistently throughout the original text.

a mixture of dread and wonder, as if one sought to penetrate the mystery of its being, learn what were its thoughts, if any it had, while looking back into the depths of a human eye. There is something so oppressive in that half-animal, half-intelligent expression, that tempts one to believe in the doctrine of metempsychosis;[1] as if those huge and uncouth forms concealed the imprisoned souls of the unhappy, who thus look mutely from their prison-houses, to ask of us sympathy and condolence.

CHAPTER IV.

A youth as tall, as straight as I,
As quick a quarry to descry:
A hunter skilful in the chase,
As ever moccasin did lace.—HOFFMAN.[2]

When Minaree raised the entrance to her cabin the next morning, a parcel, rolled in the thinnest bark of the birch tree, and tied with wampum, lay at the threshold, with a bouquet of fresh water lilies. She brought them to the couch of Margaret, saying, "Tecumseh would take away the light of my eyes."

Margaret smiled mournfully, and a blush stole upon her cheek. She undid the parcel. It was a robe of delicate feathers, exquisitely wrought. She looked upon the inside, and beheld a small turtle painted upon the lining, with a rattlesnake sleeping upon a rock. The device told her it was from the hand of Kumshaka, for the token of Tecumseh would have been the same animal in the act to spring.

Minaree seemed gratified at the mistake—"Kumshaka will help to paddle the canoe, and gather in the corn—he will smile in his cabin, and talk with his children. He is a good hunter, and much venison will be found in his wigwam."

The girl re-enclosed the parcel, and sinking carelessly upon her couch, desired Minaree to carry it to the cabin of the donor. The good woman looked disappointed; but so accustomed was she to yield acquiescence to the wishes of Margaret, that she did so now mechanically.

---

1   Transmigration of the soul from one body to another, as in reincarnation after death.
2   Charles Fenno Hoffman (1806–84), "Kachesco—A Legend of the Sources of the Hudson."

Henry Mansfield was the first to observe the package at the cabin door of his host, and his knowledge of Indian customs at once revealed the secret.

"What! Kumshaka rejected by the maidens! Had it been Eliskwatawa, or Tecumseh, I should not marvel—or even myself; but I thought Kumshaka the idol of the girls of his tribe. Tell me the name of the cruel fair one."

The youth, though evidently annoyed at the raillery of his companion, could not resist the flattery it implied, and he walked before the door with his arms folded, occasionally glancing complacently at his own fine proportions, and the trinkets that adorned them.

"Tell me the name of the cruel fair, and she shall never have bead or ribbon from the hands of Henry Mansfield. Even the Swaying Reed, proud as she seems, could not resist a gift like this, and from such a giver."

"The Swaying Reed, like my two brothers, lives in the greatness of her own thoughts. Few would dare send gifts to her cabin. She is too proud and too beautiful for love."

So saying, he threw a quiver of arrows over his shoulder, and plunged into the forest. The day was one of unclouded beauty— the sun moving onward in its majesty, leaving, as it journeyed west, the sky of its pathway blue—intensely and beautifully blue, like a sea of azure, on which the eye rested with a sense of quiet luxury. The long, shrill notes of the locust arose like an alarum[1] in the still woods, and was then silent. The butterfly poised itself long upon the blossoms; and the mute dragon-fly, with its mottled wings, darted everywhere over the still pools, in the very ecstasy of its bliss. The saucy squirrel sat with its tail erect upon the branches, and held its nuts with infantile dexterity, the shells rattling upon the dry leaves beneath. It was the very Sabbath of nature—its fullness of repose, when the human soul goes out in sympathy with it; and its own growth in the good and the spiritual, is as unmarked as the silent operations of the great mother, when thus she seems to rest, and yet is elaborating her beautiful creations.

Kumshaka stalked onward, the one discordant link in this chain of harmony; for even the deer had laid aside its timidity, and was reclined upon the margin of the streams where the trees clustered

---

1　A warning or alarm, especially a call to arms.

thickly; and a solitary panther had stretched itself upon a huge limb of an oak, its claws retracted, its head upon its paws, and its terrible eyes winking with the quietude of a cat. Instantly, as the chief perceived it, she raised her head, and began to rip the bark with her talons, for instinct had revealed the presence of a foe. The chief adjusted an arrow, without once moving his eyes from those of the beast, and, true to the skill of years, it leapt to its very heart. The panther sprang forward with a fierce and appalling roar, that waked up the silent echoes, and sent terror to the hearts of the feeble. Kumshaka had sprung to one side, and he watched the impotent rage and the frightful writhings of its dying agony with a sense of delight. In his own rage and disappointment, the repose of nature appalled him; but his own hand had produced, in its stead, a state akin to himself, and the consciousness gave him joy. If he might never win the love of the Swaying Reed, his was the power at least of causing her the pangs of suffering. If she loved not him, wo to whomsoever might win her love. The vengeance of Kumshaka might never slumber. He would pursue them with his hatred till life should be a burden of misery. For her sake, too, others of her sex should know the agony that unrequited love can inflict; and his eye kindled as he thought of one, the beauty of the tribe, who had long loved him in vain. He took an intense delight in dwelling upon all that aggravated his own sense of misery, because it assured him that Ackoree had suffered the same.

In the two days that intervened between his arrival in the village, and the departure of the chiefs for Vincennes, Mansfield found abundance of amusement among the simple inhabitants. A few trinkets and yards of gay ribbon established him as a favorite, and gave him access to every wigwam.

Observing a group of maidens seated in a thicket on the verge of the river, plaiting baskets, he joined them, and witnessed the grace and ease of their motions. At a little distance, the elderly matrons were engaged in coarse work of the kind, their children creeping about in the green grass, or crawling to the water side, where they splashed it about with bursts of noisy merriment. The air was excessively sultry, and the inhabitants were mostly gathered on the banks of the stream, where a light wind broke it into ripples. A boy of some dozen years appeared sustaining the feeble steps of a woman, nearly blind, and bowed with age. He assisted her gently to a seat in the shade, and disappeared amid murmurs of approbation. "He will be the glory of his tribe. Children shall learn goodness from him, and wisdom shall be found in his path," with similar exclamations, were on every lip.

Mansfield looked about, and almost blushed at the color of his own skin. "This is the people," he thought, "whom our nation regard with so much abhorrence, and hunt from the earth. Surely the language of the Saviour may not be inapplicable to them—'The foxes have holes, and the birds of the air have nests, but the' poor Indian 'hath not where to lay his head.'[1] What is the value of a territory to us, compared with the infringement of rights we are bound to respect, and local attachments that ought to excite our reverence? A country based upon injustice can never prosper. The blood of the red man will call from the ground as did that of Abel of old, and wo to us when the great Parent shall demand, 'where is thy brother?'"[2]

Oppressed with these reflections, the gaiety of the girls, pursuing their light employment, grated upon his feelings, and he regarded them with emotions similar to those which a spectator must feel at the cheerfulness of one about to be led forth to execution. There was so much of ease and abandonment to the quiet happiness of the moment in all their looks and manners, that it would seem as if care and anxiety had never found entrance among them. The playful remark, and low, musical laugh relieved without disturbing their voluptuous indolence, and only lent a new grace to the softness of the lip. The careless play of the small fingers seemed rather in obedience to an instinct of nature, than an effort of the will.

Margaret had just completed a small basket of exquisite color and finish, when she presented it to Mansfield, saying, "Let this remind the white man that peace is to be found in an Indian wigwam."

Kumshaka was leaning against the bole of a tree, bitterly regarding the group about him, when the action and voice of Margaret aroused him, and he turned his fierce eyes upon her, and a scowl lowered upon his brow. Margaret was unmoved, except perhaps a prouder expression grew upon her lip, and a slight look of defiance gleamed from beneath the dark lashes of her eye.

"Beautiful, mysterious girl," broke unconsciously from the lips of the youth. Margaret returned his impassioned look with one of cold

---

1 Jesus' words, with "poor Indian" substituted for "the Son of Man" (Matthew 8:20; Luke 9:58).
2 The Lord to Cain, who has murdered his brother Abel (Genesis 4:9).

indifference and the blush that faded from her cheek gave place to a fearful paleness, and a sharp expression of suffering. Conscious of his error, awed by the simple majesty of the girl, and yet desirous to return some token of remembrance, he took a small hoop of gold from his finger, and with a manner most provokingly and unaccountably awkward, begged she would wear it for his sake. Margaret withdrew her hand, and bending her head over the osiers in her lap, replied, "The Swaying Reed takes her gifts only from the Great Spirit, but a drop hath fallen upon the fountain of her heart to remain there for ever."[1]

Moved in spite of himself, he turned away and beheld Kumshaka bending over, as if to catch the very breathing of the beautiful girl, and his countenance expressive of the most intense pleasure. Margaret had witnessed the same thing, but she gave no token of her consciousness. A moment more, and the proud and gratified chief stood erect, and was carelessly replying to some light remark of a forest girl. Mansfield at once understood the secret of his evasion in regard to the history of the girl. When Margaret rose to return to her cabin, he followed by her side, hoping to ascertain something of her history, and certainly with an indefinite wish that she should be rescued from her woodland life, and be restored to society. Margaret moved on with her cold and calm manner, scarcely glancing at her companion.

When they reached the arbor of vines, she paused for a moment, and then motioned him to the wicker-chair, while she remained standing. The young man, too courteous to permit this seated himself upon the turf, and she occupied the rejected seat. More than once he attempted to break the awkwardness of silence, but the large dark eyes of the girl, fixed upon his face, and the composure with which she regarded him, operated like a spell. Of all the pretty nothings that had hitherto crowded upon his lips, not one would come at this bidding.

"The white youth has forgotten the purpose of his coming," at length said the maiden.

"No, no; but I know not how to say it—you are not one of this people, your looks, manner, all betray it—Can I not procure your release? Will you not return to the settlements—I—I—"—he blushed

---

1   Forever, which is consistently written as two words in the text.

and hesitated—at this moment a sharp whizzing cut the air, and an arrow quivered in the trunk of the tree just above his head. Mansfield sprang to his feet, and looked forth; nothing was visible—ashamed at his perturbation at what might have been entirely accidental, he returned to the arbor. Margaret retained her position unmoved, and a careless smile rested upon her lips.

"The white man is safe," said the girl, "the arrow was only sent in warning. The Swaying Reed is beloved by the tribe, and none may dare to take her away. She is her own mistress, and goes and comes at the bidding of none."

"But you are not one of them—I heard you called Margaret, and your looks are not such as to deceive. The white mother weeps for her lost child, and children miss her at their sports. Can the white girl be happy here, away from her people? Let me seek out her parents and restore them their child."

While the youth uttered this in a deep earnest voice, the maiden fixed her sorrowful eyes upon his face, and there was a slight quivering of the lip, betraying the presence of emotion. But she did not interrupt him, or change her position of tranquil indifference; and yet she seemed to listen, pleased at the language of her own people.

"None are left to mourn for the Swaying Reed. Blood hath swallowed the fire from her hearth-stone. None will weep for her. She is happy with her red people. The Great Spirit is here in the solitude of the woods to take care of her;" and she arose to depart.

Mansfield took her hand respectfully. "But, maiden, there is a voice powerful alike in the forest or city—the Indian will lay his offerings at the door of your cabin, and who will counsel the lone girl? who will protect her?"

Margaret withdrew her hand—one instant her eyes fell beneath his, and a burning blush mantled her cheek; then she raised them to the blue sky, pointed upward, and was gone. A low laugh, uttered at the very ear of the youth, caused him to turn, and he beheld the glittering eyes of Kumshaka, peering through the leaves of the vine.

"Doth the honey of the white lips sink into the heart of the forest girl? The Swaying Reed is no white maiden to be lured by smooth words. She has no love for gay robes and trinkets—and turns away from the spoils of the chase—even the scalps of war may not win her. She has a great soul. She looks all night upon the stars, and will tell us their language. When the Great Spirit layeth his broad shield over the moon, at her prayers he moves it aside, little by little, till it is left to shine again and light us to the chase. When the star with its long fiery train appeared in the sky, she warned us that war and bloodshed should appear. My brothers ask counsel of the maiden, for strange wisdom is upon her lips—but love hath no place in her heart."

The chief had leaned against the smooth bole of a tree, and gave utterance to his thoughts in a low and measured cadence, like one communing with himself.

Mansfield, baffled and perplexed, full of a strange interest in the mysterious maiden, so gifted and beautiful, and throwing the power of her own greatness over the strange people who had adopted her, turned away from the chief almost with abhorrence, while he thus acknowledged his attachment for one so unlike himself. He felt as if the very circumstance of her having awakened an attachment in such a mind, unrequited though it evidently was, were like a stain upon her purity. All the virtues and accomplishments of the chief were so many crimes, when the possibility occurred to his mind, that they might at some time plead in his behalf to the heart of the white girl.

CHAPTER V.

Love knoweth every form of air,
   And every shape of earth,
And comes, unbidden, everywhere,
   Like thought's mysterious birth!—WILLIS.[1]

Human passions are the same everywhere, whether amid the splendors of a palace or the homeliness of a savage wigwam. In the one, the conventionalisms of polite society prompt to their concealment; in the other, the subtle motives of revenge, policy or pride, produce the same result. Love is everywhere the tyrant, and his supremacy is everywhere acknowledged. The delicate girl, whose bosom swells beneath its silken bodice, and whose tears wet her embroidered pillow—whose jeweled brow throbs beneath the dainty hand that supports it; is moved by the same passion that sways the untutored girl

---

1   Nathaniel Parker Willis (1806–67), "The Annoyer."

in the solitude of the overhanging woods, with her heaving breast, swelling its zone of shells and robe of miniver.[1] The smile of hope is the same—the fear, the doubt, the long deep agony of despair are one and the same. Let the mystery of the heart be wrought out where it may—its hopes, its fears, its passions are the same. It might not be difficult to imagine the whole universe one mighty heart, with its great throbbings, its rapid pulsations, its breathless pauses, and its flood-gates of passions; and each separate person a miniature resemblance of the whole.

As the day declined, on which Mansfield held his interview with Margaret, she sought the repose and coolness of the river bank, for scarcely a breath of air stirred the leaf of the trees, that hung motionless upon the branches. The sky was without a cloud, and the red rays of sunset still lingered like a robe of crimson in the west. The distant hills grew blue and indistinct, save where, at the west, they lay bold and dark against the sky, and one tall peak hung like a white cloud in the horizon. The river was smooth as a mirror of steel, and every object upon its brink was penciled upon its bosom with a softness and fidelity, operating like fascination upon one, looking down upon its clear depths. A solitary water-fowl had stationed himself upon a rock, and so still and motionless did he remain, that his shadow below looked like the reflection of a sculptured bird, standing as the genius of the place. Margaret descended the verdant bank, for so luxuriant was the soil that vegetation continued to the very brink of the water, every stone and uncouth root being draped with its heavy coating of moss, into which the foot pressed as into a velvet carpet. Winding round the little promontory before mentioned, the river widened, forming a beautiful basin, sheltered by tall trees, that even at midday cast a refreshing gloom over the waters. The vine, springing from amid the rocks and dipping its roots into the stream, sent forth its long twisted arms, embracing the old trees, and mingling its cheerful foliage with their sombre hues; then springing away arch above arch, presented from the centre of the basin a lofty dome, rising far above its bosom, and admitting occasionally a glimpse of the blue sky through the clustering leaves. A bald eagle, that had stood for hours upon the naked branch of a gnarled oak, spread forth his broad pinions, fanned the air slowly, and soared off into the thin

---

1 White fur.

atmosphere, as if the hush of the earth and sky had been too deep and beautiful for him to disturb.

Margaret descended the bank, intending to seat herself upon a shelf of the rocks, worn by the action of the water at the time of high freshets in the spring of the year; but a light splash of the water, as if a pebble had been cast into it, caused her to look over, and she beheld the place occupied by Ackoree, the beauty of the tribe, who sat collecting the pebbles at her side, and casting them impatiently into the stream. She had loosened her moccasins,[1] and dipped her feet into the water, where they gleamed up from beneath. Her unbound hair also floated off in long dark threads, sprinkling the river, and as she stooped over the water, her brilliant eyes looked up with wild and sparkling radiance. When Margaret stooped over, her face also was reflected from beneath. Ackoree turned her head, and a frown darkened her brow. Gathering her feet from the water, and wringing the drops from her hair, she was about to depart, when Margaret detained her. "The white girl crosses my path everywhere," she muttered in a low voice, as she concealed a string of coral beads beneath her robe.

"Nay, Ackoree, do not hide them, they are the gift of the youth from the white settlements. But sit here, and tell me why you call me the white girl; you are not used to such a term."

Ackoree smiled scornfully, and pointed to the water beneath, where the images of the two girls were reflected, each in her marvelous beauty; the one tall and reed-like, with the high, round forehead, the compact features, the large dark eyes, and thin chiselled nostril, the rich hair waving in long curls, and that air of sleeping passion; which contrasted finely with the angry, almost fierce, expression of her companion. The other, less in height, and fuller in proportion, with her long jetty hair falling in heavy masses nearly to her feet, and her figure bent over to the stream, the eyes flashing with their terrible beauty, the nostrils dilated, and the lip parted in scorn. A moment they stood in the position we have described, and Ackoree dropped her attitude of scornful attention, and stooped to tie the moccasins upon her feet.

"Ackoree," said Margaret, in a low voice, "do you love this white stranger?"

---

1   While the original text alternates between "moccasons" and "moc-casins" in reference to the soft leather shoes, I have standardized the spelling to "moccasins."

Ackoree had bent upon one knee, while she adjusted the moccasin, and she now sprang to her feet.

"Love him! what, him who gives tokens to all the maidens, and then seeks out the girl of his own color to whisper the tale of his love? No: Ackoree is too proud for that."

"Sit by me," said Margaret, "and I will tell you more of this." She spoke so low and calmly, that the girl did as she desired, and looked into her pale face with an expression of surprise.

"The youth, Ackoree, is one of my own people, and I felt a strange sympathy in hearing the utterance of my own language, but I do not love him. He urged me to return to my people—but he spoke not the language of love. Do not, Ackoree, call me the white girl—do not look coldly upon me, for I am alone with your people, alone on the earth—there is none, no not one, to love me"—and the tears gushed through the long slender fingers she had pressed to her eyes.

Ackoree was softened, and pulled the wild flowers at her feet, unconscious of what she did. At length she cried, "Margaret is too proud to love one of the red men; she despises the warriors of the tribe."

A burning blush stole over the face of Margaret, and she turned her eyes from the scrutinizing glance of her companion. In a moment the fierce passions of Ackoree were awakened.

"Aye, I see it all; the Swaying Reed loves—but revolts at the thought of dwelling in a hunter's cabin—of being the wife of the despised Indian. Had Kumshaka—been"—

Margaret laid her hand gently on the robe of Ackoree, and inhaled a long breath, as one relieved from sudden pressure.

"Ackoree—hear me. I shall never be a wife. The Great Spirit has so decreed. Am I not a daughter of the tribe? Have I not been treated with indulgence and reverence? Why should I despise those who have cherished me? Ackoree, you wrong me. You send an arrow to the fawn that lieth panting at the stream, already pierced with many darts."

"But you love the chief, Kumshaka," interrupted the other eagerly.

"No, never, Ackoree—I can never love him. Does the chief know that the beautiful Ackoree regards him with affection?"

The girl dropped her head upon her bosom, and a smile stole to her lips. She did not reply, but the string of coral had slipped from its concealment, and a part of it lay upon her bosom. She seized it eagerly, and was about to dash it into the water, when the few rays of light falling upon its brilliant color, revived that native love for ornament, so predominant in the sex, of whatever condition, and she sat with her eyes fixed upon it for a moment, and then threw it over the neck of Margaret. Her companion suffered it to remain, and Ackoree's eyes kindled with delight as the rich, deep hue of the bauble contrasted with the fairness of her neck and shoulders. And then it would seem that a sudden jealousy awoke in her mind, for she turned her head and half whispered, "Would that Ackoree were as fair."

Margaret restored the beads to the neck of the maiden, and they arose from the shadow of the wood, each with a lighter heart. Ackoree, relieved from the suspicion that Margaret loved Kumshaka; and the other, rejoiced to learn the state of her companion's heart, as she thus hoped to be relieved from the importunities of the chief.

CHAPTER VI.

> I look'd on the maiden's rosy cheek,
>   And her lip so full and bright,
> And I sighed to think that the traitor, love,
>   Should conquer a heart so light.—MRS. EMBURY.[1]

The morning had arrived on which the embassy to Vincennes was to take its departure. The area in front of the village presented a scene of activity and preparation, motley in the extreme. Tall warriors were engaged in painting their bodies in the most formidable manner, and ornamenting their heads with decorations warranted by their bravery or skill, and the choicest robes were brought forth for the great occasion. War-clubs and spears, bows and arrows, all in the last state of perfection, were piled about, and the long mystic pipe, with the odorous weed, was carefully bestowed, the one emblem of peace in the midst of all warlike preparations. Pouches filled with dried fruits and venison, were brought forth by the women, as provision for the march; trusting mostly, however, to game that might be killed on the way. The youth indolently watched the progress of preparation, while the boys adorned themselves in grotesque imita-

---

1   Emma Catherine Embury (1806–63), "The Maiden's Story."

tion of their seniors; amid shouts of merriment snapping their tiny bows, discharging arrows, and shaking the hoofs of the wild deer, while they advanced and retreated in semblance of battle, raising with shrill voices the war-whoop of the tribes. Horses tethered in the vicinity, gave notice of their presence by loud neighs and tramping, that swelled the tumult of preparation.

The dew still hung upon leaf and twig, and the threads of the spider, traveling from shrub to shrub, swung laden with gems, glittering in the morning sun. The early carol of the birds had hardly died away, when Tecumseh gave the signal to commence their march.

Tecumseh appeared, clad in that stern simplicity which accorded best with the character of his mind. He wore neither scalp nor colored quill; but a silky robe of the beaver, girded by a belt of wampum, hung in massive folds about him, in its simple dignity, resembling the Roman Toga. Upon his helmet appeared the plumes and other tokens of his rank, which the nobleman of the woods assumes as testimonials of his merit, in the same way as the champion of knighthood binds upon his person the various insignia of the orders to which he has been admitted; nor would the unworthy assumption of the one excite in the public mind more contempt and indignation than the other.

Slowly, and in silence, the chiefs moved on—the rays of the morning sun lighting up the jetty crest, and playing upon feathery robe and pointed spear. Women and children were collected to witness their departure; and on a rising ground might be seen the tall form of the Prophet, spreading out his arms with the skin of the rattlesnake aloft, and chanting a song, the burden of which seemed to be death to the violators of oaths. The deep measured cadences came upon the ear of the retreating party when far on their way—now in low guttural notes of sorrow, now prolonged to the wail of heart-rending wo; and anon rising to the shrill and rapid intonation of triumph.

Henry Mansfield lingered behind to exchange a farewell with Margaret, and to urge, if possible, her return to the settlements.

She laid her hand within his, saying, "May peace be the portion of my white brother," and was about to depart.

"Stay one moment," said the young man; "say only that I may use my influence to procure your release; that you may be prevailed upon to return to the settlements. This mode of life must be revolting to you—say only that you will return."

"Never," she replied; "my fate is fixed;" and waving adieu, she suddenly disappeared, just as the glittering eyes of Ackoree gleamed through the shrubbery that surrounded them.

"Aye," said the Indian maiden, "the white girl loves the red chief; she will never return to her people—she will dress the venison of the hunter, and work his moccasins. Is the thought sweet to the white man?" and she laughed a bitter and taunting laugh.

It would be difficult to analyze the feelings of the youth, while the beautiful, but fiend-like girl, gave utterance to this mixture of truth and falsehood, solely as it would seem to torture her hearer. When she ceased, she threw the string of coral at his feet, and departed with the same cruel laugh.

Henry kicked the bauble aside, and followed the retreating army with a listlessness and heaviness of feeling which he in vain tried to dispel. He was not in love; of this he was quite sure: she was too cold, and too proud, to awaken such a sentiment; and yet this very manner, to one accustomed to the smiles of ladies, awakened an interest he could not deny—the stronger it may be, from the wounding of his self-love.

From his own sense of mortification, it became easy to reproach the cause of it; and he blamed the perversity and distortion of taste that made her adhere to this wild life, as evidences of an inherent depravity of mind. But then came up the image of her calm, sad voice, and that infinite grace and dignity of manner, that seemed to act as a spell upon all who approached her, awing even the rudest of the tribe into respect and submission. He felt the suspicion to be as unjust to her as it was unworthy of himself. Giving spurs to his horse, he sought to lose the sense of depression by the rapidity of his movements.

There had been still another spectator to the interview we have described. Scarcely had Mansfield retired from the ground, when Kumshaka picked up the beads and followed [the] retreating youth with his eyes, while a vindictive smile gathered upon his countenance. Ackoree was at his side, and a kindred expression grew upon her own.

"The white girl delights in those of her own color. She will return, like the bird lured from the woods, to her own haunts. She does well to talk of peace to the red man—it is to save her own people."

"True, true," cried the chief; and he looked for the first time with admiration upon the cruel girl, whose feelings corresponded so well with his own.

Ackoree saw the interest she had awakened, and desirous for

sympathy from the chief, if it were but the sympathy of revenge, she continued:

"Does the white girl love the white youth? or is her love fixed upon one of our own people?" And then, as if speaking to herself, she added, "no, she despises the Indian. It is well. The fawn seeks not companionship with the wolf; nor the fox with the beaver." Ackoree fixed her bright eyes upon those of the chief, and slowly dropped the lids, while a sigh stole from her bosom.

Whether it was that the rejection of his suit had extinguished his attachment for Margaret, or the beauty of Ackoree had made its impression; whether the import of her words, while they half revealed her own attachment, had also produced their effect upon his judgment and fancy, or all combined to produce the result, we will not affirm. Certain it is, however, that as the chief fixed his eyes upon the speaking face of the girl, it was with an expression not to be mistaken; and when he threw the rejected coral over her neck, Ackoree raised her eyes to his face with a look of wild delight, and bounded away with the coyness and transparent artifice of an untutored heart. The chief bent his plumed head to catch the last glimpse of her retreating figure, and then speaking to himself, said—

"True, each delights only in its kind. But let the Swaying Reed dare to love another, and she shall know the vengeance of the Indian. Ackoree is most beautiful, but she has not the loftiness and wisdom of the Swaying Reed. She shall bring the game to the cabin of Kumshaka. He will sit at rest, and mark the glitter of her eyes, and the white girl shall sing the songs of her people, and her voice, choked with sobs, will be like the sound of waters in the still night: sad, but pleasant to the ear."

CHAPTER VII.

Oh, woman; lovely in thy beauty's power!
Thrice lovely when we know that thou canst turn
To duty's path and tread it with a smile.—MRS. C. GILMAN.[1]

When General Harrison invited Tecumseh and the Prophet to meet him in council at Vincennes, he expressly stipulated, that they should

---

1 Caroline Howard Gilman (1794–1888), "A Sketch."

appear with but few followers; a request which probably would have been complied with, had it not been for the knowledge of Tecumseh that Winnemac and other chiefs, violators of the oaths of confederation, had sought refuge from the penalty of their crime with the white authorities of Vincennes. Under these circumstances, he chose to appear with a force sufficient for his own protection, and to awe the obnoxious chiefs. Accordingly the inhabitants of the country, already terrified by repeated acts of violence, which even the influence of Tecumseh was insufficient to prevent, and which the crooked policy of Winnemac served to encourage, were appalled at beholding four hundred warriors, painted and fully armed, on their way to the infant city of the west. The terrified inhabitants closed their doors, and prepared for defence; workmen left their utensils in the field, and sought a place of refuge; children gathering fruit by the way side, might be seen huddling together in mute terror, their wild eyes gleaming out from amidst vines of shrubs to which they had fled for concealment.

At the suggestion of Mansfield, Tecumseh encamped his army in a wood, at a short distance from the city, while he should report their arrival to General Harrison.

He did so accordingly, and the next day was appointed for the holding a council. In the meanwhile, Mansfield amused himself by going about the settlement, observing the changes which a few months had produced, exchanging congratulations, and becoming acquainted with many who had recently sought protection in the city; for the news of the great number of warriors collected at the town of the Prophet, had spread a panic throughout the country, and driven many from their insulated farms to the more compact settlement at Vincennes. The humble dwellings of the emigrants were hospitably opened to the fugitives, and filled to overflowing.

Passing in the neighborhood of one of the houses on the outskirts of the place, he was attracted by the peculiar air of thrift and neatness evident in all its arrangements. It was a large sized log-building, compactly constructed, and surrounded by an enclosure in which vegetables of all kinds were growing in the greatest luxuriance. Woman's taste was visible in the rude piazza over which clustered the wild vine, and the abundant sweet-brier that shaded the small windows, draped with curtains of the purest white. Morning-glories festooned the shrubs, and the chamomile, tansey, wormwood, and other medicinal shrubs, evinced rural skill and forethought. In the rear, where a ledge of rocks broke from the rich soil, might be seen pans of brown earthenware, left to scald in the sun. Tubs and bowls of wood, rounded at the angles, and white with careful scouring, and the snowy churn inverted, with its dash crossed upon the bottom, were arranged upon a neat platform of raised timber. A pole, supported by two upright sticks notched at the top, was hung with long skeins of blue and white yarn, and a young, brisk-looking woman was sprinkling water upon linen cloth, spread to bleach in the sun.

Henry stood admiring this picture of rural comfort, drawing up the images of the inhabitants to his mind's eye, and had just convinced himself that the fat, curly-headed babe that sat in the doorway, now patting its shapeless hands together, and crowing to the poultry that cackled about the door; now venturing on all-fours to the verge of the white sill, and cautiously reaching over to the step below; then prudently retreating at the vague presentiment of bumps and bruises to be encountered in the attempt to go out, must be the property of the young woman whom he had seen sprinkling water upon the yarn; when out rushed a little urchin of some half-dozen years, quite red in the face, and looking very fierce and determined. He was followed by a young woman of perhaps twenty, whose finely-moulded features and graceful air struck him with a perplexing sense, that he had seen the same somewhere before. He soon became amused in observing the little scene before him, and ceased to notice the girl.

"I say, Alice, I will go—so let go my hand, I tell you; I will go and see the Injins, and you can't stop me."

"But, Jimmy, don't go, don't; I will tell you a story about them, if you won't. Look at me Jimmy, I know you love me."

The child stopped struggling, and let her retain his hand, though he still worked the fingers uneasily, and looked with open mouth into her face, which had now become quite colorless.

"Tell me the story quick, Ally, for I mean to go soon as you're done; and make it short, Ally."

"No, no: you must go in first."

"I won't, I won't; let go, I say;" and the boy jerked away his hand and ran off with his eyes wide open, looking back at Alice, and screaming, "I will, I will," at the top of his lungs. In the midst of his career[1] he was arrested by a sun-burnt, cheerful-looking farmer, in

---

1   Charge at full speed.

his shirt-sleeves, who quietly raised him from the ground and swung him over his shoulders, where the boy hung, his feet sticking straight out, and his face red and swollen in his impatient struggles to free his arms from the man's grasp.

By the time they had reached the door-step, the young woman was standing there with water-pail in hand, and her naturally good-natured face gathering into something like a frown.

"That boy will be the death of us yet; he wears poor Alice to death, with his tantrums."

"Not quite," said the father, patting her cheek playfully, and glancing at the grotesque image of the child over his shoulder; and then swinging the baby on his back, he seated himself on the door-sill.

The young woman looked on, half smiling, and yet half determined to be pettish: "I tell you what it is, Mr. Mason, if that was my child, I would whip him smartly every time he got into these tantrums, till I broke him of them."

Mr. Mason very gravely brought the child over his knee, and holding his clothes tightly down, said, "There, Anny, there's a chance for you; pay on well."

Instantly the buzz of a small linen-wheel was suspended, and a thin, wrinkled old lady, with her spectacles pinning back the border of her white cap, appeared upon the scene.

Holding up her shrivelled hand, with an attitude of defiance, she cried in sharp broken tones—

"Let her lay the weight of her hand upon the child of my poor Mary, and she will rue the day. And you, John Mason, is it you that can so soon forget the love of a father?" and she half spoke and half shouted in a cracked voice, and with a taunting smile about her mouth,

"A mother's a mother all the days of her life—
A father's a father, till he gets a new wife."

All this time she was pulling vigorously at the child, who clung to its father's knee with the tenacity of a young bear.

"Don't, Grandmam, don't," said Anny, observing a shade of displeasure upon the face of her husband. "Nobody wants to hurt the child, do let him alone."

"No, and nobody shall hurt him, mind that, Ann Spaulding, mind that," hissed out the old woman, giving a desperate pull at the boy, that laid them both upon the floor. The child sprang to his feet and ran, but not till the grandmother, enraged at the accident, and the perversity of the child, had applied a well-aimed blow upon his shoulders, which quickened his speed, and sent him to the door-step, where he sucked in his breath, and burst into a sort of hysterical laugh.

Anny drew him toward her, and gently smoothed his hair, and this last winding up of the affair in his behalf, produced one of those strange reactions to which we are all liable, and the little fellow laid his head in her lap, and burst into sobs and tears.

Mr. Mason laid his arm over the shoulder of his young wife, and began to tickle the cheek of the babe as it drew its nourishment from her bosom, kicking its feet and winking its bright eyes in efforts to repel the approach of slumber. Instantly the child sprang from its recumbent position, sending the white fluid over the face of little Jimmy, who was about to sob himself to sleep, and Jimmy's griefs were at once forgotten; he buried his head in the baby's lap, and they tickled and struggled together, while the parents looked on with a quiet smile.

"I do wish she wouldn't call me Ann Spaulding," said the wife in a low voice to her husband.

Now, whether the old lady's senses were in reality keener than what she was always willing to allow, or whether her passion had stimulated them to unwonted activity, or whether there is really a consciousness in the individual when he is the subject of remarks from others, as the common opinion seems to countenance, we will not stop to consider; but no sooner had Ann made the remark, than the old lady cried out from the wheel—

"Mind how you talk about me, Ann Spaulding. I shall call you by your name. You've no right to the title of my poor Mary, four months after her body was laid in the grave—in four months, before she was cold, and the grass could take root over her coffin. Take heed to yourself, I say:" and she began to sing the old song of Lady Isabella's tragedy,[1] in a shrill cracked voice, selecting it would seem, those verses in which the obnoxious word, step-mother, most frequently occurred, groaning out the syllables with peculiar zest.

---

1   An anonymous ballad, "The Lady Isabella's Tragedy; or, The Step-Mother's Cruelty."

"Therefore her cruel step-mother
  Did envye her so much,
·That daye by daye she sought her life,
  Her malice it was such.

She bargained with the master-cook
  To take her life awaye;
And taking of her daughter's book
  She thus to her did saye."

After leaping over the intermediate stanzas, she broke out in a
shriller voice at the scene where the bereaved Lord returns from
the chase, and calls for "his daughter deare to come and serve his
meate;" and when she is nowhere to be found, he vows to neither
eat nor sleep until she is forthcoming. At this crisis, the old lady
recommenced—

"O then bespoke the scullion-boye,
  With a loud voice so hye,
If now you wid your daughter see,
  Pray Sir, cut up that pye;

Wherein her flesh is minced small,
  And parched with the fire;
All caused by her step-mother,
  Who did her death desire."

From this she jumped to the catastrophe, which was screamed
out with a peculiar tone of satisfaction.

"Then all in blacke this lord did mourne;
  And for his daughter's sake,
He judged her cruel step-mother
  To be burnt at the stake."

All this time poor Anna's tears were falling upon the cheek of
her babe, and Jimmy, lulled by the monotony of the tune, and unconscious of its import, had fallen asleep upon her lap. Mr. Mason,
having quietly drawn the door to, was saying all that kindness could

dictate to soothe the outraged feelings of his wife, who tried to smile, in spite of the pain she experienced.

Henry retired, wondering at the strange perversity of the human heart, thus wantonly to dash the cup of happiness from the lips of another, because it has ceased to be mingled for ourselves. He thought of the apparently unfavorable position for the growth in virtue in the little group he had seen, and yet here were all the evidences of its existence. He had witnessed tenderness, and forbearance under provocations, trifling, it is true in themselves, but yet the more galling from their very littleness, and their frequency of recurrence. We arm ourselves with fortitude for the endurance of great trials, and glory, it may be, in tribulations, as the test of our power and the evidence of our virtue; but it is, after all, in the constant, every-day trials of life, that the real excellence of the character is to be tried. Few are called to heroic acts of virtue, but all suffer more or less the daily martyrdom of life. It is probable that virtue assumes a more distinct and positive character in the midst of hindrances, and therefore all the obstacles it meets in its progress contribute to its development.

While the youth moved homeward, philosophizing as he went, some trifle broke the thread of his reflections, and presented to his fancy the image of the fair girl who had first appeared in the cottage scene. Her air and countenance haunted him with a strange conviction that he had seen something analogous somewhere, but when or where he could not fix upon his memory. He retraced his steps to the cottage, hoping to catch a glimpse of the unknown, and thus to restore the links of association.

As he neared the dwelling, he saw the old lady seated upon the door-sill alone, while from within were heard the vigorous play of the infant's lungs, holding its breath, and then relieving itself with those reiterated screams that seem to challenge instant attention; but the old dame listened with great composure, if not satisfaction, for a smile lurked at the corners of her thin lips, that seemed to say, "It is no flesh and blood of mine: let it cry."

Presently Mr. Mason and his wife appeared, each bearing pails of milk filled to the brim, the subsiding foam bubbling upon the surface. Alice walked by the side of Mrs. Mason, carrying a small pail containing what is technically called the 'strippings,' being the last milk of the animal when the more abundant supply has been exhausted.

Accosting them with that freedom tolerated in new communities, Mansfield desired a drink of the milk to allay his thirst. Mrs. Mason was about to comply with his request, when the sound of her child's cries fell upon her ear, and she set down her pail and started upon a full run to the house.

Alice presented her pail to the stranger, with a slight blush upon her cheek; and to his grateful acknowledgments she returned a graceful inclination of the head, and a smile, the composure of which again perplexed him as something he had seen elsewhere. While making these observations, he had time to notice the roundness of the white arm, bare to the elbow, and the delicate symmetry of the figure, simply clad in a blue gingham frock, so exactly fitting, that the elegance of the bust became visible, notwithstanding the high drapery that concealed all but the white throat. Her hair was combed nearly plain from the forehead, and braided upon the back, two glossy curls being left to fall behind each ear.

Mr. Mason had placed his pails upon the grass, and was ready to start off upon any topic which might be broached; the weather, the crops, the Indians, or what not.

"Alice is a nice tidy gal," said he, following the eyes of the youth.

Henry colored, and stated his perplexity as an apology for observing her.

"Very like," said the other; "it's mighty strange to me how folks that's nowise akin will look so alike. In the same stock it's nowise strange, but in the matter of strangers, 'tis mighty puzzlin'."

Henry assented, and added, "And yet, the greatest mystery after all, is, that among so many inhabitants as there are in the world, all with the same features, there should be such infinite combinations, all resulting in individuality of form and expression."

The farmer looked a little perplexed, though he had certainly caught the idea.

"I'm thinking, sir, it is because the great Maker never is at a loss. Look at the leaves upon a tree; you will never see any two alike, nor any two blades of grass with the same streaks. Now, if a man makes a machine for any purpose, every one of the kind is after the same pattern, and just like it. He can't change, and yet have the same thing; but God can."

"Is the young woman, Miss Alice, a relative of yours?" asked Mansfield, after a pause; feeling, perhaps, that the subject was growing a little too philosophical.

"No, no; she's an orphan. She has neither kith nor kin in the whole world. They were all killed by the Injins, I dare say you've heard of the murder of the Durand family."

A sudden flush mantled the brow of Mansfield at the recollection of the mysterious maiden he had seen at Tippecanoe, and the likeness, and yet unlikeness, of the two; for nothing could be more dissimilar than the cold, haughty bearing of the one, contrasted with the winning gentleness of the other. And yet there was the same contour of features, the same smile, and the same intonations of voice.

"Are you quite sure, that none were saved? Might not a part have been carried into captivity?"

"No: they were all butchered; their house burnt down, and their bodies charred like cinders."

Saying this, he took up the pails, desiring Henry to return to the house with him; adding, "but you must not say anything about this conversation to poor Alice, for it has gone well-nigh to kill her now. And here are these painted varmints come now to kill us, for what I know."

Mansfield excused himself, and retired; but not until he had promised to pay his respects again to the family.

CHAPTER VIII.

The summer sun is flaming high—
    She from her lattice hangs,
Pines she for home and distant lands
    With disappointment's pangs.—MRS. SIGOURNEY[1]

Mr. Mason had, some years before, emigrated to the west, bringing with him a young and affectionate wife and her mother: for Mary was an only child, and she could not find it in her heart to abandon her aged parent. The infirmities of the old lady's temper were well known; but Mary, always accustomed to them, and habituated from childhood to submission, probably felt them less than others; and the less, it may be, because her mother lavished all the affection of which she was capable upon this, her only child, and the only object

---

1   Lydia Howard Huntley Sigourney (1791–1865), "Lady Arabella Johnson."

left to love. Mrs. Jones was always ready to arraign, in set terms, any omission of tenderness on the part of others, while she reserved the whole right of tormenting her to herself, being her natural parent.

We ought to have included, in the enumeration of the goods and chattels of the thrifty young farmer and his notable wife, a young girl of perhaps a dozen years, whose orphanage[1] had been consigned to the alms-house; her well-to-do relatives all declaring they had children enough of their own, and care enough of their own, without taking charge of the children of others. Had the relatives of the child been poor, they might have been better able to understand the value of human affections; and the motherless babe, cast upon the world in the widowhood of the poor mother, would have found a home in every heart, and the scanty crust had been imparted with the grace of a willing mind. But, unfortunately, the case was otherwise; and the little Anna became the property of the public, and was consigned to the matronly charities of the good woman who superintended this department of the institution. Here she was taught to read and write, to do needlework, and perform all domestic duties, and being of a cheerful disposition, and quick to learn, she became a great favorite. When, therefore, Mr. Mason proposed to take her into his own family, or, in other words, have her 'bound' to him until the age of eighteen, the good woman parted with tears in her eyes, and gave her a Bible, as a special token of her good will and approval.

Anna soon became as much a favorite in the family of Mr. Mason, as she had been in the almshouse, and as invaluable in household matters. In truth, she had no reason to find fault with her condition, if we except the trials to which the ill-humor of Mrs. Jones, the mother of Mrs. Mason, subjected her. But Anna's goodness of heart was proof even against these, and she was never known to rebel, except in one instance, when, after years of submission to the opprobrious epithets of the other, she one day declared solemnly she would "never again—no never, do anything she was ordered to do, under the name of work-house gal."

The old lady took the hint, and substituted in its place Ann Spaulding, which being her real name, she could not complain of, though she would rather have chosen the more affectionate appellation of Anny, always used by her employers.

---

1   Orphanhood; her years as an orphan.

Soon after the arrangements we have named, Mr. Mason determined to remove to the west; the rich and luxuriant soil of that region holding out incalculable inducements to the farmer, accustomed to the scanty crops of our eastern shores. Anna accompanied them, and here her patience, cheerfulness, and abilities, were beyond all price. Poor Mary's health declined under the effects of the climate, and Anna watched over her with the solicitude of a sister. With endearments and caresses she strove to wile her from that sickness of the heart, that too often comes over the exile in his last moments, when he pines for the land of his birth, to breathe once more the air of his childhood, and to lay his head to rest as he did in years gone by. Oh, who can foretell that weariness of the heart, which absence from the familiar scenes of our early and innocent days brings to the way-worn pilgrim! Who calculate the strength of the bands that bind him to home?

Mary was too gentle and loving to bear the rude tempests of life; she could never smile while a shadow lay upon her sunshine; her soul was made up of love and tenderness, and it went forth in its lovingness to the bird and the blossom, the moss upon the rock, and water of the lapsing brook. These were beautiful to her in all places, but doubly so in her native place. Her thoughts were there, clinging, in the fondness of memory, to every nook and dell endeared by the recollections of childhood, and when she turned her cheek to slumber she was there in her visions. This could not last. Day after day her strength declined, and at length she died, leaving her only child to the care of Anna, imploring her to guard its infancy, and be a mother to it. Anna promised every thing; and, in the fullness of her sorrow, was ready to do any thing by which she might testify her affection for the dead. Day and night she devoted herself to the helpless infant, anticipating its many wants with the tenderness of a parent.

Mr. Mason could not be insensible to the goodness of the affectionate and devoted girl. He felt solitary and depressed, and insensibly found himself lingering by the side of Anna to caress his child, unaware that the earnest kindness and unconscious smiles of the humble maiden were bringing relief to his sorrow. Anna regarded him as her guardian, and, in the simplicity of her heart, exerted all her talents to please him. She never dreamed of the result. He was in affliction, and she strove to comfort him. She had always been mindful of his comfort, and now that he was alone and in sorrow, she became doubly so. One evening she had sung little Jimmy to sleep in her arms, and the child lay upon her lap, its sleeping face turned to the light; Mr. Mason seated himself beside her, and implored her to become, in reality the mother of the child, even as she had been in kindness. Poor Anna looked half bewildered into his face, and burst into tears. For the first time in her life she felt that she was a servant.

"No, oh no," she answered. "I am your servant, bound to do your will as such. I cannot be your wife." And she buried her face in her hands.

Mr. Mason was greatly shocked. It was true 'indentures' had been drawn up and duly signed, but the paper had been locked up in a drawer in the old black-walnut desk, unthought of for years. Mrs. Jones had undoubtedly helped to keep the memory alive in the mind of the poor girl; but neither herself nor Mary had ever regarded her in any other light than as an equal in the family; one bound to them by no ties other than those of mutual kindness and affection. Mr. Mason arose, and taking the papers from the desk, threw them into the flames, and besought her to regard herself only as the friend of Mary, and to become his wife, and the mother of his child.

Anna was for a while silent, and during this silence, such a picture of opposition on the part of Mrs. Jones, so much of petty annoyance, and daily intangible persecution presented itself to her mind, that she turned from the prospect with a feeling of horror; and she begged him to drop the subject now and for ever, adding, "I could never, as your wife, submit to the degrading treatment I now receive."

Mr. Mason understood her, and he walked the room in painful agitation. Respect for Mary had enabled him to endure patiently all the ill-humor of her mother; but was it now his duty to see the peace of his family destroyed by one whose claims were so doubtful? He wavered for a moment, and then again addressed her.

"Anna, I might say that Mrs. Jones will seek a home elsewhere; that she has no right to expect one here, only as she can bring peace to the household. But, Anna, the law of God forbids us to cast out the widow, and her that has no helper. She must remain. I will wrestle with God in prayer, and he will make the path of duty plain and pleasant before me."

Anna listened with surprise to the commencement of Mr. Mason, but as he went on, a smile of approval grew to her lip, and she held out her hand confidingly, saying, "All will be for the best. Duty can never point but one way at the same time, as you have often said.

Should my presence bring you discomfort, I will go out from you, as did the bond-maiden of old."

Mr. Mason's brow contracted sharply. "Do not, dear Anna, ever speak of bonds again," and he stooped down, and for the first time in his life, impressed a kiss upon her burning cheek, and then left the room, for the step of Mrs. Jones was now upon the threshold.

Anna was undoubtedly sincere in her rejection of Mr. Mason, but his subsequent powers of persuasion were by no means inconsiderable, if we may judge from the fact, that, six weeks after, she was duly installed as mistress of the mansion; and little Jimmy began to call her mother, to the great annoyance of his grandmother, who called her "Ann Spaulding," with more vehemence than ever. She even, in the first transports of her rage, threatened to leave the house for ever; and in fact did, to the great grief of Anna, go for a few days to the house of a neighbor, declaring she could never submit to see another in the place of her "poor Mary." It is probable that the transitory fit of benevolence and neighborly kindness on the part of the hostess, soon evaporated, when thus heavily taxed; for the old lady returned, more out with the world than ever, declaring her determination to remain and protect little Jimmy from all ill-usage. Anna was glad of her return, whatever might be the motive, for she could scarcely have absolved herself from blame had she left the house on account of her marriage.

Years passed away, and Anna was even beyond her expectations, a happy wife. True she had her trials, for what woman is without them? but then her cheerfulness and unfailing good temper were of themselves a perpetual source of happiness, and with Anna there was never but one way, and that was the right way, and she had a perception to discover it as by instinct.

Little Jimmy was a lively, self-willed boy, whose attachment for his step-mother increased just in proportion as it gave discomfort to his grandmother. It must be that the sense of virtue is deeply rooted in the very constitution of the human mind, and that it is its nature to discover its affinities just as chemical compounds repel or assimilate together. This principle may be stronger in some minds than in others; for some become the victims of untoward circumstances and mal-education, while there are others that nothing can corrupt or degrade; whose path is onward in spite of all obstacles, led by the inward light alone, which God has implanted in the human heart.

Mrs. Jones was always saying, "No step-mother shall ever lay the weight of her finger upon the child of my poor Mary," which Mrs. Mason had no desire to do; yet her unvarying firmness and kindness of manner insured his obedience, and Mr. Mason was careful to uphold her authority. Jimmy, therefore, became, as it were monopolized by his grandmother, whom he teased and caressed, amused and annoyed, as suited him best. Sometimes, having provoked her ire by his childish love of fun, he would flee to Anna for protection, who would envelope him in her robe, and whirling round and round good-naturedly, screen him from the effects of her wrath, till even she would laugh at the thrilling merriment of the child; for it is difficult for even the most irascible long to retain their anger against a lively child, however wayward he may be.

Notwithstanding these somewhat discordant materials, few families were more cheerful and happy than the one we have described. The out-breaking of passion on the part of the old lady were things counted on and expected, and therefore of less effect, while the equanimity of the remainder was an unfailing source of contentment.

Mr. Mason had been educated in the rigid school of Presbyterian sanctity; and though a shade of severity might mingle itself with his religious belief and Sabbath-day observances, it could not for a moment interfere with the habitual cheerfulness of his deportment. Now that he was debarred from the public worship of his Creator in a temple consecrated for that purpose, he found the overhanging woods and the blue canopy of heaven a more worthy dome in which to offer up the sacrifice of a humble and believing heart. Away from the actual temptations of life, too, he was apt to observe closely the workings of his own mind, and he learned to detect errors, to combat evils, and to settle cases of conscience with a skill that the most subtile casuist might have envied. Every Sabbath he read aloud passages from the few books that ornamented the walnut desk, consisting of two or three Bibles; one of great size, embellished with mysterious-looking cuts of wood, and being protected with a stout covering of sheepskin in addition to its original binding. There was besides 'Doddridge's Rise and Progress,' 'Mason on Self Knowledge,' 'Scougal's Life of God in the Soul of Man,' which was an especial favorite, 'Pilgrim's Progress,' 'Fox's Book of Martyrs,' with hideous illustrations, and an old Commentary and Concordance for the study of the Bible. There were also a few books of a miscellaneous nature, which Mr. Mason was wont to denominate 'secular,' such as 'Weems' Life of Washington,' 'Life of Marion,' 'Goldsmith's England,' and the 'Campaign of the Grand Army,' &c. &c.[1]

Night and morning he was accustomed to read a portion of Holy Writ from the great Bible, when little Jimmy was taught to sit perfectly still, and even the grandmother seemed to feel the softening influence of family worship. She bowed her head upon her hands, while her son-in-law, erect, with his two hands resting upon the pummels of his chair, uttered the strong and fervent petitions for a pious heart, often couched in the elevated and mystical language of scripture.

CHAPTER IX.

The very echoes round this shore,
   Have caught a strange and gibbering tone;
For they have told the war-whoop o'er,
   'Till the wild chorus is their own.—S.B. GOODRICH.[2]

In sketching the family of Mr. Mason, we have, in part, anticipated events, and must go back to the period of the second marriage, when the relations of the natives with the whites had begun to assume, even then, appearances of hostility. Acts of violence were not rare, the uncertain tenure of land, and the scattered condition of the population, enabling them to be perpetrated almost with impunity. Necessarily subjected to the disadvantages of a territorial government, removed at a distance

---

1   These are books with which Oakes Smith grew up and that were known by familiar, shortened titles due to their widespread popularity. The first set of books offer spiritual guidance and explain Christian principles within a Protestant tradition, written by authors who were also preachers: Philip Dodderidge (1702–51), John Mason (1706–63), Henry Scougal (1650–78), John Bunyan (1628–88), and John Fox or Foxe (1516–87). Mason Locke Weems (1759–1825) wrote bestselling biographies of American Revolutionary heroes George Washington and Francis Marion celebrating their virtues and heroism, in some cases with apocryphal stories such as Washington's chopping of the cherry tree. After the English history written by Oliver Goldsmith (1730? –1774) for the general reader, the last is a French history of the Napoleonic wars by Bernard Castillon (d. 1837). The source text's spellings "Masen" and "Scongal" have been corrected for clarity.

2   Samuel Griswold Goodrich (1793–1860), "Lake Superior."

from the sources of the law, the infrequency and perils of travel rendering communication with other parts of the country next to nothing; the
inhabitants were compelled as it were to take the administration of justice
into their own hands, and there is reason to fear it was often of an unwar-
ranted and summary character. When it is remembered, likewise, that
an almost universal prejudice existed against the 'poor Indian,' that he
was regarded as a prowling beast of the woods, divested of the attributes
of humanity, and having no claims upon its sympathies, there can be no
doubt that often, very often, the tender mercies of the whites were cruel.

The population of this part of the country consisted of emigrants
from all parts of the Union, intermingled with foreigners, whom the
tumults of European politics[1] had compelled to seek security and
repose amid the solitudes of the western world. Many of these were
French, and they and their descendants, from the ease with which
they accommodated themselves to the circumstances of their lot,
becoming almost one with the savages, adopting their costume and
sharing their perils, were less obnoxious than those of any other nation. Many of the French clergy, too, men of ardent piety and great
courage in the cause of their divine Master, had labored in their
midst, and left the impression of their kindly humanity and untiring
Christian devotion.

The family of Durand was of this description. Living upon the
out-skirts of the white population, having but little intercourse with
them, shunning observation, and yet averse to companionship with
the natives. He was, in fact, a man of stern and unyielding integrity,
of severe, almost fanatical, views upon religious subjects, making
it rather a life of penance and physical abasement, than of internal

---

1   Beyond the religious and political conflicts in England leading to Puritan
    migration, Oakes Smith calls attention to a larger colonial history by
    focusing upon the French, who left Europe for similar reasons but first set-
    tled in a different manner than English "plantation" of families in agricul-
    tural communities. Jesuit missionaries, *coureurs des bois* (woods-runners),
    and fur traders ventured throughout the Great Lakes region, living among
    Indians and learning their languages and customs. Oakes Smith also
    alludes to the history of the Huguenots, French Protestants who suffered
    religious persecution in a strongly Catholic nation. The Edict of Nantes
    (1598) attempted to resolve this conflict by granting Protestants limited
    tolerance, but its revocation in 1685 created a hostile climate and a wave
    of Huguenot emigration. Oakes Smith is connected to the Huguenots
    through her maternal grandfather and was sensitive to religious struggles
    beginning in childhood (see Appendix A1).

spiritual worship. Early disappointments, it was said, had driven him from society, and shadowed, if they had not unsettled, the balance of his mind. He gave evidence of considerable literary attainments, and his small dwelling contained articles of luxury and elegance little to be expected in such a place. A single black servant was of all work in the household, and seemed bound to the family by no ordinary ties of attachment. He was never weary, never fatigued, when aught could be done to promote their comfort.

Mrs. Durand was a slender, delicate woman, whose affection for her husband was so blended with timidity, as to make it doubtful whether the feeling did in reality exist. It was hinted that this had not always been the case, but that strange passages had transpired to make her what she was. Certain it is that a painful apathy chilled her faculties, except where her feelings were elicited in behalf of her children, then she was all tenderness and devotion—her soft eyes radiant with love, and her low voice meltingly sweet. There was wondrous fascination in the half-indolent, half-impassioned grace of her manner, which the spectator could never forget. The few that had seen her felt that she was no less beautiful than unhappy, and had not failed to observe the strange mixture of gentleness and fear with which she would raise her eyes to those of her husband, and then allow them to fall again under the deeply fringed lid. Her history was a mystery, and all felt it must be a painful one. She was the mother of three children, and her attachment for them could in no wise surpass that by which they were regarded by their father, especially the second daughter; who was said to inherit more of his looks than the rest, and much of his pride and loftiness of character.

Thus were they circumstanced, when a party of savages, in the broad light of day, and without provocation, fell upon the house, and mercilessly butchered its inhabitants. Alice, the oldest daughter, escaped, she could hardly tell how. She recollected witnessing, in part, the horrible work of destruction, and then she became insensible. Upon recovery, she found the house in flames, the dead bodies of her friends partially consumed, and the shadows of evening beginning to fall. Weak and bewildered, bereft of happiness and almost of reason, she turned mechanically to the direction of Mr. Mason's, that being the nearest family with which they had held any communication, although that was many miles distant. The particulars of that long and dreary journey through the untrodden forests, the perils from savage beasts and savage men, can never be known. Alice only retained a vague impression of darkness and hunger, weariness and sleep; of long, long, journeyings, borne down with a fatigue that seemed scarcely to be endured; of fierce, glaring lights, like balls of fire, and hideous tramplings, and midnight howlings. How she was preserved, and how led through that desolate wilderness, can be known only to Him who heareth the young ravens when they cry, and who tempereth the wind to the shorn lamb.[1] We can only picture to ourselves the feeble steps of the lone child, her slumbers beneath the midnight canopy upon the leaves heaped by the winds, and believe that the wing of Him who never slumbereth was spread over her, and 'behold Angels ministered' to her.[2]

Anna was just barring the door for the night, when a faint knock and a low wail fell upon her ear. Breathless with terror, she fled to her husband, believing it to be the panther, which is said to imitate the voice of human suffering in order to delude his prey. Mr. Mason then laid aside his book and opened the door, when the form of a child, with its hands spread out, fell prostrate before him. He raised her in his arms and carried her to the light, and for a while all believed that life was extinct. Slowly she returned to consciousness, but so enfeebled, that for many days all nourishment was given her with a spoon, as a nurse would feed a sick babe. Then fever and delirium succeeded,[3] and she lay long, verging upon the very threshold of the grave. The story of the disaster became spread abroad, and excited great sympathy; for the beauty of the lady, and the mystery that enveloped her, left much for the imagination, and through that medium awakened universal commiseration. It was a fearful tragedy; years of sorrow, of concealed, heart-felt wo, with its close of blood and death.

Anna nursed the poor orphan with untiring solicitude, soothing her delirium, and calling her back to life and hope with all that love could suggest. She felt a double sympathy for her, as well for her great sufferings as her state of orphanage, thereby recalling the painful passages of her own life. Youth and its tenacity of life at length prevailed, and the lone child, with her pale, sad face, became

---

1   From Psalm 147 and a common proverb.
2   From Psalm 121 and Matthew 4:11.
3   That is, fever and delirium followed, with her illness becoming more severe.

everywhere the companion of Anna. She clung to her as if fearful that this last stay might be removed, and she be left utterly desolate. She seemed indeed too fragile, too sensitive and loving for a creature of earth, and her mild eyes and quiet smile had in them something almost too spiritual. Gradually her health became established and her cheerfulness returned, though the unbidden tears often sprang to her eyes, and her friends knew it was in memory of those who so fearfully perished. Mrs. Mason found in her a friend and companion, whose amiable and elevated thoughts helped to relieve the homeliness of household duties, to invest them with the dignity of moral sentiment, and make things, vulgar in themselves, assume a degree of elevation by the motives that dictate their performance. Even the ill-humor of Mrs. Jones became mitigated under the influence of her gentleness; for they ceased to regard it as an error to be cured, but the natural consequence of age, and its many infirmities, its solitude and hopelessness, demanding renewed tenderness and forbearance on the part of others.

CHAPTER X.

There stood the aged chieftain, rejoicing in his glory!
How deep the shade of sadness that rests upon his story!
For the white man came with power—like brethren they met;
But the Indian fires went out, and the Indian sun has set.
—MRS. L.L. FOLLEN.[1]

It had been arranged by General Harrison, that the council should be held in a small grove apart from the settlement, partly because the city afforded no convenient place of shelter, public buildings being at that time unknown, and partly to relieve the anxiety of the inhabitants, who beheld with dismay the numerous assemblage of dusky warriors in their immediate neighborhood.

It was a still, sultry day, in the month of August, when the members of the council made their appearance upon the ground; General Harrison, in the simple garb of the West, accompanied by his aids and a guard of a dozen men. It was an imposing spectacle, when this handful of men seated themselves in the midst of two hundred

---

1   Eliza Lee Follen (1787–1860), "Sachem's Hill."

warriors, armed and painted, conscious of their superior numbers, stung by wrongs and disappointments, and resolved upon redress. When all were assembled, Winnemac and his warriors placed themselves by the side of General Harrison. The Shawanese neither by look nor motion betrayed surprise, and the treacherous Potawatamy scrutinized them in vain.

When all was arranged, General Harrison opened the council in a concise speech, in which he urged Tecumseh to explain his claims upon the ceded territory, and demanded the cause of his hostility to the friendly chief, Winnemac; closing with an allusion to the warriors present, calculated to allay any feeling of resentment or suspicion which they might be supposed to entertain.

Tecumseh listened apparently with deep interest, and when he had ceased, arose to reply. His voice was calm and exceedingly sweet in its varied modulations, and he gathered up the thread of discourse with a tact and eloquence worthy of the most accomplished orator. His action was at first subdued, and full of the lofty composure, of the great subject which engrossed him; but as his theme enlarged, the voice and even the person of the speaker seemed to dilate with it, and he went on gathering volume and power, like the torrent in its course drawing to itself the waters of many streams, till it rolls onward to the ocean a mighty river!

"Brothers: The bird will sing all day upon the branches, content with its own melody—the bee will go from blossom to blossom, seeking the store of sweet drops—and each is content with its own. The deer sports itself in the moonshine, and the beaver looks off from its mud-house—both are content. They disturb the rights of none. They wish to be undisturbed. But go to the nest of the bird to tear its young from their home, and the helpless becomes strong. Rifle the home of the bee, and you feel its sting. Tear the fawn from the doe, and it turns at bay. The beaver will retreat through many windings, and when retreat is no more, it stays to perish with its young. Thus is it with the red man. I will not recount his wrongs, I will not tell of the white man's weakness, and his wants; when he held up his hands to the poor Indian and asked for bread. I will not tell how the red man spread his skins to succor him, and his venison to give him strength. I will not tell of this. But look abroad—did not the Indian succor him? Lo, the whole land is wrested from the red man, and he is driven from the very soil where once the white man begged for a piece of earth in which to lay the bones of his dead. The white man has chased his red brother across the Alleghanies, and now he must come at bay. The weak is to grow strong in self-defence. He is to gather up the ashes of his dead, and here, on his own hunting-grounds—on the hearth-stones of his cabin, with his women and children about him, he is to stand on his defence. The Indian will do it. Here he must live; or if he must die, it shall be here, on this soil—this grant of the Great Spirit—here, with his women and his children about him. If he perish, the smoke of his cabins shall go up and light the great prairies; and if the white man carries his plough here, it must be over the graves of the last of our people!

"Brothers: We are weary of blood. The corn that we eat is red with blood; there is blood upon the leaves of the tree; the flower is streaked with blood. We are weary of slaughter. We would bury the tomahawk deep in the earth; the rain and the dew should fill it with rust, till it should be no more found. But we dare not bury it. We wear it at our belt, that the white man may remember that the Indian has a weapon, and he will use it; but only to defend his own land—his own cabin fire. Let the white man stay where he is, and the tomahawk is quiet in its place: let him step his foot but its length further, and it is red with his blood. Let him remember this.

"Brothers: The Great Spirit has taken a cord, and has bound all the red men together. They have all spread out the hand, and grasped each the hand of his brother. There is one great chain of red men, with linked hands, from the big lakes to the warm waters of the south. The whole land west of the great mountains belongs to this one people. No tribe shall again say, 'This land is mine—I will sell it for strong drink, and muskets, and blankets,' for it is the property of the whole. The Indian shall not be driven from his fields and hunting-grounds, because strong drink has taken away his heart. He is bound by the great bonds of our people to defend and preserve it. We are no more many tribes—we are one people.

"Brothers: The whites were once many tribes: they were feeble. Ships came over the big waters, and armed men to rob them. They united for defence: they became a strong people, and their enemies hurried away. So it is with the red man: he was once many—now he is one."

Turning to Gen. Harrison, and addressing his discourse particularly to him, he went on:

"Brother: You have been told that we desire war. It is false. The Indian is only resolved to defend his own. There is now one great union of the tribes. We must be treated as one people: our land belongs to the whole: our Great Father at Washington must treat us as one people: we shall make peace or war as one people. I shall visit our Father at Washington, and tell him of the union of the tribes, and he will put a stop to this bartering of our rights. He will meet us as the messengers of a great people. He will put up a barrier to hold back his people. He must do it, for the Indian has now taken his stand—he is fixed to the soil.

"Brother: Should he fail to do this—should he put his hand behind him, when his red brother crosses the Alleghanies, and offers the pipe of peace, it must come to blood. He may sit over the mountains, and drink his wine and smoke his pipe, and you and I must fight it out.

"Brother: You ask why we call upon the members of the Council of Fort Wayne to answer for their conduct.

"Brother: They had taken the oath of confederation, whose penalty was death. They had clasped the hand of fellowship that made us one, and death only can restore the links. They have done robbery, in selling what was not their own, but had become the property of the whole. They have bartered, for things that decay in using, the everlasting rights of our people—the old hills, and broad hunting-grounds, willed us by the Great Spirit. Death only can wipe out the guilt. The Crooked Path only sees the sunshine of to-day: he looks not at the shadows of yesterday, nor the black clouds gathering upon the distant mountain. He sees only the smoke of his own pipe. He must die!

"Brother, I have done."

Turning to seat himself, the chief found no place prepared for him; which, General Harrison perceiving, instantly sent him one, saying, "The white father desires you to be seated."

The proud lip of Tecumseh curled with scorn, and he replied:

"The sun is my father, the earth my mother: I will repose upon her bosom;" and he seated himself upon the earth.[1]

The reply of General Harrison was mild and conciliatory; but

---

1   This scene captured the public imagination and was widely depicted and variously interpreted, as evident in comparing Oakes Smith's telling of the story to Hall's version in his campaign biography of Harrison (see Introduction, pp. 22–24, and Appendix C1).

he had to do with an acute reasoner, and one having truth and justice on his side. He refused to recognize this new feature in the negotiations with the Indians, and contended that the chiefs who attended the Council of Fort Wayne, were the rightful owners of the land there ceded, and had received a fair equivalent therefor. He knew nothing of the union of the tribes, and declared that the great Father at Washington would never recognize their pretensions. The union was a dream. Such a thing could not exist—could not be recognized.

A smile, half mournful, half incredulous, rested upon the face of Tecumseh, at the close of this address. He sat, with his arms folded upon his bosom, involved in painful reverie, when he was roused by the voice of Winnemac, who entered upon his defence. Tecumseh arose, and vehemently stretched forth his hand:

"Let not the traitor dare to speak here, and to this assemblage, of his crime. He shall appear before the council of his own people, and plead there. He has broken his oath, and must answer for it to those who helped to administer it."

Observing a determination in the chief to go on, Tecumseh's tomahawk leaped from his belt, and he sprang forward, as if about to sink it into the brain of the traitor chief. His followers obeyed the same impulse, and stopped short, as their leader, always preserving the command of his passions, even while he seemed to give them rein, paused midway in his advance.

General Harrison unsheathed his sword, and calmly pronounced their deliberations at an end; uttering, at the same time, some words of reproach, that, for a brief moment, sent the fierce blood to the cheek and eye of Tecumseh; but immediately his proud form was erect and composed, and, waving his hand to his followers, he put himself at their head, and slowly retired from the council-ground.

The report of the tumultuous close of the council, created not a little of terror in the minds of the inhabitants. Weapons of every description were brought from musty retreats, and made ready for service. Sundry kettles of water, with dippers of goodly length, might be seen boiling, ready for use, and pokers and tongs were stationed by the doors, while broomsticks suddenly grew into great demand. When the troop, in a long file, paraded the streets of the infant city, it was hushed and motionless, as if under the influence of some powerful spell. More than one musket might be seen protruded through one of the two holes cut in the top of the doors, evidently for the purpose of letting in light, and letting out light also, in the shape of a rifle shot: but now the vibratory motion of said muskets gave strong indication of the state of nerves incident to the holder. Windows and shutters were closed, and not a child visible, except where the wild eyes of some daring little urchin were seen peering through holes in the shutter, made in the form of a heart, whither he had climbed, by the aid of tables and chairs, to get a sight of the show, or the battle, as the case might be. But the troop silently wended their way to the camp, and the inhabitants cautiously crawled out from their concealment, each casting an inquiring glance at the scalp of his neighbor, to see if that appendage still retained its allegiance. When the night closed in, precautions were not neglected, for many were assured that this appearance of quietude was only a feint, to throw them from their guard; and the stillness of the night was reserved for the attempt at destruction. Some of the more adventurous, among whom was Henry Mansfield, visited the camp at night, and were witness to the order and discipline that prevailed. It was a pleasant sight to behold the brisk fires sparkling in the green woods, the torches gleaming in long streams of light, and the dusky warriors collected in groups, or wrapped in skins, composed to undisturbed repose, while the sentries remained motionless as the huge boles against which they reclined. The night wore on in its quietude and beauty, with nothing to disturb its repose.

CHAPTER XI.

> The monarch rose in musing mood,
> And silent for a moment stood,
> Wrapp'd in himself, as though he sought
> To grasp some hidden, vanished thought,
> Which, rayless, vague, and undefined,
> Still seems to flit before the mind.—SEBA SMITH.[1]

The more Mansfield pondered upon the resemblance of the two girls, the more probable did it appear to him, that one of the Durand family might have escaped, and have been carried into captivity;

---

1   Seba Smith, "Powhatan; A Metrical Romance, in Seven Cantos" (Canto First).

while the burning of the house rendered it difficult to ascertain the fact from the partial destruction of the bodies by the flames, and wild animals attracted to the spot.

Full of these convictions, desirous to ascertain the truth, and yet fearful of awakening hopes that might never be realized, he hesitated what course to adopt. At length, bethinking himself of the little basket presented him by Margaret, he determined to take it with him, and call upon the family; making it in one way, as circumstances might direct, the vehicle of communication.

The door of the dwelling was open, and, as he entered the little gate, he observed the family motionless about the room, and caught the sounds of Mr. Mason's voice, reading the Scriptures. He spoke in deep and solemn tones, as if every word of the divine Psalmist, all the fervency of petition and humility of self-abasement, were echoed from his own heart. "Enter not into judgment with me, O Lord, and deal not with me according to my transgressions."[1]

It was now too late to retreat, for Mrs. Mason quietly beckoned him to approach, and Alice in silence pointed to a chair beside her, blushing slightly, and covering her eyes with her hand, while the reading went on. Mr. Mason appeared unconscious of his presence. The babe aroused, and gave two or three lively springs in its mother's lap; but Jimmy sat with his head back, his mouth open, and staring with great perseverance at the new comer. When the chapter was finished, Mr. Mason laid the Bible reverently aside, and uttering the words, "Let us pray," the whole family rose up, and continued standing over the back of their chairs, while 'the saint, the husband, and the father' prayed.[2] It was a simple, beautiful acknowledgment of the Divine presence in that little dwelling, and even Mansfield wondered at the fervency of his own feelings, as his thoughts went up with that devout wrestler in prayer in the quietude of the evening twilight. He at first wondered at the evidently sincere confession of errors and "short-comings in duty," from the lips of one whose life was apparently so blameless; but reflection soon taught him that errors are not to be estimated merely by the eternal manifestation of them, but by their presence in the heart. One's sense of wrong-

---

1   Psalms 143:2 and 39:8.

2   Slightly misquoted line from the poem "The Cotter's Saturday Night" by Robert Burns (1759–96), in which "The saint, the father, and the husband prays."

feeling, producing a sense of wrong-doing, in proportion as the standard of moral excellence is exalted or otherwise.

The half-reckless and unreflective life he had hitherto led, seemed suddenly checked, and the holiness of the atmosphere he now breathed, come down like a refreshing, and a new beauty upon him. He cast his eyes around upon the little family, and beheld the softened look of the old dame, the hushed spirits of the gay boy, and Mrs. Mason, who had seated herself in the discharge of her maternal duty, was looking down upon her sleeping child, a soft smile about her mouth, her eyes full of maternal love, and that whole air of quietness and content which can only spring from a heart filled to the brim with its unpretending happiness. Alice, too, was at his side; her form slightly inclined, the round lips compressed, and a holy composure resting upon the sweet face, as far as it was left visible by the small hand pressed upon the eyes.

When Mr. Mason at length pronounced the word "Amen," the youth started, as if the straying of his thoughts from the sacred duty for which he had risen, were known to all present.

Mr. Mason now came forward and shook him heartily by the hand, and the rest of the family joined in the expressions of a hospitable welcome. It was evident that the labor of the family closed with the setting of the sun, for all the implements of industry were carefully bestowed in their appropriate places. The wheel of the old lady was placed in a corner, behind the cradle of the babe, and Mrs. Mason's scissors and skein of thread were hung on one nail that supported the little looking-glass, while on the other hung a pin-ball and her thimble. The table beneath was scoured to the last degree of whiteness, and on the carefully folded linen cloth, might be seen the open spectacles of the grandmother. A small birch-bark box, wrought with the quills of the porcupine, curiously colored, contained a silver thimble, some cotton, the MSS.[1] of some old verses neatly copied, and knitting needles, with the stitches of a little stocking for the babe. Jimmy soon laid hold of the basket and carried it to Alice for her to admire. Its delicate construction attracted all eyes, and when Jimmy returned it to the owner, in obedience to the commands of his mother, Henry desired him to carry it to Miss Alice, and ask her to keep it, adding, "It was the

---

1   Abbreviation for manuscripts.

gift of a young girl at the Indian town, remarkable for her resemblance to herself."

"Alice don't look like an Injin," said the child, stopping short.

Alice colored, and looked up in some confusion.

"Oh, no: it was not an Indian, but a—" (he was about to say beautiful, but he checked himself, and added) "a white girl, who seemed to have been adopted by the tribe."

Alice half rose from her chair: "Did you say she resembled myself?" she asked faintly.

"Remarkably; except that she was taller and darker."

"It is Margaret!" murmured the poor girl, in a scarcely audible voice, and sinking into a chair with a face pale as marble.

The good Anna came to her assistance, and Mansfield blamed his awkwardness and precipitancy in giving utterance to his convictions. When restored to consciousness, Alice desired him to describe the girl he had seen; and she listened with a trembling of the lip, a painful, earnest expression about the eye, and an anxiety of the brow, that showed that self was entirely forgotten in the interest excited by the detail. When he dwelt upon the haughty expression about the lip, Alice shook her head, "Oh, no: Margaret was so light, so joyous; and yet, when teased, she would look proud and queenly, and never cry like children of her own age. She must be greatly changed."

Placing a finger upon her brow, she bent her head as in deep thought, as if striving to restore the severed links of memory. At length she commenced in a low voice, and with the manner of one forcibly dragged back to the contemplation of horrors which he would fain avoid, and without raising her eyes from the floor.

"Yes, I think I see now how she was saved. I was always fearful and timid, but Margaret was brave. I shrank from the tempest and the lightning, but Margaret delighted in beholding all that was wild and terrible. I could never see a savage without a shudder, as if I felt the edge of the tomahawk; but Margaret had learned their dances, would adorn herself with their ornaments, and listen to their wild tales. We had been out gathering berries, when the sound of shrieks and yells caused us to turn homeward. We reached the house just to behold the babe dashed against a tree, and my mother—but I can say no more. Half in weakness, for my limbs refused to bear me, and half in cowardly fear, for my flesh winced as if the plunge of the knife were in my own body, I sank down by a pile of wood near the house, and remained concealed. Bitterly have I deplored that moment of weak terror. But the noble and intrepid Margaret hastened forward, and laid hold of the savage hand about to take the scalp from the head of my father. I shall never forget the laugh of the Indian as he dropped my father's gray locks, and seized the long curls of my sister: I grew dizzy, a mist came before my eyes, and a sensation as if a cauldron of burning lead were poured upon my brain. But I forced all back and looked on. I saw a tall powerful chief approach, with uplifted hatchet—Margaret stretched out her pale arms, and rushed forward, with wild and staring eyes. I saw no more. A mortal sickness came upon me, and when I awoke I was deathly cold, the house was in flames, and the Indians gone. I looked in the spot where I had last seen Margaret. I could find no trace of any—all, all were gone. There was nothing left but blood, blood everywhere; and there it was upon the tree, and there was a few hairs from the head of the dear—dear babe. I grew wild and reckless, and wished I too had died; and yet, would you think it, when I thought of the terrible mode—of the cold, sharp steel, I rushed away into the woods in search of life—for it struck me that the savages might return. Now that I recall all the circumstances of the case, it is more than probable that Margaret's fearless demeanor might have won the admiration of the Indians, and have induced them to spare her."

Alice ceased, and all thought it at last appeared plausible. Mr. Mason, however, cautioned Alice to think calmly upon it, for after all, it might not be Margaret; and if it were so, nothing could be gained by undue solicitude, while if it were not, all the time spent in anxiety would be just so much waste of life; for, he added, "every moment should carry with it right and good thoughts, or it is worse than lost to us."

"I am sure it is Margaret," said Anna, "I feel if it must be so, and somehow, when that is the case, I know just how things will come out," and she put her arm about the waist of Alice and laid her cheek upon her shoulder. Alice felt too intensely and painfully for tears, but she sat helpless, and breathing short, her face pale as ashes.

"Never worry," said the old lady, "I am sure 'tis little Margaret. But just think how she'll be changed: She's half Injin now, there's no manner of doubt. She's as good as lost, you see, for she'll never come back again to live like other folks. She'll be kind of wild, and like to wander in the woods, and hate all manner of work, you see. I remember there was Sam Shaw; he was carried off by the Injins, when he was nigh about ten years old, and he lived with them till he was nigh on to thirty, and then his folks heard that he was alive—so his brother started off to bring him home. At first Sam wouldn't come, but when he was told about his poor mother who could never forget him, and who had grown gray in her trouble for him, Sam couldn't help feelin' it, and he come home. But 'twas a dreadful sight. He come home, you see, with his blanket over his shoulders, and leggins on, and a belt with his scalpin'-knife and tomahawk, and head stuck chock full of feathers. His poor mother threw her arms about his neck, for she knew him for all that, and kissed his cheek and mouth; and don't you think, there stood Sam, bolt upright, and never moved an arm, or said a word, only a foolish kind of look about the face. It enymost[1] killed his mother. He wouldn't never hear no preaching nor praying, and nobody could make him learn to read. He couldn't lay in a bed no how, and used to get up before day-light and go off a shooting. Sometimes he would shoot the neighbor's pigs and poultry, and if they said one word, the next night he'd shoot more. He never would go to work, but there he set all day, smoking, smoking, and saying nothing to nobody. His mother took on terribly; things couldn't last so long, and at last she died. The very next day Sam was missin'. He left all his clothin', and took his gun and blanket, and 'twas supposed he went back to the Injins; but nobody knew, for he was never seen after."

All listened to the recital with a sort of painful apathy, and Alice never raised her eyes from the floor. When she ceased, Mr. Mason replied—

"It may be as you say, grandmother, for it is no ways likely that she will appear as if brought up with the whites; still I am thinking that girls don't forget such things so quick as boys. Somehow they never lose these little nice ways, when they once get them, and Mr. Mansfield says she seems nowise like an Injin."

"O let us not talk of it," said Alice, "but she must be brought home. Can we devise no method?"

---

1 Eenamost or eny most (Americanism): even almost; nearly.

"I will go myself to the Indian town," said Mansfield, "and do all I can to restore her."

Alice raised her eyes full of gratitude, to his face, and then they fell and tears gathered beneath the lids. The youth could not but look upon her sweet pale face, and he thought again how like it was to Margaret's, and yet how much it lacked that lofty look and bearing which added so much to the interest of the other.

CHAPTER XII.

For vain yon army's might,
While for thy band the wide plain owned a tree,
Or the wild vine's tangled shoots,
Or the gnarled oak's mossy roots
Their trysting place might be!—LUCY HOOPER.[1]

Unwilling to lose, any opportunity to conciliate the powerful influence of Tecumseh, General Harrison resolved to pay him a visit at his encampment, in the hope that he might be won over to the American policy.

Tecumseh received him courteously, and motioned him to a seat upon the turf beside him, at the same time that he presented the lighted calumet in token of friendship. General Harrison was a brave man and familiar with Indian customs, and he seated himself with a single attendant, unarmed in the midst of these warriors of the woods, armed to the teeth. He was well aware of the effect likely to be produced on their wild and generous natures by such tokens of confidence; and he remained for some time smoking the pipe in imitation of their own taciturnity. Occasionally, the two leaders cast looks of scrutiny upon each other, but each was an adept in the power of guarding the expression of the face, and nothing could be gathered. In the meantime the Indian fires were lighted in various directions, and the game, secured by the dexterity of the hunter and trapper, was in process of preparation. Flitches of deer, with squirrels, rabbits and other small game were suspended on wooden spits, or roasting on the coals, while those of the party whose repast was over were amusing themselves in adorning their persons, or in

---

1   Lucy Hooper (1816–41), "Osceola."

the many games so much in vogue with a rude people. Gradually the gamesters removed from the vicinity of the older chiefs, who had seated themselves in a circle about Tecumseh and the white General; and the low hum of their voices, mingled with the singing of the birds, and the crackling of the fires.

The shells of the squirrel rattled down upon the old leaf beneath the tree, and the night-dew still gemmed the filaments of the spider, and weighed down the head of the wild blossom. The mist from the river and the level prairie was sailing lightly off to mingle with that of the great lakes, while in the direction opposite the sun, the sky reposed like an immense dome of deepest azure. Softly above the trees arose the slender spires of thin smoke, as if many altars had been reared in the great wilderness to burn incense to Him, who is invisible.

General Harrison laid his pipe aside, and Tecumseh assumed an attitude of attention.

"Brother: We heard your talk of yesterday with regret, for we thought you had been bought over to the English; that you are becoming the foes of our white Father, the President.

"Brother: We are told that the war-belt has been sent around among the tribes, and that you only wait the movements of the British to come down with all your people to kill our women and burn our villages. Tecumseh is a great chief, but he is trying to blow smoke into the eyes of his white brothers. He talks of peace when he is planning for war. He talks of a union of the tribes for their own security, when he is planning to fight against our Father, the President, and to aid his foes."

Tecumseh replied calmly, though a fierce light burnt in his eye, and there was a slight expression of scorn about the lip.

"Brother: The path of the white man is crooked like that of the snake in the grass. The red man has tried the same path; but now it is straight forward like that of the arrow from the bow. The white man cannot understand it. He covers his face with his hand, and then says he cannot see. He puts his fingers in his ears, and says he cannot hear. Let him open his eyes and ears, and his heart will understand.

"Brother: Once the tribes were a great people, their smokes went up from a thousand hills; they were like the leaves upon the trees. They are passing away. The fox is crouched in his wigwam. The moss is thick upon his council-stones. The vine clingeth about the spear of the warrior, and the old canoe rotteth beside the lake. We are bowed and feeble. We look away to the hills, and behold the spirits of our people gathering in the land of shadows. We see them departing like the wings of the bird when storms come upon the earth.

"Brother: The Great Spirit hath revealed his will to his children. He hath bound us in one brotherhood. He opened the eyes of his red children, to perceive that his white brothers were crowding him from the earth. The plan of our white Father, the President, in buying our land, is like a mighty water that will swallow up the red men. The union of the tribes is a dam to hold it in check—to keep back this mighty water. It is no dream. The tribes are one. We will sell no more of our land.

"Brother: You have evil counsellors. They tell you we are leagued with your enemies, the British. It is false. There is no treaty except that which binds the tribes into one. If you and the British go to war you must fight it out. The Indian will fight for neither. What have we to gain by your wars? Nothing, but to be still more weakened, and then to fall a prey to one or the other of you. No: the Indian will defend his own hearths, his own graves, and only hear the roar of your battle afar off.

"Brother: The wampum-belt has been sent amongst the tribes, but it is in amity. It is the pledge of faith between us, and it means too, that we will fight against you or the British, whichever shall molest us. Respect our rights and you have nothing to fear. Plant your foot upon the red man's soil and it is felt from the Lakes, to the mouth of the great river Mississippi."

Tecumseh was followed by others, who replied at length to the charges of Harrison, and dwelt long upon the aggressions of the whites. The General, finding it vain to hope for any arrangement in accordance with his own views, arose to depart.

At this moment, Mansfield, who had accompanied him, beheld Mr. Mason and Alice approaching the spot. The former addressed them without hesitation, while Alice stood a little apart, looking anxiously upon the array of dusky warriors.

"Good morning, Gineral, you're stirrin' airly this mornin'. These varmints seem to be mighty still here. Don't you think the're hatching some plot to butcher us?" and then, without waiting for a reply, he went on.

"This young woman here is named Durand. She was one of the family murdered by the Injins, and now she is persuaded that a sister of hers is among them; only because Mr. Mansfield saw a white girl living there who happened to look like her. But I am more thinking it may be one of those French gals, that seem to like the Injins about as well as the whites. Howsomever, nothing would do but she must come out here to see Tecumseh about her, and see what can be done to bring her back."

The General addressed her courteously, and returned where Tecumseh remained standing against the trunk of a tree.

Instantly, as Alice beheld him, she exclaimed, "It is the very chief to whom my sister fled for protection:" and then, forgetful of all but her own anxious thoughts, she addressed him.

"Tell me, O chief, were you not of the party that destroyed the family of Durand?"

The warrior at once dropped the expression of apathy he had before worn, and started forward with a look of fierce displeasure, the attitude of a tiger about to spring upon his prey: "Tecumseh wets not his tomahawk in the blood of women and children. Who can point to the cabin fired by his hand? or show the scalp of an old man among his trophies?"

Assuming his wonted look of dignified composure, he folded his arms and looked upon the face of Alice, as she stood shrinking, yet resolute to pursue her holy mission. Slowly a smile grew upon the face of the chief, one of those inexpressibly beautiful smiles which rendered him so remarkable. His lips parted, displaying teeth white and even, and he waved his hand in token of silence as he was about to speak.

"Did not the maiden creep beneath a heap of wood, her lips red with the wild berry, and cheek white and cold, and there behold the death of her kindred?"

"Most true," replied Alice, "I was fearful and selfish. But O! bitterly, most bitterly have I deplored. Margaret was bold and generous, and she plead¹ to preserve the life of those she loved. She held up her arms to you—did you spare her? does she live?" She spoke in a deep tremulous voice, her features contracted into an expression of intense anxiety, her breathing short and hurried, as if life itself hung upon her reply.

Tecumseh seemed willing to sport with her emotion. He appeared studying the lineaments of her face as it was raised to his own, and his reply was clear and studied.

---

1   Pled or pleaded.

"Tecumseh goes to war only with men. The blood of a child never stained his weapon. He heard the shrieks of the dying, while the followers of Winnemac, the friend of the white man," and he glanced derisively at General Harrison, "had sunk their tomahawks into the skull of their white friends. I beheld the maiden in her paleness and terror as she lay concealed, and the noble girl who would have saved the scalp of her father. Tecumseh spread his shield over her, and she was safe!"

During this recital Alice had gazed upon him with parted lips; when he ceased she breathed heavily, and would have fallen to the ground, had not Mansfield sustained her. Pressing her hand to her brow, and declining further aid, she arose and again addressed the chief.

"Can my sister be restored to us? Will she not leave her wild life, and come to live with us again? We are both desolate. Let us dwell together. I will go with you, and she cannot refuse the pleadings of a sister."

As she uttered this she laid her hand within that of the chief, and looked up with an expression akin to that of her more daring sister, repeating, "I will go with you."

Tecumseh's brow relaxed with another of those winning smiles as he replied,

"There spoke the spirit of the Swaying Reed. Margaret is brave and beautiful—her step is light as the fawn's upon the hill. She has the eye of the hunter, and the heart of the warrior. Wisdom is upon her lips. Why should she be confined to the toil of the white man's cabin? Her free soul would spurn the thraldom. Leave her, maiden, to the freedom and happiness of the life she leads. Why should the bird be imprisoned? Why would you stop the freedom of its song? Margaret is a daughter of the woods, let her remain."

"Still I will go with you," persisted Alice. "She cannot refuse me. Oh! no, no: she will remember our mother's tears, our mother's prayers, and she will return;" the tears gathered in her own eyes, and she turned to conceal them.

"The maiden shall go with me," replied the chief, "and she shall be safe."

"It must not be," eagerly returned Henry Mansfield; "for if she goes I will be her protector."

Alice looked up, and a blush overspread her cheek and neck.

"I feel that I shall be safe under the protection of this generous chief. It were not maidenly to receive other aid. Mr. Mansfield will surely pardon me if I reject it."

The youth felt the propriety of what she said, and yet he shuddered to think of the perils to which she might be exposed in her journey through the wilderness with such an escort; the hazard from surprise, from skirmishes with ambushed foes, and the fatigues and sufferings of a long journey to one delicately nurtured, to say nothing of the dangers of a residence with them, and the improbability that Margaret would be prevailed upon to return to the settlements. All these things crowded upon his mind, and filled him with perplexity. The more he thought upon it, the more preposterous did the project appear. Its terrors grew upon the imagination every moment, and when Alice placed her arm within that of Mr. Mason, waving him a cheerful good morning, he followed her retreating figure as that of one doomed to unknown suffering.

He returned to the city, silently, by the side of General Harrison, inwardly resolving to follow the natives to Tippecanoe, and as far as possible shield the footsteps of the devoted girl. The good General came to his aid by proposing to make him the bearer of a message to the chiefs, recommending Miss Durand to their protection. He hinted, too, the propriety of delaying his departure, as well from respect to Alice as public opinion. The youth of course acquiesced, but deprecating in round terms the baseness of idle scandal, and the propensity of the world to interfere with that in which it had no concernment. His feelings softened again as he thought of the maidenly refinement of Alice; her gentleness combined with dignity; the dignity not of manner, which can be easily assumed, but that which arises from native innocence, the majesty with which goodness is always wont to invest her votaries. He recalled her smile, the tones of her voice, till the course that she would have dictated became the best of all others, and the one to be adopted by himself.

CHAPTER XIII.

We in one mother's arms were locked—
   Long be her love repaid;
In the same cradle we were rocked,
   Round the same hearth we played.—CHAS. SPRAGUE.[1]

Mrs. Mason looked in the face of Alice sadly for more than a minute, without speaking, when told of her determination to seek her sister

---

1   Charles Sprague (1791–1875), "The Brothers."

in the Indian settlement. She then gently undid her bonnet, divested her of her shawl, and stroked the soft hair upon her brow tenderly, as she would caress a sick child.

"Poor dear child," she said, "you are ill. I will make you a drink of herb tea, and put you to bed, and you will soon be better. Your hands are cold, and head burning hot. These troubles are too much for you, poor child. Grandmam, please touch the cradle with your foot, while I take care of Alice."

"I must be ready to go at early dawn," said Alice, as she looked round upon the familiar room; and it may be the thought crossed her mind that she might never return, for tears gathered in her eyes, and she bent down to kiss the cheek of little Jimmy, who was regarding her with open mouth.

"Have you gone crazy, Alice?" said the child, speaking low, and peeping at a little distance.

"Crazy? no indeed; what made you think so?"

"Why, mother says you are, and she shall watch you, so you shan't go to the Injins."

"No, James, I am going to bring home a dear sister. The Indians won't hurt me."

"They will, they will;" returned the boy, beginning to cry. "They will take your hair off your head, and roast you alive. Don't go, don't go:" and he clung his arms around her neck, weeping and sobbing.

"Dear Anna," said Alice, observing her about to make the herb tea, "don't make anything for me. I am perfectly well. I need nothing. Indeed, Anna, I am in my right mind. Is it strange that I, an orphan, with no kindred upon earth, should go a long journey, and encounter perils to recover a sister? That I should go into the wilderness to seek that which was lost? Indeed, Anna, can you not conceive how delightful it would be to have a sister?"

The young woman took her babe from the cradle, and threw her apron over her face to conceal her tears, for the old lady was regarding her with a fixed and bitter look.

"Nay, Anna," said Alice, approaching her, "you must not weep; you have been a sister to me, and I have loved you most tenderly. You have done everything to make me happy, and the Almighty will bless you for it. But, Anna, the face of Margaret gleams upon me as it did in our childhood, when our father laid his hands upon us in blessing, and my poor mother pressed her lips to ours. Oh, Anna, is it strange that I, who have been so terribly bereaved, should go far to seek the only relative left on earth?"

Anna pressed the hand of Alice, but she could not speak for weeping, and the old lady scowled still more upon her.

"No, child," she said, "it's nowise strange you should want to go and find your sister, and if Ann Spaulding had any kind of feeling, she would not think it was. I advise you to go, you'll never be the worse for it."

No sooner had Mrs. Jones commenced her reproaches, than Anna's tears were dried as if by magic. She wiped her eyes, and removing her apron, replied,

"I am sure, Alice, you don't think I meant to blame you for anything. But when you spoke so tenderly of a sister, I thought of myself." Here her tears flowed afresh. Suppressing them with an effort, she went on. "I thought if I only had a relative in the wide world, I would do just so. I would go into the woods, miles and miles. I would suffer hunger and fatigue, anything to tell them of my attachment, and to win their love. But oh, Alice, strangers are often kinder to us than those of our own blood. Can't we, by being loving ourselves, teach children to love?" and she drew little Jimmy to her side and kissed his cheek.

"I am sure, mother, I love you," said the boy, "and Alice, and father, and grandmam, and the baby;" and he began to tumble and frolic with it as he spoke.

"And we all love each other," said Mr. Mason, as he entered the door, and hung his hat upon a peg behind it. "I do wish, Alice, you would abandon this project. It seems to be so dangerous; and Mr. Mansfield says if you will, he will go back to the town and see if he can prevail upon her to return to us."

Alice blushed deeply. "You know he told us that she declared her determination never to return. I must go. I must see her. She grows every moment more dear to me; and if she will not come with us, I must stay with her."

"That is rather cruel, Alice," said Mr. Mason, reproachfully.

"Pardon me, I meant not so. I do appreciate all your kindness; but you cannot tell how my heart is drawn out in love to that companion of childhood."

"Say no more, Alice, say no more. I do understand all you feel; and I know that He who tempers the wind to the shorn lamb will make all things work together for your good. Let us assemble around the family altar, and ask His blessing upon all that we do." Taking down the large Bible, he read the beautiful and affecting language of the Saviour as given by St. John, "Let not your heart be troubled," &c,[1] then laying aside the sacred volume, he, with more than his ordinary fervency, poured out his desires before the Infinite, the Great Father, who knoweth all our wants, and is ever ready to impart wisdom and strength.

When Alice retired to her bed, it was with more of hope and happiness than she had known for many years. She could think of Margaret only as the same ardent, joyous being she was at the time of their cruel separation, and she doubted not her heart would as readily respond to the language of affection. Then, she thought of the young stranger who had so kindly interested himself in her behalf. She tried to think it but the dictate of common humanity; but still she dwelt upon his noble features, his manliness, and kindness of manner, till even his image grew indistinct in the shadowy visions that gathered around her slumbering pillow.

With those in the middling classes of life, benevolence is not confined to its mere expression: it goes forth into active kindness, and prompts to a thousand offices of love and forethought, scarcely dreamed of by those who entrust everything to the care of servants. The simple wardrobe of Alice was arranged entirely by Mrs. Mason; for in the tenderness of her solicitude, she would scarcely allow Alice to do anything for herself. The old lady busied herself in preparing dough-nuts and other little dainties for her use on the journey, sewing them into the white napkin with her own trembling hands.

It was a sad day when Alice mounted the steed prepared by Mr. Mason, and bade adieu to the little family. Many were the tears shed, and the last words of caution and advice; and then, when the sound of her horse's feet died away in the distance, Anna threw herself upon her bed, and sobbed as if her heart would break. She wondered more than ever that she could have parted with her, and she felt how lonely would she herself be in the long summer days when her husband was away in the field, and she should have no one to speak to, no kind face to which she might appeal when wearied with the ill-humor of the old lady. Even the old dame sat rocking her body back and forth, occasionally giving utterance to a deep groan, and an ejaculation, "It is the Lord's will."

---

1 John 14:1.

Mr. Mason took his leave as the Indian cavalcade commenced their march. When it was rumored that Alice Durand was going to the Indian village in search of a lost sister, many of the inhabitants of the city came out to get a glimpse of her sweet face, and to utter a benediction upon her innocent head. Though personally known to few, her misfortunes were known to all; and scarcely a dry eye followed the beautiful white girl, as her slight figure disappeared in the distance, where she rode beside the stately form of Tecumseh.

Henry Mansfield had not ventured to say adieu, and for a while Alice looked searchingly among the crowd, hardly daring to say even to her own heart, it was for him; but when he came not, a faint sigh stole from her lips, and she inwardly said, "I ought not to have expected it." She had known so much of sorrow, that disappointment never came unlooked for. In the meanwhile, Henry stood apart, leaning against a tree, his arms folded across his breast, and his face pale as marble. He looked upon her white cheek and slight frame, and shuddered to think of the sufferings to which she might be exposed. When General Harrison gave her his paternal benediction, he envied him the privilege and the assurance which his age and character imparted, and thought how he should have stammered in uttering the simplest thing at such a time. Slowly the crowd dispersed, each with his own comments, and all ominous of evil. Many were the glances sent to catch a last glimpse of the fair girl; and her beauty, her gentleness, and misfortunes became the more impressive, as perils thickened about her. So Death, the great scorcher of living hearts, buries the faults of the dead only to open the eyes of the living to their own, and all errors are the more glaring as the spirit brings 'all things to recollection,' whatsoever was lovely in the departed.

Alice had mingled but little among them, and her face was scarcely known; and now, as they beheld it for the first time, and in the act of self-sacrificing affection, it became invested with a mysterious and spiritual beauty, which all were ready to believe ominous of the doom that awaited her.

Mansfield saw and felt all this, and the tears started to his eyes as he thought his should be the privilege to be with the sweet girl in the long and perilous march, to shield her from evil, and anticipate her wants; and so respectful should be his attentions, that even Alice, delicate and maidenly as she was, should receive them as from a brother: for was she not as a sister to him? He trembled as he thought; for the emotions awakened by her calm and simple beauty, were so unlike those from beholding the more radiant Margaret, that he was sure they could be no more than the tenderness one would feel for a gentle and suffering sister.

Tecumseh had sent on the main body of his warriors in advance of his own little escort, that was to accompany Alice; and he now adapted his pace to her comfort, with a refinement worthy of a higher state of cultivation. Alice, though apparently timid and distrustful, had still all a woman's fortitude and resolution, when thrown upon her own resources. As the dangers of her situation grew upon her imagination, and, in the solitudes of the forest, appeared greater than they were in reality, she felt her own nature grow strong within her, and resigned herself to her situation with a spirit prepared for any emergency. She looked in the face of her noble conductor, and read there so much of all that is best in the human heart, that a strange and unlooked-for sympathy took the place of that awe with which she had hitherto regarded him. She saw him choose out the smoothest and most sheltered paths, that the low wood or the burning sun might not incommode her; and that, too, while his followers dashed on, regardless of all impediments. In fording the streams that swept across their path, he took the bridle of her horse, and led him through the torrent, gratified to perceive in her no womanly tokens of fear. At noon, he spread skins for her to repose under the shadow of the woods, and brought water with his own hands from the brook, as she partook of their simple repast. His words were few, but always in a voice low and winning, with that same remarkable smile, that contrasted so strongly with the usual sad and even stern expression of his face.

They had emerged from the woods, and were in the outskirts of a prairie, that undulated far off upon the horizon like a sea of verdure, when Tecumseh paused upon the elevation they had gained, and cast his eye over the broad prospect that opened before them. In the rear, growing dim and indistinct in the distance, appeared the clustered dwellings of the white settlers, with their waving fields of grain and cultivated enclosures. At their right swept far off a forest of green trees, as yet untouched by the axe of the settler; the old primeval woods reposing in the dim majesty of many centuries, and their giant arms outstretched in the regal pomp of by-gone and uncounted years. At the left were vistas in the green woods, bright streams, smiling and singing onward in the summer light, sheets of water in which the water-fowl dipped its beak, and the trees stooped down to the very brink, as if in love with their own images reflected in the crystal beneath. The smoke of the Indian wigwam went up like a scarcely perceptible mist in the thin air, and through the long perspective might be seen herds of deer, with their antlered heads proudly elevated, and their penciled limbs scarcely visible in the speed of their motions. In front was the great prairie, relieved by a long line of hills painted upon the horizon, and the mist that hung over the great lakes disposing itself into clouds of every variety of form, stretching high up into the azure vault, or reposing like fairy isles in a sea of blue.

Tecumseh drew to the side of the maiden.

"Is it not a worthy inheritance?" he said, as he stretched out his arm, and circled slowly the glorious picture beneath them.

"Beautiful! most beautiful!" responded Alice; and in the gush of her enthusiasm, the tears gathered to her eyes, and she turned from the beauty of the earth and looked in the face of her noble conductor.

Tecumseh regarded her with a saddened smile; and Alice felt, were it not for the majesty of his sorrow, she might have dared to pity the chief, whose thoughts she knew were dwelling upon the former glory of his people, and their present feebleness and decay. As it was, she could feel nothing but a strange admiration and sympathy. Her eyes fell slowly, and a sigh escaped her bosom. The chief moved not, but he answered the sigh heavily.

"Maiden, the white man is spared, only that the Indian remembers that such as thou art dwell with him. But the Indian's wrongs are many and great. Look around us: all that you behold was once his: it was the gift of the Great Spirit. He built his fires and pursued his game, and there was nothing to make his heart faint. But it is past. The Indian is an outcast and a wanderer. The white man marches up with fire and sword, forward, forward: and the deadly bullet is sent before him, and the warriors retreat, shielding their women and their children, and falling down to die in the vast wilderness; and the few that are left will be lost in the great waters of the setting sun."

This was uttered in a deep, solemn voice, with slow, melancholy action; and, in its dying close, Alice seemed almost to behold the extinction of the tribes. She clasped her hands over the saddle, and looked wonderingly up as the chief went on. His eye kindled, and his action assumed greater animation, though he never for a moment forgot the gentleness of the fair girl at his side.

"But, maiden, the Great Spirit has decreed that his children shall no more flee like the deer before the hunter. He has commanded them to drive the whites to the other side of the great mountains, and there hold them at bay. The white man must leave the Indian to hold this side of the mountains as his own. The Indian hath planted his foot; it is the soil of his fathers. He will build his smokes here— die here; or blood will come of it!"

Alice turned pale, as the picture of burning dwellings, and slaughtered inhabitants, presented itself to her eye, and she replied earnestly: "The red chief is generous; he is humane; he will not dip his hands in human blood. He has mothers, and sisters, and children among his own people, and he will have compassion upon those of his white brother."

"Nobly hast thou spoken, maiden; Tecumseh delights not in war. He will visit our white father at Washington, and tell him to stop the purchase of our lands. He will remove his people quietly into his own land, and leave us ours. The high mountains must be a wall to divide the red man from the white: they are not the same people—they cannot live together. True, maiden, we have wives and daughters; and it is for their defence that the Indian has united to become one people. But, think you, when the white man bends his lips to the cheek of the beautiful, that he remembers the Indian is drawn to the maidens of his own people with a like emotion? No, no! he is but as the wild beast that prowleth in the desert, to whom love and gentleness are unknown."

Alice bowed her head, for she felt there was too much of truth in what he uttered. Tecumseh mused a moment in silence, and then, giving the reins to his horse, they entered upon the prairie. Desirous to change the current of his thoughts, Alice ventured some inquiries as to Margaret. She raised her eyes timidly to the face of her dusky guide, and a momentary fear came over her; but the thought of Margaret again assured her, and she spoke.

"Is Margaret beloved of the Indian maidens? Is she joyous and beautiful? or has she ceased to be the gay, proud girl that we once loved? Oh, if I could see her look as she once did! hear her speak and see her smile, as she did when we were children together, life would be too blissful!"

The chief listened with a smile. "The Swaying Reed is beautiful; hers is the beauty of the wild blossom, the smile of the sun when he stealeth through the leaves to play upon the still waters, and the wind awakens it to dimples. Her voice is sweet as that of the spirit-bird, that singeth all night amid the branches. The maiden is proud, and wise, for the Great Spirit talketh to her in her slumbers."

"But has she forgotten to worship the God of her fathers—to bow down to the one only true God?" asked Alice, earnestly, as she, for the first time, began to feel that the bonds of sympathy might have become weak between them.

A shade stole over the features of the chief. He was silent for nearly a minute before he replied.

"The Swaying Reed worships the Great Spirit, but not like her white fathers upon bended knees and with loud words, in temples reared by skilful hands, with the music of many voices. No! she folds her hands upon her bosom, and in the solitude of her own thoughts, in the calm of the great woods, her spirit goeth forth, and mingleth with the universal spirit, till she is a part of all that is good and infinite about her. The broad arch of the overhanging sky, with the light of innumerable stars—the green earth, with its old woods and bespangled blossoms; the drapery of many clouds, and ascending mists, are to her a temple of adoration. The sound of many waters, the melody of birds, and the swaying of trees, send up their tones of worthiest music; and her thoughts blend in the midst, like the sweet offering that the sleeping plant sendeth upward as the shadows of evening gather about it."

Alice listened, enchanted by the fervor and unlooked for elo-quence of the chief; and, for a moment, she could not but feel how much more worthy were the temple he had described, than the most gorgeous tabernacle reared by human hands—the worship from such an altar,[1] than the most elaborate ceremonial of human institutions. Still she would rather have known that Margaret, mindful of early instruction, had knelt by her bed night and morning, and prayed, as had been their wont in childhood. This vague and solitary worship,

---

1 Oakes Smith describes a similar altar in her autobiography (Appendix A1, p. 254).

did it really exist, seemed to her pious mind, always accustomed to times and forms, so precarious, that she hardly dared to call it worship. Gradually the impression of abstract truths faded from her mind, and slowly a fearful surmise gathered upon it, assuming form and distinctness. It passed over her like an unearthly chill; and so palpable did it appear, that she felt as if a fearful gulf already separated the lost and beloved from herself, and from all companionship and sympathy. She looked upon the chief, with his manliness and beauty, his winning smile, and melodious voice; his passionate, and yet subdued eloquence; his humanity, and yet well-known courage in battle; and as all these things gathered upon her fancy, his person seemed to assume still more of majesty and beauty; and she grew sick at heart, as she thought how unlikely it was that a maiden like Margaret, ardent, proud, and enthusiastic, should resist so many attractions, when deprived of the society of her own people, and subjected entirely to their influence. A sylvan picture gathered upon her mind's eye, of a cot away in the woods, in the midst of vines and gushing waters, and Margaret standing at the door in robe of skins, and armed with bow and quiver. Margaret seemed already lost to her for ever, so vivid became the picture, and she spread out her hands for support.

Tecumseh looked upon her with amazement; and, lifting her from her horse, placed her gently under the shadow of the trees—for they had reached one of those little islands, as it were, of trees, that occasionally rise, like the oasis of the desert, in the midst of the surrounding wilderness of verdure.

"I have seen a strange dream," said Alice, recovering. "I thought Margaret had ceased to love her own people; that she would no more return to us. I saw her away in the wild woods, proud and beautiful, but in all respects like an Indian maid."

Tecumseh's eye gleamed with a wild and startling brilliancy. He looked off into the blue space, and a smile almost of triumph rested upon his lips. It may be that a new dream came to his own spirit—one that, in the midst of his ambition, and labors of patriotism, had never before distinctly came to his eye. *He* beheld, too, the vine-covered wigwam, the beautiful girl in her sylvan robes, and the eye growing more radiant at his own approach. Alice felt that her worst suspicions were confirmed, but great was her relief when the chief replied.

"Fear not, maiden, that the Swaying Reed has learned to weep, and to love. She is alone with her own thoughts,"—he might have said more, but Henry Mansfield, emerging from a clump of trees, reined up his steed by their side, and he was silent. A glad smile for an instant lighted the face of Alice, and a crimson blush overspread cheek and brow. Tecumseh greeted the youth with one of his blandest smiles, and the party again sat forward.

It would be uninteresting to follow their route through that wild and beautiful wilderness; to describe their encampments for the night, and the tender and respectful attentions bestowed upon Alice through the long journey. As they approached the village, the sun was near its decline; and the rich crimson tints were spread out upon the river, and lighted up vine and tree from the sombreness of their repose, as if a trail of glory delightedly lingered about the green earth. Alice felt her heart beat wildly as she approached, and her breath came thick and heavily. A thousand pictures were presented to her mind, gloomy and disheartening, till she grew exhausted at the contemplation. Tecumseh conducted her by the river path to the bower before described, in which he knew that Margaret would be likely to repose at this hour of the day. Alice caught a view of a maiden half reclining in the shadow, caressing a white fawn at her feet; and she saw that she raised her eyes, blushing deeply at the entrance of the chief. He stepped aside, and revealed the form of Alice. Margaret's radiant eyes assumed an expression of searching interest; her bosom slightly heaved, and she became deadly pale. Still she neither spoke nor moved. Alice rushed forward, and knelt by her side; and, putting her arms about her neck, whispered, "Do you not know me, my own dear, dear Margaret?" She felt herself slightly repulsed—the girl sighed heavily, raised her eyes reproachfully to those of the chief, and fell fainting to the ground.

Alice felt a dizziness and sickness of heart gathering about her, and all her dreams of attachment and sisterly sympathy seemed suddenly to evaporate in thin air. She groaned heavily, and pressed her hand to the cold brow of Margaret.

"Oh, God! that we should be spared for this. Margaret, dear Margaret, say but one word—say that you love me, and I will return again through the wild woods, and trouble you no more."

Margaret's cold eyes were fixed upon her face without a single token of recognition. Her hands were clasped, and her brow contracted, and yet there was no look of severity, nothing but a fixed, long look of utter wretchedness.

Alice burst into tears and was silent. Suddenly a painful thought crossed her mind.

"Oh, can it be? Do I behold you, Margaret, but a wreck of your better nature; the victim of cruelty and oppression?" and she again drew her to her bosom and kissed her white lips.

Margaret gently repulsed her, and turned away her head. But the fire came to her eye, and she held up her delicate hand as if to say, "Do these look like bondage or cruelty?" Alice turned appealingly to the chief.

"The Swaying Reed hath been like the blossom sheltered in its green covering, and away from the breath of the storm."

Margaret rose up, and with tottering steps approached the cabin of Minaree. As her eye rested on the face of Ackoree, the beauty of the tribe, her step became firmer, and a portion of her former pride gathered about her motions. Alice followed mechanically behind her, feeling as if the golden bowl[1] of existence had been suddenly dashed to the earth. What was all the beauty of earth and sky to her, all of human hope and happiness, when the one only staff on which she had ventured to lean was thus thrust from beneath her. The friendly chief looked pityingly upon her, and gave his arm for support, but she turned away saying, "Leave me to die, for life is a weariness." Entering the cabin, she seated herself upon the skins, motionless and tearless. The good Minaree spread her repast before them, but neither could speak or eat.

The twilight faded away, the bright stars came forth, and the full moon stole in through the open portal, revealing the two sisters, awake and motionless, each full of her own wild and troubled thoughts. Each was deathly pale, and each felt and marveled at the strange repulsion that was thus separating two whose childhood had been so full of sympathy. The torch of Minaree had been long extinguished, and her regular breathings betokened the depth of her slumber. Alice arose and looked forth, and she shrunk with awe from the wildness and beauty of the scene spread out before her; the dim forest approaching the very threshold, and the sound of the fox, with its sharp barking, and the long, melancholy cry of the

---

1   Ecclesiastes 12:6.

owl, uttered almost at her ear. Near the banks of the river, motionless in the moonlight, and thrown into bold relief by the sparkling waters, appeared the statue-like form of a warrior, keeping watch over the slumbering village. All was so hushed and gloomy in its midnight grandeur, that her own desolateness weighed the heavier upon her spirits. Closing the portal, she exclaimed, "Oh, my God, that I should have forgotten thee in this hour of trial!" And she sank upon her knees, in the very agony of prayer, uttering the sorrows and the desires of a stricken heart. Her voice was tremulous, and choked with tears. As she went on, the soft arm of Margaret encircled her neck, and she whispered, "Alice, my dear, dear sister?" Their lips met, and they wept long upon the bosom of each other; and when sleep stole to their lids, it found them clasped in the embrace of childhood.

CHAPTER XIV.

A loneliness that is not lone,
A love quite withered up and gone.—J.R. LOWELL.[1]

Shortly after the return of Tecumseh, the party, which he had sent off to intercept, and, if possible, capture Winnemac and the other treacherous chiefs, returned from their unsuccessful enterprise. The wily chiefs knew too well the dangers to which they were exposed, to omit any precautionary measure. It required the most experienced observation, and the keenest instinct of the savage, to detect the almost imperceptible trail. But it was detected and followed with the certainty and keenness of the bloodhound in pursuit of its prey. The crushed blossom and the tangled grass, though restored to their original position, could not escape the practiced eye of the Indian. The twig slightly bent, the moss imperceptibly rubbed off, were so many guides to direct his footsteps. As he neared the foe, the whirring of the partridge alarmed in its covert, and the quick wing of the wild bird, as it hurried away, told of his vicinity. The crack of a twig, the rustle of the dry grass which he alone could distinguish from the foot of the wild animal, admonished the pursuer to move warily, or he himself might be betrayed. Each party fed upon the dry

---

1   James Russell Lowell (1819–91), "Rosaline."

provisions of his pouch, or such berries as appeared in their path, without venturing to light a fire, as the smoke would tell the tale of proximity. At night, the pursuing party beheld the other sleep, with weapon in hand and a trusty and vigilant guard. The orders of Tecumseh were, strictly, to shed no blood, as the motive might easily be misapprehended; and he had resolved to bring the chiefs before a grand council of the whole confederated tribes, and there, in the united presence of the representatives of those whom they had wronged, pronounce their condemnation, and offer them on the shrine of Indian patriotism.

For the purpose of assembling this great council, Tecumseh proposed to summon the various chiefs to a meeting upon the banks of the Wabash. He earnestly besought his followers to adhere to the principles of pacification; to disregard those British agitators, who, taking advantage of the growing hostility between the two countries, were desirous to conciliate the aid of the northern tribes, as powerful auxiliaries in a frontier warfare. He represented to them in glowing colors, the perils to be hazarded, and the small prospect of advantage to be gained by joining themselves to either of the belligerent parties. They were a nation by themselves, with interests to be promoted, and rights to be maintained, and he besought them to peril nothing by an indiscreet participation in the coming troubles. An uncompromising neutrality was their safest and best course. He urged upon them the necessity of study in the arts of war, the practice of their national games and festivities, and all those exercises, whether of war or peace, that were necessary for their improvement or security.

Eliskwatawa enforced the instruction of his brother by rites and incantations, for the voice of the Great Spirit had mingled with the visions of the night, and represented to him the future glory of the tribes. He had beheld cities and towns, rivalling the prosperity of the whites, gradually filling the great valley of the Mississippi, and a people prosperous and happy, rejoicing in equable laws, and free from the vices of the white man. He had looked upon the stars, and they in their courses fought against the white man.[1] Wrong to the Indian, injustice of every kind, and war and bloodshed were preparing a fearful retribution for the white man. The storms and frosts

---

1   [Oakes Smith's note:] "The stars in their courses fought against Sisera," seems to be a beautiful astrological allusion.

of winter were passing away, and the tribes were rousing themselves from their long slumber, and ready to go forth in the strength of other years. The massasauga lay no longer coiled in the cleft of the rock, feeble and inanimate, but with glittering eye, and radiant hue, rolled itself onward, with neck erect and fang ready to strike its deadly poison into the veins of its foe.

Kumshaka listened to the fervid eloquence of his brothers, in gloom and silence. New and vindictive passions were at work in his bosom, and he inwardly resolved that at least Tecumseh should be dashed from his proud pre-eminence, let the consequence be what it might. What to him were the dreams of ambition, the glory of his people, who brooded in selfish discontent over his own disappointed hopes, and dark plans of revenge. He had preceded Tecumseh on his return to the village, and half in idleness, half in awakened interest, had sought out Ackoree.

He found her on the bank of the river, slowly drawing a net to the shore; her small fingers grasping the threads; her long hair falling forward, revealing the faultless neck and shoulders on which glistened the coral beads, which he had placed there. The sound of steps arrested her, and still holding the net through which the scaly captives were just visible, she held back her long hair, and turned partially round. Her bright eyes gleamed with more than their wonted brilliancy, and the ready smile was upon her lips; again dropping her hair, she playfully yielded the net to the chief, and seated herself upon a projecting rock while he drew it to the shore. This done, the chief seated himself by her side, and played with the long glossy threads of her hair.

Ackoree was even more than ordinarily gay, and her clear laugh floated away on the air, and stirred up the gratified echoes. And what seemed surprising in one so gay and giddy, she required a full account of the proceedings of the late council, and the probable course to be adopted by the tribes. While her companion went on with the details, all the levity in which she had hitherto indulged, disappeared from her manner, and she listened with composed and engrossed attention; when he ceased, she replied slowly, without raising her eyes from the ground,

"So, then, the fang is to be extracted from the massasauga, that he may shake his rattles, but do no mischief. Tecumseh would bury the hatchet, lest its edge should terrify his white bride."

"The white girl who has just entered the village, is nothing to Tecumseh. She is the sister of the Swaying Reed."

"Very true; but Tecumseh is much, very much, to the Swaying Reed:" and she fixed her eyes stedfastly upon the face of the chief, to see what effect her words might produce.

He drew in his breath, and his eyes glittered with the intensity of the serpent about to spring upon its victim; clenching the locks of hair firmly in his hands till the indignant beauty colored with rage, he demanded in husky tones what she meant. "Have they dared to love?"

Ackoree disentangled her hair, and uttered a low scornful laugh; for rage and jealousy were both at work in her bosom.

"Dare! why should they not dare, what Kumshaka had dared before them? The Indian is to dwell side by side with his white brother, that the white bride may be at ease in her wigwam."

"And the voice of the Great Spirit, and the language of the stars are only to help out an affair of love!" said the chief, bitterly. "I will expose their jugglery. The Indian is duped by his own leaders. The confederation is but a device to make him powerless and to protect the whites." But even while he spake the blood rushed to his cheek, for his heart gave the lie to his lips.

Ackoree saw that her poison had taken effect, and assuming an air of gentleness and composure, she laid her hand upon that of the chief, and replied, softly,

"Tecumseh is wary and powerful. Would the chief rush unarmed into the very jaws of the panther? Would he seek the den while the dam is by to guard it? Surely, it were better to wait till she is out in quest of prey."

Kumshaka caught at the idea with avidity; for, vain and impulsive, he readily adopted the suggestions of others, thereby saving himself the labor of investigation. He looked admiringly upon the vindictive girl, and the activity of the like passions operated as a bond of sympathy between them. Taking her passive hand in his, he replied,

"Thou art most beautiful, Ackoree, and wisely hast thou counselled. Tecumseh will depart to assemble the great council, and then shall be the time to act. If the white girl becomes his bride, the scalps of her people shall line the entrance to her wigwam."

Ackoree withdrew her hand. "Kumshaka follows a shadow. He is in pursuit of the bow that rests upon the tops of the trees, but vanishes as he draws near."

"I will follow it no more. The Swaying Reed is as nothing to me, except as she can feel my vengeance. But tell me, Ackoree, how do you know of their love?"

"We stood together when your party returned to the village. Tecumseh was not with you. I looked into the face of the white girl, and she knew it not. The heart of the white girl could be read upon her cheek, for the blood went and came, and her eye wandered from chief to chief, and then was fixed long upon the woods, to see if he came from thence. 'Tecumseh has not returned,' I said. She tried to smile, to speak, but my eye was upon her, and she felt that I knew all. She turned away and was silent."

She had scarcely finished her recital, when a harsh voice was heard to utter her name several times in a peevish accent, and Ackoree, obedient to the summons, gathered up the net and hastened away.

CHAPTER XV.

Oh, long shall I think of those silver bright lakes,
    And the scenes they revealed to my view,
My friends, and the wishes I formed for their sakes,
    And my bright yellow birchen canoe.—H.R. SCHOOLCRAFT.[1]

The morning after the arrival of Alice, Margaret arose lightly from her slumbers, while the sun was as yet invisible above the horizon. Minaree was already abroad, and there was no one to observe emotions which she might otherwise have concealed. She remained long, stooping over the form of her sleeping sister, as if analyzing every feature, to see how well it harmonized with the recollections of her childhood. As she continued to gaze, her bosom heaved with sighs, and tears stole from beneath her lids. Memories almost obliterated awoke to new life, and she lived once more, in the midst of love and happiness in that sweet home away in the deep woods. The voices of childhood came to her ear, and she heard again the language of prayer. Clasping her hands, the sacred duty sprung to her lips. It was a lovely sight to behold that proud and beautiful girl, in her strange wild dress, bowing in lowly devotion over the

---

1   Henry Rowe Schoolcraft (1793–1864), "The Birchen Canoe."

form of her sleeping sister, whose presence had awakened all the gentle harmonies of her nature.

An unwonted softness stole over her manner, displacing a portion of that coldness and pride which had won for her not less the admiration, than the reverence of the rude people in whose midst she had been thrown. She took the garments of her sister, and examined their, to her, singular construction; for though she had never entirely forgotten the costume of her earlier days, and had in some measure adapted her own garments to it, yet the recollection had become dim and indistinct. She placed her small foot within the slipper, and walked back and forth, evidently pleased with the symmetry it helped to reveal. Alice turned in her departing slumbers, and Margaret restored the garments to their former position, and seated herself to comb and brush her abundant hair, using for the former purpose bones of the fish, skilfully inserted in a piece of wood. The brush was made of the stiff hairs of the buffalo, richly wrought with the quills of the porcupine.

Alice opened her eyes, and spread out her arms to embrace her, but Margaret only indicated her consciousness of the motion by a smile, as she continued her occupation. Minaree soon entered with fish, for their morning repast, which she proceeded to roast between two flat stones covered with coals. Alice herself prepared a cake to be baked in a similar manner. Margaret brought in fruits, and a vessel of water, and another containing a beverage prepared from the sap of the maple. The breakfast was spread upon a rude low table, at which the two sisters were seated, while Minaree chose to take hers in her lap, not precisely in the manner in which ladies take their tea when 'carried round,'[1] as it is called, but bearing a strong analogy thereto; thus showing in these two opposite situations in life, as well as in all others, that extremes always approximate. Margaret looked timidly in the face of her sister, for she had not forgotten the usages of her early life; and Alice folded her hands, closed her eyes, and in a low voice pronounced an appropriate grace.

Alice found the resources of the cabin much greater than she had anticipated. Margaret had instructed Minaree in many things unknown to her people, and the good woman, being naturally of a patient and thrifty turn, had busied herself cheerfully in preserving

---

1   Handed to guests who are not seated at a table.

many things for winter use, which could only have been suggested by the superior resources of Margaret. These were stores of grapes dried carefully in the sun, bearing no mean resemblance to imported raisins; honey from the wild bee, preserved in gourds, covered with thin leaves of the birch bark; sugar from the sap of the maple tree, in vessels of bark; and berries of different kinds made into sweetmeats; dried fish and venison; a small delicate fish of the trout kind, which was considered a great luxury. It was first prepared by immersing it in the oil of the bear, while fresh, for a few days, and afterward putting them away in gourds sealed, and then cased in clay and dried in the sun. In this way they were excellent for a great length of time, improving by age. There were also pulse, corn, and wild rice, as also a species of wild wheat, which could be converted, by means of pounding, and afterward grinding between flat stones, into excellent cakes.

Alice soon helped Margaret to improve the taste as well as the comforts of her cabin, by the manufacture of many things which her superior ingenuity and experience suggested. Henry Mansfield, and even the young men of the tribe were ready to construct frames for their wicker-chairs, and helped Minaree not a little in making a more ambitious table; for so winning and gentle were the sisters, that they felt a new pleasure in promoting their comfort, perhaps the more, that many articles afterward found their way to their own cabins; to say nothing of the nice cakes furnished for the breakfast of some young warrior, prepared by their own hands, and borne by the faithful Minaree. The good woman was slow to adopt improvements for herself, but gratified in everything that imparted pleasure to her foster-child; and when, after many days of labor, she beheld one side of her cabin covered with a rush mat, and chairs and a table, on which lay the Bible of Alice, and a rude chest with robes, belts, and moccasins, carefully disposed, her joy knew no bounds. She saw Margaret open and close the lid, seat herself upon the chairs, survey herself in the small glass, re-arrange the combs and brushes, walk across the mat, and then look full of smiles into the face of Alice.

Suddenly she ceased the little pantomime, and her face grew sad; a heavy sigh escaped her, and she stood pale and motionless. Alice would have embraced her, but she repelled her approach, and taking down her bow and quiver, hastened from the cabin. Alice followed her proud and graceful figure, as with light and bounding steps she disappeared in the dim woods, and covering her face with her hands,

burst into tears. All the little comforts of civilized life, which she had
endeavored to bring about her sister, thereby to awaken a desire for
them, and to lure her imperceptibly back to her old associations and
pleasures, she felt had served as a momentary gratification, exciting
wonder rather than affection; and she felt she was still wedded to
her wild life. Other suspicions, too, were gaining strength upon her
mind, and her own loneliness weighed heavily upon her.

Scarcely had the sisters one morning completed their repast, when
Tecumseh, accompanied by Henry Mansfield, entered the lodge.
Alice gave her hand to the chief with an open smile of pleasure, and
Margaret coldly laid hers in that of Mansfield. Both blushed deeply
and seemed embarrassed. Tecumseh's stay was short, for he was
about to start upon his journey for the purpose of assembling the old
men of the different tribes, and his time was precious. Turning to
the sisters he said in a voice, tremulous, and deep, "When Tecumseh
returns, the white maidens will be away with their own people; but
let them not forget that the poor Indian spread his mat to shelter
them, and brought this game to give them life. Tecumseh had broken bread with the white man, and he could never forget it."

Margaret's cheek was very pale. Alice arose earnestly, the tears
gathering in her eyes, and taking the hand of the chief in both of
hers, she replied—

"We can never, never forget your generosity, and with us, Tecumseh will be the name for all that is noble, and excellent. We will pray
always that the Great Spirit may bless you, and reward you for all
that you have done for Margaret."

Tecumseh bent his head, and the plumes of his helmet concealed
his face. When he turned to take his leave of Margaret, she had left
the cabin. Leaving Alice, he bent his steps to the arbor of vines on
the bank of the river.

Margaret had buried her face in her hands, and lay prostrate upon
the leaves of the floor, while low sobs burst from her lips. Tecumseh
raised her from the ground, and remained silently and sadly regarding her. Had he spoken—Margaret might have wept on, for her
heart was now open for the reception of sympathy, and unwonted
emotions were stirring in her bosom; but his silence served to call up
her native pride, and she stood up, and flung back the curls from her
brow, and the tears from her eyes, as if hers were a nature to which
weakness, and the melting mood of womanhood were unknown.

Tecumseh's eye kindled with admiration. "Tell the white man," he said, "that the Swaying Reed learned her pride in the wild woods, and her freedom and nobleness under the clear sky, and by the many waters of the red-man. Tell him, too, that Tecumseh will watch for the happiness of the Swaying Reed, and for every tear that falls from her eye, shall answer a drop from his heart. If her eye grows dim, or her step heavy, Tecumseh will be there to avenge her wrong. Tell him too, that the Swaying Reed has been to Tecumseh what the shower is to the earth, the sun to the blossom, or the bird to the forest. She has been the one star in a night of storm: that when she is gone, the light will have gone out upon his path."

Margaret trembled violently.

"Tecumseh, I shall never return to my people. I will live and die here. I would that Alice had never heard of my existence, that she might be spared the pain of this."

Tecumseh shook his head. "Nay, nay, the white maiden will long for companionship. She will be like the bird alone in its nest, and she will listen to the melody of love. She would spurn the red man, for he cannot woo her as would one of her own people, on bended knee, and with honied[1] words;" and as he spoke his voice was low, and his eyes mournfully fixed upon her face.

Margaret blushed deeply, and she raised her speaking eyes upward. Tecumseh sprang forward with a wild expression of pleasure. He took her trembling hand in his, and bent his expressive eyes to those of the fair white girl, and for a moment seemed to abandon himself to a new and unexpected source of happiness. Recollecting himself he went on—

"No, no: Tecumseh will not be the one to bring a shadow upon the brow of the white maiden. The bird will long for the sound of its own woods, for the rocking of the tree on which its nest was first built. Tecumseh will not take the blossom from its home in the pleasant sunshine, to see it wither alone in his own cabin. Evil is coming upon Tecumseh, the blackbird is always above his head, and as he came to the village, he found the massasauga dead in his pathway. Sorrow is falling upon him, for the spirit-bird sang all night upon his roof." He pressed the hand of Margaret to his heart, and left the bower.

---

1 Honeyed or sweet.

Margaret remained in the attitude in which he had left her, long after he had disappeared; she gave utterance to no wild burst of anguish, she did not even weep: a heavy sense of misery weighed upon her; a cold pressure lay upon her young heart, as if hope had suddenly and almost undefinedly taken its departure. One by one she disengaged the tangled threads of thought, and there came the image of Alice, with her eyes fixed in displeasure, almost in abhorrence upon her, and then there was the noble chief, with his eyes telling so much of love, and deep and abiding sorrow. She heard voices and footsteps approaching, and elevating her figure to its full height, she went out to meet Alice and Henry Mansfield with a manner from which all emotion had disappeared. Still she was not at ease in their presence. She felt the pressure of manners and associations to which she had been unaccustomed, and they affected her with a painful sense of inferiority. Margaret drew herself proudly up, and retreated within herself, holding communion with the wild romance, awakened by wood and water, and the depths of the blue sky. They had seated themselves upon the bank of the river and all were silent, as if the beauty and quiet in which they reposed had closed even the avenues of speech.

It was a sight rare and picturesque in that sequestered spot, to see those two sisters, each in her distinctive loveliness, seated side by side, vainly essaying, as it were, to join once more the links of mutual sympathy and love which had been so cruelly dissevered.

The face of Alice was pale, yet composed in its sweet sad expression, and a tear seemed trembling beneath the lid of the clear blue eye. Margaret's cheek was flushed, and her brow, higher and broader than that of her sister, was thrown backward, and the short upper lip curled with an expression of discontent, if not of scorn. Her dark, deep-set eye, with its long curved lash, was moving impatiently from object to object, as if she felt already the trammels of artificial society, and longed to be once more a free dweller of the wood, to follow alone the impulses of her own nature. She felt too, from the looks and manner of Alice, that she had become an object of gentle compassion to her, and she revolted from the position. When, therefore, Alice gently smoothed her clear brow, sighing heavily; Margaret's cheek flushed, and she arose hurriedly from the grass, and turned half angrily away; for she could not understand how the knowledge of so much that to her appeared useless, and even enfeebling to the human character, should stamp upon its possessor the rights of superiority.

What were the studied conventionalisms of society to the freedom, and grace, and native buoyancy of the wild dweller of the woods? And what were the artificial words of those, who year by year filled their brains with the ideas of others, making it as it were only the receptacle of other men's thoughts, to the untutored outpourings of those who spake only as the spirit gave them utterance? Who learned their vocabulary from the spontaneous operations of their own unshackled minds; and the teachings to be learned in the great school of nature, the language of the midnight stars, the chiming of many waters, the swaying of the old wood, and the hoary grandeur of the everlasting hills! What was the blind devotee to human creeds, to him who, bowing in the freedom and majesty of his own nature, worshiped in the singleness of his heart, that great and invisible Spirit, whose presence he felt diffused upon every side of him?

Margaret failed to perceive the right of the civilized to arrogate aught of superiority, and the gentle melancholy of Alice served only to attach her the more strongly to the freedom of savage life. She returned to the cabin, and shortly after made her appearance with a pair of paddles, followed by old Minaree bearing the canoe. They descended the bank, and launched it upon the river, Minaree holding it by the stern till all was ready. Margaret beckoned for Alice to accompany her, and she timidly prepared to follow. Margaret's eyes danced with delight, and she struck the paddles lightly upon the waters, as if to say, "she cannot do this," and her pride became reconciled.

"Shall I come, too?" said Mansfield, still holding the hand of Alice, who was really terrified as she seated herself in the bottom of the canoe, and felt the ripple of the water beneath the thin birch.

Margaret assented, and he took one of the paddles to assist in propelling it over the waters. Light as the fairy nautilus it sped along the river, and Margaret's long slender fingers lay upon the paddle, as she threw aside the bright waters that flashed and fell like a shower of diamonds at the every motion of the oar. Her joyous laugh rang out upon the woods that overhung the river, as she gaily challenged the speed of her companion, and even Alice grew fearless, as she observed the ease and security of her companions. They had left the village long behind them, and the river which had been growing narrower now suddenly turned, leaving in the centre a small island, covered with low trees down to the dip of the water; separated from the main on one side by a narrow channel, over the rocky bed of which flowed a stream of water like a thread of silver dropped in the sunshine; on the other, the channel was broad and still, moving gracefully around the fairy isle, making a diminutive basin, deeply shadowed by the surrounding woods.

They were still under the lea of the little isle, and about to emerge once more upon the open river, when Margaret laid down her paddle and motioned her companions to silence. Mansfield smiled as he observed her fix an arrow to her bow, and following the direction of her aim, beheld far up the stream a deer that had come down to drink, standing in a startled attitude, with foot lifted, and head turned upon one side, listening if aught *had* indeed disturbed the slumbering echoes. The shaft leapt from the bow, and bounding forward the animal sprang into the river, dyeing it with its blood. A faint scream escaped the lips of Alice, and she looked almost with horror upon Margaret, as she sat with her lips slightly compressed, a gratified smile playing about the mouth, and calmly watching the struggles of the expiring animal. In the agony of its sufferings it had swam quite across the river, and with drooping antlers it attempted to ascend the opposite bank, but its strength failed—it staggered forward and fell to the earth, quaffing the waters that laved its distended nostril.

"Nobly done," exclaimed Mansfield, as the daring girl dashed the water aside to near her victim.

Alice covered her eyes with both hands, as they neared the dying animal, where it lay staining the green bank with its blood, giving utterance to faint sobs, and its full eyes expressive of its patience and its agony. "Oh, it was cruelly, most cruelly done. Dear, dear Margaret, say you will never kill another!"

Margaret looked displeased and disappointed, and she turned almost contemptuously away, and sprang from the canoe to the bank. Carelessly disengaging the arrow from its side, the animal gave a faint spring, raised itself upon one limb, quivered convulsively, and was dead.

"Oh, Margaret, you must leave this wild life, and go with me, and become gentle and womanly; you will learn to sit quietly in the house and read and sew, and we shall be so happy, shall we not, dear Margaret?" said Alice, drawing her hand within her own.

Margaret withdrew her hand and smiled scornfully, but was silent.

"Tell me, dear Margaret, will you not go with us?"

"To sit all day in the house, and do useless work, and read words, that mean nothing," said Margaret, with flushed cheek; "never—never!"

"But Margaret, you will learn what the great and good have thought before us, and there will be pleasure in that."

Margaret shook her head. "They were creatures like ourselves, with like thoughts and feelings, and how shall we delight to read their words? No, Alice, it is folly; let us be free here in this great wilderness, and rejoice in the beauty around us, but let us not be chained down by the opinions of others. I cannot go with you to your poor life; stay with me, and we can be happy."

Alice felt that the eyes of Mansfield were upon her, and she blushed deeply. Why should she not stay here in the populous and beautiful solitudes of nature, away from the restraints and arbitrary usages of society, and live with Margaret in the innocence and freedom of their own thoughts, with the simple children of nature? She hesitated to reply.

"No, Margaret, we all desire improvement; it were but selfishness to remain here, away from duty, and from human ties"—she blushed and stopped, for she had uttered what she would fain recall; but she went on—"from the ties that bind us to our creatures; should we remain here, we should die neither wiser nor better than we are now, and that must not be."

"And we should be no worse, Alice; nor can I see why we cannot do good to the Indian as well as the white man:" and she tapped with an arrow impatiently upon the small moccasin that covered her foot.

"Think of our mother, Margaret, how it would have grieved her to think of your living here in the midst of savages."

Margaret's cheek reddened with an angry flush.

"Say no more Alice. I cannot go. I am resolved. You but call me back to misery, the more intolerable that many eyes behold it. You awaken recollections too painful. Think you, when tears are upon my cheek, and sorrow at my heart, known only to the Great Spirit, that I could brook strange eyes to look upon me, and ask, what is the matter? The Indian will sit all day by the side, and utter nothing, when grief is at the heart of his friend. He weeps, and is silent; but the white man will talk, talk with a cold unfeeling heart, and dry eye. I want no words. I must be alone. Our mother, oh, I have seen her weep, weep in the bitterness of sorrow, and yet she was gentle and loving like you, Alice, and can I hope for greater happiness? No, no: the world is full of tears, I will shed them here. What matters it, that the grave is made with many prayers, or dug in the wild woods; the spirit returns to Him who gave it, and life and weeping are at an end."

She spoke in a tone of deep feeling, and Alice felt that Margaret was the victim of sorrow deeper than the loss of friends, or the separation from society. She followed the haughty girl in silence to the canoe, and when Mansfield whispered, as he seated her therein, "Alice, there are smiles as well as tears in life, sunshine, or there could be no shadow," she smiled through her tears, and felt that there must be much in life for which we would wish to live; that suffering but gives a zest to enjoyment, and that many of our purest pleasures are but the results of previous suffering.

CHAPTER XVI.

But on the sacred, solemn day,
And, dearest, on thy bended knee,
When thou for those thou lovest dost pray,
Sweet spirit, then remember me.—E. EVERETT.[1]

The first Sabbath spent by Alice in the Indian village was clear and mild, the morning sun shone upon the grass heavy with dew, and the damp leaves of the trees glittered with a thousand beautiful hues, for the breath of autumn had passed over them changing their color, but as yet few were displaced. The distant hills, and slopes of the river, looked as if some gorgeous drapery had been drawn over the rich earth. The shrill voice of the locust came out from the clustering foliage, and the cricket's sharp and cheerful notes lingered long upon the ear. A group of hunters were out on the banks of the river ready for an excursion toward the lakes, and the merry voices of children at their sports in the village area, told that all days were alike to these dwellers of nature.

Alice took her Bible from the table, and drawing Margaret to her side, commenced reading the sublime truths of the Saviour contained in the sermon on the mount. Margaret responded to every word in a low voice, her eyes closed, and her head leaning on the shoulder of Alice. As the reading went on, a tear fell upon the sacred page.

---

1   Edward Everett (1794–1865), "To a Sister."

Alice looked up, and kissed the cheek of her sister. "Margaret, I had not thought you would remember all this."

"Oh, Alice, how often we have repeated them in childhood at the knee of our mother; and since I have been here in the woods, they have been fresh in my memory, and I have acted from them."

"And yet," said Alice, "you have forgotten much, very much of our religion."

Margaret dried her eyes. "I remember all that is of value to us. The desire to do what is right, the love of God, and the hope of a better life. Alice, don't perplex me with what I cannot understand. The holy Saviour, who taught as never man taught, I remember went out into the desert to pray, and loved the woods and mountains, and surely we may worship the Great Spirit acceptably here."

"Yes, Margaret, but the Saviour returned again to the dwellings of men, to soothe the afflicted, and to strengthen the tempted. John, who came to prepare the way for him abode in the desert, but the holy Saviour fled not from the trials or dangers or life."

"Say no more," cried Margaret, "I know you mean that I am fleeing from the duties of life while here; but you forget that the Indian is the work of God like ourselves, and has claims upon us." She arose from her seat, and taking down her bow, was about to leave the cabin.

"Oh, Margaret, do not, I beseech you, desecrate the Sabbath while I am here. Let us spend one day, at least, as we did in childhood—it may be the last we shall be together on earth."

Margaret was softened, and she seated herself again by the side of Alice, and listened to her sweet voice with a smile of happiness. Even Minaree closed her eyes where she sat upon her mats, and seemed gratified at the low murmuring cadences. When the reading ceased, the two sisters were for a while silent; and at length Margaret said—

"Alice, why should you not stay here with me, and why should not this be our home?" Alice did not reply, and she sunk her voice to a whisper, and went on: "You would stay, Alice, I am sure you would, but for this white youth." Margaret did not raise her head from the shoulder of Alice to look in her face, but she felt her breath was short and quick, and she knew the blush was upon her cheek. Twice Alice attempted to speak to deny the charge even, but the words would not come to her lips, and she at length turned to Margaret and said—

"Margaret, I dread to think there may be some secret cause that detains you here in the woods, away from our people and the true worship of God. Speak, dear Margaret, tell me that it is not so, that you do not love—Tecumseh," she said slowly.

Margaret started from the shoulder of Alice, as if an arrow had entered her breast; her cheek and neck were crimson, and her eyes flashed beneath their long black lashes. She looked one instant in the face of Alice, and then left the cabin. The skin that concealed the entrance had hardly ceased its vibration, when it was raised again, and Margaret looked in, and sternly fixed her eyes upon her sister.

"Tell me, Alice, that you will never, never name that again, or we part for ever. Promise me;" she repeated, observing that Alice hesitated to speak.

Alice knew that her suspicions were verified—that Margaret must henceforth be as a stranger to her, and the tears gathered in her mild eyes, and she said faintly, "I promise, dear Margaret."

Margaret again dropped the skin, and Alice buried her face in her hands and wept long and bitterly. The fond hopes she had cherished in the reunion and affections of her sister were at once darkened—a shadow lay upon her brightest anticipations. The sister whose memory she had so long cherished, turned coldly from her proffered love, and in the panoply of her pride repelled all tenderness or familiarity. And yet Alice felt she could not have listened to the tale of such an attachment; her nature would have revolted to hear one thus nearly allied to herself, disclose a love for one of a race so different from their own, and whom she had been taught to regard with abhorrence.

Weeks passed away, and the gay drapery of the woods faded from the trees, the yellow leaf lay gathered in heaps by the side of the hillocks, or borne along on the eddying winds rustled in melancholy music. The grass became dry and crisped in the early frost, and the shrill autumnal winds sounded through the naked trees. In the early light of morning, it was a fair sight to behold the gray limbs of the trees penciled against the red sky, and the fields from which the harvest had been gathered, showing myriads of tiny spears made by the frost, as the loose soil crumbled with moisture. Often and strongly had Mansfield urged the departure of the sisters, but nothing could shake the determination of Margaret to remain with her adopted people. Alice used argument and persuasions of every kind, but she was alike inflexible to every appeal; and the youth now besought Alice to return to her home, and leave

Margaret to the course of life which she had chosen. But Alice still believed that persuasion and perseverance might be effective, and she could not abandon her. She shrunk, too, with maiden delicacy, from a long journey through the wilderness with only the youth to protect her. These motives weighing upon a nature naturally sensitive and timid, finally made her resolve to remain through the winter in the Indian village.

Mansfield had already staid beyond the time prescribed, and it was now necessary that he should take his departure. He besought Alice to return with him. In a few words she acquainted him with her determination. The young man turned pale with surprise and anxiety.

"Let me implore you, Miss Durand, to reflect upon what you may suffer. The precarious nature of Indian supplies, the hazards from cold and sickness, to say nothing of the perils from their caprice and superstition."

"But remember," said Alice, with a smile, "my sister will be exposed to all these in case I leave her here."

"Oh, no: she will be safe, she is accustomed to them—she is as one of them."

"Do not urge me," said Alice, gently, "I feel that I cannot leave Margaret. All that she may be called to encounter, I must endure with her. Indeed, I apprehend no danger, the Indians are kindly disposed, and ready to promote our comfort."

The brow of the youth contracted, and he brushed back the thick curls from his brow with an air of irritation.

"Alice, pardon me, but I cannot leave you here—you are dearer to me than life itself, and I cannot endure the thoughts of this cruel separation."

Alice trembled violently, and her cheek turned from red to pale, but she did not speak for nearly a minute.

"She is my sister, most tenderly beloved, and she must not be abandoned."

Then rising from her seat, she proffered her hand unreservedly to the youth, saying,

"Till we meet again, my thoughts and prayers are yours;" her voice trembled, and as she raised her meek eyes upward, a tear was upon the lids.

Mansfield drew the slight form to his bosom and imprinted a kiss upon her pure brow, with a reverence and love that had little of earthliness in it. For a moment Alice yielded to the embrace, and then responding to the fervent "God bless you" of the youth, she disappeared behind the screen that concealed the couch of herself and Margaret. For one brief period she wished her resolve might be recalled, that she might return to the kindliness of society, and she sunk upon her knees blessing that Power that had made the voice of duty strong within her, and removed the power of temptation ere her strength had forsaken her. When Margaret entered she greeted her gaily, and told her that she should remain with her, and learn to weave baskets, and paddle the canoe, and plait belts of wampum. In return, Margaret promised to apply herself to needlework and reading, and be like a white girl in quietude.

exchange

CHAPTER XVII.

Come with the winter snows, and ask
  Where are the forest birds;
The answer is a silent one,
  More eloquent than words.—HALLECK.[1]

As the winter wore away, appearances of decided hostility on the part of the Indians to the white settlers began to manifest itself in the village. Preparations for war were daily made, and the subject discussed openly, and in council. Their numbers, too, were daily augmenting, and the Prophet, unaided by Tecumseh, found it difficult to control the restless and fiery spirits assembled around him. Added to this their increasing numbers, sometimes induced a scarcity of provisions, compelling parties of them to start upon expeditions for relief, aimed too frequently against the defenceless inhabitants of the frontier. On their return they brought with them horses, cattle and garments known to be plundered from the whites, and more than once Alice turned pale at beholding a white scalp depending from the belt of some lawless young chief.

Every day increased the gloom of their situation. The snow lay for many months piled heavily upon the ground; the wailing sound of the wind through the dry branches of the trees, and the eddying gusts about the frail tenement in the silence and gloom of midnight,

---

1   Fitz-Greene Halleck (1790–1867), "Fanny."

sounded like the shrieks and groans of the suffering and dying. Margaret, too, grew pale and restless; more than once Alice was led to suspect, that although ostensibly free, she was always an object of suspicion, and every motion subject to the strictest scrutiny; that, did she desire it, escape from the village would be impossible. Scarcely ever did herself and Margaret leave their dwelling to go out into the woods, or upon the frozen river, without encountering the sable looks of Kumshaka, or those of the vindictive Ackoree.

It was a long, dreary season, and Alice, timid and delicate, found herself now dependent upon the stronger-minded, and more courageous Margaret, not only for comfort in their trials, but often for subjects for reflection. Minaree, too, related old Indian legends and sang their wild songs, while Margaret's rich and melodious tones swelled the chorus. Nor were her sympathies unemployed in this wild and savage region. She entered the cabin of the invalid mother and assisted to relieve her sufferings. When want and sickness laid the child upon its bed of death, Alice disposed its little limbs, smoothed down the long dark hair, and wept as she listened to the thrilling dirge of sorrow raised by the bereaved. Had Margaret's faith and religious knowledge been equal to that of Alice, she would, in a like situation, have been the ardent and self-sacrificing missionary, kneeling in lowly supplication by the bed of death, and pointing to the Saviour of men as the great Comforter of the afflicted. But Alice was too gentle and self-distrustful for this; she was made rather to be cherished tenderly in the bosom of those who loved her, then to be the supporter or strengthener of others. Hers was a nature lovely and confiding, whose power could only be exhibited through the medium of her affections; one of those that the haughtiness of manhood is led to adore because its weakness and dependence is flattering to his self-love.

Margaret, in the course of her intercourse with the Indians, had not failed to impart to them many ideas of the Deity and of his ever abiding presence, more exalted and pure than those of their imperfect faith. Naturally enthusiastic, delighting in the abstract and spiritual, she had at first won their admiration, and even awe; by her bold and eloquent descriptions of the attributes of Deity, often couched in the sublime language of scripture, which still adhered to a memory tenacious of all impressions, most especially those of an elevated and impassioned nature. With intuitive tact she laid hold of the one great truth to be found in every mind however rude, that of the existence of a God, and thence strove to elevate and purify the conception; to impress upon the mind that the Creator of so much that is good and beautiful in the external world, must be a being to delight in all harmonies, most especially in those of truth and goodness. Hence, the most acceptable worship must be that which should develope in the human character qualities assimilating to himself.

Having acquired from her father some knowledge of the heavenly bodies, she was wont to mingle in her discourse allusions to them and to the objects in nature, astounding to the simple people she addressed. No wonder they regarded her as an especial favorite of the Great Spirit, and gave her credit for supernatural wisdom. From a child she had been a fearless, investigating girl, delighting in solitude and lonely meditation; and the great shock she experienced in the death of her family instead of overwhelming her, its magnitude served rather to develope the native strength and dignity of her character. Cast entirely upon her own resources, understanding as by instinct, the contempt felt by her captors for anything like weakness or tears, she at once appeared in the village, not a timid, weeping girl like others of her race, but proud and solitary, rejecting aid, and assuming from the first an air of haughtiness and superiority. They soon took a pride in her instruction, and absolved her at once from everything like labor or dependence.

Tecumseh delighted to initiate her in all the accomplishments of savage life; the choicest spoils of the chase were reserved for her cabin, and the freshest flowers gathered in rugged and unfrequented paths. In return, when the stars of night were out, and the earth was draped in green, and garnished with gems of blossoms, he would bend his head to the lips of the fair girl, and listen with delight while she told of the great and abiding Presence, who doeth all things, the great and beautiful alike; who painteth the blossom with its beauty, and upheaveth the everlasting hills—who rideth upon the whirlwind and dwelleth with the midnight stars. In the wildness of poetic fervor, she would describe the planets as the dwelling-place of the wise and the good, of those who delight in mercy and did generous deeds upon earth. She dwelt much upon the blessings of peace, of the delight of the Great Spirit in those who strove to promote it. Even the great and far-seeing reformer among the tribes, felt his views strengthened and elucidated by the eloquent language of the impassioned child. What wonder, then, that the voice and smile of one whose nature harmonized so well with her own, should have become very dear to the lone girl? What wonder, as the distinctions of society lost their impression in the lapse of years, he should have become her ideal of all that is manly and elevated in human nature? It was even so, and Margaret could not abide the abhorrence with which Alice regarded the state of her affections.

Often, in the silence of those long winter nights, the sisters were aroused by the wailings of some bereaved mother (for this was a season of great mortality among the children of the tribes,) who, with unbraided hair and robes loose in the midnight storm, was out removing the snow from the grave of her little one, while her tremulous voice sent up the dirge for the dead, in words like these:

"How wilt thou dwell in the spirit land, my beloved? Who will bring thee food, and spread the skins to shelter thee? Thou art alone. I see thy little hands beckon me away, for thou art cold and hungry. Would that I might go to thee, for my breasts are full of milk, and I would warm thee in my arms. Alas! the night wind is about thee, and the cold snow is thy covering. I put my head to the turf, and hear thy feeble wailing. My child! my child! why didst thou go!"

This propensity of the savage to transmit the physical sufferings of this to the invisible world, was to the last degree revolting to the mind of Alice. It may be, that she felt more repugnance for the error in point of faith, than compassion for the sufferings which it implied; for she had learned to attach great importance to the tenets of the religion she professed, without the ability to perceive that this vague mingling of spiritual and physical qualities in the mind of the savage, when he contemplated the invisible world, was the natural consequence of the difficulty felt by the human mind in fixing itself upon pure abstractions, especially in a rude state, where animal wants become an engrossing subject of contemplation, owing to the difficulty of supplying them.

Various motives impelled the subtle and vindictive Kumshaka to throw himself in opposition to Tecumseh. He had never heartily enlisted in the policy of confederation, which his brother had so much at heart, having been impelled thereto rather by the force of example, and that power by which a strong mind naturally controls the weak; while his own love of ease, disinclination to reform of every kind, as well as his innate levity of character, disqualified him from the labors and sacrifices necessary to promote it. All imbecility is apt to be vindictive. Motives that, to the strong, must bear proportional magnitude, to such, are often of the most trivial character; a disappointment of any kind, trifling in itself, and common to all, is enough to arouse the most baneful passions, and instigate to revenge, deadly as the hatred inspired. Kumshaka saw himself supplanted everywhere—in the field of battle, in the council-hall, and lastly, in his love. He had now a motive for action. His faculties even acquired a keenness of perception, a subtlety of combination, while, thread by thread, he wove the tissue of his revenge. He found in Ackoree a kindred spirit, whose devices were always ready for his use. It would be vain to pretend that he loved the girl: it were a desecration of terms; for the bond of sympathy between them was not that of the high and holy attributes of the soul, which alone deserve the name of love, but that fearful compact by which evil passions seek their affinities, and enjoy a horrible pleasure in so doing. Ackoree, with a woman's penetration, saw their relations to each other, and she took a wild pleasure in sometimes assisting, sometimes foiling, his machinations. In torturing him, she gratified her own wounded pride; in assisting him, she helped to crush a rival.

It was Kumshaka that promoted the numerous aggressions upon the whites, hoping thereby to provoke a collision, which must for ever destroy the links of confederation. He affected to think the project impracticable, and the sooner the red man threw off its restraints the better. How could materials so discordant, be made to conjoin? How could a people perpetually at war with each other, stimulated by wrongs yet unrevenged, be made to forget their animosities, and smoke the calumet about one great council-fire? It could never be. The blood of the slain would cry out for redress and the hatchet would leap from its burial. Or, suppose that the red men everywhere should unite, should become one people, must it be for peace? Rather let them become one, that their strength may be great, and they able to drive the white man from the earth. It was thus that Kumshaka incited the warriors; at first casually, in the chase, or about the coals of the wigwam, and then more openly. Cautiously did he attack the motives of Tecumseh; but the chief was away, and there are few generous enough to defend the absent. Gradually, he insinuated suspicions as to the motives of his policy with the whites. A feeble girl alone, he pretended, was sufficient to interpose between the white and the red man.

At first, he was heard with incredulity; but the iteration of surmises, the proposition for a course of conduct more accordant with their natural characters, gradually wrought conviction among those little accustomed and little desirous to think for themselves.

It was in vain that the Prophet represented the power and resources of the whites, their superiority in arms and mode of warfare producing fearful odds against them; that their only bond of security, of existence, even, as a people, consisted in this union and repose. Peace and consolidation alone could preserve their existence as a people. His followers were unable to take this dispassionate view of things. They felt the pressure of present evils, the memory of recent wrongs. They knew not how to interpose great moral and political relations, that should henceforth be a barrier and a defence. They lacked that far-seeing wisdom to perceive the utility and glory of measures, that should convert a feeble and dispersed people, divided, oppressed, jealous of each other, and jealous of the whites, into a powerful and prosperous whole. They were like the insane man, who would throw himself naked upon the thick bosses[1] of the mailed giant.

Margaret saw the impending storm, and herself urged the Prophet to dispatch runners to facilitate the return of Tecumseh, and warn him of the perils that threatened the cause he had so much at heart; but Eliskwatawa was loth to confess that Tecumseh could do more to avert the impending evil than himself. It may be too, that even he felt some degree of jealousy at the great popularity of his brother, and was willing to interpose a check; for when did ever the devoted patriot find himself aided by others as pure-hearted as himself? When did he find followers ready to cast aside the mantle of selfishness, and join in the holiness of the cause, forgetful of all emolument and all person ambition? Whatever might have been the motives of the Prophet, whether those of rivalry, or the result of inactivity, he certainly yielded to the current of public opinion, which he had ceased to control, and tacitly acquiesced in their departure from originally adopted principles.

Margaret wept in secret grief to behold this whelming of the wa-

---

1   Studs or other projecting ornaments on armor.

ters over the ark of Indian safety. Often did she wish it were possible for her to seek Tecumseh, and warn him to return; but whither bend her steps? where, in the solitudes of the western valley, hope to find him, who alone could endure the safety of the tribes? Her own faith in the permanency of the confederation became weakened, since but a single man served to hold it together, and with him it might be dissolved. Incited by a spirit akin to his, she wished the power had been hers to assume the right to govern in the solemn council, and to punish those who should be treacherous to the cause. Sometimes a strong energy impelled her to put herself at their head, and, by the force of her own will, awe them to submission: but her youth, the timidity of Alice, and the gentleness of her sex, forbade the measure. She felt a noble sympathy in what she knew would be the sufferings of Tecumseh, as if the magnitude of his griefs were her own likewise. She asked no more for the emotions that governed her; she felt their purity, their elevation, and that they carried her out from the dominion of self into companionship with greatness and virtue, in whatever shape. This was enough. She had no petty cares, no debasing passions, to divide and weaken the empire of her soul, and her thoughts were absorbed in sublime contemplations. From the holiness of her own emotions, she learned to judge of those of Tecumseh. She remembered the ominous import of his words, "Sorrow is coming upon Tecumseh," and she felt herself already admitted into the sanctuary of his griefs; for when we share the sorrows of our friends, we leave the outer court, and enter into the holy of holies of the human heart.

Love, with Margaret, was a part of her adoration for all that is noble and exalted in human virtue, the earthly realization of those attributes of perfection, with which in an infinite degree we invest the Deity. Such a love serves, more than all other exercises of the human faculties to ennoble the heart of its possessor. It was not the creature of passion and impulse, swayed by jealousy, and extinguished by neglect; it was a holy and enduring flame, requiring no foreign aliment, fed as it was from the fountain of her own innocent and exalted nature. It was like the hidden flame of some unrevealed crater, invisible till the tempest and the earthquake should develope its existence.

She remembered the sorrowful words of the Chief. "Evil is coming upon Tecumseh, why should he take the blossom from the sunshine, to see it wither in his own cabin?" and she knew that she was beloved; that in all his wanderings his thoughts reverted to her. She felt the consciousness of this, in the still midnight, when she held sweet communion with him, for she knew that their spirits commingled. And now, that the forebodings of prophecy were daily becoming reality, she acknowledged a holier bond of sympathy drawing their hearts together. True, they had not talked of love; there were no personal endearments to be remembered with a thrill in after-times; but what were these to a mind like hers, that dwelt upon that internal and holy sympathy, the union of mind with mind constituting the pure essence of love! His sorrows had become her sorrows, and she folded her hand upon her bosom and wept, and they were tears of blessedness. Love is religious in its nature, when of that holy kind which alone properly deserves the name. Who is there in the blessed consciousness of being beloved, whether by maid, friend or child, that has not felt his nature drawn out into fuller acknowledgment of Him who is Love itself, as if the soul were inhaling its own appropriate element? So was it with Margaret; she felt a clearer understanding of the Invisible Presence, an enlargement and dignity of nature proportionate to the depth of her love. She had looked into the deep fountains of her own soul, and seen there the records of her own immortality.

CHAPTER XVIII.

All this in her had wrought no change,
  No anxious doubt, no jealous fear,
But he meanwhile had words most strange,
  Breathed in my gentler *Nal*-hah's ear,
Which made her wish that I were near.—HOFFMAN.[1]

Alice had been for many days ill, very ill, and often in her despondency had she thought she should die, there in those wild solitudes, with none but Margaret to receive her last sigh; and yet so hopeless had she become, that the thought of death was pleasant to her. She pictured to herself the swelling turf under the shadow of the old trees, and the warm pleasant sunshine resting upon it, the meek flowrets

---

1 Hoffman, "Kachesco" (see p. 67, note 2), in which the name appears as "NULKAH," not "*Nal*-hah."

clustering there as if in love, and the birds giving out their sweet music as knowing that the sleeper beneath delighted in all harmonies. The leaves of autumn too heaped by its side, and the cricket chirping in their midst, while the bright river should roll beneath uttering for ever its dirge-like melody. The character and manners of Margaret were so unlike what she had anticipated, so unlike those with whom she had associated, that she was unprepared either to appreciate or understand them. Accustomed to forms and the daily routine of medium life, she had no standard by which to judge of the daring intellect, and unshackled strength of opinion which characterized her sister. Meek and gentle in her nature, distrustful of herself, and accustomed to spread out her hands as it were to win the support of others, she shrank from the self-sustaining intrepidity of the other as something to be feared and distrusted. Her love too, retiring and timid, needed more to sustain its fervor than did the same passion in the breast of Margaret. She beheld her sister firm and undoubting in her attachment, requiring nothing to sustain it but the fervency of her own nature, neither seeking or perhaps expecting the possession of its object, content to exist in its own blessed unconsciousness; while she herself was full of doubt and anxiety, marveling much that he who had spoken of love should so long abandon her to silence and neglect. Perplexed and disappointed in all things, her health had languished beneath the struggles, and now she felt as if there were little in life to desire. As her system became daily exhausted and she thought herself nearing the last dread bourne,[1] she was astonished to perceive how Margaret's strong and elevated faith, divested from all dogmatisms, and human creeds, helped to relieve her from the terrors and hesitancy engendered by the stern doctrines in which she had been educated. She learned from Margaret, to estimate the character of the soul by the purity and elevation of its desires, and to take comfort from a consciousness of a growth of goodness in herself.

Margaret was unwearied in her attentions upon her sister, and Minaree exercised all her skill, which was not inconsiderable, in procuring remedies which her own experience had taught would be efficacious. Herbs and roots were compounded by her into refreshing and strength-imparting beverages, and she taxed her culinary lore in preparing delicacies of various kinds for her relief. Under the united

---

1   Boundary; destination.

efforts of Margaret and Minaree her health gradually returned, and leaning on the arm of her sister she was able to reach the bower of grape vines on the bank of the river. She seated herself upon the wicker-bench and cast her eyes out upon the blue sky, and the river smiling in the sunshine. Margaret had gathered for her a few early violets which she held between her thin pale fingers. Twice she looked in the face of her sister and attempted to speak, but the effort was unavailing and she burst into tears. Margaret was affected, and she put her arms tenderly about her waist and drew her to her bosom.

"Speak, dear Alice," she said, "Margaret is not proud now as she used to be, and she can feel for the weak and suffering. Alice would tell of her white lover; let her speak, for Margaret will listen as doth the bird to the singing of its mate."

A blush mounted the pale cheek of Alice, but it faded away as she replied—

"I fear, Margaret, I shall see him no more, that he has forgotten me; but should he return, Margaret, you will show him my grave, and perhaps he will weep over it. You may tell him too, that I prayed for him to the last." Her voice was choked by sobs, and she ceased.

Margaret looked wonderingly in her face, as if she were doubtful of having comprehended her aright.

"What mean you, Alice, that he may have forgotten you? did he not say you were dearer than life to him?"

Alice colored at the reproof. "Yes, Margaret, but it is long since we have met, and he may have changed ere now."

Margaret colored with a slight look of scorn: "And so you call this love, Alice? Doth the bird talk of distrust to its mate? Is its song made up of discontent? Doth the flower repine that the sunshine is long away? Rather doth it not fold its leaves meekly, waiting till the shadow be past? Alice, Alice, this is selfishness, not love. Love is the going out of self and becoming absorbed in the being of another, and there can be no misunderstanding of that other self, for their natures are one."

"Is it so, indeed?" said Alice musingly. "Help me to so believe, Margaret, for I am sadly weak and distrustful. Must we live, dear sister, in the midst of woods and waters, and in the shadows of great mountains, apart from our species, to preserve our own natures unperverted? Are your feelings, Margaret, primeval and chaste like the freshness of undegenerate man, or only those of the crude demi-savage, to whom the refinements of life are a weakness and a restraint?"

Margaret's cheek again reddened, but she only said, "Look, Alice, into your own heart, and behold how pure may be its emotions, and then judge of mine. The innocent need not distrust. Have you ceased to love Mansfield now that he is away? Then why imagine that he should forget you? If he is long absent, it may be caused by a thousand various motives other than those of forgetfulness. The distance is very great, and the hazards many; besides, I doubt now whether he would be permitted to enter the village. It is evident that war is determined upon, and the measures of our people are always secret. No future intercourse will be allowed between the white and the red man."

Alice turned deathly pale, for till now she had not fully understood the danger of her situation. "O Margaret," she exclaimed, "can we not make our escape?" She grasped Margaret's arm wildly, for a suppressed laugh sounded close to her ear.

"Come in, Ackoree," said Margaret carelessly, and the girl entered the bower and stood before the sisters, her glittering eyes expressive of the utmost satisfaction.

"So the Swaying Reed talks of escape. Can the bird that looks into the eyes of the serpent, escape? Can the beast, whose trail the huntsman has followed day by day, hope to escape? No more can the white girl escape Ackoree. Tecumseh is long absent. He must be dead. Kumshaka will be the chief of the tribe, and Ackoree his bride."

She stepped to the side of Margaret, and, stooping, looked into her very eyes, and continued in a low, husky voice—

"The Swaying Reed, too, shall be his, and the bond-maid of Ackoree."

Alice gasped, and fell fainting on the breast of her sister.

Margaret laid her gently upon the turf, and turning to the girl, drew herself proudly up, and even the fierce eyes of Ackoree fell beneath her stern, indignant look.

"Ackoree is a fit wife for Kumshaka, for he is vain and spiteful; but she dare not rest a finger upon the person of the Swaying Reed: the Great Spirit hath given her a charmed life, which cannot be harmed. Tell Kumshaka he dare not look into her eyes—it were death to him. Let the shadow of Ackoree be taken hence."

Awed by the haughty tone of defiance assumed by Margaret, and the victim of that superstition to which she alluded, the girl turned slowly away, as at the bidding of a supernatural agent.

Margaret assisted Alice to her couch, and then calmly detailed to her the necessity that she should summon strength of mind to repel every weakness, as the surest means of protecting themselves from the malice of Ackoree. She could feel no sympathy for the suffering, but might be awed by the daring of those who could summon a spirit stronger than her own. She besought Alice to endeavor to regain her health, and promised that when sufficiently firm, she would seek with her the white settlements.

Alice embraced her tenderly, and expressed her surprise, as well as delight, at her determination. While they were yet talking, an Indian youth, of beautiful and manly promise, raised the skins of the entrance, and glancing smilingly around, stood hesitating. Margaret beckoned with her hand, and he entered and stood before her. He looked admiringly at the sisters, as he stood with his hand beneath his robe, smiling archly, as if to sport with their impatience.

"The Brave may deliver his message," said Margaret.

It is probable the term so skilfully applied, had its effect, for his look grew composed, and his form elevated, and, taking a parcel from beneath his robe, he laid it at her feet; then pressing his hand not ungracefully upon his heart, he retired.

Margaret took up the package, and parting the fillets that confined it, revealed skins of the rarest texture, and an arrow, on which was inscribed a rattle-snake in the act to spring, and four moons. The maiden colored deeply, and sat looking upon the gift, nor once glanced at her sister. Alice remarked her, and wondered that she should feel so much more of sympathy for Margaret than she had hitherto done; but love is the great leveller, and she now almost participated in the emotions of her sister.

She pressed the hand of Margaret: "Tell me, sister," she said, "what does it mean?"

Margaret started at the tone of tenderness; but she replied frankly, "It means that I am beloved, and that he will be here in four moons."

"It is from Tecumseh?"

Margaret motioned in token of assent, and turned away, fearful that Alice might say more.

The package had been brought by one of the parties that had that day entered the village—probably one of the new converts to the views of the great leader—who had thus come to join his forces, and been entrusted with the commission.

Under the promise of Margaret, that she would seek with her the white settlements, the health of Alice began to amend rapidly, and many were the little preparations she began to make in reference to their departure. She pictured to herself the sorrow of Minaree when abandoned by her foster-child, and her heart was filled with tenderness. She made many articles of comfort and convenience, expressly for her use, in gratitude for her kindness to herself and Margaret. The maidens and matrons of the village came in for a share of her remembrance, and she gave them tokens of her good will. The children were assisted in the construction of new toys, and their simple expressions of affectionate interest received with renewed tenderness. Then she would picture to herself what must have been the anxiety of the excellent-hearted Mrs. Mason at her protracted absence, and her delight to welcome their return, till the imagination almost became a reality to her.

CHAPTER XIX.

He ceased. Her eye was on him—and the blood,
In rush tumultuous from the citadel,
Spoke from her forehead as it swept her frame.—MELLEN.[1]

A few weeks after the incidents described in the last chapter, the sisters had retired to their couch, wondering much at the protracted absence of Minaree, who was always the first at night to dispose herself to slumber. The tumult of the village had ceased, the children were hushed to repose, and the games of the youth suspended. All was silent, except the leaders of the people, who were assembled in the great council-house, to discuss measures of public import. Margaret had fallen into her first slumber, and dreamed that she was about to leave suddenly in quest of Tecumseh, to reveal to him the state of affairs at the village, and the treachery of Kumshaka, when the hand of Ackoree was placed

---

1 Grenville Mellen (1799–1841), "Rebecca and Ivanhoe."

upon her shoulder: often as she attempted to move, the maiden held her back. She started up, for she became aware that a touch was indeed upon her shoulder. It was that of Minaree. She laid her hand upon her lips in token of silence, and motioned her to leave her couch. Margaret followed her to the other side of the cabin, and Minaree looked sadly in her face.

"The arrow will reach the heart of Minaree, through the body of her child," she said tearfully.

Margaret was silent, while she went on: "Tecumseh is a great chief. They say he is dead, and that he did not love his people. They say he sought for peace with the white man, because of his love for the Swaying Reed."

She would have said more, but Margaret waved her hand impatiently. She arrayed herself in a sumptuous robe of rare feathers, bound the wampum about her slender waist, and tied the moccasins to her feet. She twined a tuft of feathers amid her abundant hair, and, thus accounted, looked like some proud maiden of their own race, upon whom the Great Spirit had lavished beauty exceedingly. Drawing the elastic bracelet over her round arm, which was otherwise naked to the elbow, she left the cabin. Minaree watched her motions till all was complete, and then quietly disposed herself to slumber.

Kumshaka was in the midst of an impassioned harangue, in which he seemed to have caught a portion of the fervid eloquence of his brother. There was the same power of appeal, the same affluence of diction, and force of argument; but the spirit that, in its elevation and far-seeing prophecy, lent a holiness to the every utterance of Tecumseh, was far from resting upon the lips of the speaker. He was powerful—for jealousy and revenge had lent him their aid—and he spoke from the burning energies of his own vindictive passions. Yet few of his hearers understood the nature of his inspiration, while the good of the tribes, and hatred to the white man, were the burden of his appeal.

In the midst of one of his most glowing periods while his hand gracefully swept the circle about him, and his glowing eye turned from side to side, his voice faltered, his eye fell; for there, with a proud, calm dignity, stood the Swaying Reed at the threshold, confronting him with a look in which cold and biting scorn was the predominant expression. Thrice he attempted to rally, but the freezing look of the haughty girl was upon him, and he could not resist its influence. Mortified and enraged, he pointed his quivering finger forward, and between his clenched teeth uttered—

"Behold the bait for which Tecumseh would sell his people. Behold the serpent that hath crept into the lodge, to sting its victims."

All eyes were turned upon the lone girl, where she stood—one hand grasping the folds of her robe, her head thrown back, revealing the short compressed lip, and the small chiselled features, pale and statue-like in their fixed and calm expression. One moment she confronted the gaze of that agitated multitude, and then slowly advanced to their midst. Even Kumshaka stepped back, awed by her quiet majesty; for she quailed not at the fierce eyes bent upon her. As she prepared to speak, she looked round upon the dark group, and the ready blood mantled cheek and bosom, but her voice was clear and untremulous in its intonations.

"The Shawanese have taken the massasauga as the emblem of their tribe. A noble reptile, that first warns its victim of danger: ere it strikes, it proclaims the peril. Then who would look for treachery in a Shawanee? Who would look for a secret blow upon the defenceless, from the arm of a Shawanee, and that defenceless one a brother? The shadow of Tecumseh is not found in the village. Moons grow large in the heavens, and fade again from the sky, yet it comes not. Doth Tecumseh pursue his game? doth he feast with the youth of his people? doth he dwell at ease, and the wants of his people forgotten? When did ever Tecumseh disport himself, and the red man was as nothing to him? Let not the chief with lying lips talk of the treachery of Tecumseh; that he would be at peace with the white man, and sacrifice the good of his people for the smiles of any maiden. The chief knows it is false. Kumshaka looked upon the Swaying Reed, and felt her scorn. Before it had turned his heart to bitterness, he was an advocate—cold, indeed—for who would look for the bravery of the warrior or the eloquence of the orator from Kumshaka? Yet he was an advocate for the measures of Tecumseh."

As she alluded thus to the chief, her cheek reddened with maidenly shame, and a derisive laugh burst from the assembly, in the midst of which the discomfited chief withdrew.

"Let no one impute unworthy motives to Tecumseh. While the youth of the tribe are at rest, Tecumseh is all day on the march; his feet are weary with travel, and his eyes heavy with watching. The dews of night are upon his robe, and the stars listen to his paddle, as he goes down the rapid river. He sleeps within the sound of the cataract, and the Great Spirit cometh to him in dreams. In after years, when the Indian shall have become a great people, old men shall tell of the wisdom of Tecumseh, and children shall tell of his toils and sufferings. The Great Spirit is with him. He came to him as he lay an infant upon the earth, and touched his lips with a living coal. Thence came the wisdom and the eloquence of his tongue. Tecumseh is not dead. He is calling the Great Council of the tribes, to judge the treacherous Winnemac and his friends, and to consult upon measures to be adopted for the good of our people. He is not dead. The Great Spirit will give you a token by which ye shall know that he still lives. In four moons he will be here. In token whereof, look out upon the full moon. Not a cloud is in the sky; yet the Great Spirit hath caused his shadow to pass over it; and as that shadow shall pass from its face, leaving it clear and beautiful in its brightness, so shall all shadows pass from the fame of Tecumseh."

All eyes followed the direction of those of the maiden, and there, upon the lower limb of the moon lay a dark and heavy mass, even like the dread shadow of the Eternal, and the whole multitude looked on with awe and terror.

Margaret had observed the phenomenon on her way to the lodge, and was at no loss to understand its nature;[1] familiar with the character and superstitions of the people she confronted, she felt no hesitancy in turning it to her own use. As she quietly stole from their midst, the youth of whom we have before spoken walked by her side, and as he looked reverently from the shrouded moon to the still face of his companion, he whispered,

"The Great Spirit hath touched the lips of the Swaying Reed: She hath the heart of a red maiden, and wisdom as from the spirit land."

Kumshaka attempted no further open attack upon his brother, but the poison he had infused did not fail of its effects. The policy so urgently recommended by Tecumseh had been interrupted, and the great accession of numbers at the village rendered the discussion of principles and the enforcement of pacific measures next to impossible. Every day witnessed their departure from the primitive habits hitherto adopted, and all the mystical rites and supernatural agency of the Prophet were insufficient to lead them back, to preserve the

---

1 A lunar eclipse.

good order of the village, or protect the whites from their atrocities. He had listened like the rest of his people to the solemn appeal of Margaret, with amazed wonderment; too wary to exhibit his emotions, he beheld the verification of her prediction with the cool indifference of one accustomed to sport with the credulity of others, and who is sure that however mysterious the charm may appear, still the solution must be simple to the initiated.

At night, when the village was hushed to repose, he came to the cabin of Minaree, and beckoned Margaret to follow him forth. She stood with him by the river side, the full moon resting upon the figure of the maiden, with her pure brow gleaming in its light; the soft wind lifting up the curls from her bosom, her hands calmly folded, and eyes raised fearlessly to the face of the towering chief, who leaned carelessly upon a huge club, and regarded her with a searching look. Neither spoke for many minutes. At length the chief commenced in terms of reproach:

"The charm of the maiden was not well wrought. Why did she so long delay the return of Tecumseh? He should be here now. Eliskwatawa would see the maiden work her charm. She will do so and hasten his return."

Margaret's eye kindled, for she felt the suggestion to be equivalent to a command. At another time she might have frankly confessed the source of her information, as would have been more in accordance with the natural candor of her mind; but now she understood too well the danger of her situation, to hazard anything that might contribute to her own influence. She confronted him awhile with a calm, almost indignant look. Then turning her eyes to the still moon, she replied:

"Let the Prophet look upon the calmness and beauty of that pale face, and read the destinies it reveals. Let him turn to the stars and understand their teachings. They speak a language to him who can understand. Floods and storms, the tempest and the earthquake, death and disaster, are all shadowed forth in their fearful teachings. Wise men have read them, and foretold the destinies of nations. Sages, for thousands and thousands of years, have studied the language of the midnight stars, and told what should be. And what they have foretold has been as the revelations of the Great Spirit. Men have heard and trembled. What they foretell is not to be changed. It is the immutable fate. Let not the chief ask for the exhibition of charms. The Swaying Reed deals in none. She reads and understands. She hears and is silent."

During the utterance of this her voice became deep and energetic, and the blood rushed to her cheek; she yielded to a vehemence of manner that relieved in part the wrong she felt she was doing her own nature in thus assuming the position of imposture. The Prophet's keen eye was fixed upon her as if he would read her very soul; but the dauntless girl quailed not beneath his searching glance. It would seem that a strange awe grew upon him as the moon lay upon her white face, radiant with the fervor of her emotions, for he spake in a low, reverent voice:

"The Prophet will sit at the feet of the Swaying Reed, and learn the mysteries of the stars. When they utter their midnight talk, he will listen and understand. Let the Swaying Reed reveal the secret of her power. Eliskwatawa would cause the moon to veil her brightness, the stars to dim their luster, and appear again at his bidding. He would awe the people with strange prodigies. He would speak, and behold the Great Spirit should lay his shield upon the moon's face. Speak, maiden, for thy wisdom is that of the spirit land."

Margaret fixed her sorrowful eyes upon the face of the chief, and felt even as if a ray from the Eternal had penetrated the recesses of her soul, revealing the one shadow upon her own temple of truth; still the teachings of her father had, perhaps, afforded as much of astrology as the pure science of Astronomy; and these mingling with the enthusiasm engendered by woods and mountain solitudes, had infused a belief in the mysterious influences of nature, that made the language she adopted in reality but little at variance with her own faith. Her answer was solemn, and according to the convictions of her own heart:

"The Swaying Reed can impart no power to the Prophet. The stars, in their stillness and beauty, have a language audible to him who in the lowliness of truth bows before the Great Spirit. Thus have the old men of other times spread their gray locks to the midnight wind; have fasted till the flesh no more hindered the going forth of the spirit—prayed till the Great Spirit uttered itself in their own, and then were the heavens opened; they heard the melody of the stars, that mysterious and beautiful melody, revealing the destiny of men and the fate of empires. The vistas of moons and suns opened before them in their eternal courses of gladness, singing responsive to the heart of blessedness, that throbs in the great universe. Let the Prophet fast and pray as did these, and then learn that his will can neither stay nor alter their courses. The voice of the Almighty alone can speak and they obey. Let him, if he would learn their utterance, veil his face with awe, and behold them in their majesty! The tempest rageth beneath them and they look forth again calm and undisturbed. Can the Prophet at his will bid the whirlwind uproot the oak of a thousand years? Can he cause the sun to appear while the black cloud hangeth in the heavens? Can he look to the earth, and cause the blossom to come forth; or the lily upon the stream to blush at its own whiteness? Behold, it is the Almighty that quieteth the earth with the south wind. How then can the Prophet hope to speak, and the moon and the stars shall obey him?"

As she ceased, she glided lightly away, leaving the wondering chief gazing into the depths of the shadowy sky, with a new sense of its marvelous beauty. A holy influence stole upon his heart, an utterance of the Deity within responding to the voices that called to him from the glory and loveliness of the external world. His dim thoughts partially penetrated the thick veil of ignorance and superstition, and beheld the purer light of truth and goodness. Long time he stood communing with his own nature through the agency of that spread out before him, feeling mysterious enlightenments, new and wondrous, there, amid the holy solitudes of midnight.

CHAPTER XX.

Beside the auld hearth she hath cherished for life,
Silent and sad sits the lonely auld wife;
Time hath left many a trace on her brow,
But grief hath not troubled her spirit till now.—J.L. CHESTER.[1]

Meanwhile, the inhabitants of the frontiers were suffering daily from the outrages committed by the disorderly assemblage at Tippecanoe. The dispersed and homeless inhabitants found a refuge in the infant city of Vincennes, which became the rallying point for men indignant at repeated atrocities, and resolved upon revenge. All eyes turned upon Harrison as the deliverer of the West. His well-known influence over the savages, and moderation in the management of affairs, inspired hope and confidence. Remonstrances on his part were made to the natives, but without effect. No messenger was per-

---

1 Joseph Lemuel Chester (1821–82), "The Lonely Auld Wife."

mitted access to the village. The General Government, roused by the growing hostility, dispatched troops for the defence of the frontier, and the whole territory wore the aspect of a military ground. Mansfield found himself constantly occupied in public duty, and he found relief only in the assurance afforded him, by straggling parties of the natives, that the sisters were secure and well. Various missals[1] which he trusted would reach Alice through the same medium, were either lost or destroyed, for none ever reached her. In the discharge of his services, it had been necessary for him to repair to Washington, which, at that time of bad roads and unfrequent travel, was a journey of no small enterprise, and detained him some months. On his return, finding the aspect of affairs still more threatening, his fears were increased as to the safety of the sisters. The calls of his country were many and urgent—the times seemed approaching a crisis, when the native or the white man must yield his position. In case of collision, he knew well the first victims of the war would be any whites that might be with the Indians; they would be offered to the manes[2] of those that should perish in battle. Troops even now were prepared to advance upon Tippecanoe, and he trembled for the fate of the two girls. Unable longer to support his anxiety, he determined to effect their escape before the commencement of hostilities. For this purpose he threw up his commission, resolved at all hazards to penetrate to the Indian settlement. He believed their escape would be more easily effected in this private and friendly manner, than if demanded as a public measure. Difficulties augmented on every side, and in every view, but he believed this the least obnoxious.

Mr. Mason had not been inactive in attempts to relieve them, but all had been ineffectual. When therefore, informed of the resolution of his young friend, he replied, instantly addressing his wife:

"Anny, I must go with the youth, and the Lord will be with me. These are perilous times, Anny, and evil must not befall the maiden. What saith the scripture? Is it not that he who had an hundred sheep, left the ninety and nine, and went out into the wilderness to seek

---

1   Likely intended to be "missives"—written letters or messages—rather than "missals," which can refer to any books of prayer or devotion but is a term associated more specifically with the missal used by Roman Catholics in the celebration of Mass.

2   Ancestral ghosts or spirits honored as deities; souls of deceased loved ones in Roman mythology (usually capitalized Manes).

that which was lost? Did the shepherd ask who will keep the ninety and nine? Verily the Lord was their keeper; even so will he keep the household of him who trusteth in him."

Anna turned pale, and pressed her child to her bosom, for their dwelling was one of the most exposed in the city. Nevertheless, such was her reverence for her husband, her habitual submission to his will, that she never for a moment doubted the propriety of the course he adopted. Mr. Mason felt less anxiety in leaving home at this juncture, as the city would be left under the protection of troops, and every house had in part, been converted into an armed garrison. Weapons and munitions of war were ready for defence, and men slept with the loaded musket at their side, prepared for any emergency. Timid women taxed their imagination as to the best course to be adopted in case of an alarm, and embraced their children at night as those whom death might separate at any instant. Cheeks were steeped in tears in the midst of perturbed slumber, as the forebodings of the day presented in dreams, the horrors of death and slaughter, the tomahawk and flame.

Mrs. Mason had suffered exceedingly in her anxiety for Alice, magnifying the hardships and the dangers to which she had in reality been exposed. Her repugnance to the race, imbibed by education, and a knowledge of their atrocities, had caused her to invest them with everything that is revolting, and unfitted her to judge dispassionately of the treatment to which they had been subjected, or to detect the redeeming traits of their character. Often when Mr. Mason presented the "lone orphan, the tender lamb in the midst of wolves," as he was wont to designate her, before the throne of mercy, his voice became choked with emotion, and Anna would respond with a flood of tears. Her own prayers also were uttered with a fervency wondrous even to herself. Every incident of the day, brought her freshly to recollection. Were she happy, Alice were needful to participate in her happiness; sorrowful, she needed her sweet look of sympathy.

Mrs. Jones suffered equally with the rest. She felt the want of the winning sweetness of Alice to lure her from a sense of her infirmities, and make her feel again the sunshine of the earth. Her form became daily more wasted, and an unnatural softness crept over her. Often would she wipe her dim eyes with the corner of her apron, her shriveled hand trembling with age.

There is always something painfully touching in the grief of the aged. The shaking of the wasted hand, with its sallow skin and prominent veins; the scanty supply of tears, and the sigh, which no longer comes as a relief, but deep and heavy has become in truth a groan, wrung as it were, from the very vitals; the hand is no longer pressed upon the eyelids as if weeping brought its own consolation, but wanders uneasily about the garments, now smoothing the folds, and now pressed against the loose girdle. The foot is moved in quick restless taps upon the floor, and the eyes are never turned as if expecting sympathy from others. Alas! who is there that is ready to lay the aged and stricken head upon his bosom, and smooth the gray locks, and kiss the furrowed brow, that has known the weariness and the sorrow of many years. There is something awful in the weeping of the aged. They are those that have known the full bitterness of life; have beheld the beloved of youth pass to the land of spirits; have known the folly of earthly hopes; have found the canker at the root of every promise, and the golden fruit turned to ashes of bitterness. Love, and youth, and hope, and glory, all the chimeras of life, have passed away, and they live on like those ancient summits, that from their sterileness, and riven aspect, tell of former light and flame, though their fires are long since extinguished. No wonder, then, that we are prone to turn fearfully away from the sorrow of the aged—to feel there is something awful in the revival of human passions, in those who are supposed to have survived them. No, no; it is for the young, the hoping, the beautiful, to weep and find a response in every heart; the brow of the aged can repose alone upon the bosom of its God.

Mrs. Mason, besides her own cares and anxieties, found abundance of exertion necessary in order to relieve the growing infirmities of the old lady. The winter had been unusually severe, and she suffered from the many complaints incident to age. From the departure of Alice, a listlessness had crept over her, that told plainly the absence of the sweet girl lay heavily upon her heart. She would sit for hours watching the flakes of snow as they sailed slowly to the earth, turning their diamond points to the light, or driven by the wind, swept in eddies around the dwelling. At the least sound, she would hurriedly wipe her spectacles and look earnestly in the direction of the door, as if expecting her to enter. At first she turned peevishly away from the proffered kindness, and delicate attentions of Anna, but as her feebleness increased, she began to yield to them a silent acquiescence. At last her nature so much softened, that she called her Anny, and began to crave small attentions from her in the manner of a querulous child. The first time she addressed Mrs. Mason by the familiar and affectionate name of Anny, the good woman was so affected, that she burst into tears, and gently pressing her lips to the shriveled cheek of the other, she whispered—

"Thank you, grandmother, I was sure you would love me."

The old lady half pushed her aside, saying "Go away child," but she wiped a tear from her eyes with the end of her thumb, and her thin lips quivered, though she compressed them very tightly over her toothless jaws to conceal her emotions.

After the departure of Mr. Mason, she became still more the victim of restlessness and peevish impatience. The eager exercise of her senses seemed to have imparted a preternatural activity to them. Sounds hitherto inaudible to the decaying organs, became keenly perceptible, and even the sense of sight began to improve. Many were the devices adopted by Anna to dissipate the tedium of absence; patchwork of curious and intricate patterns was commenced, and the old lady for a while would become absorbed in its construction; when this became wearisome, she planned the manufacture of various articles of the dairy in which Mrs. Jones could assist; among these were cheeses variously colored, and improved by the addition of rare buds. She even became a reader, and in addition to her instructions of little Jimmy, read the whole of Pilgrim's Progress aloud, ostensibly to amuse the child; but the grandmother never failed to put her spectacles to the top of her cap, fold her arms, closely crossed upon her thin waist, and lean forward in absorbed attention. Anna was full of household affections, and gentle benevolence, and where the heart is thus disposed, ways are never wanting for the exercise of its propensities. Even little Jimmy learned as if by instinct to amuse and gratify her, and the baby would creep across the room, and grasping her apron climb to her side; there he would stand swaying by the frail support, till his words and smiles won her attention. Anna at such times did not call the child away as many would have done, for the old lady rarely took any notice of it, as the very act would have conveyed a reproach; but she allowed the child of four-score, and the infant of a year to adopt their own course, and in time they became friends together, and delighted to interchange caresses.

CHAPTER XXI.

Proud maiden, with thy pale, imperial brow,
And thoughts too lofty for a world like this—
The cup of life, dark drugged as it is now,
Were meter for thee, than the cup of bliss—
No meaner crown is thine
Than that which fame shall twine.—MS.[1]

The doctrine, that without the shedding of blood there can be no
remission of sin, announced in the written revelation of God, hath
found a response to an original sentiment found in the mind of all
nations, however rude or uncultivated. In whatever way it came
there, whether by immediate inspiration, preserved by tradition,
or growing out of that intuitive sense of justice, teaching us that a
penalty must be paid for all wrong-doing; from whence springs the
hope, that the sacrifice of the pure and holy may procure its remit-
tance, it is unnecessary now to inquire; suffice it, that such is the
fact. The savage, suffering from famine, from pestilence, or defeat
in war, at once recognized the principle, and believes that the accumulated sins of his people have provoked the anger of the invisible
powers, and a sacrifice must be made in order to propitiate them.
He selects an animal which he believes suitable to the occasion; or,
if the case is urgent—he is desirous to avert great evil, or to procure
great good—a solemn sacrifice is made of a human victim; a captive
taken in war, whose death shall appease the manes of the departed,
and win the favor of the invisibles.

It had been the wish of Tecumseh to do away these sacrifices,
but the people, regarding them as an essential part of their religion,
acquiesced only while there was nothing in their affairs that would
render them of consequence. The Prophet, belonging more immediately to the priesthood, was unwilling to part with anything in
ancient usages, that should add to the impressiveness of their ritual.
The custom had partially gone into decay, but when Kumshaka
proposed its revival, and, in a paroxysm of extraordinary sanctity,
urged its necessity in the present period of famine and approaching
hostilities, he was at once ready to adopt the measure. It would seem,

---

1   Unknown source; possibly from an unpublished manuscript by Oakes
    Smith.

that the brothers understood intuitively who was to be the victim, for none was named, and preparations were immediately made for a great feast, preparatory to the sacrifice. The next day Margaret received a small reed, with mysterious characters thereon inscribed, which she at once understood as the ceremony of invitation to a sacred festival. Alice saw her array herself with unwonted care, and with many preparatory ablutions, take her way to the great hall of council.

An immense fire was kindled in the centre of the lodge, and the sacred weed filled it with its fumes. The Prophet, in full canonicals,[1] swept the circle, chanting in a low voice, and holding aloft an immense rattlesnake, which the hunters had found in the woods. The old men and chiefs of the tribe were seated next the flame, and the outer circles were occupied by the assembled multitude. On the entrance of Margaret the crowd opened, and the Prophet pointed her to a place among the elders of the tribe. Spreading out his two hands, with the snake across them, the Prophet commenced.

"Didst thou perish, O manitou, to foretell the doom of the Shawanee? The hunters beheld the conflict with terror. The black snake towered aloft, and thou didst ring the alarm. Fierce was the struggle. Ye did lash the air in your fury; and your scales clashed like the spears of the warrior. But the folds of thy foe were about thee; twined like the binding cords of the canoe. Thou art dead. Such is the fate of the red man. The white man binds him in his chains, and he is powerless. He lies like the manitou of the Shawanee, dead upon the earth. Shall he revive? Will life return to the massasauga?"

"Life shall return!" shrieked a voice at the threshold. Margaret covered her eyes at the terrible apparition. It was Ingaraga. A hundred years had quenched the light of her eyes, and bleached the raven of her hair. Her flesh was wasted and cadaverous, and her nails protruded from her fingers. She turned her sightless eyes over the multitude, and spread out her bony hands. She shook her head from side to side, as if to catch some sound, though death had long since come upon the organ; in so doing her white hair, which reached nearly to her feet, encircled her like a shroud, from which peered the shriveled face, thin and diminutive, and the quenched[2] eyeballs.

---

1 Garments prescribed by religious law for clergy when officiating, as by the canon law of the Roman Catholic Church.
2 Extinguished.

"Life shall return!" she continued, approaching the fire, and lifting the serpent from the ground; "Life shall return, even as it doth come to the massasauga!" Scarcely were the words uttered, ere the snake coiled itself, its tail vibrating so as to be almost invisible, and its red jaws distended. Taking a twig she carried in her hand, she played from side to side, retreating to the open air: the serpent followed her motions as if by enchantment.

Ingaraga returned, her white hair streaming over her shoulders, and with a velocity almost supernatural, she thrice circled the flame, and cast therein powerful charms. She stopped short, and staggered heavily, exhausted with the effort; her chest heaved, her frame quivered, and her face fearfully distorted. At first her words were inarticulate, but at length her cry wrought itself into language frightfully vehement and shrill.

"Wo—wo, to the red man! He hath forgotten the worship of his fathers! His fields are barren, and the game flieth from his grounds! His young men are feeble in battle; and the arrow goeth crooked in the chase! A black mark is upon him—he is doomed to death! Wo—wo! The eagle's nest was upon the rocks! Up where the lightnings played, and the strong winds battled! He looked off upon the prairies, and down upon the big lakes: for his prey was upon every side. The wings of his children were thick, and their sound as the voice of the tempest! A foe crept to the rock, and hurled the young into the depths beneath! The cry of the old eagle went up, and it was heard like the thunder in the dark clouds—calling together the fiery bolts! There was the rushing and shivering of wings, and the tumult of battle!"

Her voice was lost amid inarticulate mouthings—a white froth gathered about her lips—she swayed, heavily forward, and lay writhing upon the earth. The Prophet assumed the tone of prophecy.

"The eagle's nest shall again appear upon the rock; the bones of his prey shall be heaped beneath him, and he shall look forth in his might. The altars of the Invisible have been deserted—there is no blood upon the stones—the fire has gone out, and moss creepeth where the fresh victim should bleed. The Shawanee will return to the worship of his fathers. Behold! the Great Spirit hath prepared the victim! He will be pleased with his children, and their glory shall return."

Margaret's cheek assumed an ashy paleness, and her breath came heavily, for a sure instinct revealed to her that Alice was the victim designed. Hurriedly she revolved the possibility of escape: but how, with the vindictive Ackoree and the subtle Kumshaka to watch their motions? How, too, when the superstition of the people would lead them to watch vigilantly the victim designed for the altars of their gods? Scarcely knowing what she did, she arose from her seat, and cast her mournful eyes about the assembly. She heard a low laugh, which she knew to be that of Ackoree. The Prophet spoke.

"Let not fear come to the heart of the Swaying Reed. The sun will long dance upon her pathway, and she will be as the voice of the Great Spirit to his red children."

Margaret felt as if a film were gathering over her eyes; the place whirled about her, and the faces of the multitude changed to fearful and grotesque images. Her throat was parched, and a strange ringing came to her ears. Pressing her hand heavily upon her brow, she at length found utterance.

"It is well. The white girl must die."

Kumshaka arose from his feet, and confronted her searchingly. "Let not the Swaying Reed hope that the white girl will escape. She is doomed!"

Pale as marble, heart-stricken as she was, a portion of her former spirit lent its fire to her eyes, and curl to her lip.

"The Swaying Reed neither hopes nor desires escape. Whence comes the new sanctity of the weak chief? Whence his courage? It is that he may work the death of a lone girl. He will bring ruin upon his people to gratify his own hatred. The white girl must die. Hath the Prophet listened to the stars? Hath the Great Spirit come to him in dreams, and called for one to bleed for the people? So be it. Let the victim be brought to the altar; but let her not be dragged thither with streaming eyes and tears. Let no shrieks and wailing be heard, when ye sacrifice to the Great Spirit. Ye ask a victim."

There was a death-like pause. Margaret left the circle of chiefs, and stood in the area in front. Her face was utterly bloodless: the small clasped hands were like cold white statuary, and her breath so light that it lent no motion to her chest. Fearful was the contrast where the curls of her long dark hair lay upon her bosom. Low exceedingly, and sweet, were the tones of her voice.

"Ye ask a victim. Lo, I come!" and she raised her eyes upward with an expression of holy patience. "Let me be laid upon your altars. Would you make a welcome sacrifice to the Great Spirit, it must be a willing one. Not with terror, and many tears; but one who would willingly die for the good of the tribes. Behold me. What is there in life to bind the Swaying Reed to earth? She longs for the spirit land. There is no light in her path. She has loved the red people, why should she not die for them? But the timid maiden must not die. No evil must come to her. She must be sheltered like the infant of few moons. Let me go with her to our people, and the Swaying Reed will return and die in her place."

There was a murmur of applause, interrupted by Kumshaka. "Think you the bird, escaped the snare, will return to it again? The pale maiden must not escape."

Margaret's lip curled with bitter pride. "There is no truth in the heart of the chief, and he cannot read it in the hearts of others. Before one moon I will return, unless the Great Spirit should sooner take me to himself." And she took the lighted calumet, laid her hand upon her heart, and blew the sacred smoke upward, and then cast a piece of the weed into the flames at her feet.

"It is enough," said the Prophet. "The Swaying Reed shall go with the timid maiden. She dare not break a vow made to the Great Spirit. In one moon she will be here."

"Should she fail," returned Kumshaka, "let her listen in every wind for the arrow of Kumshaka—see in every shadow the passage of his form—and lie down every night, sure that he is by, ready for the death."

Margaret listened with a faint smile, and with slow steps left the feast, for the food was upon the coals, and many and solemn were the rites still to be observed. She was now to prepare Alice for escape, and yet conceal from her the fearful pledge by which it had been procured. Her foot had lost its elastic spring, and she moved with that kind of retarded speed with which the dreamer attempts to struggle forward, and yet feels himself drawn to the earth. There was a strange bewilderment about her senses, and she found herself at every moment collecting the links of thought; turning her mind backward, to see what was the secret of that heaviness that grew upon her—whether it were a reality, or but the impression of a too vivid dream. 'The new moon, wi' the auld moon in her arms,'[1] hung upon the verge of the horizon, but she scarcely beheld the thread of

---

1 From the anonymous ballad "Sir Patrick Spens."

silver, so prepared was her mind to observe the shadow it embraced. Leaf and blossom were at rest; the stars looked down beholding themselves in the river, but their very tranquility was oppressive, so much did the hopelessness of life speak to her heart. She leaned against the entrance of her cabin, scarcely conscious she did so, looking abstractedly into the dimness of the woods. The moon quivered for a moment upon the tops of the trees, gleamed faintly through the dense foliage, then left all to silence and gloom—yet she regarded not the change. Tongatou touched her hand.

"The feast will be long—Kumshaka has a false heart. The maidens must escape ere the chiefs shall call for blood. Tongatou will go with them."

Margaret entered the cabin. Alice was sleeping soundly; and as she held back the screen, the dim torch-light fell upon her sweet face, the round cheek resting upon her arm, and the brown hair scattered in profusion over her shoulders, the long lash sweeping its graceful curve. Margaret listened to the light breathing, half in wonder that aught human could look so much like blessedness.

"Alice," she said, and she started at the unearthly tones of her own voice. Alice arose, looking with surprise at the ashy paleness of her sister.

"We must away, Alice; I will go with thee to thy people."

Alice felt they were in deadly peril, for the voice and look of Margaret revealed it, but she staid for no questioning; she embraced her, and silently prepared for departure. When she laid her hand upon the Bible, Margaret's cold fingers were upon her own, and she whispered, "Let it remain."

Alice remembered long that deathly touch, and pale sorrowful face. They left the cabin in silence, for even Minaree lingered at the feast, unsuspecting the early departure of her foster-child. The river, swollen by recent rains, rolled on with a deep, heavy swell; and the sound of the rapids above added to the gloom. At this moment a fish leapt upward, and fell back with a long, heavy plash. She grasped the arm of the chief, wild with terror.

Tongatou shook her off fiercely. "The pale girl has nothing to fear, while the Swaying Reed shelters her."

Margaret's native energy came to her assistance, for she saw that the generous youth in his heart despised the helpless timidity of Alice, natural as it was, and condemned her for being, though unconscious of the fact, the cause of her own destruction. She therefore put her arm about her waist, and placed the skins to shelter her with the tenderness of a mother; and then took one of the paddles to assist in propelling the boat. Alice shuddered to contemplate the gloom of the young chief, as the bright star light revealed his face; and there was something, too, appalling in the still pale face of Margaret. Hour after hour, Alice looked upon her, and she remained the same, with her passionless brow, and sad, sweet mouth, bending her slight form mechanically to the dip of the oar. At length, Tongatou took the paddle from her hands; she resigned it passively, and, as he motioned, she placed herself at the side of Alice. She seemed chilled to the heart, but spoke not, and scarcely breathed. Alice was certain she did not sleep, for when the morning blushed in the melody of light, and a response burst from bird and blossom, she remained the same—cold and motionless.

All day the canoe moved onward, now in the shadow of dense forests, and now by the side of the prairie, where vine and blossom bent over to the refreshing waters—a wilderness of beauty. Blossoms! beautiful—most beautiful creations of the Eternal! How the heart expands with delight at beholding ye, and the lips unconsciously utter the language of thankfulness. Surely—surely the creator must delight in the beautiful, for everywhere, on earth, sea, and sky, hath He affixed its impress; and then, that man might share in his beatitude, he hath indued[1] him with this most ennobling and joy-imparting faculty. They are the joy and the mystery of childhood; and blessed are they who, in their meekness and purity, suffer no 'glory to depart from the earth!'[2] Blessed creatures! ye toil not, neither do ye spin; and yet who shall be like ye in glory? Ye minister not to the base wants of the body; your mission is to the soul—to the higher inward sense, to be expanded hereafter. Children of the desert! of else waste and desolate places, ye appear to glad the eyes of the invisibles; and, if perchance man goeth forth, how doth tears gush to his eyes at beholding thus the foot-prints of infinite benevolence! Meek dwellers of the rocks! ye cling confidingly to the rugged bosom, content with the tears of the morning, and its first blush of

---

1 Endowed.
2 Possibly a reference to Ezekiel 10:18, but the language in this paragraph strongly echoes Luke 12:27–31 and the Sermon on the Mount, including the Beatitudes, in Matthew 5–7.

light. Ye are content whether the rain or the sunshine be upon ye, happy in the blessings of existence. The vale and the mountain, the pure water, and the dim forest, have each their beautiful dwellers; for by them do the angels record upon earth the presence of gentle and holy hearts, made manifest by the flowers upon its bosom.

Often as the canoe approached an opening in the forest, making way for the passage of a stream scarcely visible, except by its long trail of verdure, herds of startled deer appeared in the distance, retreating to the woods, or off over the prairie. The practiced eye of the youth detected the nature of the country, and the doublings of the stream, and when to bear the canoe across portages of perhaps a half-mile, thus to avoid a circuit of many. It was a long, dreary route to one like Alice, to whom the grandeur, the silence, and wild solitudes of wood and mountain, brought only images of gloom and apprehension. Nothing relieved the native taciturnity of Tongatou, and a calm, settled melancholy rested upon the face of Margaret. She was gentle exceedingly; and more than once, when Alice looked up, she perceived the eyes of her sister fixed tearfully upon her; and when she would have spoken, and asked her why, Margaret smiled faintly, and motioned her to silence.

CHAPTER XXII.

Are we not exiles here?
Come there not o'er us memories of a clime
More genial and more dear,
Than this of time?—TUCKERMAN.[1]

It was now the third night of their journey, and they had not as yet encountered a human being. More than once a thin column of smoke betokened the presence of the hunter or the pioneer; but at such times they moved on in silence, nor struck a fire, or shot an arrow, till the indication became lost in the distance. It was one of those quiet, beautiful nights, when the heart seems to feel the presence of the Eternal visible in his creations, and we are led unconsciously to speculate upon what we are, and what we may be, when we go out and claim our affinity with the unseen but all-pervading

---

1 Henry Theodore Tuckerman (1813–71), "Il Penseroso."

presence. Alice, faint and weary, had fallen asleep immediately upon the spreading of the skins for the night; Margaret, half reclining, was beholding the moon, over which thin clouds were spreading a veil of gossamer. Tongatou regarded her long in silence, and then he seated himself at her side, and addressed her.

"Will the Swaying Reed remain with her people? She will bring light to any cabin."

Margaret fixed her eyes sternly upon him.

"Does the chief think there is no truth in the heart of the white maiden? The Swaying Reed belongs now, neither to the white nor the red people. She is given to the Great Spirit."

"Tongatou will not counsel the maiden, he knoweth her wisdom. When Tecumseh shall return, his cabin will be desolate. If it be the will of the Swaying Reed, her red brother will bear her away to the valley of the great river, and build her wigwam where none shall find it but Tecumseh. No evil shall come upon her, for Tongatou will guard it night and day, and she shall dwell in peace. Why should blood drown the melody of the Swaying Reed? Let the blossoms gather about her nest, and the sunshine rest upon it."

Margaret listened, smiling faintly, and as her eye wandered over earth and sky, their beauty came again with a new love to her breast. The sylvan lodge with its rest and security, seemed a pleasant vision to her eye, and spoke in tones of appeal. Then came that strange clinging to life, which even age, with its withered hopes, is known to feel; how much stronger then the young and trusting! But a deeper and holier principle reigned in the heart of the lone girl, teaching her that truth is holier, and more to be sought than repose or even life itself. When at length she replied to the youth, it was with a strong and holy purpose of heart.

"The Swaying Reed, has learned to look away from the sunshine of earth, and find her delight in thoughts of the spirit land. The sound of many voices cometh to her ear, and they tell of rest and blessedness where the storm or shadow cometh not. They tell of stars in their myriads and glory, and of skies unbounded reposing in blueness and beauty. I float away in a wilderness of blue; there is delight in motion, in existence, for the soul is unshackled in its flight. The same voice that spoke to Tecumseh of war and disaster, spoke also to the ear of the Swaying Reed. The spirit bird that sang upon the roof, was sent to warn her of her fate. Why should she seek to shun it? She may not now, for her pledge is given to the Almighty. She is ready to depart. It will be death only, be the mode what it may, and why should she shrink therefrom? The Swaying Reed must die. She would not escape, and for the sake of a few longer draughts of air, carry herself about a living lie! No: it were daily death!"

She turned to the face of the sleeping Alice, and it may be, wished that hers had been a like nature to weep and smile, and slumber in forgetfulness; to hold out the hands for support from others, rather than rely upon herself; to yield to circumstances, rather than shape out her own destiny. But such had not been the character of her soul, and suffering and trial had been proportioned to the strength of her endurance.

"Tongatou," she resumed, "I feel upon me the shadows of another world. I feel its vastness, its infinite silence. While I listen with awe to that eternal hush, faint low music cometh to my ear, now heard, and now lost, like the far-off notes of the night bird. Alice talks of spirits in that land of shadows, of companionship, and love; but as for me, I have striven to penetrate its mysteries, almost in despair. I cannot believe because others believe. I must feel it in my own soul. The blossom appears and dies; another comes in its place, but the same one appears no more. Is it so with us? Others come where we have been, and shall we appear in another land? O, Tongatou, these are great mysteries: I am willing to die that I may understand them. Alice reads the Book of our faith that tells us we may live for ever; and she never doubts. I have been away from its pages, and must find the assurance elsewhere. Our people all believe in a Great Spirit; in a life after death. Tongatou, it is the voice of the Great Spirit, speaking in the heart he has made. It is the calling of spirit to spirit. If there were nothing beyond death we would never have desired aught. We believe, because we have been made so to do; it is our nature. Tongatou, I fear not to die by thy people, and there may be virtue in it, since it will save Alice, and may bring good to the tribes. It is a small thing to die, and live again—to sleep and awake."

The youth looked in the face of the inspired girl, and though he but dimly comprehended what she had said, yet the best impulses of his nature had been awakened, and the tears came to his eyes.

"Tongatou feels, that the Great Spirit hath talked with the Swaying Reed, and told her of the land of the spirits. He will think more of it now, and when the Swaying Reed shall be there, will she not sometimes come and sit upon the roof of Tongatou, and sing of the spirit land? He shall remember her voice for ever, and her music will sink into his heart. He will know even in the spirit-bird, the voice and the eyes of the Swaying Reed."

"Alas!" said Margaret, "I know not aught that shall be hereafter, but I can never cease to love all that is generous and good in the heart of my red brother. Methinks, I hear in my heart the utterance of the Great Spirit; let us commune with him!"

She folded her hands upon her bosom, and remained long in silent meditation. Tongatou sat with his eyes fixed, as if striving to penetrate those mysteries of which she had spoken.

Margaret fearlessly slept by the side of Alice, and the youth continued his watching till the young dawn awoke them to another day's journey. They had rested upon a point of land projecting deeply into the water, covered with birch, sycamore and other hard-wood trees, and the morning awakened the grove to one universal gush of melody. In the shoals of the river the patient heron waited motionless for its prey, and the wild duck trimmed its plumes and swam at ease upon its bosom. The air was warm and quiet, the shadows from beneath looking as distinct as objects above. It was a sweet secluded spot, and the waking of inanimate nature in this little dell, was like the unclosing of an infant's lid, while the smile of its angel dreams is yet lingering about its mouth.

Tongatou addressed a few words to the ear of Margaret, to which she seemed to assent, for he concealed the canoe in the thicket, and proceeded upon a route diverging somewhat from the direction of their course. Alice perceived it and demanded the cause.

"The red man must do honor to the graves of his fathers," replied Margaret.

She would have remonstrated, but the very looks of Margaret were of a kind to command, and acquiescence had become habitual to the timid sister. She walked on by the side of her companion, till weariness compelled her pause; while they took some refreshment, she observed the chief examining the ground before them with great scrutiny. She became alarmed. "We have struck upon a trail," explained Margaret, "and Tongatou is trying to learn what has preceded us."

Tongatou returned, and informed them that the same path had been traveled by two upon horseback, and each led a horse.

"Are they red or white men?" asked Margaret.

"One is a white."

"How have you learned all this?" said Alice, surprised at the minuteness of the detail.

"I know that two of the horses are unbridled, for they have browsed upon the herbage in passing. One of the men is white; for, where he had alighted, the foot was turned outward: he is young; for his step is long and firmly set."

The color came to the cheek of Alice, as the possibility occurred to her, that Henry Mansfield might be on his way to restore them to their friends. Impressed with the idea, she followed her companions with a quicker pace, and with something of her former vivacity. Hope suggested a thousand pleasant images, and lent a new beauty to the objects around her. The green wood became greener, and the blossom brighter in her pathway.

CHAPTER XXIII.

> I look around and feel the awe
> Of one, who walks alone
> Among the wrecks of former days,
> In dismal ruin strown;
> I start to hear the stirring sounds
> From the leaves of withered trees;
> For the voice of the departed
> Seems borne upon the breeze.—PARK BENJAMIN.[1]

All day they pursued their journey: sometimes in the direction of the trail, and then again divergent. As night approached, they left it nearly at right-angles. The moon was sending down her beams of silver beauty, lighting the shimmering woods, when their guide came to a halt in the vicinity of a mound of earth, raised in the midst of the forest. It was nearly circular in its form, and of considerable extent, and in many parts covered with trees of great size. An occasional projection indicated parts of a more recent construction, and suggested that these slight deviations from the designed figure, were but temporary, and in time to be removed. The turf was smooth and

---

1   Park Benjamin, Sr. (1809–64), "The Departed."

green, and the mound—standing in the midst of a wide level extent of country, with no other elevation for miles about, surrounded by a dense forest—suggested impressions of reverence and grandeur. The very spirit of silence seemed to brood over this venerable relic of a by-gone and forgotten age. The moon lay upon its summit, and dense, heavy masses of shadow lay at its base. If a straggling wind found itself in this solitary vale, it crept hushingly beneath the pendant leaf, and over the sighing grass, to free itself with its gay fellows, sporting by the river brink.

The three stood together, looking in mute awe upon this record of obscurity, when all at once a flood of melody broke forth from the branches above, so full and liquid, so like the gushing forth of all sweet and sorrowful harmonies, that it might have passed for the conjoined griefs and blessedness of all that slept beneath; who had once lived and sorrowed, rejoiced and wept, and passed away where tears are no more. Awhile, the melody ceased; silence rested as before upon them; the moon looked forth in her brightness, and then veiled her face in silvery clouds, and again burst forth that gush of strange sad music.

Alice clung to the arm of Margaret, for the stillness of the night, the solitude, and that wild gush of melody filled her with awe, amounting to terror.

"It is the spirit-bird," whispered Margaret, solemnly; "it singeth ever by the sepulchres of the tribes. It sang three nights upon our roof. I knew its voice of warning."

Alice shuddered; for the whites had imbibed the same superstition, and she knew it ominous of death.

At this moment, Tongatou threw his hands upward, and bending to the monument in an attitude of grief, began to chant in measured tones. Margaret placed herself by his side, keeping time to the dirge-like burden.

"The bones of the red man are on every side. They lie in the deep woods; they sleep to the sound of many waters. They that perish in battle, sleep together, forgetful of the strife. The grass is green upon them, and the trees of a thousand suns spring from their ashes. The land is rich with their blood; it heaveth with their bones. Where shall we go, and our fathers sleep not with us? The tree that shelters the warrior in battle, sheltered old men before him. The hunter in the chase treadeth in the trail of the hunter a thousand years ago.

"Alas, alas, for the dead!
Alas, for those that go to the spirit-land!
Do they know of the deeds of brave men?
Do they delight in the glory of their children?
Do they know when we weep over their bones?"

The last sentences were prolonged to a wail, that mingled with the music of the bird, and swelled low and sadly upon the night air. It died away, and was renewed in plaintive cadences:

"Alas, for them that go to the spirit-land!
They heed not the fame of their children:
Sorrow cometh to them, and they know it not:
We come to them, and they know it not;
We call upon them, and they answer not:
Come—come! we call upon ye, spirits of the dead."

Alice covered her face with her hands, for a long pause succeeded the invocation; and on the misty canopy above, in the midst of the dim trees, and hovering over that solitary mound, seemed to her excited fancy to assemble the warriors of other days, fierce in the panoply of war; wielding spear and battle-axe, guarded by corslet and shield, with towering plume and radiant crest. Dimly and mistily they thronged in the still night, and fought again the battles of heroes. Overcome with awe, she threw her arms about the neck of Margaret, and implored her to leave a place so awful.

"Behold, it is deep midnight!" said Margaret, huskily; "speak not, for we are in the midst of the dead!" and then, as if continuing the chant, she went on:

"Hark to the voices of the dead:
The tones from the spirit-land;
They come from the dim sepulchre,
From the old and shadowy wood;
They come from the pale stars:
On the cloudy cars of the wind
We behold the dead of a thousand years!
They come like the gathering mist of the storm.

Do ye behold how the glory hath departed from your children? How the stranger is here, even in the midst of your graves? How the youth have forgotten your sepulchres? We weep, and ye know of our sorrow. We weep, and ye point to the spirit-land. We come—for rest is not for the red man—we come to the spirit-land."

As the chant proceeded, they began to slowly circle the mound, and Alice moved with them; for that unearthly bird—those sepulchral notes, uttered at the hour of night, in the midst of dimness and shadow, filled her with unspeakable fear. As the group moved onward, the barking of a dog at no great distance, thrilled her with delighted relief—it had a voice to remind her of human presence—of human sympathies; and the misty visions of the mind fled before it.

Tongatou laid his finger upon his lips, and crept silently forward; and so certain was Alice that relief was near at hand, that, notwithstanding her companion desired she should remain while the youth went forward to see from whence came the sound, she clung to the neck of Margaret, and insisted that they should follow. A slight turn revealed, at no great distance, a cloud of sparks rising in the midst of the branches, flashing and soaring upward, till they went out in the dense blackness above.

A rapid, continuous rattle, like the shaking of pebbles in a stiff parchment, caused them to recoil; for there, visible by the flame before them, lay coiled an immense rattlesnake; darting, and throwing itself forward with wonderful velocity, in search of its prey. At length, recovering itself, it remained poised, with neck towering from the midst of its burnished folds; its jaws distended, its glittering eyes like coals of flame, and its head oscillating from side to side. To the terrified eyes of Alice, the aspect of the creature changed with every vibration of its body. Now it was a heap of gems, sparkling and heaving in the moonbeams, and she felt an irresistible desire to behold them nearer, and would have done so, but that the arm of Margaret held her back. Then it was a rainbow, coiling and trailing upon the earth; anon it was a train of fire, gleaming and quivering, and endowed with vitality.

Tongatou began to address it with great earnestness, assuring it that a Shawanee could never have designed to do it harm; that if evil had been threatened, it was unknown to them. They were full of reverence for the guardian manitou of the tribe, and were ready to do anything to appease his anger. As the adjuration proceeded, Alice beheld the huge reptile lay itself down, its gray hue returned, and she now saw that another of the same species lay dead beside it.

CHAPTER XXIV.

—The moon's cold light, as it lay that night
On the hill side and the sea,
Still lies where he laid his houseless head:
But the pilgrim—where is he?—PIERPONT.[1]

Tongatou now crept with the stealthy tread of a panther, in the direction in which the fire appeared. Margaret would have remained, waiting his return, but so much did the terrors of their situation grow upon the mind of Alice, that she determined to follow him. They had accomplished nearly half their distance without alarm, when the snapping of a twig beneath the foot of Alice aroused the vigilance of the dog, and he rushed forward, barking furiously. A moment more and two men appeared, with arms presented, striving to penetrate the darkness around, to learn the cause of the alarm. Alice uttered a loud shriek, and fell fainting into the arms of Margaret.

The strangers approached, and Henry Mansfield folded the insensible Alice to his heart. Bearing her to the light, he marked with painful emotions the changes which care and sorrow had wrought on her sweet face. Mr. Mason sunk upon his knees and returned thanks with a gush of tears. Then turning to Margaret, he would have laid his hand upon her head in paternal benediction, but she shrank proudly back, and he only added,

"Bless the Lord, O maiden, that thou hast been taken from the horrible pit and the miry clay."[2]

No sooner had Tongatou found the strangers were the friends of Alice, than he threw himself upon the earth, and was soon buried in profound slumber; the more welcome, that it was the first he had indulged since their escape from the village.

Many were the inquiries of Alice as to the welfare of the little family, and she listened to the recital of their fears and anxieties on

---

1 John Pierpont (1785–1866), "The Pilgrim Fathers."
2 A reference to Psalm 40:2: "He brought me up also out of an horrible pit, out of the miry clay, and set my feet upon a rock, and established my goings."

her behalf, with smiles and tears. At every proof of tenderness, and every effort made to rescue her, the tears were in her eyes, and the most touching acknowledgments fell from her lips. For many hours after the rest of the group were buried in sleep, the quiet tones of her voice, disturbed, like a wandering note of music, the silence of the night; nor did she frown when Henry, gathering the thick robes to shelter her, placed his arm around her waist, and laid her cheek upon his shoulder. Though exhausted with travel, she felt too much of happiness while again listening to the language of affection and sympathy to admit of slumber. She wept as the youth recited his anxieties and efforts to relieve her, and the long months of suspense, amounting to agony, relieved only by the assurance from some passing Indian, that she was well. Then she wept again, as she related her own sorrows; and when the youth tenderly kissed them away, her tears were renewed, for suffering had converted her to a very child. When, at length, she lay down by the side of Margaret, it is no wonder if the youth stole a look at her pale face, and impressed a kiss upon the pure brow; for he was left to guard the sleep of the little party in that wild, solitary wood.

The arrow of Tongatou furnished the morning repast, and when it was over, Mr. Mason in accordance with his invariable custom, uttered a fervent and heart-felt prayer. There was something touching in the performance of the duty in the midst of those old solitudes; the deep and reverential voice blending its homage of praise with that of the free bird; and the green earth waked from its period of repose.

It was resolved to remain through the day, and another night in the woods, for the sake of rest; and Tongatou no sooner learned the determination, than he again disposed himself to slumber—for the precarious life of the savage, subjecting him often to protracted watchings, likewise enables him to indulge in long intervals of sleep, thereby preserving the equilibrium.

Mr. Mason regarded the cold and haughty bearing of Margaret with sorrowful displeasure. Her demi-savage dress, too, shocked him as something heathenish, and allied to the children of Belial;[1] to say nothing of its outrage upon his sense of propriety. The indolent grace of the beautiful girl, as she reclined, wrapt in her own medita-

---

1 Commonly used synonym of Satan, or the personification of evil and worthlessness.

tions, taking no note of those about her, seemed but an ill requitance for the labor expended in her behalf. More than once he attempted to address her, but the awe she inspired made him at a loss how to begin. The more he regarded her, the more was he impressed with the urgency of his duty to enlighten her as to those doctrines of which he believed her ignorant. In his own mind he could not entirely exculpate from blame, in suffering her to remain so; and he resolved, on their return, to place her offence strongly before her; for, though kind and cheerful to the last degree, in his daily life, he could not tolerate the least omission in religious observance; and here, if anywhere, rested a shadow of severity.

Seating himself beside her, he waited in vain for some token of consciousness on the part of Margaret, that he was present; but she, neither by look or motion, gave him leave to address her.

"Daughter," at length said Mr. Mason, "I perceive that thou art still in the gall of bitterness and iniquity."

Margaret turned her penetrating eyes full upon him, and read searchingly his face. Mr. Mason was abashed, and colored slightly, but in the way of duty he was not easily daunted, and he went on, though his voice was certainly louder and more determined than the occasion would seem to require.

"Daughter, wo is thee, that thou hast sojourned in Meshak, that thou hast dwelt in the tents of Kedesh;[1] thou hast burned incense under every green tree, and upon every high hill; and thou hast forgotten the heritage of Israel. Thou hast bowed down unto strange gods, and hast forgotten the Lord, the righteous. Thou hast forsaken the guide of thy youth, who would have led thee to green pastures and beside the still waters. Return, outcast daughter of Zion,[2] for behold the Spirit and the bride say come, and let him that is athirst come, and whosoever will, let him come and partake of the water of life freely."

---

1   A reference to Psalm 120:5, in which the psalmist laments dwelling among inhospitable peoples who do not share his faith in God and desire for peace: "Woe is me, that I sojourn in Mesech, that I dwell in the tents of Kedar!"

2   In this context, an exile separated from Jerusalem—that is, from both her homeland and her religion. The quotation that follows from Revelation 22:17 is used to extend an invitation to return to Christian community and faith.

While he thus addressed her in the inspired language of scripture, Margaret listened as to remembered music; but when he added, "I know thy pride and the naughtiness of thy heart, and that thou wilt rather eat chaff with the swine than return to thy father's house, where is wine and oil, and bread enough and to spare:" her eyes flashed, and she half arose from her seat; but impelled perhaps by awakened curiosity, she again sunk back upon the heaped up leaves. Mr. Mason went on.

"Let me hear thee cry, 'Lord, thou art the guide of my youth.'[1] Let me see thee cast thy idols to the moles and the bats, and these garments, which are the filthy rags of heathenism, cast aside for the more seemly robes of a Christian maiden. Let me see thee clad in the garments of righteousness, and adorned with a weak and quiet spirit, and prostrate at the foot of the cross, cry mightily on the Lord, thy Saviour. Yea, cast thyself down, for I perceive thy spirit is full of all pride, and wrath and bitterness."

Margaret arose proudly from her seat, and motioning that none should follow, was soon lost in the thick woods. It was many hours before she returned, and when she did so, her cheek was pale and her eyes swollen with weeping.

The next morning, when the first tinge of light broke upon the forest ere the bird had lifted its wing or shook a drop of dew from its nest; Tongatou, who had watched through the night, awoke Margaret from her slumbers. She arose, and gazed long and earnestly in the face of Alice, with hands clasped and the tears streaming from her eyes. Long—long memories were awakened; their childhood, their cruel separation and last meeting, with dissevered sympathies, secret sorrows, hopes, fears and perils. Alice must never know the horrors of her death, never know what she herself had escaped. This reflection imparted a degree of firmness, and she turned away, denying herself a last embrace—a last farewell. She had proceeded but few paces, when she returned and gazed in mute tenderness upon the sweet face, which she should see no more on earth. Alice stirred slightly, and she stooped down and pressed her hand upon her side hushingly, as a mother would caress the restlessness of a child; she bent her lips to her cheek, and unconsciously whispered, "Dear, dear sister! may the Almighty comfort you." Alice felt a tear fall

---

1   Jeremiah 3:4: "Wilt thou not from this time cry unto me, My father, thou art the guide of my youth?"

upon her cheek, and she started wildly up, and grasped the garment of Margaret—the whole truth flashed upon her mind. Wildly she clung to her neck, and implored her to remain.

"Alice, it cannot be. It had been better had we never met again on earth; but now we meet no more. The decree has gone forth, and we part for ever! Oh, Alice, when you think of me, let it not be with anger and reproach, as of one whose heart was cold and dead, and who loved a wild life better than she loved friend and sister; who went back to it for the sake of her Indian lover, to dwell in peace in a forest wigwam: but think of me as one who bore a great sorrow at her heart; and yet it was strong, fearing nothing however terrible; but think of me, Alice, as one who loved you better than life itself!"

The tenderness of this appeal was too much for the exhausted powers of Alice, and she fainted upon her bosom. Margaret gently laid her upon the turf; she kissed her lips, cheek, and brow, held back the long dark hair and looked into the pale inanimate face; gave her one long, last kiss, and rising mournfully to her feet, spread her hands one moment over her, as if in blessing; waved them toward the wondering group, and plunged into the dense woods. Mr. Mason's first impulse was to follow in pursuit; but a warning arrow from Tongatou admonished him to forbear.

"The Lord be praised, that I warned her yesterday," he ejaculated; "had I not done so, I had been as a faithless watchman on the citadel of Zion, and verily the blood of her soul had been found upon the skirts of my garments. Like the Israelites of old she remembered the garlics and flesh-pots of Egypt, and loathed the spiritual manna."[1]

By the aid of branches of the trees, covered with skins and suspended between the two led horses, a comfortable litter was prepared, on which was borne the almost lifeless body of Alice. It was a sad journey of tears and hopeless sorrow. She felt as if all her labor had been in vain, and it was not till busy recollection brought back the memory of the growing tenderness of Margaret, and the evident enlightenment of her religious views, that she could find one ray of consolation. Then she remembered her request that the Bible should remain, and wondered that she had not before suspected the reason.

---

1   In Exodus 16:3, before God sends nourishment in the form of manna, the discontented Israelites complain of their hunger to Moses, remembering the pots of meat and other food they left behind on their flight into the wilderness.

Then would come the conviction that Margaret was lost, lost to her for ever, and her tears flowed afresh. Now that she was gone, memory, as in the case of the dead, restored all the noble, the excellent and unselfish nature of her sister, casting upon them the bold and distinctive light of another world; and all that was unlovely, if such there were, retired into the shadow or totally disappeared. When she attempted to recall her features to her view, she could only bring back the beautiful face, beaming with that last look of tenderness, and the radiant eyes suffused with tears. Then, too, the presence of Mr. Mason had awakened many points of faith into vivid distinctness, which had become partially obscured by her long residence in the woods, where human creeds were undreamed of. Calling to Mr. Mason, she hinted her fears that she had not been at sufficient pains to ascertain the true state of her sister.

"I fear so too," said Mr. Mason, with a severity unusual to him, and which brought a frown upon the brow of Mansfield. "I fear so too; for I found in her little of the meekness that should become a believer in the meek and lowly Jesus. But if you have clearly pointed out the true way, and she refuses to follow it, the consequences of rejection must rest upon her own head; you are free from all blame in this matter. But I—"

"Alas!" said Alice, "she was so full of lofty thought, and a strange exalted religion, that I could never talk with her. She was the teacher, not I."

Mr. Mason scrutinized her countenance suspiciously—"I should be sorry to feel, Alice, that thou art straying from the flock. Thou art but a tender lamb, and must be carried in the bosom of the good shepherd. Remember, that he who putteth his hand to the plough and looketh back, is not fit for the kingdom of heaven."[1]

Mr. Mason persisted in completing his warning, notwithstanding many angry shakes of the head on the part of Mansfield; and Alice could only reply with her tears, for she was becoming bewildered in language that conveyed to her but little of definite meaning. From Margaret, she had learned to take a more elevated and comprehensive view of the great doctrines of human faith and duty; and in her present debility she feared, that what in the wil-

---

1 Luke 9:62.

derness had appeared as freedom and truth, might after all have been nothing more than delusion.

When the little party wound around the rude road cut through the forest on their way home, Mrs. Mason was standing at the door, evidently in the vague hope of witnessing their return. Little Jimmy started upon a full run to meet his father, and Anna caught the baby from the old lady's arms, kissed it and hurried to the door; then in again, turning round and round in the bewilderment of her joy; put the child upon the floor, and then rushed from the house, and throwing her arms about the almost unconscious Alice, bore her like an infant into the inner room and laid her upon her own bed. The pale hands of Alice were clasped over her neck and they wept together. The old lady stood by wiping her eyes with her trembling hands, and then putting down her spectacles to gaze upon her altered face, and elevating them again to the border of her cap to wipe away her tears. Jimmy began to scream very loudly, and the baby joined in concert.

A refreshing draught was now prepared by Anna, and the poor girl was left to repose.

"Where is Margaret?" inquired both Anna and the old lady, at the first moment for observation.

Mr. Mason went on to relate the whole of their adventure in the woods, together with what he had otherwise learned, concerning Margaret, from the lips of her sister. Upon which the old lady repeated in full the history of Sam Shaw, with suitable comments, to which all listened with the utmost kindness and apparent interest, notwithstanding they had heard the same story, and the same conclusions, from the lips at least fifty times before. But when is ever a story wearisome to benevolent ears, if coming from the lips of a child in the budding of its existence, or from the child of fourscore upon whom has fallen the sear and the yellow leaf of human life.[1] She turned her eyes from one to the other in assurance of approval, and when her subject had become exhausted, and the vanity of earthly expectations pressed home to her heart, she laid her head against the high back of her chair, and closing her eyes began to sing,

---

1 From Shakespeare's *Macbeth*, echoing Macbeth's description of his life in old age as "fall'n into the sere, the yellow leaf" (Act 5, Scene 3).

"How vain are all things here below!
How false and yet how fair!
Each pleasure hath its poison too,
And every sweet a snare."[1]

Many were the weeks of severe illness that followed upon the return of Alice. At times she was delirious, and her sweet and tender appeals to Margaret, in which she implored her not to forsake her, and return again to the solitude of the wild woods, brought tears into the eyes of all present. Then she renewed the terrors and perils of their flight from the village, and that long wearisome journey. She would deplore her own want of strength and resolution, and wish that like Margaret she were undaunted, and persevering. At length her disease yielded to the faithful nursing of Mrs. Mason, and great was the rejoicing, when she was able to be seated in the common room, bolstered up in the old lady's great arm-chair. But the subject of Margaret was one to call up the most painful emotions, and it became tacitly interdicted by the family.

CHAPTER XXV.

And oh, when death comes in terrors, to cast
His fears on the future, his pall on the past;
In that moment of darkness, with hope in thy heart,
And a smile in thine eye, "Look aloft," and depart.
— J. LAWRENCE.[2]

Margaret, accompanied by Tongatou, traveled on in silence; her hands folded and drooping before her, and her tall, slender figure realizing painfully her Indian cognomen of the Swaying Reed; for her footsteps were languid and vascillating, and she moved mechanically forward, without noticing the impediments in her pathway. Once, when they had come to a small brook, that babbled over its rocky bed, its pure waters sparkling and flashing in the sunshine that peered through the dense branches, she stopped and laved[3] her

---

1 From Hymn 2:48 by Issac Watts (1674–1748), "Love to the creatures is dangerous."
2 Jonathan Lawrence (1807–33), "Look Aloft."
3 Washed.

cheek and brow, and partook of its refreshing drops. As her own colorless cheek, thin and worn, met her eye, she said mournfully to her companion—

"The Swaying Reed is very weary. Would that she might lie down in the great woods, and pass to the world of spirits. Her heart is sad. There is no light upon her path."

Tongatou wept. "Shall Tongatou paddle his canoe down to the white settlements? He will wear the moccasins from his feet, he will follow the sun behind the mountains of the west, and forget to eat and to sleep, if he may bring joy to the heart of the Swaying Reed."

Margaret looked in his face, and tears were in her eyes.

"Tongatou has a kind heart; and the Great Spirit loves it. But the sunshine will be no more in the path of the Swaying Reed. Would she were at rest; for she is very—very weary."

Tongatou prepared their repast, but Margaret was too ill to eat. She lay down upon the earth, and a heavy sleep gathered upon her. He spread the skins upon the heaped leaves, and wove together the branches of the trees for a shelter; and then he lifted her in his arms, and placed her in the lodge. Margaret opened her eyes, and smiled faintly; but she had no power of utterance.

It was an affecting sight, to witness that rude son of the woods nursing the sick girl in that dreary solitude with the tenderness of a brother. He poured water upon her burning temples, and held the birchen cup to her parched lips. When she mourned in her uneasy slumber, he soothed her as a mother would a sick child. The mazy roots and shrubs, which the experience of rude life had ascertained to be salutary, were compounded into beverages for her use. Charms were wrought with care and skill, and poured out upon the earth at the hour of night, under the influence of the full moon; that, as they were absorbed into the dry earth, the disease might disappear from the suffering girl.

The third day she lay motionless, breathing short and heavily, with half open eyes and face pale as marble. Tongatou thought her hour of death had indeed arrived, and he sunk down upon his knees beside her, and wept freely.

"Very beautiful wert thou, O maiden of the sunny brow," he murmured, "but the shadow of the Great Spirit is upon thee." Impelled by an impulse he could not control, his tongue burst forth in prayer to the God of the white maiden. Margaret opened her eyes and beheld him kneeling at her side. Touched by the simplicity and fervency of his appeal, she also wept; and when he ceased, she laid her thin hand in his and said—

"Tongatou is very kind. The Great Spirit has heard his prayer. But O, the damp heavy pressure that has been upon me. I feel as if I had been through the dark valley of death."

Tongatou wept at the tones of her voice; with a delicacy and refinement that a more cultivated mind might have envied, he prepared all things for her comfort. Combed out the long tangles of her beautiful hair, smoothed the skins beneath her head, and laid fresh blossoms upon her pillow. When the night came on, he laid himself at the door of her lodge and watched while she slept. In the tenderness of her gratitude, Margaret called him "Brother." Tongatou was more than rewarded, for Tecumseh called him by the same name.

One night Margaret was awakened from slumber by a loud crash, that seemed to shake the very earth with terror. The elements were warring fearfully, and the red bolt had shivered a tree beside her. The rain was pouring in torrents, and the murky darkness of the night lay like a dense pall upon the earth, relieved only by the fierce glare of the lightning, that revealed the wild swaying of the branches and disrupted trees, reeling in the darkness. The lone girl, exhausted by sickness, felt a strange terror overcome her, and she called loudly upon Tongatou.

"Brother, I will sit by thee, for this darkness and storm are terrible."

Tongatou gathered the skins about her, and seated himself at her side. "Is fear known to the Swaying Reed? Tongatou thought she had never known it."

"Brother, I am like a leaf that shivers in the autumn blast—I shall soon be carried away."

"Tongatou will seat himself away," said the youth in a trembling voice, "for the words of the Swaying Reed sink too deeply into his heart." A flash of lightning revealed the ghastly face of her companion, and Margaret, mistaking its cause, gently detained him.

"Tell me, brother, what it is that you mean. Is sorrow in the heart of Tongatou?"

He sighed heavily and was long silent. A terrible suspicion flashed upon the mind of the lone girl, and she dropped the hand she had seized.

"Tongatou is very sorrowful. He loves the Swaying Reed, but she loves him only as a brother. Tecumseh and the Swaying Reed have both called him brother. He is worthy of their love; but let not the voice of the Swaying Reed be so like the wind through the pine trees, for it goeth to the heart of Tongatou."

Margaret felt no terror at this frank avowal from the lips of the young savage, for her own innocence and purity were shield and buckler, and she knew too well the honor and generosity of the man with whom her lot had been cast, to feel aught of fear. She gently desired the youth to remain at her side till the perilous storm should be past. Tongatou obeyed, and more than an hour they remained silently watching the progress of the tempest.

"The white girl is as one from the spirit land, to her red brother; will she not talk of that place of shadows?"

Fervently did Margaret dwell upon the glory and beatitude of that state, whose happiness the human heart has failed to conceive. She told of the blossoms by the tree of life, that fade not nor decay; she told of the pure waters, and the melodies that shall never cease; of that diffused and ineffable light, that could dim the brightness of sun and moon and resplendent star; of the Power that should reign for ever and ever, undisturbed by storm and tempest or the fierceness of human passion. As she went on, her voice became deep and musical in the earnestness of her description, and the youth remarked:

"The voice of the Swaying Reed is as that of the spirit-bird. When Tongatou shall be away in the lone woods, he will be filled with joy. He may behold the Swaying Reed, in that heaven of which she has told him, for the heart of Tongatou is very sad."

"Brother," said Margaret, "the Great Spirit hath laid his hand upon the Swaying Reed, and she will pass away as the mist from the hills. But Tongatou will remember that she pitied and deplored his love."

The next morning, the sun glittered upon the drops depending heavily from the trees; the birds that had been all night rudely tossed in their frail tenements, shook the spray from their wings, and rejoicing that the peril were past, burst forth into a new and wilder strain of melody; the squirrel sprung chattering from branch to branch, and the rabbit poised its ears, cast around its wild brilliant eyes, and leaped in the very gladness of its heart. The trees, that had been so rudely shaken, swayed lightly as if trying the firmness of their roots, while those that had been torn from the earth leaned heavily against their companions as if in quest of sympathy.

Margaret was so much recovered as to be able to follow Tongatou a considerable distance in the direction of the river, but her steps were slow, and ere night she was obliged to repose and sleep again in the shadow of the old woods. When at length they had reached the river, the fresh winds rippling its surface, and the heaving of its waters, filled her with a portion of her former vivacity, and she plied the light paddle with a beaming eye, and the bright hue upon her cheek; but she was soon obliged to lie down in the bottom of the canoe and trust to the guidance of Tongatou.

They had been gliding on under the shadow of the trees, whose dense foliage limited the view to a vista of the river above and below them, and a bright gleaming of the sky, when the opening of the prairie permitted a more extensive prospect. Tongatou balanced his paddle and arose hastily, for a dense cloud of smoke, in the direction of the village, hung heavily in the atmosphere. Again bending to his task, and assisted by Margaret, they rapidly made their way in the direction. Slowly, in immense volumes, arose the black vapor, rolling and swelling along, bearing itself upward like a vast pyramid, till it reached the higher regions of the air, when it sailed off like a floating banner in the blue sky. As they approached, straggling bands of savages were seen encamped in the marshes and on the banks of the creeks, feeble and worn, the children crying for food, and the woman making loud lamentations for the dead and dying.

At another time Margaret would have approached them, but now she was aware that a battle had been fought between her own people and the red man, and her own doom so near its accomplishment demanded speed.

When the canoe stopped in the little cove beside the grape-vine arbor, Margaret beheld the flames just kindling upon the cabin of Minaree. The brand had been applied by a soldier who lingered after the departure of his comrades, whom the insulated dwelling had escaped. She rushed forward in time to secure the Bible of Alice, and then stood to witness the destruction of her last place of refuge. In the distance, she could behold the retreating party, and hear their war-notes of triumph, as they marched onward, leaving a thousand women and children, starving and defenceless, to perish amid the ashes of their wigwams. The wounded and the dead were heaped together, and the red glare of the flames rested fearfully upon their livid faces.

The battle of Tippecanoe had been fought, and she stood amid the ruins of its homes. The flames spread to the adjoining groves, and in the darkness of the night the towering flame, as it embraced some monarch of the woods, sent forth a thousand tongues of light, darting and writhing like fiery dragons. Slowly as the sounds of the retreating army died away, came in the dispersed inhabitants, and crouched themselves in groups about the smouldering ashes. Each family selected the hearth-stone that had once been its own, and a wild song of lamentation broke from every lip. Here might be seen a wife stanching the blood from the wounds of her wounded companion, while the filmed eye and laboring chest showed it must be in vain. Children were clinging to the mother, who had dragged herself hither to die—a new-born infant partaking of its first and last tribute of life, for the dying groan of her who had given it life mingled with the shrieks of her children. Here might be seen a young mother clasping the dead body of her first-born, pierced by a wandering bullet, refusing to believe life were indeed extinct, and she alone in her sorrow, though hunger, and cold, and death were in reserve for herself.

Margaret moved onward to where a heap of ashes alone remained of all that was once hers. A shriveled and half-naked figure was crouched amid the ruins, holding her bony hands over a heap of coals that remained upon the hearth. She had placed a few kernels of corn to parch, and as Margaret approached, she clutched at them eagerly, with a laugh of savage triumph, like the growl of a wild animal. It was Minaree. Margaret looked in her face, but a bewildered, idiotic stare was her only token of recognition.

Tongatou had prepared the bower by the river for the repose of Margaret, and she divided her skins with Minaree. As she led her into it, the poor creature seemed in part to recollect her foster-child, for she smoothed down her hair many times, as if the operation gave her pleasure, smiling and weeping at the same time. Then she laid herself down for a moment, to rest; but she arose again and looked at Margaret, caressing her thin hands, and gazing piteously in her face. It was shocking to behold the ravages of disease and famine, for she was wasted to a skeleton.

The next morning, when Tongatou laid a piece of venison at the door, Margaret prepared it quietly, lest Minaree should awake. When all was ready, she gently shook her by the arm. It was stiff and cold. Poor Minaree was dead! Margaret laid the venison aside, contenting herself with a draught of cold water; for so nearly were the threads of life spun out, that their wants were scarcely felt. She took a fearful pleasure in looking at the cold still face of the dead, as prefiguring what she should soon be; and the sight of its mortality helped to give palpability to her meditations. Her thoughts followed in pursuit of the disembodied spirit, so recently gone forth on its eternal flight. She shed no tears for herself or others; for what had she to do with human emotions, to whom the mysteries of the unknown world were so soon to be revealed. She rolled the skins about her foster-parent with her own hands, and bound the kerchief over her gray locks. She shuddered not at the cold, rigid, marble touch: for there was relief in knowing that poor Minaree would be spared the agony of witnessing her own death. She helped Tongatou to prepare the grave in the midst of the arbor which Minaree had helped to adorn; she rounded the green turf above it, and then wearily laid her head upon it, as her last place of repose.

CHAPTER XXVI.

And the blue wave upon the beach dissolves,
Like woman's hopes and manhood's high resolves.
—AMELIA B. WELBY.[1]

All day Margaret remained motionless, wrapt in deep and awful meditation. The shadows of the eternal world pressed heavily upon her, dense, vast, and almost rayless. "When man dieth, shall he live again?" she repeated again and again, and an echo from her inward self responded, "Death is but the rending of the veil[2]—to desire is to realize, to hope is to enjoy. It is the going forth of the occupant only that leaves the tenement to decay." The Bible of Alice was beside her, and yet she did not open it, for unacquainted with the evidences for its authority, she distrusted at this time, so fraught with fearful interest, all evidence, except that which she gathered from the world about her, and the great evidence founded on the character of her

---

1   Amelia B. Welby (1819–52), "Time."
2   The veil of the temple is torn in two upon Jesus' death, which opens the way for human salvation (Matthew 27:51; Mark 15:38; Luke 23:45).

own inward nature. She believed, because it is a part of the constitution of the human soul to believe, and the belief is the argument for its immortality. A holy calm grew upon her, and she closed her eyes, humbly resigning her spirit to the Infinite. 'The wind bloweth where it listeth, and ye hear the sound thereof, but cannot tell whence it cometh nor whither it goeth: so is every one that is born of the spirit.'[1] She closed its pages in thought. No more can we tell whence cometh or whither goeth the soul. But we feel that when it shall be born into its spiritual life, more will be revealed. She read again, 'The kingdom of God is within you,'[2] and mused, it is an everlasting kingdom. Again, 'The flesh profiteth nothing; it is the spirit that giveth life.'[3] "Holy Father," she exclaimed, "I believe in what thou hast said; for it is in harmony with the desires and necessities of the human soul. Surely thou wast a teacher sent from God."

The shadows of evening gathered upon the earth, and low, fitful gusts stirred the branches. She raised her eyes upward, and again the new moon hung its silver barque upon the verge of the horizon. She arose and left the arbor. Tongatou met her at the entrance, and addressed her.

"The glory of the Shawanee has departed. Why should the Swaying Reed die for a dead people? Let her depart in peace."

"The pledge of the white maiden must be redeemed," she replied, solemnly.

An immense fire had been kindled in the centre of the ruined village, and groups were dispersed about it of men, women, and warriors escaped from the perils of defeat. When the pale girl appeared in their midst, murmurs of surprise at first, and then of triumph, mingled in the crowd. Here was a victim; one of the very race that had brought such suffering upon them, whose death might appease the dead, and upon whom they might wreak their revenge. Margaret paused not till she reached a group, in the midst of whom she beheld Kumshaka and the Prophet. Standing before them, she pointed her pale hand to where the moon lingered with its slender beam.

"The moon has filled its horn and disappeared, behold it is here again. The white girl has redeemed her pledge." She stood with folded arms and eyes bent upon the ground.

---

1 John 3:8.
2 Luke 17:21.
3 John 6:63.

At any other time such generosity would have won applause, even here in the midst of untutored nature; for the sentiments of virtue are universal. But now they were stung by recent defeat, and by loss and suffering; and to their superstitious vision the period demanded more than ever a victim. Slowly uprose the cry of death, gathering volume, till one fearful appalling yell awoke a thousand echoes. Margaret stood unmoved; her meek hands folded, and her face still and colorless. The Prophet led her to the midst, bound her unresisting hands to the stake, and commenced the preparatory rites.

There was a motion amid the outer crowd, a swaying and confused voices. A warrior leapt into the midst, and with a blow severed the cords of the victim. A faint cry burst from the lips of Margaret, and she fell into the arms of Tecumseh. It was but one moment of weakness, and she arose and stood up.

Fiercely did the chief eye the group of dispirited and traitorous warriors. Even the Prophet quailed before it, and Kumshaka withdrew deeper into the crowd. Tecumseh perceived it, and shaking his finger at the craven chief, he commanded him to remain. After a pause, in which the crackling of the flame and the rustling of the leaf alone were audible, in that hushed assemblage he spoke.

"I have been told all. Ye have severed the belt that should have bound our people together. Ye have provoked the rage of a people stronger than we, and with your own hands have dug the graves of your children. But tell me here with your own lips who hath counseled this? Who is the traitor to his people?"

"Kumshaka!" whispered the paled lips of Margaret.

"Kumshaka!" burst from the whole assemblage.

Scarcely had the words passed the lips, ere the tomahawk of Tecumseh flashed above his head, and the traitorous brother lay dead at his feet.

Margaret's eyes followed the gleam of the instrument, and she remained in the very attitude she had assumed, her eyes fixed in mute horror upon the body of him upon whom justice had been so summarily administered: her cheek ashy pale, and her figure like a statue endowed with life and breath, but denied the power of motion.

Tecumseh cast his eyes mournfully over the ruined village, and blackened woods, and the feeble remnant of his tribe. Where were now those great hopes that were to elevate his people? that far-seeing policy that was to place them among the nations of the earth? that union and peace that were to ensure their strength and perpetuity? Where were his own dreams of future glory and happiness? All—all were lost. As he looked abroad, the spirit of prophecy sprang to his lips.

"The doom of the red men has gone forth. The hunter shall cease from the chase, and the warrior from the field of battle. The mounds of the dead shall be levelled to the earth, and the graves of our fathers forgotten. The wigwam shall become a den for the fox, and the vine creep over the ruined canoe. The path to the spirit land is thronged with our people. They come from the great lakes, the valleys of the east and the west, and the sunlight of the south. They move their heads sadly as they move onward, and point to the land that is lost to their children. The Indian has no home upon the earth. Lo he has passed away, and his name is forgotten."

He folded his robe over his bosom, and stood lost in thought. At length he turned to Margaret, and took her cold hand in his. She moved not. He laid his hand upon her brow, it was like the touch of marble. The strong man groaned heavily. One moment he pressed the slight figure to his bosom, and then laid it upon the grass. He severed one lock of the long, beautiful hair, and turned away to the solitude of the forest.

Ackoree held back the powers of life, while the last fearful tragedy had been enacted, and she now stooped down and laid her hand upon the heart of the insensible Margaret. It beat faintly, and a savage joy lit up her fierce eye.

"Ackoree is glad that the white girl lives. She would have her suffer long."

She gazed into the open, unwinking eye, and held her cheek to catch the light breath.

"The white girl has been as wretched as Ackoree, and it does her heart good," she whispered, in husky tones.

With the battle of Tippecanoe, perished the great scheme of Indian confederation, which had so long been the forlorn hope of Tecumseh. But the scheme, conceived and upheld only by his own personal influence, was doomed to failure ere it was well completed. Had he been the foe to any other people, Americans would have been ready to do justice to his memory; but time will remove the prejudices that must always cloud the fame of a reformer, and when the name of the last Indian shall have been inscribed upon the scroll of eternity, monuments will be reared to his memory. Reflecting that Metacom, Pontiac,[1] and Tecumseh struggled for the very boon, for which our fathers bled and died, liberty for their wives and children, their names will be inscribed with the great and good of all ages, who have sought to do good for their country. The circumstance of failure will not detract from the ability with which their plans were conceived, or the devotion with which they yielded themselves to a great mission. They will cease to be enemies, and become patriots.

CONCLUSION.

Stoop o'er the place of graves, and softly sway
    The sighing herbage by the gleaming stone;
That they who near the church-yard willows stray,
    And listen in the deepening gloom, alone,
May think of gentle souls that passed away,
    Like thy pure breath, into the vast unknown,
Sent forth from heaven among the sons of men,
And gone into the boundless heaven again.—BRYANT.[2]

Four years elapsed after the incidents of our story. The battle of the Thames had destroyed the strength of the northern tribes, and the death of Tecumseh annihilated the bands of confederation. After the battle of Tippecanoe, he had made one more last effort at peace and union; but that had been its death-blow. His own marvelous eloquence, bravery, and great personal influence, for a while promised success, but they were unavailing. His people lacked hearts to feel as he felt, eyes to see as he beheld, and wisdom to understand the connection of events, and the promise and revealings of the future. He had stood, a solitary watcher in the strong tower of Indian safety; and when he fell, the beacon-light was extinguished, and for ever.

The characters of our story remained the same, allowing for the

---

1   The Wampanoag leader Metacom or Metacomet of Pokanoket
    (c. 1638–76), known by the English name of "King Philip," and the
    Ottawa leader Pontiac, or Obwandiyag (c. 1720–69) are both known
    for their resistance to European colonization—to the extent that two
    colonial wars bear their names: King Philip's War (1675–76) and
    Pontiac's War, also called Pontiac's Conspiracy or Rebellion (1763–66).
2   William Cullen Bryant, "The Evening Wind."

slight changes, which may have been already anticipated. Mrs. Jones abandoned the spinning-wheel, except at long intervals, when a day of bright sunshine, a brisk fire, and a peculiar harmony between atmospheric and nervous influences, awakened a sense of juvenility, when its brisk buzz might again be heard, and her trembling hand seen guiding the irregular thread, which afterward was duly exhibited to every visiter that might make his appearance. In general, however, she was seated in her large chair, on the warmest side of the hearth, her fingers slowly and mechanically busied with her knitting-needles, a work of the hands only, in which sight was unnecessary; and its monotony suited the quietness of decay. Occasionally, her lips moved, but whether in sympathy with her hands, or in the involuntary utterance of thought, as the child thinks aloud, is uncertain. When roused by the kindly voice of Anna, she would lift up her dim eyes, smile, and move her hands hurriedly, like a child taken by surprise. She now talked but little, and took small note of what passed about her; yet she always called Mrs. Mason, Anny; or when some buried memory arose from its sepulchre, awakening emotions of tenderness, she called her "Darter," which never failed to fill the eyes of both with tears.

Mrs. Mason's family had somewhat increased, but as her husband's worldly goods had also kept steady progress, nothing had impaired the hearty cheerfulness of her temper. She was wont to exhibit occasionally her wedding-dress, as a miracle of diminutiveness, compared with the ample size of those that now enveloped her goodly person; for Mrs. Mason had increased materially in size, as all hearty, good-natured women will, who are well to do in the world, and have little mental effort, except that which is prompted by ready sympathy, and active, confiding benevolence. She now employed 'help' constantly; and her children were always the tidiest, the smartest, the healthiest, and most daring to be found anywhere. Her notability, too, found ample employment in helping Alice, now Mrs. Mansfield, in the management of household matters. Were she ill, it did one's heart good to see with what alacrity Mrs. Mason donned her best cap and apron, and repaired thither to nurse her like a child, and absolve her from all care of the household. She never had a baking without a portion being kept in reserve for Alice, who reciprocated her kindness by presents of smart caps, and collars, and tunics for the little Masons.

The home of Alice was a pleasant cottage on the banks of the Wabash, and, just as she desired, close to her excellent friend, Mrs.

Mason. Her cheek had resumed its hue of health, though a slight expression of sadness lingered about the pure temples and the gentle lips, blending with that quietude of air that betokened a heart at rest. She was happy, as a wife, gratified in all her affections, needs must be. She was gentle and loving, trusting and meek; and the lot of such is always blessedness. She was still uncertain as to the fate of Margaret, and the thought of her often brought a pang to her heart. It was the one thorn to remind her that the blossoms of earth are thus armed.

It was the musing hour of twilight, when the repose stealing upon the earth predisposes the soul to reflection, and we feel, if ever, the beautiful propriety of scripture, that represents the patriarch going forth at even-tide to meditate. Alice was seated thus; and a beautiful child, of perhaps two years, weary with the busy sports of the day, stood at her knee, robed in its loose night-dress. Presently, it folded its chubby hands together, and lisped forth an evening prayer, while the roguish eyes were winking all the time, in vain efforts to keep them closed.

Little Margaret, for such was her name, wore the compact spiritual features of her aunt, and the dark, abundant curls looked the same that had waved over her shoulders in childhood. Even the turn of the head, the curve of the lip, were the same; and there, too, breathed her stateliness of air.

The door opened, and a moccasined foot appeared upon the threshold. Alice put by the child, and hastened forward. It was Tongatou! He was much changed, but his noble and generous bearing remained the same; and she welcomed him as a friend, and preserver. The child began to play with the plumes of his helmet, and she looked on, longing, and yet fearing to ask of Margaret. The chief took the fearless child in his arms, and gazed long and earnestly in its face.

"It is the spirit of the Swaying Reed," he at length said, and he turned away to conceal the tears, that sprang to his eyes.

Alice wept, but it may be they were tears of relief, as well as of sorrow. She seated herself by his side, and begged he would tell her all. Little Margaret hid her face upon her mother's bosom, and wept likewise; for a sorrowful tone, and a sad countenance awaken sympathy, even in the heart of a child.

When he revealed the secret of their escape from the village, and the devoted truth that impelled the return of Margaret, she sobbed aloud.

"Noble and generous girl, how could I so much have mistaken

her! But tell me, Tongatou, had it been otherwise, would she have returned to our people?"

The chief evaded the question, and went on to tell of the ruin that met them on their return, the appearance of Tecumseh, and the strange long sleep of the Swaying Reed.

"Thank God, she escaped that death of torture. And it was for me that she suffered all this—nor asked for reward, nor sympathy. Mysterious, and beautiful spirit! how unlike thy unworthy sister!"

The chief went on. "For many, many days the Swaying Reed neither moved nor spoke, but there was warmth about her heart, and we knew the spirit had not gone forth. Strange fear came upon us, for she had been as one from the spirit land. At length all was cold and still. Tongatou knew not till now, that her spirit was preparing to enter the body of the white child," and he stooped down over the sleeping babe, to read anew the evidence, and then went on.

"Our people will never believe she is dead, and they tell of her as one that is suffered to remain out of love to the poor Indian. Tongatou has heard her song at night, and heard her voice speaking to his heart. Tecumseh slept all night upon the grave of the Swaying Reed, and he felt that she came to comfort him. But he never smiled. His heart had long been dead. The sorrows of his people, and the death of the Swaying Reed broke the strength of the strong man. Tongatou bore him from the field of battle, and laid his body by the side of the Swaying Reed. Tongatou will dig his own grave at the will of the Great Spirit, and rest by his side. He has built his lodge there, and all night the spirit-bird sings upon the roof."

Opening his mantle he produced a small box, which Alice instantly recognized as having once been Margaret's. From this he took a long glossy curl, and held it to the light. "This I found in the bosom of Tecumseh; a part is buried with him, and this must sleep with Tongatou. The book of the white girl is here; he has no need of it:" and he presented the relic to Mrs. Mansfield. She clasped it to her bosom and wept freely, for the simple memorial and the recital of the chief, had restored at once the look and very tones of her sister, and the whole of her sad, suffering destiny.

When she lifted up her head, she was alone.

END OF THE WESTERN CAPTIVE.

INDIAN TRAITS:

THE STORY OF NISKAGAH[1]

---

1   Two years before *The Western Captive*, Oakes Smith (as "Mrs. Seba
Smith") published this captivity narrative in the popular monthly
magazine *The Ladies' Companion*. The story fictionalizes an historical
event that circulated both as example of Indian nobility and barbarity,
and Oakes Smith's interpretation offers a nuanced perspective, shaded
with ambiguity. It appeared in the July 1840 issue that also included
the first installment of *Mary Derwent; A Tale of the Early Settlers* by
Ann S. Stephens, who like Oakes Smith would go on to publish several
Beadle and Adams dime novels with Indian tales.

When a Pawnee Loup Brave has become weary of inaction, and desires to lead in some daring adventure, he may, according to the customs of his tribe, retire from the village, and erect, from the branches of trees, a temporary lodge, suspend, in some prominent place, the belt of wampum, and then seat himself quietly to smoke his pipe, certain that the adventurous and chivalric spirits about him will soon collect, and be ready to participate in any peril. If the leader be brave and popular, his volunteers are assembled with far greater celerity than a Highland gathering,[1] or the flocking of feudal retainers around the Barons of the olden time. In this way, too, the greatest secrecy prevails, as no one can know the object of the Brave, till it is his will to reveal it. The term, Brave, is an epithet of distinction conferred only upon those who have become renowned for their military prowess.

In the summer of 18—, the son of old Knife,[2] Chief of the Pawnee Loups, residing upon a branch of the Platte River, was observed in this way to retire from his people. The young chief, though scarcely upon the verge of manhood, was already distinguished in all the skill, daring and hardihood of an accomplished savage warrior, and had earned the envied appellation of *the bravest of the Braves*.

It was in vain that the beautiful wife of the Chief timidly approached the lodge, and tossing her infant before him, sought to engage his attention. He motioned her away, and resumed his pipe, neither by look nor gesture betokening that he marked the drooping sadness of her eye, and the lingering of her footsteps, as she turned to depart.

---

1   An event celebrating Scottish and Gaelic traditions, including athletic competitions.

2   Corrected from "Thife," as the story clearly refers to Knife Chief, or Lachelasharo, and his son Man Chief, or Petalesharo (c. 1797–c. 1832), of the Skidi, also known as the Pawnee Loup or Wolf Pawnee. In 1821, Petalesharo became a celebrated hero in the East when the story circulated of his rescue of a Comanche maiden from human sacrifice: in Washington, DC, his portrait was painted by Charles Bird King, and students of Miss White's Select Female Seminary presented him with a medal inscribed "To the Bravest of the Brave." In her autobiography, Oakes Smith writes, "Few who see the eagle-feathered head on our pennies know the story of this Achilles—this Hotspur of the woods, than which there is no more gallant legend connected with our Indian population—Petilosharo, like Pocahontis, had developed a higher perception of the higher and more beautiful claims of humanity, than had been awakened in the hearts of his people" (*HL* 366–67).

It may well be supposed that he remained not long in solitude. The best and bravest of the tribe sought his retirement—one by one they entered the lodge, took down the belt of wampum from the buffalo horns upon which it was suspended, drew it slowly through the left hand, restored it to its position, and then seated themselves beside him.

When the requisite number had assembled, the ceremonies preceding an adventure of the kind, commenced. Fastings and prayers, with mystical and varied incantations, were observed for many days. No one returned to his cabin to exchange greetings with his wife or kindred; every thing yielded to the solemn preparations of the warrior. They threw themselves, at night, upon mats of skin, and awaited the visitations of sleep, for then the Great Spirit would descend, and in dreams, make known his will to his children.

Morning came—the Pawnee Brave sprang from his couch with a flashing eye, his natural bearing of fierce defiance made still more terrible by the streaks of black paint upon his visage, which had been put on for the ceremonial. Grimly the chiefs eyed one another; for their dreams had been wild and disconnected, and the voice of the Great Spirit had failed to reach the ears of his children. The Chief advanced, his eyes gleaming red from beneath his helmet, and stretching forth his arm, upon which rattled the quills of his feathered robe, he thus addressed them:—

"Warriors, all night I could hear the whispering of the Great Spirit, but the words were borne away by a strong wind. I tried to listen, but I could not. There is a serpent in our midst. Let him depart."

His hand dropped by his side, and he stood with foot advanced, head inclined, and looking fiercely upon the group before him. Slowly a young warrior arose, and left the lodge.

A smile of derision passed over the face of the youthful Brave, and a low guttural expression of scorn escaped the lips of the grim chieftains. The recreant Brave had but lately married his bride, and in the silence of midnight he had stolen to her side. Thus had all their incantations been counteracted, and the expedition delayed.

All day were the warriors engaged in their mysterious rites, practiced with renewed and awful solemnity. The dim shadows of the old woods rested upon the lonely lodge, the pale stars looked down, and the night-breeze trembled into silence, while the Great Spirit passed over them, revealing his will.

When the morning came, the leader stood ready to disclose his intentions. He spoke of a tribe, distant a journey of many days, by whom their warriors had once been defeated, and the insult remained unavenged.

"Warriors, upon the land of our foe were many saplings; they were small—our children might have rooted them up. They are now mighty trees, casting their shadow upon the earth. They grew with the blood of our warriors. Chiefs, the old men of our foe, tell over their scalps, and they say, this, and this, and this, is the scalp of a Pawnee Loup. Let us avenge them. The hatchet has slept till it is covered in rust. We will dig it up, and make it bright till the blood of our people is revenged."

Grimly the chiefs arose, each adorned according to his rank as a Brave, or his skill as a huntsman. The plumes of the war-eagle nodding upon their crest, and the hairs of the white buffalo, and the scalps of the slain depending from their arms and legs. The bow and quiver hung at their back, one arm supported the shield of tough buffalo hide, and the right had grasped the massy[1] spear.

The Pawnee leader eyed, for a moment, the gallant band, and then with measured pace commenced their perilous march, the towering crest rising and falling to the long, undulating step, resembling the trot of one of their own forest deer.

With unerring sagacity they threaded the pathless woods—forded the rapid torrent, and traversed the wide and monotonous prairie. As they approached the doomed village, their vigilance was redoubled. Not a twig snapped beneath their moccasins—not a shrub was suffered to remain crushed by the footstep. They laid in ambush till the last torch expired in the wigwam, and the last wail of the restless child was hushed on the breast of its mother. Then arose the wild and appalling sound of the war-whoop. The battle-axe and the arrow found their victim, and the yell of the warrior, grappling with his foe, the stifled cry of childhood, and the shrill shriek of woman, mingled with the tumult of battle, and the crackling of flames. Fierce and desperate was the strife, and fearful the destruction. Scarcely a warrior was left to the tribe, to tell the tale of death. The Pawnees weary with labor, and laden with trophies, mounted the horses of their foes, and prepared to depart.

Beside the Pawnee leader rode a beautiful captive he had spared in the battle. Her father, rushing from his dwelling, had encountered the Paw-

---

1 Massive.

nee Loup upon the threshold, and a long and desperate battle ensued. The Chief fell, and the victor found within, a matron sheltering a child in her bosom, and her daughter by her side. The maiden approached the Brave with a faint smile, saying, "Would you kill a Squaw?" The uplifted weapon fell to his side, and the cabin was spared.

The captive was scarcely fifteen, yet had she sprung to the maturity and rounded outline of early womanhood. A world of passion seemed slumbering beneath the dreamy lids, and there was a litheness of motion, and gleamings of vivacity through the voluptuous indolence of the untutored girl, that might have won the admiration of more cultivated observers. Her dress was a snowy robe, made of the skin of the mountain goat, ornamented with the quills of the porcupine, gorgeously colored. Leggins[1] and moccasins of the same material, and similarly adorned, the springing curve of the latter giving promise of a small, elegantly formed foot. Her long, abundant hair, parted from the forehead, fell in braids far below the girdle. She managed the small restive animal which she rode, with a skill and dexterity not unmarked by her captor, who might thence be pardoned the display of the like accomplishment in the presence of one so fair, and so well qualified to appreciate it.

Dauntlessly all day did she ride beside the Pawnee Loup, a captive, yet with a lofty bearing, an air of proud indifference, that neither sought nor repelled sympathy; threading her way through the dense forests, galloping over the prairies, and plunging her horse into the stream to ford the rivers that impeded their progress. At night, she slept upon her couch of skins, nor dreamed of danger. The accidents of death and captivity were too frequent in the history of Indian life, to elicit much emotion, and the separation from her kindred was little different from what it would probably have been, had this been her bridal excursion, as scarcely ever did a maiden of her tribe marry one of their own people. True, her captivity might close in torture, and a lingering death, but she was a child of the woods, with a native apathy as to all evils in the possible future, and when trial should come, was ready to meet it in any shape, with a spirit worthy of her race.

Once she placed her fingers upon the gray-haired scalp of an old man, that hung at the girdle of the Brave, and said in a low voice, "It was my father's."

---

1   Leggings.

A flush passed over the brow of the Pawnee Loup, and he looked earnestly in the face of the poor girl.

"He died the death of a brave chief," he at length replied.

"Yes," responded the maiden, mournfully, "but he has no son to avenge his death; his memory will be like the leaf of autumn when it is dry. Would that Niskagah had been a son!"

They had now approached within view of the village. It stood upon an elevated plain, rich in pasturage, the river sweeping by in front, with its perpetual beauty, and untiring melody, and flanked by a heavy forest, undulating in the distance, draping the hills in verdure, and lovingly embracing the little lakes that sparkled in the sunshine, like diamonds scattered in the great wilderness. The party came to a halt, while a messenger was dispatched to the village with notice of their arrival.

Instantly all was commotion, and a multitude approached to escort the victorious chiefs to the council lodge. The women brandished the weapons of war, elevated the trophies of victory, and led the way with cries of exultation. The wife of the leader conveyed the captive to her own cabin, presented her with parched corn and venison, and spread the mats for her repose.

Solemnly and in silence assembled the chiefs in council, to hear the result of the expedition, and determine the fate of the prisoner. The Pawnee leader gave the particulars of the enterprise, with a brevity becoming the character of a chief, already renowned, not only for his skill in battle, but wisdom at the council hall. Revenge, rather than plunder, had been the incitement to action, and they had returned, laden with the scalps of the foe, and a daughter of the chief of the tribe, to await the will of the council board. The warriors of their foemen had fallen in battle, and women and children alone remained to tell, in after years, of the deadly vengeance of the Pawnee Loup.

It was the great festival of the Buffalo Hunt, but a mortality had appeared amongst them, and the animals were sickly and scarce, and hardly rewarded the labor of the hunter. Their Medicine men had hinted at a solemn sacrifice necessary to appease the wrath of the malignant spirit.

An old man arose, trembling with age, his hair white with the frosts of a century. He bowed heavily upon his staff, and cast his dim eyes over the assembly.

"Brothers, I am an old man; the hunters that went with me to the chase, have departed. The warriors that followed me into battle, are not. The sapling that I bent when a child, is now a gnarled tree, grey with the moss of years—such am I. Many suns ago, the evil spirits destroyed our game as they do now. We had forgotten to do them honor. Then we offered a human sacrifice at our great festival, and they were appeased, and the buffalo and the deer came down to drink in our rivers, and fed upon the great prairies. The Great Spirit has reserved the captive maiden, that his children may do what is right."

Low sounds of applause spread over the assembly, and when the chiefs separated, it was to prepare, the next day, for the great sacrifice which should avert the evils that threatened the tribe.

Niskagah was in the cabin of her captor when told of the fate that awaited her. An instant flush mounted to her cheek and temples, as if a pang had forced the blood, in a strong current, from the heart, and then it retreated, leaving in its place a fearful pallor. She raised her dark eyes imploringly to the face of the Pawnee Loup, but she met only the stolid look of an unsympathising heart. Ashamed of her weakness, she raised herself to her full height, threw back the masses of her jetty hair, and addressed him in a tone of defiance.

"Niskagah is the daughter of a great chief—she fears not to die. The Pawnee Loup is a brave chief—he took the scalp of an old man;" and she laughed in scorn.

For a moment lightning seemed to dart from the eyes of the young chief; and then he folded his arms and moved not while she continued—

"The Pawnee Loups know not how to torture their enemies—they are faint-hearted. They should have spared our chiefs to teach them. Our young men had eaten the hearts of the Pawnee Loup warriors; it made them strong. Every chief had the scalp of a Pawnee Loup at his girdle. Would Niskagah might die by the hands of a brave people— but the Pawnee Loups are faint-hearted—they cannot torture her."

The night came on, burdened with wind and rain. The tall grass of the prairies undulated like the vexed waters of the ocean, and the river, swollen by the mountain torrents, roared over its rocky channel, foaming and tumultuous. Niskagah arose from her bed of skins, and looked forth into the darkness of the night. She thought not of escape, for she had witnessed the defence of the village, and knew the attempt were useless. She was alone amidst the solitude of the night, and the wild uproar of the elements, and now her woman's nature returned, and she pressed her hands upon her brow, and wept bitterly. All that instinctive clinging to life that belongs to humanity in every condition, pressed upon her, and made her recoil from the prospect of its speedy termination, with all the wildness of terror. The mode, too, protracted and horrible, glared up before the eyes of the lone girl, and her flesh already palpitated under the torture of the burning pitch, or quivered under the knife. The pride of her race, and the daring bitterness of her own proud spirit forsook her, now that she was alone with none to witness her weakness, and powerful—very powerful became her woman's nature, with its shrinking dependence, its dread of solitary suffering, and tendril-like reaching for support. It may be that a vague dream of rescue from her gallant captor haunted her imagination, but she remembered his cold, unsympathising look, and the long night wore on, and still he slept. Hope died within her, and gave place to a wildness of excitement, and she rushed forth into the tempest.

Passing a cabin door, she was arrested by low moans from within, and companionship, even in suffering, drew her towards it. Suddenly a young mother raised the skins that concealed the entrance, and stood in the tempest, her long hair streaming in the wind, and she gave utterance to her sorrow in words like these:—

"Alas! why didst thou leave me, my child? My bosom is full of nourishment; why didst thou go? Who will nurse thee, my infant—who comfort and shelter thee? I cannot stay in my cabin while the cold wind is blowing about thee, and the rain sinking into thy bed. Thy skins are wet, my child, and thy cheek is cold and damp. Come to my bosom! Let me feed thee, and dry the rain from thy hair. I cannot rest in my wigwam—I cannot be warm and sheltered, whilst thou art cold in thy little grave."

Then she sank down upon the threshold, and uttered low wailing. It was the first sorrow of the young savage, the grief of the untutored mother at the loss of her first born.

Niskagah envied the lot of the unconscious child, that had thus gone to the land of the spirits, ere it had known the bitterness of life. Yet the grief of another had allayed the excitement of her own heart, and she returned to the cabin, with the renewed apathy of her people, and the gleamings of hope that can never quite desert the young heart. She slept long and soundly, and awoke only to the sound of the wild birds as they blithely hailed the purity of the morning. The heavy dew weighed down the herbage, and the clouds rolled away where the mountain tops seemed to beckon their coming. The river poured on with its swollen waters, chafing its rocky bed, and its hollow voice was heard where it plunged down a chasm of rocks, sending up a volume of spray, upon which the morning sun was showering rainbow gems, and crowning it as with a diadem.

The wife of the Pawnee Loup presented the captive with venison and fruits, but she motioned her away, saying, "Niskagah will talk with the Great Spirit—she will soon be in the land of shadows," then turning her face to the wall, she folded her robe over her bosom, and awaited those who should lead her to the stake.

All things were in readiness. Women were there, eager with expectation, and children, awed by the presence of their seniors, looked breathlessly at the elevated stake and instruments of torture.[1] Warriors were there adorned with paint, and the trophies of battle, and helmets nodding with plumes, but conspicuous in the midst was the son of the chief, with the eagle crest towering above the chiefs of the tribe. Wildly did the Medicine Man pursue the preliminary ceremonies, singing chaunts in a low, guttural tone, keeping time with measured step, and then tossing his arms in the air, raising his voice to a piercing scream, the bells of his robe jangling, and scalps fluttering in the wind. At length bounding from the ground, he returned, slowly leading in the victim, her wrists crossed meekly before her, and her unbound hair falling like a black veil nearly to her feet. Her step was feeble, and her lips compressed, as if to crowd back all memory of weakness.

As she approached the stake, she raised her eyes timidly from the ground, and encountered those of the young Pawnee Loup. Instantly the shrinking girl became the proud child of the woods, sending back the gaze of the eager multitude with a look of fearless defiance, and approaching the instruments of torture with a step almost of alacrity. A shout of exultation burst from the crowd at the noble bearing of the prisoner.

There was a rush—and the whole multitude sprang to their feet. The Pawnee Loup had bounded into the arena, and borne the captive from their midst—and off over the broad prairies, and up by the roar of the cataract was seen the tall form of the warrior, and the robe of

---

1   Writing of "Pawnee Barbarity" and the ceremony of ritual sacrifice to which Oakes Smith's story alludes, Henry Rowe Schoolcraft describes the torture of a 14-year-old captive Sioux girl by Pawnees who burn her with fire, shoot her with arrows, and cut off her flesh with knives before she finally succumbs to death (*Oneóta* 20–21).

the fearless maiden, as their fleet horses panted for the desert. Not a bow was strung, nor javelin poised. It was an impulse from the Great Spirit, which it were impious to counteract. Rapidly and in silence the fugitives pursued their flight. The Pawnee Loup scarcely glanced at his companion, as she gave the reins to her steed, and kept by his side, fearless and unhesitating, her eye dancing with renewed hope and happiness, and a smile playing upon her lip as they welled up from her young heart. At night, when the Chief spread her skins, in the shadow of the great forest, and watched her slumbers at a distance, Niskagah slept with the security of a child. When she awoke, she laved[1] her face in the brook that bubbled at her feet, and braided her abundant hair, using it for a mirror. Seven days had they pursued their perilous way through the wilderness, greeted only by the howl of the wild beast, and the barking of Wish-ton-wish,[2] when Niskagah knew they were approaching the country of her own people.

They were now on the outskirts of the forest, and the Chief pointed to the hills behind which arose the smoke of their cabins. Niskagah heard him in silence. When he turned to depart, she laid her hand timidly upon his arm, and with the pathos of nature, said—

"The home of Niskagah is desolate. Grass grows in the foot-path of our warriors, and the council-fire is extinguished. The hunter has ceased from the chase. The blood of our chiefs is still wet upon the threshold. I would not behold it."

"Niskagah is a proud maiden," replied the Brave. "She will be Chief of her tribe, and she will teach her young men to take vengeance on the Pawnee Loups. Niskagah must be the wife of a great chief, who has many wives, for she would scorn to cook his venison, and make his wampum belts and moccasins."

The girl sprang to his side, all the passion of her nature beaming from her dark flashing eyes. The Chief bent his looks admiringly upon the beautiful girl, and her lids fell under his ardent gaze. Her head drooped, and her voice was low and sweet.

"Niskagah is proud; she is the daughter of a great chief—but she is not too proud to love—and love would make her very gentle"— and her round lip quivered with the timidity of her sex.

It may be that the Pawnee Loup remembered his own fair bride, singing a lullaby to his child—for he turned, away, and Niskagah

---

1   Washed.
2   Prairie dog.

remained motionless till the forest hid him from her view, and then in weariness and solitude sought the ruins of her village.

When the Brave returned to his own council hall, none questioned his right to do as he had done. He was wise in council, and brave in battle, and his will had the authority of law. But his wife saw the growing gloom upon his brow, and that her own smiles could not dispel it. His wigwam was lonely, and the game he killed in the chase, went to the cabins of others, for he had few to eat it. She tried often to give utterance to the thoughts of her heart, but they died upon her lips. But she had determined on the great sacrifice, for her love sought only the happiness of its object.

She had nursed her infant to sleep, and laid him on the skins beside its father, and then in a low voice she said—

"The Brave grows weary of his cabin—it is lonely. Niskagah is very beautiful, and she loves the Pawnee Loup."

She said no more, but pressed her lips to the cheek of her child, and when she raised her head, a tear had fallen upon it. The Chief took her to his bosom, and the wife wept long and bitterly. Yet she urged his departure, for she saw the beauty of the captive was still fresh in his memory.

With woman, love is ever the same, whether in the halls of elegance and refinement, or the simple cabin of the savage—it is still true to its nature—still self-sacrificing and enduring; twining flowers and verdure about the shrine of its idol, while its own heart is desolate and broken.

MACHINITO, THE EVIL SPIRIT;

FROM THE LEGENDS OF IAGOU[1]

"The Pagan world not only believes in a myriad of gods, but worships them also. It is the peculiarity of the North American Indian, that while he believes in as many, he worships but one, the Great Spirit."—(*Schoolcraft.*)

---

1 See Henry Schoolcraft's introduction to Oakes Smith's telling of this legend in "Idea of an American Literature based on Indian Mythology" in Appendix D4.

CHEMANITOU, being the master of life, at one time became the origin of a spirit, that has ever since caused himself and all others of his creation a great deal of disquiet. His birth was owing to an accident. It was in this wise.

METÓWAC, or as the white people now call it, Long Island, was originally a vast plain, so level and free from any kind of growth, that it looked like a portion of the great sea that had suddenly been made to move back and let the sand below appear, which was the case in fact.

Here it was that Chemanitou used to come and sit, when he wished to bring any new creation to the life. The place being spacious and solitary, the water upon every side, he had not only room enough, but was free from interruption.

It is well known that some of these early creations were of very great size, so that very few could live in the same place, and their strength made it difficult for Chemanitou, even to controul[1] them; for when he has given them certain elements, they have the use of the laws that govern these elements, till it is his will to take them back to himself.

Accordingly, it was the custom of Chemanitou, when he wished to try the effect of these creatures, to set them in motion upon the island of Metówac, and if they did not please him, he took the life out before they were suffered to escape. He would set up a mammoth or other large animal, in the centre of the island, and build him up with great care, somewhat in the manner that a cabin or a canoe is made.

Even to this day may be found traces of what had been done here in former years; and the manner in which the earth sometimes sinks down [even wells fall out at the bottom here,] shows that this island is nothing more than a great cake of earth, a sort of platter laid upon the sea, for the convenience of Chemanitou, who used it as a table upon which he might work, never having designed it for anything else; the margin of the CHATIEMAC, (the stately swan,) or Hudson river, being better adapted to the purposes of habitation.

When the master of life wished to build up an elephant or mammoth he placed four cakes of clay upon the ground, at proper distances, which were moulded into shape, and became the feet of the animal.

Now sometimes these were left unfinished; and to this day the green tussocks, to be seen like little islands about the marshes, show where these cakes of clay had been placed.

---

1   Control.

As Chemanitou went on with his work, the NEEBANAWBAIGS (or water spirits,) the PUCK-WUD-JINNIES, (Fairies[1]) and indeed all the lesser manittoes,[2] used to come and look on, and wonder what it would be, and how it would act. When the animal was quite done, and had dried a long time in the sun, Chemanitou opened a place in the side, and entering in, remained there many days.

When he came forth, the creature began to shiver and sway from side to side, in such a manner as shook the whole island for many leagues. If his appearance pleased the master of life he was suffered to depart, and it was generally found that these animals plunged into the sea upon the north side of the island, and disappeared in the great forests beyond.

Now at one time Chemanitou was a very long while building an animal, of such great bulk, that it looked like a mountain upon the centre of the island; and all the manittoes, from all parts, came to see what it was. The Puck-wud-jinnies especially made themselves very merry, capering behind his great ears, sitting within his mouth, each perched upon a tooth, and running in and out of the sockets of the eyes, thinking Chemanitou, who was finishing off other parts of the animal, could not see them.

But he can see right through every thing he has made. He was glad to see them so lively, and bethought himself of many new creations while he watched their motions.

When the Master of Life had completed this large animal, he was fearful to give it life, and so it was left upon the island, or work-table of Chemanitou, till its great weight caused it to break through, and sinking partly down it stuck fast, the head and tail holding it in such a manner as to prevent it from going down.

Chemanitou then lifted up a piece of the back, and found it made a very good cavity, into which the old creations, which failed to please him, might be thrown.

He sometimes amused himself by making creatures very small and active, with which he disported[3] awhile, and finding them of very little use in the world, and not so attractive as the little Vanishers, he would take out the life, holding it in himself, and then cast

---

1   [Oakes Smith's note:] Literally, little men, who vanish.
2   Spirit beings or gods.
3   Frolicked.

them into the cave made by the body of the unfinished animal. In this way great quantities of very odd shapes were heaped together in this *Roncomcomon*, or "Place of Fragments."

He was always careful to first take out the life.

One day the Master of Life took two pieces of clay and moulded them into two large feet, like those of a panther. He did not make four—there were two only.

He stepped his own feet into them, and found the tread very light and springy, so that he might go with great speed, and yet make no noise.

Next he built up a pair of very tall legs, in the shape of his own, and made them walk about awhile—he was pleased with the motion. Then followed a round body, covered with large scales, like the alligator.

He now found the figure doubling forward, and he fastened a long black snake, that was gliding by, to the back part of the body, and let it wind itself about a sapling near, which held the body upright, and made a very good tail.

The shoulders were broad and strong, like those of the buffaloe, and covered with hair—the neck thick and short, and full at the back.

Thus far Chemanitou had worked with little thought, but when he came to the head he thought a long while.

He took a round ball of clay into his lap, and worked it over with great care. While he thought, he patted the ball upon the top, which made it very broad and low; for Chemanitou was thinking of the panther feet, and the buffaloe neck. He remembered the Puck-wud-jinnies playing in the eye sockets of the great unfinished animal, and he bethought him to set the eyes out, like those of a lobster, so that the animal might see upon every side.

He made the forehead broad and full, but low; for here was to be the wisdom of the forked tongue, like that of the serpent, which should be in his mouth. He should see all things, and know all things. Here Chemanitou stopped, for he saw that he had never thought of such a creation before, one with but two feet, a creature who should stand upright, and see upon every side.

The jaws were very strong, with ivory teeth, and gills upon either side, which arose and fell whenever breath passed through them. The nose was like the beak of the vulture. A tuft of porcupine quills made the scalp-lock.

Chemanitou held the head out the length of his arm, and turned it first upon one side and then upon the other. He passed it rapidly through the air, and saw the gills rise and fall, the lobster eyes whirl round, and the vulture nose look keen.

Chemanitou became very sad; yet he put the head upon the shoulders. It was the first time he had made an upright figure. It seemed to be the first idea of a man.

It was now nearly night; the bats were flying through the air, and the roar of wild beasts began to be heard. A gusty wind swept in from the ocean, and passed over the island of Metówac, casting the light sand to and fro. A heavy scud was skimming along the horizon, while higher up in the sky was a dark thick cloud, upon the verge of which the moon hung for a moment, and then was shut in.

A panther came by and stayed a moment, with one foot raised and bent inward, while he looked up at the image, and smelt the feet, that were like his own.

A vulture swooped down with a great noise of its wings, and made a dash at the beak, but Chemanitou held him back.

Then came the porcupine, and the lizard, and the snake, each drawn by its kind in the image.

Chemanitou veiled his face for many hours, and the gusty wind swept by, but he did not stir.

He saw that every beast of the earth seeketh its kind; and that which is like draweth its likeness unto himself.

The Master of Life thought and thought. The idea grew into his mind that at some time he would create a creature who should be made not after the things of the earth, but after himself.

He should link this world to the spirit world,—being made in the likeness of the Great Spirit, he should be drawn unto his likeness.

Many days and nights, whole seasons, passed while Chemanitou thought upon these things. He saw all things.

Then the Master of Life lifted up his head; the stars were looking down upon the image, and a bat had alighted upon the forehead, spreading its great wings upon each side. Chemanitou took the bat and held out its whole leathery wings, (and ever since the bat, when he rests, lets his body hang down,) so that he could try them over the head of the image. He then took the life of the bat away, and twisted off the body, by which means the whole thin part fell down over the head, and upon each side, making the ears, and a covering for the forehead like that of the hooded serpent.

Chemanitou did not cut off the face of the image below, he went on and made a chin, and lips that were firm and round, that they might shut in the forked tongue, and the ivory teeth; and he knew that with the lips and the chin it would smile, when life should be given to it.

The image was now all done but the arms, and Chemanitou saw that with a chin it must have hands. He grew more grave.

He had never given hands to any creature.

He made the arms and the hands very beautiful, after the manner of his own.

Chemanitou now took no pleasure in his work that was done—it was not good in his sight.

He wished he had not given it hands; might it not, when trusted with life, might it not begin to create? might it not thwart the plans of the master of life himself!

He looked long at the image. He saw what it would do when life should be given it. He knew all things.

He now put fire in the image: but fire is not life.

He put fire within, and a red glow passed through and through it. The fire dried the clay of which it was made, and gave the image an exceedingly fierce aspect. It shone through the scales upon the breast, and the gills, and the bat-winged ears. The lobster eyes were like a living coal.

Chemanitou opened the side of the image, *but he did not enter.* He had given it hands and a chin.

It could smile like the manittoes themselves.

He made it walk all about the island of Metówac, that he might see how it would act. This he did by means of his will.

He now put a little life into it, but he did not take out the fire. Chemanitou saw the aspect of the creature would be very terrible, and yet that he could smile in such a manner that he ceased to be ugly. He thought much upon these things. He felt it would not be best to let such a creature live; a creature made up mostly from the beasts of the field, but with hands of power, a chin lifting the head upward, and lips holding all things within themselves.

While he thought upon these things, he took the image in his hands and cast it into the cave.

But Chemanitou forgot to take out the life!

The creature lay a long time in the cave and did not stir, for his fall was very great. He lay amongst the old creations that had been thrown in there without life.

Now when a long time had passed Chemanitou heard a great noise in the cave. He looked in and saw the image sitting there, and he was trying to put together the old broken things that had been cast in as of no value.

Chemanitou gathered together a vast heap of stones and sand, for large rocks are not to be had upon the island, and stopped the mouth of the cave. Many days passed and the noise grew louder within the cave. The earth shook, and hot smoke came from the ground. The Manittoes crowded to Metówac to see what was the matter.

Chemanitou came also, for he remembered the image he had cast in there, and forgotten to take away the life.

Suddenly there was a great rising of the stones and sand—the sky grew black with wind and dust. Fire played about the ground, and water gushed high into the air.

All the Manittoes fled with fear; and the image came forth with a great noise and most terrible to behold. His life had grown strong within him, for the fire had made it very fierce.

Everything fled before him and cried—MACHINITO—MA-CHINITO—which means a god, but an evil god!

The above legend is gathered from the traditions of Iagou, the great Indian narrator, who seems to have dipped deeper into philosophy than most of his compeers.[1] The aboriginal language abounds with stories related by this remarkable personage, which we hope to bring before the public at some future time. Whether subsequent events justify the Indian in making Long Island the arena of the production of Machinito or the Evil Spirit, will seem more than apocryphal to a white resident. However we have nothing to do except to relate the fact as it was related.

As to these primitive metaphysics, they are at least curious; and the coolness with which the fact is assumed that the origin of evil was accidental in the process of developing a perfect humanity, would, at an earlier day, have been quite appalling to the schoolmen. E.O.S.

---

1   Oakes Smith describes Iagou as "an Indian storyteller" (22) in her
    novel *The Salamander: A Legend for Christmas* (1848). In *Oneóta*,
    Schoolcraft writes that Iagou "is the god of the marvellous, and many
    most extravagant tales of forest and domestic adventure are heaped
    upon him" (458).

BELOVED OF THE EVENING STAR:

AN INDIAN LEGEND

CHAPTER I.

Then list the legend long since heard
Beside the Red man's winding river,
What time the wilds and forests lone
Were held by right of bow and quiver.

Emma C. Embury.[1]

Every place of any picturesque pretension has its "Lover's Leap," a cliff, high and rugged, shelving over a boiling flood, which became at one time the scene of a thrilling tragedy. Strange that an emotion of such universal import as Love, should be treated with so little reverence by the constitution of society; that a sentiment involving so much of human happiness or misery, affecting health, intellect, and life itself, should be the subject for gibes and jokes, instead of being met, as it should be, with solemn and holy thought, and deep, earnest reverence, as of a mystery belonging to the soul itself and not to be profaned. Laws are made not to guard the sacredness of this necessity of our being, but to guard inviolate the sacredness of contract. "This ought ye to do, and not to leave the other undone."[2] We all weep over the wrongs and sorrows of loving hearts; history, literature, the dweller of the palace, and the peasant beside the "stile," each and all are alive to the same sentiment, and suffer the same griefs, yet no man has said to his neighbour, "Come, let us see if we cannot do something to right this great human wrong; let us see to it that the congenial stand only in relation, and thus do away the greatest temptation to evil in the minds of the weak and the erring."

The Ken-dus-keag is a narrow tributary of the Penobscot in the State of Maine. Having at one time by some great convulsion forced itself through the primitive rocks of that region, its banks are left wild and broken, seeming altogether too majestic for the foaming, noisy little trough of water gurgling beneath. Two miles from the city of

---

1   Emma Catherine Embury (1806–63), "The Star Flower: A Forest Legend." Embury's poem and Oakes Smith's "The Acorn; A Forest Legend" are both collected in *The Forest Legendary; Or, Metrical Tales of the North American Woods*, edited by John Keese (New York: W. Van Norden and J. Adams, 1845).
2   Matthew 23:23; Luke 11:42.

Bangor is a cliff upon its margin, something more than two hundred feet in height, which bows itself towards the opposite shore, whose dissevered rocks still yearn for their old companionship. Here is the place where one given to romance would be sure to look for some fine old legends, some tale of stirring adventure or beautiful sentiment, to give vitality and human interest to what might else be the waste place of nature. Accordingly we find the story of Mequa (the Squirrel, literally), the graceful Indian of the Penobscot, already associated with the spot long before the European had looked upon its beauty, or made its bright waters subservient to the purposes of thrift.

Mequa was not a native of this region, but a girl taken captive after the defeat of one of the tribes farther to the north. She was originally designed for sacrifice; but her exceeding grace, her vivacity and tenderness, so won upon the hearts of her captors that the ceremony was delayed, and finally passed out of mind. Unlike the maidens of the tribe into which she had been adopted, who were laborious, patient of fatigue, and content to be the slaves rather than companions of their warrior and hunter lovers and husbands, Mequa openly refused such bondage, laughed at the burdens attempted to be forced upon her, and with such pretty petulance shrunk from wigwam toil, that she soon became the privileged pet of the tribe. In return she wrought moccasins and belts with unequalled skill and elegance, she arranged wampum for the warriors, and ornaments for the squaws in a style of excellence they had never before witnessed, so that Mequa became to these children of the woods indispensable, in the same way that an accomplished milliner is so to the more civilized women of our cities.

Coquettishly fond of ornament herself, she never appeared unadorned with feathers and shells, wild berries and furs of the choicest kind; indeed, she must have been to the Indian mind what a rare piece of art is to the civilized, a thing to be looked upon with delight and admiration disconnected with the ordinary emotions of humanity, for the pleasuring and the adorning of Mequa became the delight of the tribe. The name they had given her indicated their perception of her character. Mequa, the Squirrel, was in truth as freakish, as gay, as whimsical, as coquettish as this rarest masquerader of the woods, and withal as graceful, as loveable, as pertinaciously attachable.

One of the whims of Mequa was to sleep in the summer nights

within a cave, still to be seen to the right of the cliff. This cave is large enough to hold five or six persons; it is open towards the water side only; below the floor the bank is nearly perpendicular, from the sides of which spring trees of the largest size, so as to hide the mouth entirely from one unacquainted with its existence. The access is difficult on account of the steepness of the shore, but the spot is sheltered and most lovely when once secured. In the days of Mequa, when the forest was unbroken, the river unshackled, and nature in her primitive glory, it might well tempt a wayward girl to its secure and most tranquil retreat. Here the birds yielded a wilderness of melody, the sunbeams glinted upon the leaves, and the wind, which found no lodgment within, tilted the branches of the trees, and whispered all day in the pines on the hill top. The steady roar of the falls lent a monotonous melody, relieved at intervals, by that changeful sound, as if a new gush of accumulated water gave them a deeper voice.

This freak of Mequa's passed in the tribe as a freak, to all but Pusános, the Panther, who saw something covert and mysterious in this solitary retreat. Pusános was the son of the old chief of the tribe, a youth as agile, as alert, and as deadly too, as the creature whose name he bore. He had long been the secret lover of the girl, and no one doubted his love was returned with a singleness and devotion peculiar to one with such individuality of character as Mequa; yet it was most true that she took delight in teasing her lover, in exciting his jealousy, and affecting for the whim of the moment sentiments entirely foreign to the reality. No sooner did she find Pusános uneasy at her bower in the cave, than she became the more pertinacious in her disposition to go there. What was at first the pretty daring of a wayward girl, became in time the weapon of a woodland coquette.[1]

Whether it was that a fear of her lover grew gradually upon the mind of the girl—for indeed he became stern, silent, and observant of her motions—or whether there might have been real mystery, is now needless to inquire, for it was observed that she became daily timid and sensitive, regarding the young chief with an expression of such soulful tenderness, so entirely unlike her

1   [Oakes Smith's note:] This cave remains as above described. The people in the vicinity call it the Devil's cave. We trust hereafter they will call it Mequa's cave, as being more sonorous to "ears polite."

former gayety, that the coldness and reserve of Pusános was the more surprising. Indifferent to her ornaments, listless in her motions, the dainty qualities of character, which had won for her the pretty appellative of Mequa, seemed fast departing from the wild-wood beauty.

At the period of the change we have just described, Mequa, in the exuberance of her mischief, or in the recklessness of her despondency, had slept three successive nights in the cave. The third morning she came forth pale and trembling, with her wampum girdle bound around her arm, and an arrow in her hand dabbled in blood. Returning to the lodge of her foster parents, she sat down in the farthest part alone, and weeping bitterly. Accustomed to her many moods, the old woman contented herself with wrapping the skins together beneath her head, and asking of the wound. Mequa returned no answer excepting by her tears and holding up the arrow which bore upon it the totem of Pusános. All day the poor girl sat in this wise, uttering no word of complaint. As the night approached she went out and sat down by the council-fire in the centre of the village. Surprised at this strange act, the elders gathered about the spot and waited silently an explanation of her will.

CHAPTER II.

'Tis the middle watch of a summer's night—
The earth is dark but the heavens are bright:
Nought is seen in the vault on high
But the moon and the stars and the cloudless sky,
And the flood which rolls its milky hue,
A river of light in the welkin blue.

Drake.[1]

For three years the hunting grounds of the tribes had been nearly desolate of game. The hunters pursued it through long and perilous ways, but the supply had been too scanty to meet their wants. Vainly had sacrifices been made; all spells and incantations proved of no avail; the women grew sullen, and disheartened, while the

---

1   Joseph Rodman Drake (1795–1820), "The Culprit Fay."

men, weary of their complaints, and enfeebled by the famine, began to talk of a removal farther west. Mequa had scarcely seemed able to comprehend the sufferings of the people, for she was the foster daughter of an expert hunter, and beloved as she was by all around her, she found a supply always ready for her needs; she had kept herself free from anxiety from the natural hopefulness of her character, which found itself incapable of comprehending an evil till it was forced upon her, and because as yet she had suffered little inconvenience. Now, however, she appeared weighed down by the sufferings of the people. A conviction of want and misery, protracted and increasing, seemed to have fallen with stunning effect upon her mind.

Drawing her robe about the wounded arm, and folding her small wrist and hand over it, she arose and stood before them. She attempted to speak, but the words refused to leave her lips, and her breast only heaved with inarticulate sounds. At length she raised her head and cast a searching glance through the group. Pusános was not there, and the glare of the torch hid him from her view as he stood with his back against a hemlock, with foot and head advanced, watching her strange proceedings. Recovering firmness, Mequa went on, though her face was ashy pale, and she trembled in every limb.

"Three nights has a vision appeared to the eye of Mequa. Three nights has a youth fair as the moonbeams, still and solemn, come down from the Evening Star and bid me follow him. 'You must leave the tribe, Mequa,' he said, 'for I have blighted the corn and dispersed the game for your sake, and they will perish unless you leave them.'" "I will go away," continued the maiden, "I will bring no more evil upon the tribe."

The Chiefs had no doubt the Great Spirit had thus signified his will to the girl, and they sat long with heads reverently bent, suffering her to depart without a word. As she left the circle and came into the shadow cast by the great trees which flanked the settlement, Pusános sprang across her path. Mequa looked up in the face of the stern young chief, and stood, so calm, so sad, so utterly bereft of all save her deep inward woe, that even he, who had folded his arms and bent his proud eye scornfully upon her, relaxed his severity, and stooped his head to read the strange, mournful expression of her eyes. She did not move, but her lips trembled, and a tear which swelled under her lid remained there as if without its fellow.

"So then Mequa follows the youth of the Evening Star," at length the chief uttered bitterly.

The girl sprang forward and clasped her fingers upon his arm, and looked up searchingly into his face, as if a dim terrible truth grew upon her mind.

"I follow the will of the Great Spirit," she at length uttered falteringly.

"And who was the fair youth stealing with honey-words to the ear of the false-hearted maiden?" whispered Pusános.

"Mequa is very foolish, but she is not false; she goes to her doom for the good of your people," she answered mournfully, for indeed grief seemed to have deprived her of the power of resentment.

Pusános shook his head, and with a quick motion tore the robe from her wounded arm.

"Think you the Panther had set his fangs thus unless assured of wrong? Mequa shall not go forth—she shall be the scorn of her sex."

The girl dropped her arms to her side, and stood for a moment as if crushed and broken-hearted at the tone and words of her lover. At length she lifted her head, with its sweet earnest air of indignant spirit, and said, "Mequa would know the meaning of Pusános."

"Oh nothing, only that she loves this youth of the Evening Star."

"Mequa is doomed by the Great Spirit; she dare not love any more. She must pass as does the foam from the cataract, the mist over the river; the moonbeam when it steals out from the glen, and leaves all to blackness and grief."

The solemn tones of her voice, and the truthfulness of her look fell like a chill upon Pusános, and he murmured, "You do not love me, Mequa."

She burst into a flood of sorrowful tears, but was silent.

"Hear me, Mequa; three nights have you slept in the cave, and three nights have I sat all night upon the bank with the Ken-dus-keag between us. I saw you enter, heard your voice singing alone to the falls, and, Mequa, three times did I behold the youth of whom you speak steal adown to your resting-place. The third night I sent an arrow, which should have pierced the heart of the false-hearted maiden."

Mequa redoubled her tears. "I thought it was but Weeng.[1] I knew not the youth of the Evening Star came to me, although I saw him descend in my dreams. Oh, Pusános, will he take me from thee? In the Spirit Land wilt thou not find me?"

"Had you loved me, Mequa, you had not slept in the cave of Weeng. Even the stars above had not dared to love the chosen of Pusános, had she been true of heart."

Mequa wrung her hands bitterly. "Poor, foolish Mequa!" was all she could say.

"No, Mequa—you were full of weak fancies, and now all is lost. I could not trust you, even should you bring me the great shining stone of the White Hills, which though near at hand, as you climb the cliff, is for ever seen upon a more distant peak when the summit is gained.[2] But mind me, Mequa, do not attempt to escape. The arrow of Pusános shall find you if but a step from the village."

Passing on a few paces he turned back, and saw her still upon the spot, with her sweet eyes fixed upon him. He returned, and would have led her away, but she shrank from his touch, and looked imploringly into his face, saying,

"Let me go, Pusános, it is the will of the Great Spirit; I would save thy people from further harm. If I may not go, let the arrow of the Panther finish his work; why should Mequa perish by fire and torture?"

The Chief shuddered and bounded forward, as if even then his strong arm were enough to shield her from harm, although his heart was filled with the bitterness of distrust.

"Oh that Mequa had died with her people! Why should she live? Where is the joy of her heart? Where is the light of her path? She is alone in her grief—no eye weeps for her—no heart pities her—her dreams are evil, and yet her heart is not bad—Oh that she might die!" She had cast herself upon the ground, and in this way gave utterance to her emotions.

---

1   [Oakes Smith's note:] The Indian god of sleep.
2   [Oakes Smith's note:] "The Carbuncle of the White Hills" is often referred to in Indian legends, and the common people of that region have many vague and romantic stories connected with attempts to discover its existence.

CHAPTER III.

White man! I say not that they lie
Who preach a faith so dark and drear,
That wedded hearts in yon cold sky
Meet not as they were mated here.
But scorning not thy faith, thou must,
Stranger, in mine have equal trust.

Hoffman.[1]

A month went by, and the sufferings of the tribe were daily increasing. The chiefs wondered at the stay of Mequa after the announcement she had made. No one doubted the truth of the revealment, and people began to scorn the girl who shrank feebly from the mission of the Great Spirit. They looked when she should go forth to her solitary doom, and leave them again to the smiles of the Spirit of Good. They came to her wigwam, and demanded that she should be given up by her foster parents for the welfare of the tribe.

Mequa heard the tumult of voices, and she came to the door of the lodge. All shrank back with surprise, so pale and so changed had she become. They could still see the full lustrous eyes of the graceful Mequa, the sweet earnest mouth; but her cheek was thin, and her form swayed in its feebleness like a reed in the storm. Casting her mournful glance over the group, she saw not the person of the Panther, and a deadly chill grew upon her, for she thought of the tortures of the sacrifice to which she supposed herself doomed. But no one laid grasp upon her, and she stood with folded hands, waiting when they should speak.

"Mequa will obey the will of the Great Spirit," she said meekly, observing that all were silent. Passing through the group, she took her way to the cliff upon the banks of the Ken-dus-keag, which was within the area of the village. The people followed at a distance, not doubting that she would now obey the voice of the vision which had commanded her to leave her adopted tribe for the good of the people.

Her steps were feeble, and as she went on, tears, silent and hope-

---

1   Charles Fenno Hoffman (1806–84), "The Vigil of Faith, A Tale of Aboriginal Mesmerism."

less, fell from her eyes. Sometimes she stopped as if even then she clung to the idea that Pusános would save her, for she sent keen glances to the woody covert, and up the ravine, from whence she had so often seen him emerge in her days of gladness. But he came not, and she pursued her way alone, with the people mourning, yet demanding her doom.

Reaching the verge of the cliff she stood long peering down into the roaring mass, not in terror of the fall, for she gave back no repining glance, but as if communing with the solitude and immensity of the great world, from which she must depart. At length she lifted her eyes upward, and then it seemed as if the silvery mist which hung over the river veiled her in, and she floated downward, falling, and yet sustained.

As the day closed in, the hunters, laden with spoil, were entering the village, and Pusános was the first to detect the group in the rear of the cliff. Casting aside the burdens of the chase, he sprang with long bounds to the spot, just as the form of Mequa sank downward. One moment the light figure of the youth was poised upon the verge; one moment fixed and statue-like he stood between the spectator and the red warm light of the horizon; and then the cold gray headland loomed up as it was wont, and the river rolled beneath, chafing the rocks with its never-ceasing flow.

The people uttered a cry of grief, for the youth and maiden were the beloved of the tribe. As they lifted up their eyes, the clouds parted, and the new moon in the form of a silver bow, faint and slender, appeared as if hanging from the sky over the spot where the lovers had disappeared, and by its side was a bright star, white and most beautiful, and they knew it was Mequa, beloved of the Evening Star, who thus nestled at the side of Pusános, whose bow was placed in the heavens to protect the maiden so gentle and loving. Since that time, whenever the moon comes forth thus in the heavens, a slender bow with one meek star at her side, the Indians say it is Mequa and Pusános, and at such times they offer sacrifices to the memory of her, who through her gentle offering of herself brought them a fruitful harvest and an abundance of game. When she thus appears beside her lover, it is an omen of good.

It is not unusual for an Indian to dream in the way described in the above legend; that some great sacrifice, some immolation of himself, or some journey or labour is demanded of him for the public good, and the mandate is religiously obeyed. To shrink from the mission, to disregard the voice of the Great Spirit made audible in dreams, is considered to the last degree wicked and cowardly. Whatever evils may afterwards befall the individual or the public, would be regarded as a penalty for his impiety. It is curious to trace the analogy in this to the belief of the ancients, when dreams were treated with solemn reverence, and oracles were consulted to expound their terrible and momentous signification. We talk indignantly of the impositions practised in this way upon the multitude, and laugh at the absurd meanings thus attached to the vagaries of a heated and will-enfranchised brain; but it is more charitable, and more in accordance with the facts of human development, to suppose that the interpreter of dreams and the consulter of oracles were both alike deluded by the vagueness of mystery in which the human mind delights; that the mummeries[1] of the priest were practised less from the intent to deceive, than to produce a state best adapted to the purposes of clear vision. We are fast casting aside the crude shackles of superstition, and God only knows how much of the best part of religion is going also—its simpleness of faith, its earnest and affectionate hold of the heart, which clings to it with the tenacity of the Patriarch when he said, "I will not let thee go except thou bless me."[2] The cold intellectual assent of the understanding, however high in the abstract, is poor in comparison with that life-giving grasp which, though dimmed by excess of faith, is yet the grasp of one who feels a great and overwhelming human need.

Surely it is not well to make our religion, as the tendency of the age is, a matter for logical deduction, a subject for seventh-day speculation, when it should be a daily and hourly craving of the heart, a going forth of the spirit to commune with spirit, a beautiful lifting of the veil of the temple to behold the mystery and glory within. The instinctive faith of the child-man is better than this, "who sees

---

1 Ceremonies.
2 Genesis 32:26.

God in clouds and hears him in the wind,"[1] and who in the dimness of his reverence, gropes amid omens and dreams, in the blind fear of slighting the intimations of that all-pervading power, which he "ignorantly worships."[2]

---

1   Alexander Pope (1688–1744), *An Essay on Man* (1734), Epistle I, lines 99–112: "Lo, the poor Indian! whose untutor'd mind / Sees God in clouds, or hears him in the wind; / His soul proud science never taught to stray / Far as the solar walk or milky way; / Yet simple nature to his hope has given, / Behind the cloud topp'd hill, an humbler heaven; / Some safer world in depth of woods embraced, / Some happier island in the watery waste, / Where slaves once more their native land behold, / No fiends torment, no Christians thirst for gold. / To be, contents his natural desire; / He asks no angel's wing, no seraph's fire; / But thinks, admitted to that equal sky, / His faithful dog shall bear him company" (London: John Sharpe, 1829).

2   Acts 17:23, "For as I passed by, and beheld your devotions, I found an altar with this inscription, TO THE UNKNOWN GOD. Whom therefore ye ignorantly worship, him declare I unto you."

FROM "THE SAGAMORE OF SACO:

A LEGEND OF MAINE"

Never was country more fruitful than our own with rich materials of romantic and tragic interest, to call into exercise the finest talents of the dramatist and novelist. Every cliff and headland has its aboriginal legend; the village, now thrifty and quiet, had its days of slaughter and conflagration, its tale of devoted love or cruel treachery; while the city, now tumultuous with the pressure of commerce, in its "day of small things"[1] had its bombardment and foreign army, and its handful of determined freemen, who achieved prodigies of single handed valor. Now that men are daily learning the worth of humanity, its hopes and its trials coming nearer home to thought and affection; now that the complicated passions of refined and artificial life are becoming less important than the broad, deep, genuine manifestations of the common mind, we may hope for a bolder and more courageous literature: we may hope to see the drama free itself from sensualism and frivolity, and rise to the Shaksperian dignity of true passion; while the romance will learn better its true ground, and will create, rather than portray— delineate, rather than dissect human sentiment and emotion.

The State of Maine is peculiarly rich in its historically romantic associations. Settled as it was prior to the landing of the Pilgrims, first under Raleigh Gilbert, and subsequently by Sir Ferdinando Gorges,[2] whose colony it is fair, in the absence of testimony, to infer never left the country after 1616, but continued to employ themselves in the fisheries, and in some commerce with the West Indies, up to the time of their final incorporation with the Plymouth settlement. Indeed the correspondence of Sir Richard Vines,[3] governor of the

---

1 Zechariah 4:10.
2 Sir Ferdinando Gorges (c. 1565–1647) was an early investor and patent holder in colonial New England, a founder and governor of the Province of Maine who did not himself travel to America. Gorges was a shareholder in the Popham Colony in Maine, which was undertaken in 1607 with the 25-year-old Raleigh Gilbert (c. 1583–1634), second in command to George Popham (1550–1608). After Popham's death, Gilbert became the leader of the short-lived colony, which lasted little more than a year and was abandoned in 1608.
3 The English colonist Richard Vines (1585–1651) was also employed by Gorges to advance settlement in Maine after the Popham Colony failed. In 1616–17, Vines successfully passed the winter in Maine, as instructed by Gorges, in an attempt to establish the feasibility of enduring the region's climate.

colony under Sir Ferdinando Gorges, with the Governor of Plymouth, leaves no doubt upon this head; and it is a well known fact that the two settlements of De Aulney and De la Tour[1] at the mouths of the Penobscot and Kennebec rivers, even at this early age, were far from being contemptible, both in a commercial and numeric point of view. Added to these was the handful of Jesuits at Mont Desert, and we might say a colony of Swedes on the sea-coast, between the two large rivers just named, the memory of which is traditional, and the vestiges of which are sometimes turned up by the ploughshare. These people probably fell beneath some outbreak of savage vengeance, which left no name or record of their existence.

Subsequently to these was the dispersion of the Acadians, that terrible and wanton piece of political policy, which resulted in the extinction and denationalizing of a simple and pious people.[2] The fugitive Acadians found their way through a wilderness of forests, suffering and dying as they went, some landing in distant states, (five hundred having been consigned to Governor Oglethorpe[3] of Georgia,) and others, lonely and bereft, found a home with the humble and laborious farmers of this hardy state, whose finest quality is an open-handed hospitality. These intermarrying with our people here, have left traces of their blood and fine moral qualities to enhance the excellence of a pure and healthful population.

Then followed the times of the Revolution, when Maine did her part nobly in the great and perilous work. Our own Knox[4] was commandant of the artillery, and the bosom friend of Washington: our youth sunk into unknown graves in the sacred cause of freedom; and our people, poor as they were, for the resources of the state were then undeveloped, cast their mite of wealth into the national

---

1   Acadian settlements governed by Charles de Menou d'Aulnay (c. 1604–50) and Charles de Saint-Étienne de la Tour (1593–1666).

2   The French colony of Acadia included what are presently the Maritime provinces and eastern parts of Quebec and Maine. The expulsion of the Acadians by the British began in 1755.

3   James Edward Ogelthorpe (1696–1785), founder of the colony of Georgia. Admiral John Reynolds (c. 1713–88) was governor of Georgia when the Acadian exiles arrived.

4   Henry Knox (1750–1806) was a military officer under George Washington in the American Revolutionary War and the first Secretary of War in the United States.

treasury. Northerly and isolated as she is, her cities were burned, and her frontiers jealously watched by an alert and cruel enemy. Here, too, Arnold[1] sowed his last seeds of virtue and patriotism, in his arduous march through the wilderness of Maine to the capital of the Canadas, an exploit which, considering the season, the poverty of numbers and resources, combined with the wild, unknown, and uncleared state of the country, may compete with the most heroic actions of any great leader of any people.

A maritime state, Maine suffers severely from the fluctuations of commerce, but is the first to realize the reactions of prosperity. Her extended seaboard, her vast forests, her immense mineral resources, together with a population hardy, laborious, virtuous, and enterprising; a population less adulterated by foreign admixture than any state in the Union, all point to a coming day of power and prosperity which shall place her foremost in the ranks of the states, in point of wealth, as she is already in that of intelligence.

We have enumerated but a tithe of the intellectual resources of Maine—have given but a blank sheet as it were of the material which will hereafter make her renowned in story ...

---

1   Benedict Arnold (1741–1801) was a general for the American Continental Army but is best known for his betrayal of the cause and his open defection to the British side in 1780.

KINNEHO: A LEGEND OF MOOSEHEAD LAKE

VISIT TO MOOSEHEAD—LINES TO THE LAKE—OUR CAIRN BUILT.

In the interior of the State of Maine is a large lake, which, from its supposed resemblance in shape to the head of a moose, has received that appellation. Moosehead Lake, at the time we made a pilgrimage thereto, some few years since, was in the midst of an entire wilderness, the marge[1] covered with a dense forest, and the broad, beautiful waters alive with innumerable wild fowl. We remember the moon was large, and the atmosphere at midnight had that clear deepening blue, away into the lessening stars, that always fills the soul with a sense of the Infinite.

How lovely seemed this bowl of crystal beauty amid the hills! how solemn the shadow of those ancient trees, tall, motionless, and stretching away into the unknown desert! We listened to the lonely cry of the loon and the solitary call of the moose, the voices of huge unsocial denizens of this remote and soul-stirring region, till the heart throbbed wildly at its impressive grandeur.

In front was the bald head of Kinneho,[2] a high bluff rising from the centre of the lake; far to the left appeared what is quaintly called Squaw Mountain; fifty miles to the right, Katahdu[3] stands beneath his canopy of clouds alone and regal. Islands of rare beauty, inlets bordered with white sand, "like fringe upon a petticoat," rested in the moonlight, and beckoned the fancy away to delicious dreams of wild devoted love and a lodge in the wilderness. At our feet lay a Newfoundland dog, whose eyes wandered over the lake with such a look of superhuman intelligence and content, that we were sure he shared not our enthusiasm, but had an enthusiasm of his own: not dog enthusiasm for wild goose or duck; but the scene suggested the fairest dreams of poetry and romance to his heart—the doctrines of Pythagoras[4] assumed a new truth—we were sure some faithful and devoted soul was

---

1 Margin or edge; here, of the lake, as on p. 250.
2 Mount Kineo.
3 Mount Katahdin. Oakes Smith claims to be the first white woman to climb Mount Katahdin in an account of the trip published in the *Portland Daily Advertiser* in 1849.
4 The Greek philosopher and mathematician Pythagoras (c. 570–c. 490 BCE) believed in reincarnation or transmigration of souls.

struggling up to its best form in the shape of that dog; hereafter he would emerge as a lover worthy of a Sappho or a Heloise. Alas! that we shall have passed on to another sphere before that day shall arrive!

We visited the top of Kinneho, the first white woman (Heaven save the mark) that ever touched the summit. Reader, your pardon; we have a mind to tell a fact in connection with this journey. The chances for fame are precarious, you know. Women who write now are not a few slatternly, odd, withered-looking bugbears; they make a little array of nice, dashing, elegant feminines,[1] who are capable of anything that arrests their attention; from the darning of a pair of hose to the writing of an ode, the tending of the baby, compounding of the pudding, writing an epic, or breaking a heart, each and all they do with perfect facility, address, and comfort, both to themselves and others. Each lady writer understands the power of her sister author, and so far from disparaging her or it, and being eaten up with envy, as the uninitiated suppose, she is joyous and appreciating, and foresees great good to her kind from the accumulating power of womanmind; but she does see that the chances for her own selfish individual distinction are lessened by the numbers in the field, and she begins to repeat—

"Just what you hear you have, and what's unknown
The same—if Tully's, or your own."[2]

Well, we confess our exordium[3] is something long; but we shall come to our story, our little trumpet-peal of our own corner of fame, in the process of time. What was a wilderness five years agone is now a thrifty hamlet. A steamer plies upon Moosehead; an hotel, radiant in white and green, exults over Kinneho. Poets, artists, millwrights and schoolmasters have made the desert to blossom "like the rose"—oh no! like a vigorous and expanding cabbage—its lonely romance is over. Thrift and enterprise rejoice the spirit of the worldling,[4] and even we rejoice; although the co-

---

1 Females.
2 From Alexander Pope's *An Essay on Man* (1734).
3 Introductory part or beginning.
4 A person concerned with worldly matters or material things.

verts of Pan[1] are desecrated, genial hearthstones and household voice bring gladness wherever they appear; but not the less do we roll the sweet morsel of content under our tongue, inasmuch as Moosehead was ours in her primal loveliness, wild, heroic, and most beautiful; queen-like did she sit amid the hills, unsung and unvisited, and then we ventured a stop in her praise—

TO MOOSEHEAD LAKE. *(female)*

Lake of the beautiful! solemn and still,
How art thou sleeping by mountain and rill!
    Welcome to thee,
    Primal and free!
Rarely a footstep thy silence hath broken,
Poet-lip never thy beauty hath spoken;
Screened in the wilderness lonely and far,
As we see in the north sky one only star.

Lake of the cold clime, buried in wild-wood,
Ages of solitude over thee brood;
    The plunge of the bird
    In the distance is heard;
Softly away and away dies the sound,
Lost in the glens that encircle thee round:
Thou art a creature delighting to reign
Where the light-footed snow wakes no echo again.

Lake of the dark pine! imp of the north land!
Calmly in winter thou foldest thy white hand:
    The Frost-spirit here,
    With glittering spear,
Sits at thy feet with his pale bannered host;
Lover of thine long he clings to his post.
Sound the loud blast of his bugle by night,
The breast of the "Thaw King"[2] to fill with affright.

---

1   A Greek god of mountain wilds whose form is that of a man with the horns, hindquarters, and legs of a goat.

2   Most likely borrowed from Charles Fenno Hoffman's poem "The Thaw-King's Visit to New York," published in *The New-Yorker* 1.2 (1836): 24.

Lake of the mountain home! baring his brow,
Up from his flinty bed springs Kinneho;
　　　Lo! antlered and tall,
　　　'Gainst the heaven's blue wall,
Capping the bold cliff, the stately moose stands,
Snuffing the wind that from ice-covered lands
Tells where the moss and fir-tree are growing—
Tells where the stream from the iceberg is flowing.

Lake of the eyrie! befitting thy pride,
Springs the bald eagle the tempest to ride:
　　　White-headed storm bird,
　　　Wild is thy scream heard,
Waking the desolate rocks at thy call,
Pelts the gray rain and the snow javelins fall,
Nor turns thy strong wing aside from its flight,
The tumult is gladness to thee and delight.

"Chainless

Lake of the wilderness, joy of the heart,
Chainless and curbless, how graceful thou art!
　　　Cup of the hills,
　　　Millions of rills
Bring unto thee, from forests and mountain,
Tributes of crystal from cavern-hid fountain;
Rejoiced at thy beauty, as all things delight,
When a gleam of the beautiful gladdens the sight.

We say nothing of the poetry—Heaven forefend that we should sit
in judgment upon our own offspring. We are no Brutus: we have ever
considered the virtue of the old Roman as questionable. We record
the lines only as an existing fact, preparatory to another fact which
we desire to set forth with becoming modesty. It became known
that we had worshipped at Kinneho, had sung the praises of Moosehead, and a monument was raised by our guide to commemorate the
event. The *monument was raised in honor of ourself.* Gentle reader, do
not smile; do not look in scorn upon our notation. In the hereafter,
there may be none to raise a monument to our ashes; be it so, our
cairn is built. In that wild, solitary region our pillar of stones is set
up, and men who know little of us, except that we once stood upon
that spot, keep the incident alive. Others have followed us, other

heaps of stones are piled upon the mountain; but the stout lumber-men are tenacious of our glory, and they gather together and keep our column the tallest, and point it out as something in which they feel an interest. We are content. This simple proof of remembrance amid the hills of our own State has touched our heart most nearly, and we are willing to leave to others the marble monument and noisy plaudit, while our cairn is built upon Kinneho.

And now we will to our story.

KINNEHO.

MASQUASO DEVOTED TO HER CHILD—FLIES FROM HIS CRUELTY—ORIGIN OF THE INDIAN PIPE— DISAPPEARANCE OF KINNEHO.

Squaw Mountain, of which we have before spoken, rises at the dis-tance of perhaps five miles from Kinneho. The Indian appellation is lost, and the name it now bears, uncouth as it sounds, was given it by the whites in the first settlement of the country. When the story is known which gave rise to the name, we trust Squaw Mountain will sound neither uncouth nor unlovely.

At the time that Raleigh Gilbert, half brother to Sir Walter Raleigh,[1] made a settlement at the mouth of the Kennebec River, in 1606, that region was inhabited by a powerful tribe of Indians called the Norridgewocks, a tribe second perhaps only to the Mohawks of New York. They were enterprising, hardy, and courageous in a re-markable degree, and had long held all the other clans, from the St. Croix to the Narragansets[2] (the last only being able to defy them), in complete subjection. Their villages were scattered along the whole course of the river, from its mouth even to the upper sources, and

---

1   Sir Walter Raleigh (c. 1552–1618) was not the half-brother of Raleigh Gilbert (c. 1583–1634) himself, but rather of his father, Humphrey Gilbert (c. 1539–83). All were involved in the colonization of New England: Humphrey Gilbert reached Newfoundland and claimed it for the British in 1583, paving the way for other expeditions such as Walter Raleigh's attempt to establish a colony on Roanoke Island in 1584 and Raleigh Gilbert's undertaking with the Popham Colony in Maine, chartered in 1606 and occupied by colonists from 1607–08.

2   Variant of Narragansetts.

along its many tributaries. In the hunting seasons, the shores of Moosehead, and the many lakes contiguous, afforded abundance of game, and gratified that love for the wild and mysterious which always forms an ingredient in the savage mind. Indeed, to this day, when the encroachments of the whites have done so much to change the character of the Indian, he still seeks his game in these ancient hunting-grounds, and may often be encountered in some lonely glen intent upon a luckless moose, or spearing salmon in the midst of rapids. Travelers delight in their escort; and at night, when the camp fires are lighted and the hemlock boughs spread for the night, when the pipe goes round and the wildwood feast is over, the Indian loses his taciturnity and repeats with pride, not unmingled with sadness, the stories of his people. He never pronounces the name Katahdu, which has a mysterious and forbidden import; the mountain itself being supposed the habitation of the great Spirit of Evil, who there dwells amid its lonely caverns enveloped in an eternal canopy of clouds, for the top of Katahdu is rarely disincumbered of these. It was on an occasion such as we have described that we gathered the legend we are about to relate.

Though the season was August, a sharp northerly wind was biting cold, and made the camp fire not only cheery, but absolutely essential to comfort. This fire was built of an immense pile of logs placed transversely across two, which had been so laid down as to supply the place of andirons. Our oiled tent was pretty and picturesque, and when the pale[1] was ornamented with our pistols, caps, gloves, and the numerous paraphernalia of a gipsying party, who went from pure woodland enthusiasm into the desert, it will be at once perceived that not a touch of cockneyism[2] existed amongst us, but all was true, earnest, and picturesque, not only in the members, but in the appendages of each.

The light glowed warmly upon the faces of our group: Morman examined the lock of his rifle, and then placed it within the shelter of the tent; Nannie reclined upon one elbow with an attitude worthy of a gipsy queen; the rest were cosily dispersed in various positions, while we, dreading repose, lest thought should become too painful for endurance, had lingered without watching the sparks as they ascended amid the trees, the blaze of the fire casting a white light

---

1   Wooden post or stake.
2   Squeamishness of city-dwellers unaccustomed to rural life.

upon the huge trunks. The stars were clear and tranquil, the scene so lovely, so remote and solitary; we, a handful of human beings, away from our fellows, and impelled hither neither by the hope of fame nor desire of gain, but simply because our hearts yearned for the primal in nature. An intense loneliness, such as we sometimes feel in a crowd, caused me to sigh heavily. Our Indian guide took the pipe from his mouth, and, for the first time, I saw he was near me, his bright eye, with its half-closed lid, fixed upon my face.

"The white woman has an Indian soul," he murmured; "she can close her face over her heart."

So, then, the best touch of refinement to the civilized and the savage are the same—concealment. Not the callous hardihood of the vulgar or depraved, but the Spartan, gathering his robe over his pangs and looking tranquilly abroad.

I pointed to Katahdu, behind which the slender thread of the moon was just sinking—

"Tell me of that mysterious pile," I said.

The Indian shook his head. He had now resumed his pipe, and the voice of Nannie from the tent admonished me that the air was chill, and our walk had been long and painful. Gathering my feet beneath me, I now sat watching the faces of those about me. Our Indian had settled himself near, and I could catch an occasional glance of his eye drawn to my face, as if impelled by an unwonted sympathy.

"We are in the pathway of Kinneho, when he used to visit yonder," he at length said, pointing in the direction of Katahdu.

He saw we were all eager for the story, and he went on; but I must give it in my own words.

The whole way from Moosehead Lake to the base of Katahdu is threaded by a chain of lakes, through which the Indian paddles his canoe, and at the several portages shoulders his light burden till a tramp of a mile, it may be less or more, enables him to launch it once more upon one of these lovely sheets of water. It will be seen that the great promontory which rises out of the centre of Moosehead takes its name from the principal personage of our story.

More than two hundred years ago, an old chief, who had taken a young wife late in life, became the father of a very beautiful girl, of rare wisdom, likewise, whom he called Maquaso, or the robin, because her cheek showed red through the olive hue, like the feathers upon the breast of this bird. Now this chief, besides being old, was nearly blind. It was believed his young wife had rubbed his eyes while he slept with the leaves of the poisonous hemlock, in revenge for some wrong she had suffered. Be that as it may, Maquaso, as she came to womanhood, was known to esteem her mother but lightly, while her whole soul seemed devoted to the comfort of her infirm parent.

It could not be otherwise but the graces of Maquaso would win the admiration of her people, and we find skins and venison, trophies of the chase and river, were often laid at the door of the wigwam as testimonies of love; but the presents of Muckaé (black heart) far outshone all others. Moreover, whenever the morning showed a heap at the lodge of the old chief, bearing the totem or mark of the young donor, Muckaé spurned it aside with his foot and placed his own offering within the entrance, in a manner that showed it must not be rejected. Maquaso shuddered as she saw this; for Muckaé was a bad man, whom the tribe feared; but he was at the head, and no one dared resist him.

When, at length, Muckaé asked her of her father, she made no resistance, but became his wife. Shortly after this event, her father died, and Maquaso, out of dread of her husband, dissembled her grief for him just as she did her aversion to Muckaé. But, as moons wore on, she grew more stately in manner, and more firm and violent in speech, till the bad chief in time grew half fearful in his turn. She was diligent, patient, and thrifty; his wigwam the best provided amongst the tribe; but Muckaé was morose and cruel of heart, and never a smile beamed from his face. Maquaso spread the skins and cooked his venison, but she was silent; and when the women of the tribe assembled at their feasts of the hunt and ripening corn, she was not among them.

At length, she became the mother of a boy, whom she called Kinneho. Now her whole nature was roused into action. She bathed his limbs, she trained him to courage, to hardihood, and virtue. She taught him to bend the bow, for she had often brought down game for her infirm father. With her own hand she prepared him for the chase or the battle-field, and was never happy away from his side. Kinneho was, in truth, so beautiful, that he seemed worthy of her care. Stately in height and swift of foot, with his mother's clear and vigorous intellect, he soon became first in the war party, as he had always been first in the chase. At the council fire, too, Maquaso, seated with the women, saw with delight that old men listened to his voice with deference, and often followed his suggestions.

She was still beautiful; for, rejecting the servile life that uncultured woman submits to, she had dwelt in this midst of her own great thoughts while her hands labored in the wigwam, therefore care and age had found no place upon which to leave their traces. Her husband had long since given himself up to a morose and solitary life, under pretence of having become a great medicine-man, leaving the whole care of providing for the boy to his mother.

Now whether there is that in human nature that makes it ungrateful to tenderness, regardless of what is lavishly bestowed, and covetous of that which is denied it, or whether there is a depth beyond human requital, we will not take upon ourselves to determine; it may be that moral qualities are transmissible to a greater degree than we comprehend. Whatever might be the cause, Maquaso was stung to the soul to find, as years grew upon the boy, he was morose, cruel, and sullen of heart as his father had been, rewarding her tenderness with scorn or indifference. She was far too wise and too proud to complain at this; but the women, who are always observant of each other, became aware of the fact, and it was much talked about amongst the people. At length, one morning beside the stones of the council fire was found a pair of worn moccasons, a decayed robe, and braid of hair, which were known to have belonged to Maquaso.

These tokens were designed to indicate that the owner was dead to the tribe; and when it was found that Maquaso had disappeared, terrible thoughts grew upon the minds of the people. It was in vain that Kinneho joined the search, and declared he was ignorant of her fate; his former bad repute fixed suspicion upon him, and a council was held, before which he was cited to appear. Prior to this, the young men had refused to join him in the hunt, and he was forbidden to sit amongst the chiefs who deliberated upon a war-path about to be taken against a party of their enemies who had encamped upon the river Androscoggin.

When Kinneho appeared before the council, the chiefs, one and all, arose and turned their backs upon him. The oldest man amongst them approached him, and taking the war-club from his hand tossed it into the midst of the flames, then seizing his bow, he broke it asunder. Kinneho uttered a cry of rage and defiance, and plunged into the forest.

The chiefs now started on their war-path; but they missed the courage and zeal of Kinneho. The way was long and toilsome, their enemies fierce. As they approached the vicinity, the scouts came in, declaring the numbers of their foe to be as many as leaves of the trees, for they counted as many as a dozen smokes. Cautiously did the party come on, watching each the planting of his foot, lest the crackling of a twig or the stirring of a branch should betray their proximity. As they neared, a single voice arose, clear and strong, singing the chant that betokens victory. They uttered the yell of the savage and sprang forward upon the foe. There was a dead silence, and every man stood in the glare of the flame arrested and silent.

The ground was strewn with the dead, and the reeking blood bubbled amid the ashes. Standing above the field of carnage was Kinneho, stringing the scalps to his girdle. He had kindled fires around the foe, which deceived and bewildered them, and then rushing upon them while they slept, had made them his prey. The young warriors set up a shout of approval, but Kinneho stalked forth in silence, leaving them to the feast of the dead.

At length, he fixed his lodge upon the top of the mountain in the centre of Moosehead Lake, which still bears his name. Here the tribe, in their hunts, saw all night the light against the sky, and a long streak of red across the water; but no one dared to approach him. If by chance a party met him in the forest, they fled before him; for he was known to be implacable in his rage, and the wildest stories were told of his single-headed valor.

Soon after Kinneho had established himself upon Moosehead, he observed a faint gleam of fire upon what is now called Squaw Mountain. At first, he thought this might be a tree blasted by lightning slowly consuming itself; but as night after night presented the same appearance, he resolved to learn the mystery. Perhaps he hoped to surprise a party of his people. He crossed the lake in his canoe, and drawing it up under the bank, followed the direction in which he had seen the light. He ascended the mountain with covert step; as he neared the top, he saw beside a small spring that bubbled from the rocks a rude lodge. As he stood gazing upon the scene, a woman came from the door bearing a birchen bowl, which she filled at the fountain. It was the once beautiful Maquaso, bent, emaciated, and her hair bleached to the color of the hoar frost. Kinneho rushed forward and clasped her in his arms. She looked in his face; but her eyes were wild and streaming with tears. Kinneho smoothed the white hair from her brow and strove to comfort her; but she seemed not to know him, only weeping and wringing her hands. He brought down a partridge with his bow and spread it upon the coals, in the hope it might restore her; but she only wept the more, with her eyes fixed piteously upon his face. At length they closed slowly—Maquaso was dead.

Kinneho made her grave beside the fountain, and came piously day by day with fruits and venison to comfort her in the long journey to the spirit-land. It was to the *tears of Maquaso that we owe one of the most beautiful of our August plants.* Wherever these fell, the *Indian pipe appeared, white and pure, like congealed sorrow.* The Great Spirit caused this to spring up as a memorial of her grief.

Kinneho lived more than a hundred suns in this desolate spot. His people tried to conciliate him; but he would never return to their favor. Once a year, when the Gat-gwah-da-ah, or Watchers, as the Indians beautifully term the Pleiades,[1] hung at evening in the west, he went across the chain of lakes to the Great Mountain, or Katahdu. Why he did so, how he dared to do so, no one knew; but old men believed he had made a compact with the evil powers there; but for what purpose is now lost.

At length, his fire appeared no more upon the top of the mountain. Hunters, as they peered through the trees at the marge of the lake, could no more see him, as they often had done, moving to and fro upon the bold cliff. They told how Kinneho never bent with age, how his white hair and eagle eye looked venerable yet terrible as he stood taller than other chiefs, and striking terror into their hearts. When they had watched night after night, and were sure he was not there, they ventured to cross the lake, thinking to find him dead in his lodge.

But neither chief, nor lodge, nor vestige of any kind rewarded their search. There is a fountain welling from the side of the rock (out of which you yourselves drank, Sophia and Nannie, and where the party crowned ourself Queen of Kinneho); here they thought at least to find a pipe, a bowl, or something to show that human life had been passed in so wild a spot; but the redberries clustered then

---

1   The constellation of stars known as the Seven Sisters.

as now above the clear water, and all was solitary and tokenless.

Men remembered the visits of Kinneho to the Great Mountain, and shook their heads bodingly;[1] and when it was found that the top of the cliff was covered with flinty rocks, as if they had been melted in the fire, that neither grass nor moss grew where the footsteps of the man passed, they were confirmed in their worst suspicions. They believed the stones were burned and melted under the feet of the necromancer, Kinneho, who is now confined in the bowels of the mountain.

burned himself!

---

1 With foreboding; ominously.

Appendix A: Elizabeth Oakes Smith's Writings on Her Life and Women's Rights

1. From *A Human Life: Being the Autobiography of Elizabeth Oakes Smith*, n.d. (c. 1885), MS. Elizabeth Oakes Prince Smith Papers, c. 1834–93, New York Public Library, Manuscripts and Archives Division

[Oakes Smith's *A Human Life: Being the Autobiography of Elizabeth Oakes Smith*, completed in her late years, is a 600-page manuscript held in the Manuscripts and Archives Division of the New York Public Library. Mary Alice Wyman published a modified and condensed version, *Selections from the Autobiography of Elizabeth Oakes Smith* (1924), and the unabridged text appears in Leigh Kirkland's unpublished dissertation, "'A Human Life: Being the Autobiography of Elizabeth Oakes Smith': A Critical Edition and Introduction" (1994). The source for this appendix is the original manuscript, in which Oakes Smith pieces together a narrative of her life, often pasting (and revising or annotating) print clippings from previously published pieces into her handwritten pages.]

The Place of Prayer.[1]

My Grandfather Prince I had observed early in childhood was in the habit of going out into the woods at evening twilight, alone. These woods were a natural park between the house and county road: being free from underbrush, and the trees of magnificent size it was a place of great beauty; here and there a white bowlder[2] peering through the green; rich in birds of song, and the pranks of the squirrel, and always the low hum of the wild bee. Here I used to resort for wintergreen, bunch-berries, acorns and beech nuts.

One day in rambling about I came to a lovely nook, overhung with tall trees, and beneath was a large flat stone, where the granite

---

1   MS pages 36–38.
2   Variant of boulder.

had cropped out of the soil, glittering with ising glass[1] and garnets and embellished with the cups of the ruby moss. This ledge of granite was something more than a foot in height. All around was fresh and sweet—not a noisome weed or shrub—above the branches of interlaced cathedral trees, through which gleamed the soft blue sky the air resonant with the song of birds.

I stood reverently before it, for I saw this was an Altar, a place for prayer. I too knelt down, and uttered a child's prayer not to God, but to my real father, for whom I yearned with tender affection.

On returning to the house I described what I had seen to my Aunt, and she confirmed my idea of an altar and went on to say that several years before she had come near the place accidentally & heard her father's voice in supplication.

"I beseech thee, great God, that all of my blood may be a God serving, and a God loving race: that my children, and my children's children to the third and fourth generation may be a people walking the way of thy commandments." Surely good must follow such desires. And I dwell lovingly upon this ancestor because the serene majesty of his character, was less stimulating to a sensitive child than the more vivacious, but certainly more heroic maternal grandparent, who as Capt. of the Sea, had encountered many and great perils. Many were the sea stories to which I listened with rapt attention, and childish awe.

A Sad Experience.[2]

[...] We had, as before said, a little stepsister, a fair complexioned, cheerful, engaging child of my own age, but more robust, not so sensitive either, of good, sweet temper, and quite as forward in her books as a little thing of six years ought to be. While I was perched in a high chair to make my little head visible in the "first class," Eleanor was wrestling with words of two syllables. Sometimes I was mortified at this and would offer to help her, which she rejected with a resolute "don't bother." She displayed sense in this, but it did not comport with my ideas, and accordingly, I made her the subject of my most persistent prayers, even offering God to "part with some of my forwardness if he would only bestow it upon her." I was intent in this, for I did nothing by halves.

---

1   Thin transparent sheets of mica.
2   MS pages 133–38, 144.

I presume my habits of undue thought and reflection had seriously undermined my nervous system for I became conscious of a hesitancy in my reading and recitations. "You seem to be going back," the teacher would say. Suddenly it flashed over me that God had answered my prayer. Now I watched Eleanor with scrutiny, and to my consternation found, that though I had lost, she had not gained.

But soon my thoughts became absorbed in my own mental state which must have been apparent, for I stammered and blundered down from class to class, till I stood at the teacher's knee looking at the a.b.c.s the form and names of which had faded from my mind. Mr. Butler who had regarded me as the show pupil of the school grew quite angry, I remember, and talked of using the ferule.[1] He took my hand—the blow never came for I sank to the floor in a dead swoon.

When I recovered consciousness I found myself at home lying on the bed in the "guest room" which was filled with my little mates and my mother weeping over me: all the neighbors by, and all trying to "bring me to." A painless interval followed. I remember only a delicious feeling of ease—of content: no books no prayers—only my dolls.

Gradually I must have grown strong, for I remember Phillip[2] carried me about in the garden in his arms. He was a wise helper bringing flowers to me and fruit. The first sense of discomfort that came to me was when I overheard the children of the school read—I was cutting some grasses with Phillip's knife, and in the sudden pang I cut my thumb, the scar of the wound is still visible.

From that time I must have grown stronger, and to have settled into ordinary channels of thought.

My teacher told me I would come round all right: Our Pastor, Rev. Mr. Hines, related to me what befel a classmate of his in College, who "*went back*" and forgot all his learning, and began to learn his a.b.c.s like a little child, but after a while it all came back to him, and he became a very great preacher, and a most holy man.

Such comfort, if comfort it could be called, would only be administered to a Puritan child with her deep spiritualism and incipient ambition. Even she was not comforted. A deadness, a kind of chaos came over her.

All this time my memory of what I had learned was unimpaired.

---

1   A cane, stick, or ruler for punishing children.
2   Introduced earlier as her family's servant, a "poor ignorant negro from the Island of Guadaloupe."

I had forgotten only the symbols of learning. I remembered every-thing I had ever read with a painful distinctness, and was glad to sleep, that I might not think, and I did sleep, I am told, much and often, and without dreams. I shrank from my young playmates, and dreaded grown people, who wounded my little pride by their pitying looks. Good, ignorant Phillip alone ministered gratefully, and his simple talk about flowers and birds, and my being just like them, was an inlet to something better than books. At length I was sent to my grandam, where my mental state was never alluded to, and where I was allowed to be "as wild as a young Indian," as they phrased it. In this eager, extreme, idle existence I seem to have forgotten it myself under new and beautiful experiences.

[...]

There was one feature connected with the state of mind that in-duced my mother to send me as before stated to the calm, peaceful retreat of the old Homestead, not devoid of interest in a psycho-logical point of view. I was in perfect accord with Nature.

Perfect Harmony with Nature.[1]

There was a trout brook flowing through the farm, overhung with tall oaks and beech trees, and spanned by a rustic bridge. Nothing could exceed the beauty of the spot—nothing exceed the sweet content I enjoyed sitting under this shadowy retreat flecked with the sunshine glinting through the leaves and watching the spotted trout as they darted from the shadow of the old fantastic roots and poised themselves in the amber-tinted water. The birds were not afraid to pick up the crumbs I scattered at my feet; the squirrel dropped his nuts in easy companionship, and the fox came to the verge of the wood with his little sharp bark, more like a greeting. I was one of them—I reasoned not, nor toiled—I was a child, without the child's restlessness and ques-tioning. I felt only the sweetness of existence—saw only the beautiful. I well remember when thought came to me in the way of speculation about a snake I saw gliding under the dead last year's leaves.

I began to ask myself if God could be altogether good, when he

---

1 MS pages 144–47.

made a creature without legs or arms, and I started with the conclusion that they did exist *under the skin*, to come out at some time, just as our wings were hidden, but ready for us when we became Angels. Accordingly having found a dead snake on the ledge, where somebody had killed it, I made a little grave enclosed by shingles, and buried it. For I had learned that the beetles and ants would soon pick its bones. Not many days elapsed before I examined the spot and found a beautifully prepared vertebrae, but no sign of limbs. I was shocked, and all afloat in my theories.

This sympathy with nature has been a marked feature of my life, and this, with my tendency at this early age to solitary speculations, was a natural sequence to the grave, earnest, secluded habits of my Pilgrim ancestors. Later in life this experience was in a measure renewed. In 1866, as noted in my journal, I was walking in our village, when I observed many birds flying about me. The old feeling of childhood came over me, and I held out my finger and said, *come*. Instantly one alighted upon it. A Stranger seeing this said to me:

"You have recovered your pet, haven't you?"

I replied, "No, this is a wild bird."

He observed me with astonishment, ejaculating, "It looks like a miracle." Doubtless in the days of witchcraft I should have been denounced as a sorceress. [...]

Martyrdom.[1]

When about nine years old I renewed my study of Fox's book of the Martyrs,[2] partly because children at that time had so few suitable books to read, and partly because I felt I was not in myself improving in my Portland life—growing too giddy and fond of praise. I knew from the first that I was of a flimsy make, and might not be able to bear any great pain even for a great cause, for I fainted at even a slight hurt of any kind. Accordingly I tested myself in various ways such as holding my fingers in the blaze of a lamp or candle but as I always fainted from the pain I saw that I was not at all like the martyrs of which I read.

It will be remembered that I was not in accord with my orthodox mates, and though dwelling much upon historic events I could not

---

1   From MS pages 194–201.
2   See Introduction, pp. 14–15.

be supposed to understand the mutations of empire, and brought my illustrations of events from my experience of the war of 1812, hence I concluded that the people in Rome had fallen into a similar state, and the strongest of them got the power to kill, torture and burn the weaker ones who did not think as they did, so when such people got the same power in our country they would do the same things, and I must either stick to the truth or go to the stake.

We Puritan children were methodically trained: every week, either at home or at church we were called upon to say the Assembly's Catechism[1] and answer questions in the Bible, and the replies required in the catechism caused me much suffering. I there learned about the Elect,[2] and was greatly exercised to know if I were one of them. I persisted in affirming that I was good—I was not in the least devilish—I tried to make my mates *good*, I never told a lie nor cheated in any way—I never purloined anything—I was never disobedient—never unkind, and this is to be good, and, if God does not love me he cannot be a good God. This shocked my mother, and my Aunt shook me soundly, saying I was "a little devil."

At church it came my turn to answer a most, to my mind, objectionable part of the lesson, wherein it was said something about God being justified in sending the non-elect to hell to be punished to all eternity &c. This awakened in me the necessity for protest or I might be thought to give assent to what I could not believe. It was a grievous moment to me—my usually white face grew pale—at length I articulated

"This is what is said in the book, but I do not think so," lisping the s's, which added to my discomfort.

[...]

I had read enough of history to see that there had been tyrants in the world, but I saw that the great struggles of nations were different from the

---

1 Catechism of the Westminster Assembly of Divines, likely the Assembly's Shorter Catechism (1647) designed specifically to teach Protestant children the Christian faith through a series of questions and answers.
2 Questions 19–20 in the Shorter Catechism explain the fallen condition of all humans, who can only be saved from eternal damnation through God's grace or election. God's Elect are predestined for salvation, chosen "out of his mere good pleasure," while the non-Elect will be unable to find redemption through Christ and thus left to suffer in hell.

persecution of individuals, and then I felt that I was just in the condition to do as those martyrs did. I must hold on to what I believed, or die as they did, or, what was worse, give up my truth. I was no philosopher, and had not learned the progress of the ages, but I knew that my Grandfather Blanchard was little esteemed on one point—he was a Universalist, and my Grandfather Prince had been set aside from the church for rejection of some Calvinistic[1] dogmas. People were tired of my questioning, and I was left to solve any little problems as best I could.

I knew there prevailed a deadly hostility to the Pope of Rome, and the wars of Napoleon[2] and our wars with England not well understood by a child of eight years made all possibilities possible, and I accordingly set myself to prepare for martyrdom. I knew I was weak, but I could not renounce my convictions, which consisted mostly of the simple creed, that I was good, and God ought to love me. My ancestors were steadfast people, and I must not flinch, even if I was not allowed to go to the Communion table when I got older as Grandpa was forbidden, and yet went to see others partake of it, and thought perhaps he might yet be burned at the stake.

In view of the terrible contingencies to which I thought I should at some time be subjected, I practiced, as before said, many little penances most painful to my sensitive nerves. When by any accident I received an injury I made no complaint. I ran needles into my flesh and preserved a serene countenance only happy that I did not faint. Indeed I was marvelously happy in it all—I was very tender with my brothers and sisters; I was a true Puritan, heroic child with no consciousness of merit—for much of my habitual sense of well-deserving was modified and abated by the intensity of my religious zeal. [...]

Maidenhood.[3]

This is the most beautiful and the most suggestive period of a woman's life. The girl who has sacrificed this by a premature marriage will carry

---

1   Named after the French theologian John Calvin (1509–64), Calvinism includes the doctrine of predestination and God's absolute sovereignty in choosing his Elect: God selects who will be saved, and his grace is irresistible. Universalists believe that God sent Christ to redeem the sins of all of humankind: he wills all people to be reconciled to him, not merely a predestined Elect, and in his love and mercy extends the possibility of salvation universally.
2   Napoleon Bonaparte (1769–1821), military leader and Emperor of France.
3   MS pages 243–44.

in her breast, to the end of her life, the sense of a loss—the sense of desecration. She has left the child behind her—she no longer has the mother want of a help—a supporting, and while the evolving tendrils indicate a something allied to beautiful blushes, all is indistinct and pure as the Lily upon whose petals the first rays of the morning have just stirred the golden chalice of the opening life. To lose this period—to be rushed from the cradle to the altar is to make the great life-long mistake. The following Sonnet may perhaps better express my meaning, as the uttered feelings of a girl, when the exigencies of life press heavily upon her, and she cannot recall the sweetness of untasted Maidenhood.

Sonnet.

Thou did'st bereave me of my golden days:
My heart calls backward for those girlish hours,
With which dear nature Maidenhood endowers.
Upon my head the pang of wrong always
Burns like the noon-day sun's all-scorching rays.
Oh! the crushed garlands, and the withered flowers!
The blighting damp that hung in rose-deck'd bowers!
The frost that hush'd the wood-bird's morning lays!
Oh! lost, lost joys of youth! I wear the Cross
Like some pale Nun, but not her vestal fire:
Grow moody dull like Miser o'er his loss,—
And o'er perverted duties vainly tire;—
Curse the vile lucre, and the worldly dross
That lays dear Love upon his fun'ral pyre.

My Marriage.[1]

[...] I was clad in white satin, with lace flounces—white silk hose and white kid slippers, long white gloves—white flowers amid my long golden brown hair which reached below my waist and was only confined by a narrow fillet across the forehead. Mr. Smith was almost twice my age, wore spectacles, and was very bald. He had contempt for fashionable and conventional usages, and declined to furnish the bridal ring, it esteeming a foolish appendage to a bride. My mother was much

---

1   MS pages 250–53.

chagrined at this, for she was an ultra-conventional woman, and I was in one aspect of character disposed to observe appearances, and in most others, a mere baby, no more fit to be a wife than a child of ten years.

I apprehend now it must have been a melancholy spectacle, and a sad wedding, for it was a spring thaw of snow, and sleet—the rain falling all day and all night in torrents, and the streets deluged in water. I heard it whispered more than once by the servants,

"A lowery day and a lowery bride."

It would be foolish and needless to describe the emotions of a girl of sixteen. The maid who dressed me for the occasion stepped aside, and giving me a careful inspection, exclaimed, "You are the beautifullest creter I ever laid eyes on," at which somehow, I did not smile. I was so foreign to all this: so unfit for the occasion—I, a dreamy, imaginative, undeveloped child—living my own life, in which worldliness did not form a single ingredient. My poor little head was not furnished with a fibre of the actual. I had read much, but fiction—all the old works to be found in old libraries, even translations from Goethe,[1] had not touched my simple Puritanic world, and I had read like one in a mist to whom objects are hardly at all revealed.

I had vast ideas of immaculate purity—consecration to God—living in the spirit, and being Christ-like. How could any man expect to take a Nun and make a Grizzel[2] of her? take a chalice from the ideal and convert it into a potsherd.[3] Every true, good, manly heart will feel a pang for the man who attempts this. Neither may be at fault, but the unsuitableness of the whole thing must be felt, and naturally human sympathy will go where it ought to go, with the man that runs

---

1   Johann Wolfgang von Goethe (1749–1832), the great German literary figure.

2   Griselda, the legendary character of a wife whose patience and submissiveness to her husband never falter under his cruel tests of obedience.

3   The chalice or cup used in the celebration of the Lord's Supper or Holy Communion, as Christ commanded his followers to remember him at the Last Supper (Luke 22:20; 1 Corinthians 11:25). By contrast, the broken piece of pottery recalls the warning in Isaiah 45:9: "Woe unto him that striveth with his Maker! Let the potsherd strive with the potsherds of the earth. Shall the clay say to him that fashioneth it, What makest thou? or thy work, He hath no hands?"

such risque,[1] and not with the dreamy young girl. Nor must any one reading the above conclude that I was a miserable wife, my husband a miserable man, which would be cruelly unjust to both of us. Let the reader remember I am writing of the real with its many shades.

Married.[2]

[...] Oh! the beautiful world that at once faded from my view! The world that seemed utterly destroyed—Where was its music—its learning—its travel over which I had pondered and dreamed! Where was the sacred inner consciousness that allies the Maiden to the Angels!

But I did not sink down into a melancholy moodiness. The sense of duty had always, amid all my illusions been paramount with me. I faced the music without let or hinderance.

Now a new England man is exceedingly exacting—He is bent upon having a clean, orderly, comfortable domicil.[3] I had one servant and six dependents in the shape of apprentices to the printing business, for Mr. Smith was Editor and half owner of the Eastern Argus Portland Maine.

I did not shirk my responsibilities. I superintended everything with religious pertinacity. I had been accustomed to little of this kind of work at home, but I set myself to learn like a perfect little drudge. Went daily from attic to cellar—to see that all was as it should be. Learned to patch and mend, and make. Transformed myself to an utterly different creature from what had been native to me. Duty—duty was my motto everywhere. Was all this known and appreciated! How could it be! From my dreams and illusions I had wakened to what a Puritan girl was expected to be. I did not fret nor complain. I kept "streight on"—What else was I, bred after the strictest sect of Calvinism, expected to do, or be, when the solemn bonds of the marriage covenant were upon me?

The old Puritan woman with here and there a revolt, as in the case of Anna Hutchison,[4] looked up to men in the Miltonic style

---

1   Risk.
2   MS pages 256–58.
3   Domicile; residence or home.
4   Anne Hutchinson (1591–1643), a midwife and spiritual leader who voiced her own religious views and criticism of the Puritan clergy, leading to her banishment from the Massachusetts Bay Colony.

"He for God only, *She for god in him*"[1]

and this masculine arrogance and demigodism, sat well upon the religious, dignified men of these days. Changes have come since, and women are critical now.

Myself.[2]

With no just cause for complaint I found myself in a situation so foreign to the fastidious, dreaminess of a spiritualistic creature as ignorant of the world as an infant. I had been bred in nunlike exclusiveness and purity. Earnest, and painfully conscientious, accustomed to sacrifice my own feelings to promote the well-being of others, I was totally devoid of all selfishness, and even selfism. I had not quite enough for smartness, and the Puritanic exactions of implicit obedience, left me at the mercy of any one who wished to coerce me, for I practiced "taking up the Cross"[3] with all that it implied. I was physically sound in every respect, but so sensitive, that I suffered torture, and made no sign. As I see what I was then, and realize what I was compelled to rise beyond in the developments of maternity, and the growth of larger views, it seems to me that the martyrdom for which I prepared myself in childhood has been fully realized. [...]

The Western Captive.[4]

This romance was one of the first of the cheap paper-covered publications. It had an immense sale of 2500 in four days, for the use of the Ms. for that period, I received just $100. and I had some difficulty in the matter of copy right. It will be seen that my books brought me little remuneration, while I was well paid for Magazine work, and my Sonnets, poems &c were always in demand.

---

1   John Milton, *Paradise Lost*, book 4, line 299.
2   MS page 265.
3   Following Christ (Matthew 10:38; Mark 8:34; Luke 14:27).
4   MS page 542.

Woman & Her Needs.[1]

[...] The firm of Messrs. Fowler & Wells collected the papers, Woman & her Needs into pamphlet form price 25 cents, and honorably paid me my percentage. The sale of these was very great, and it became evident that a great deal had been done by it in awakening public interest on the question of Universal Suffrage. I was flooded with letters—strangers from all parts of the country came to see me. Letters and pamphlets reached me from outre-mer.[2] Robert Owen[3] sent me his tracts for the people. Mr. Firk[4] sent me his Bible of the Reformation reformed—I sent this and many other documents to Bowdoin College, Maine. Eminent Judges and Lawyers wrote me declaring that my ground was legally tenable, and my arguments unanswerable.

But over and above this, it brought to my notice a large class of toiling, suffering women, who enduring without hope, and living without sympathy, told me of their trials, came and opened their hearts to me—told me of their temptations, their sins, their despair. Many a sad tale could I relate of these women, who wept before me bitter tears for the past, but sought me out, that they might tell me I had inspired them with a new hope.

I was the recipient of hundreds of touching letters, false in grammar and orthography, but replete with womanly thoughts and feelings. I often received little gifts of lace and flowers, sent by unknown hands, in rude penmanship asking my acceptance. Men, importuned me for money, but women did not. My literary career had not been devoid of recognition, but in this new field, designed to reveal woman to herself, I realized an inconceivable satisfaction. True many long endeared friends were vexed at me, and did not

---

1   MS pages 546–50. See excerpts from *Woman and Her Needs* in Appendix A2.
2   Overseas.
3   Robert Owen (1771–1858), a Welsh industrialist and social reformer. An early socialist and utopian thinker, Owen promoted improved conditions for factory workers and experimental, cooperative communities including one in the United States at New Harmony, Indiana.
4   The author of this text is John Finch (1784–1857), not "Firk," a follower of Robert Owen who interpreted Owenism as a true form of Christianity, rearranging the contents of the Bible into new, retitled chapters in *The Seven Seals Broke Open; The Bible of the Reformation Reformed* (London: James Rigby, 1853).

fail to remonstrate, and I was cruelly abused by the press, but I did not falter, and through all Mr. George Ripley[1] was ready with his approval, and kindly genial notes, and words which I still preserve as a precious heritage. A judicious critic, he never commended a work the more for being written by a friend, but only from the standpoint of art. Poetic tributes were not lacking, replete with a sweet enthusiasm. I was reaping the benefit of stepping outside my Puritanic bondage. Brought up as I had been, I had so much to renounce, and so much to do, that I almost danced over my freedom.

Of course while old, conventional friends, conservative and rich, were eager to show their disapproval of my views, and not over kind in their expression of it, I was cordially accepted by the best and brightest thinkers of the advancing age—Theodore Parker, Ralph Waldo Emerson, Lucretia Mott, James Freeman Clarke, Wendell Phillips, William Lloyd Garrison, and a host of others, to say nothing of literary competitors who were like Willis & Poe,[2] indoctrinated with like opinions.

---

1   George Ripley (1802–80) was a Transcendentalist, social reformer, founder of the failed utopian community at Brook farm, and a journalist for the *New York Tribune*.

2   Theodore Parker (1810–60) was a minister, Transcendentalist, and abolitionist who practiced and advocated civil disobedience of the Fugitive Slave Act of 1850. Ralph Waldo Emerson (1803–82) was a highly influential writer, lecturer, and philosopher in the Transcendentalist movement and American intellectual culture. Lucretia Mott (1793–1880) was a major figure in movements for women's rights, abolition, religious tolerance, and other social reform. James Freeman Clarke (1810–88) was a Unitarian minister, theologian, and author active in Transcendentalist, abolitionist, and social reform movements. Wendell Phillips (1811–84) was an orator who advocated for abolition, women's rights, Native American rights, and other social reform. William Lloyd Garrison (1805–79), a famous and controversial anti-slavery and women's rights crusader, was a lecturer, publisher of the abolitionist newspaper *The Liberator*, and member of various women's suffrage organizations. Nathaniel Parker Willis (1806–67) was an editor and popular contributor to magazines and periodicals, with many connections to important literary figures including Poe, Henry Wadsworth Longfellow, Harriet Jacobs, and his sister Fanny Fern. Edgar Allan Poe (1809–49) was a prolific author and major figure in the American Romantic movement, an editor, and a literary critic. Poe was a literary acquaintance of Oakes Smith, a reviewer of her poetry, and a subject of her own commentary and memoirs (see Kent Ljungquist and Cameron Nickels, "Elizabeth Oakes Smith on Poe: A Chapter in the Recovery of His Nineteenth-Century Reputation").

2. From *Woman and Her Needs* (New York: Fowlers and Wells, 1851)

[Oakes Smith published a series of essays on the topic of women's rights for Horace Greeley's *New York Tribune* between 1850 and 1851, around the same time that she began regularly participating in National Women's Rights Conventions. The essays were then collected and republished with their original title, *Woman and Her Needs*, to the success that Oakes Smith describes in her autobiography (see Appendix A1, pp. 264–65).]

CHAPTER FIRST.

"They who seek nothing but their own just liberty, *have always right to win it and to keep it*, whenever they have power, be the voices never so numerous that oppose it."—MILTON.[1]

From the moment that an individual or a class of individuals, in any community, have become conscious of a series of grievances demanding redress, from that moment they are morally bound to make that conviction vital in action, and to do what in them lies to correct such abuse. Our nature is not such a tissue of lies, our intuitions are not so deceptive, that we need distrust the truth thus forced upon the life. Wherever the pang is felt, a wrong exists—the groan goes not forth from a glad heart, and he or she who has felt the iron of social wrong piercing into the soul, is the one to cast about and demand relief. The saintly patience so often preached is but another mode of protracting the world's misery; we wrong ourselves, and we roll onward the Juggernautic[2] car that is to crush those who succeed us, when we supinely endure those evils which a strong purpose, an energetic will, and an unfaltering trust in the good might help us to redress.

Whatever difference of opinion may exist amongst us as to the

---

1 John Milton (1608–74), *The Ready and Easy Way to Establish a Free Commonwealth* (1660).

2 With reference to the annual Hindu Chariot Festival, bearing an image of Jaggarnath, one of the gods celebrated with a procession of ceremonial carriages.

propriety of the recent Conventions held in our Country,[1] called "Woman's Rights," the fact stands by itself, a handwriting on the wall, proclaiming a sense of wrong, a sense of something demanding redress, and this is fact enough to *justify the movement* to all candid eyes. Indeed enough to render it praiseworthy. For one, I am glad to see that our Republic has produced a class of women, who, feeling the Need of a larger sphere and a better recognition, have that clearness of intellect and strength of purpose by which they go to work resolutely to solve the difficulty. They might stay at home and fret and dawdle; be miserable themselves and make all within their sphere miserable likewise; but instead of this, they meet and talk the matter over, devise plans, explain difficulties, rehearse social oppressions and political disabilities, in the hope of evolving something permanently good.

All this is well, and grows naturally from the progress of institutions like our own, in which opinions are fearlessly discussed, and all thought traced home to its source. It isn't in the nature of things that any class in our midst should be long indifferent to topics of general interest; far less that such should feel the pressure of evils without inquiring into the best means of abatement. When our Fathers planted themselves upon the firm base of human freedom, claimed the inalienable rights of life, liberty, and the pursuit of happiness, they might have foreseen that at some day their daughters would sift thoroughly their opinions and their consequences, and daringly challenge the same rights.

For myself, I may not sympathize with a Convention—I may not feel *that* the best mode of arriving at truth to my own mind—I may feel its singleness of import would be lost to me while standing in the solid phalanx of associated inquiry; but these objections do not apply to the majority of minds, and I reverence their search in their own way, the many converging lights of many minds all bent upon the same point, even although I myself peer about with my solitary lantern.

These Conventions have called forth from the Press one grand

---

1   The Seneca Falls Convention in 1848 was the first women's rights convention in the United States, followed by other regional conventions and the first National Women's Rights Convention in Worcester, Massachusetts. Oakes Smith attended in 1850, took the platform at the second convention in Worcester in 1851, and became an ongoing participant in conventions and speaker for women's rights on the lecture circuit.

jubilee of ridicule "from Dan even unto Beersheba,"[1] as if it were the funniest thing in the world for human beings to feel the evils oppressing themselves or others, and to look round for redress. It would seem as if Inquiry must always come under beaver and broadcloth— it must be mustachioed and bearded—and yet the graceful Greek made the quality feminine. Truth, too, is feminine, but then she must have a masculine exponent to the modern ear, or she becomes absurd. I do not exactly see how she should be so changed when needed for our sex, from what she is when performing good offices for the other. But enough of trifling. The state of things thus appearing in our own day is just the state we might have prophesied would take place at some time. We must meet it, recognize it, and help to direct it wisely. It argues great things for Woman, and through her for the world. We have *Needs* becoming more and more tangible and urgent, and now is the time to consider what they are.

[...]

Heretofore, women have acted singly—they have been content with individual influence, however exercised, and it has often been of the very worst kind; but now, in our country at least, they seem disposed to associate as do our compeers of the other sex, for the purpose of evolving better views, and of confirming some degree of power. There is no reason why they should not do this. They are the mothers and wives and sisters of the Republic, and their interests cannot be separated from those of the fathers and husbands and brothers of the Republic. It is folly to meet them with contempt and ridicule, for the period for such weapons is passing away.

Their movements as yet may not be altogether the best or the wisest—all is as yet new; but their movements truly and solemnly point to a step higher in the scale of influence. There is a holy significance in them—a prophetic power that speaks well for themselves, and, as I before said, well for the world. It cannot be, from the nature of things, that so much of human intelligence can be brought into vivid action without some great and good result. It has always been so in all subjects that have enlisted thought— men have come from the turmoil of mental action, with new and broader perceptions, a higher and freer humanity, a better iden-

---

1   1 Samuel 3:20.

tification of the individual with his species, and why should not Woman the same?

I know it is women who sneer most at these movements of each other, and that women oftenest turn their backs upon the sufferings of each other. I do not mean the griefs or physical pains of those in their own rank and circle; far from it, their hearts are rarely at fault there; but to the cry of those ready to perish, to the needs of the erring, the despised, and neglected of their sex, they are deaf and blind. To the long, torturing discords of ill-assorted marriages, to the oppressions of family circle, the evasions of property and the lengthening catalogue of domestic discomforts growing out of the evils of society, they are *cruel, selfishly indifferent, or remorselessly severe* upon each other.

It is true they have not condemned such to the stake literally; have not roasted them alive; hung, quartered, tortured them with thumbscrews, impaled on hooks, confined in dungeons and beheaded on blocks, as men have done, the good, the great, the heroic, "of whom the world is not worthy," of their own sex: for they have been denied the power—men choosing to hold the prerogative of externally inflicted cruelty in their own hands; but they have condemned their suffering sisters to the intangible and manifold tortures which can fall only upon the spirit, and which are ten-fold more cruel than any external wrong, without once attempting to move tongue or finger in their behalf. Indeed, I have sometimes thought that women instinctively avoid each other when suffering from social ills, as if that kind of misery had something allied to a stain attached to it; and so it has in fact; the human instinct is not at fault; a *misplaced* individual is humiliated; he or she feels it in the very soul, and all that is within recoils at the wrong. *Appositeness, freedom, joy, are a part of the beautiful,* and where any or all of these are wanting, harmony is wanting, and dignity also, unless the character be allied to the sublime.

Much of this great movement of our sex argues a better and nobler sympathy for each other, the growth of a loyalty full of promise. We think we see a broader and better spirit is awakening within us, a nearer and more wholesome humanity—ill-directed it may be as yet, groping after a hidden, unrevealed good, yet the search has opened, and the good will be grasped. [...]

CHAPTER SECOND.

"I know —— has always loved her
So dear in heart, not to deny her that
A woman of less place might ask by law,
Scholars allowed freely to argue for her."[1]
HEN. VIII. Act ii. Scene 2.[2]

I have said the world needs an admixture of Woman thought in its affairs; a deep, free, woman-souled utterance *is needed.* It is the disseverance of the sexes, the condemning of the one to *in-door* thought only, to the degradation of in-door toil, far more limiting in its nature than that of the out-door kind, beneath the invigorations of air and sky, that has done so much in our country to narrow and paralyze the energies of the sex. Excessive maternity, the cares and the labors consequent upon large families, with inadequate support (when we consider the amount of general intelligence amongst us) have conspired to induce the belief that the most entire domestic seclusion is the only sphere for a woman. Our republic has hitherto developed something akin to a savage lordliness in the other sex, in which he is to usurp all the privileges of freedom, and she is to take as much as she can get, after he is served.

Now, a woman may or may not be adapted to an in-door life exclusively. There is as much difference in us in that respect as there is in men. The expanse of earth and sky have unquestionably worked enlargement upon the mind of the other sex; and, in our own, have developed from the poor serving girl of the Inn of Domremy, inured to the toils of the stable, the chivalric and enthusiastic Joan of Arc.[3] It is the making woman a creature of luxury—an object of sensuality—a vehicle for reproduction—or a thing of toil, each one, or all of these—that has caused half the miseries of the world. She, as a soul, has never been recognized. As a human being, to sin and to suffer, she has had more than an acknowledgment. As a human being, to obey her God, to think, to enjoy, men have been blind to her utmost needs.

---

1 Oakes Smith's italics for emphasis.
2 In Shakespeare's play, "your majesty" fills the blank, as Cardinal Wolsey addresses King Henry VIII.
3 Jeanne d'Arc (c. 1412–31), Roman Catholic saint and French heroine, born in the village of Domrémy.

She has been treated always as subservient; and yet all and the most entire responsibility has been exacted of her. She has had no voice in the law, and yet has been subjected to the heaviest penalties of the law. She has been denied the ability to make or enforce public opinion, and yet has been outraged, abandoned, given over to degradation, misery, and the thousand ills worse than a thousand deaths, by its terrible action. Even her affections—those arbitrary endowments imparted by the Most High for her own safeguard, and for the best being of society—have been warped and crushed by the action of masculine thought upon their manifestations, till their unadulterated play is well nigh lost.

Men have written for us, thought for us, legislated for us; and they have constructed from their own consciousness an effigy of a woman to which we are expected to conform. It is not a Woman that they see; God forbid that it should be; it is one of those monsters of neither sex, that sometimes outrage the pangs of maternity, but which expire at the birth: whereas the distorted image to which men wish us to conform, lives to bewilder, to mislead, and to cause discord and belittlement where the Creator designed the highest dignity, the most complete harmony. Men have said we should be thus and thus, and we have tried to be in accordance, because we are told it is womanly. They have said we must think in a certain way, and we have tried so to think; they have said that under given circumstances we must act after a particular mode, and we have thus acted—ay! even when the voice of God in our own hearts has called to us "where art thou?" and we have hid ourselves, not daring to reply; for with that cowardice which men tell us is feminine, we dared not face that public opinion which *men* have established—dared not encounter that ridicule which men first start, and weak women follow up—dare not face that isolation which great and true thought brings upon itself in the present pettiness and prejudice of the world.

Till woman learns to cast out the "bond-woman," her and her offspring—send them forth into the wilderness of thought, no angel *can* succor her.[1] She must cast herself down amid the aridness of thought—hungry and thirsty for the truth—she may veil her eyes, that she "see not the death of the child," even the Ishmaels of error, whence shall be born a nation, armed against its kind, even the hoariness of established falsehood, for often will she find Truth

---

1   An allusion to the exile of Hagar and her son Ishmael in Genesis 21:8–21.

revealed in a way she little supposed, and which she trembles to perceive; but let her not fear—let her trust to those intuitions, better than all the demonstrations of reason—let her think, and feel, and see, and grasp with a courage which is of God, and all will be well.

Let woman learn to take a woman's view of life. Let her feel the need of a woman's thought. Let her search into her own needs—say, not what has the world hitherto thought in regard to this or that, but what is the *true* view of it from the nature of things. Let her not say, what does my husband, my brother, my father think—wise and good and trustworthy though they be—but let her evolve her own thoughts, recognize her own needs, and judge of her own acts by the best lights of her own mind.

Let her feel and understand that there is a difference in the soul as in the bodies of the sexes—a difference designed to produce the most beautiful harmony. But let her not, in admitting this, admit of inferiority. While the *form* of a man is as it were more arbitrary, more of a fact in creation, more distinct and uniform, a sort of completeness of the material, and his mind also more of a fixture, better adapted to the exactitudes of science, and those protracted labors needful to the hardier developments of the understanding, let her bear in mind that this fixedness, this patience of labor, this steadiness of the understanding, are in conformity with his position as *Lord of the material Universe*, to which God has appointed him: whereas she was an after-creation, with something nearer allied to the heavenly. In her shape there is a flexibility, a variety, more graceful, etherial, and beautiful, appealing more intimately to that something within the soul of man, that goes onward to the future and eternal—a softening down of the material to the illusions of the unseen—her mind, also, when unstinted and unadulterated, has in it more of aspiration, more of the subtle and intuitive character, that links it to the spiritual; she is impatient of labor, because her wings are nearly freed from the shell of the chrysalis, and prompt to a better element; she cares less for the deductions of reason, because she has an element in herself nearer to the truth than reason can ever reach, by which she *feels* the approaches of the true and the beautiful, without the manly wrestlings all night of the Patriarch to which the other sex are subjected. She does not need the ladder of Bethel,[1] the

---

1   Jacob's ladder, in his dream of a stairway between earth and heaven used by angels (Genesis 28:10–17).

step by step of the slow logician, because her feet are already upon the first rung of that mystic pass-way; this is why she is bid by the arrogance of apostolic injunction to veil her head in public, "because of the Angels."[1] She is a step nearer them than her *material* lord and master. The angels recognize her as of nearer affinity.

Let it not be thought I say this lightly. Would that women would receive it as a solemn truth—that they would, out of their own souls, reject the hardness of materialism which the masculine mind engenders from its own elements, and receive cordially and meekly the truth as it is witnessed in their own souls. It was this pure, ready recipiency, this "let it be to thy handmaid as seemeth to thee good,"[2] that distinguished the Maid of Judah above the others of her sex, and enabled her to receive without questioning the Divine Birth. Overshadowed by the Holy Ghost, the mystery of Truth was born of her, and new light through her came to the world. Had we spirits like hers, perpetual youth of soul might be ours, and new and miraculous revelations of better thought, and higher beauty of life, might redeem the world again and again.

Would that women would learn to recognize their own individuality—their own singleness of thought. Let them not feel disparaged at the difference which I have recognized; it is a difference that crowns them with a new glory. We give the material Universe to men, and to those of our sex who, from whatever cause, approximate to their standard; to such let us yield ungrudgingly the way; but it is no less certain that there is a woman-thought, a woman-perception, a woman-intuition, altogether distinct from the same things in the other sex; and to learn what these are, and to act from these, is what women must learn, and when they have so learned, and impressed themselves thus through these upon the world, it will be regenerated and disenthralled.[3]

Look at the long catalogue of monstrous evils and errors that have disgraced the annals of our race, and then judge if woman had been allowed her proper share in the formation of opinion, in the making up of human judgments, would these things have been? Take, for instance, the least reprehensible of these errors, where the masculine

---

1 1 Corinthians 11:10.
2 Luke 1:38, the Virgin Mary's response to the angel Gabriel, who announces that she will conceive and bear the Son of God.
3 Set free from bondage; liberated.

mind has belittled, besotted, and bewildered itself under the aspect of sanctity; where, under the priestly garb, the monkish cowl, it has busied itself with the absurd subtleties of the schoolmen, and wasted itself with vicious tendencies of the casuist, seeking not for the best good, but searching for intricate apologies for the worst evils. Let us consider a race of men shut up in cloisters, passing their lives in vigil and prayer, idling themselves in the contemplation of beatific dreams, or scourging their bodies for real or imaginary crimes, and that, too, while the world was groaning under the vices and cruelties of their kind. Could Woman have done this? It is true women followed in their career—immured themselves in convents, outraging their humanity by monkish denials, hypocritical pretenses, or secret and monstrous indulgences; but the system did not originate with them; the whole vile theory of that species of life was the growth of the masculine intellect.

No, there is a directness, a utilitarianism, in the affections and thoughts of the woman-mind, that of itself would never have misled her; there is a tangibility in her religious impulses that leads her at once to prayer—a reality in her affections that involves the best devotedness of human love; and a solidness in her benevolence, inciting at once to good works. She has a natural going out of herself, a readiness of sympathy that prompts to relieve; while a certain buoyancy of her physique makes action more pleasurable to her than to the other sex. If she has lent herself to the evils that have outraged the world, it is because she has been cast into the background by man, and then has followed him like a slave; if she has been his aid in the cruelties that have shamed the world, it is because she has closed her own eyes and looked through his; if she has been his companion in luxuries and vices at which the pure woman blushes, it is because he has driven her to the resources of the weak in the lower orders of creation, and she has become crafty, that she might obtain power—longing for companionship, she has stepped from the rung of the ladder where she stood nearest heaven, and plunged into sensuality with him, the Lord of the material; then she, who had been his superior in the elements that most harmonize life, looking up from her debasement to the face of her companion, begged for tolerance where she before had a right to homage—pleaded her weakness as a motive for protection, because she had laid aside her own distinctive powers, and become imbecile and subservient.

Women must recognize their unlikeness, and then understanding what needs grow out of this unlikeness, some great truth must be evolved. Now they busy themselves with methods of thought, springing, it is true, from their own sense of something needed, but suggested altogether by the masculine intellect. Let us first shake ourselves from this pupilage of mind by which our faculties are dwarfed, and courageously judge for ourselves. In doing this, I see no need of Amazonian[1] strides or disfigurements, or stentorian lungs. The more deeply and earnestly a woman feels the laws of her own existence, the more solemn, reverent, and harmonious is her bearing. She sees what nature designed in her creation, and her whole being falls gracefully into its allotted sphere. If she be a simple, genial, household divinity, she will bind garlands around the altar of Penates[2] and worship in content. If more largely endowed, I see no reason why she should diminish her proportions to please an imbecile taste in society. I see no reason why she should not be received cordially into the school of Arts, or Science, or Politics, or Theology, in the same manner as the individual capacities of the other sex are recognized. They do not all square themselves to one standard, and why should we? They have a very large number engaged in sewing, cooking, spinning, and writing very small articles for very small works, designed for very small minds.

The majority are very far from being Platos, or Bayards,[3] or Napoleons. When so very large a portion of the other sex are engaged in what is regarded as unmanly, I see no reason why those of ours who have a fancy to tinker a constitution, canvass a county, or preach the Gospel, should not be permitted to do so, provided they feel this to be the best use of their faculties. I do not say this is the best thing for them to do; but I see no reason, if their best intelligence finds its best expression in any such channel, why they should not be indulged.

---

1 In Greek mythology, the Amazons are a nation of women warriors, fabled to practice the removal of one breast in order to better wield a bow and arrow.
2 In Roman mythology, patron gods and protectors of the household.
3 Pierre Terrail, seigneur de Bayard (c. 1474–1524), French military hero, called *le chevalier sans peur et sans reproche*, "the knight without fear or reproach," and *le bon chevalier*, "the good knight." Oakes Smith places Bayard with Greek philosopher and mathematician Plato (c. 429–c. 347 BCE) and French Emperor and military commander Napoleon Bonaparte (1769–1821).

Our right to individuality is what I would most assert. Men seem resolved to have but one type in our sex. They recognize the prerogative of the matter-of-fact Biddy[1] to raise a great clamor, quite to the annoyance of a neighborhood, but where's the use of the Nightingale?[2] The laws of stubborn utilitarianism must govern us, while they may be as fantastic as they please. They tell much about a "woman's sphere"—can they define this? As the phrase is used, I confess it has a most shallow and indefinite sense. The most I can gather from it is the consciousness of the speaker, which means something like the philosophy of Mr. Murdstone's firmness;[3] it is a sphere by which every woman creature, of whatever age, appending to himself, shall circle very much within his own—see and hear through his senses, and believe according to his dogmas, with a sort of general proviso, that if need be for his growth, glorification, or well-being, in any way, they will instantly and uncompromisingly become extinct.

There is a Woman's sphere—harmonious, holy, soul-imparting; it has its grades, its laws from the nature of things, and we must seek out. The pursuits of men vary with their capacities— are higher or lower, according to age; why should not those of women vary in the same way? The highest offices of legislation are filled by men of mature age, whose judgments are supposed to be consolidated by years. Among the Mohawks, a woman, who had so trained a boy that he became *elected* to the office of Chief—for this honor was not hereditary, was received into the Councils of the Nation. The Spartan women emulated the men in the terseness of their language and the hardihood of their patriotism. Often and often do we see the attributes of the sexes reversed; the woman becoming the protector and, in fact, the *bond* of the house, without a shadow of infringement upon the appropriateness or beauty of her womanhood. It is late in the day to

---

1 Disparaging term for a woman, especially one who is old, gossipy, annoying, and interfering.
2 A bird that is symbolic of a poet.
3 In the novel *David Copperfield* (1850) by Charles Dickens, Edward Murdstone is the tyrannical stepfather whose so-called firm discipline is cruel and violent abuse aimed at breaking David's will and imposing conformity.

be thrown upon the defensive. I see no way in which harmony can result in the world without entire recognition of differences, for surely nothing is gained upon either side by antagonism merely. Women cannot be so very ridiculous and absurd in their honest, hearty truth-searchings; for such are the Mothers of the Republic; and he who casts contempt upon them, endorses his own shame. If the members of his own household are exempt from solemn truth-askings, he should beware how he exults over such evidence of common-place dullness or frivolity.

CHAPTER TENTH.

"Were I the chooser, a drachm[1] of well doing should be preferred before many times as much the forcible hindrance of evil doing." —MILTON.[2]

[...]

It seems to me the very spirit of many of our laws is humiliating, and helps to lower public opinion—they are a living witness to the ignorance and one-sided views of men; and while we see him who styles himself the head of creation thus benighted, we cannot expect entire justice from him—but we can, by a noble exertion of our own true dignities, make him ashamed to enforce laws which carry with them a reproach to himself. It seems to me that a man who goes into a court of law to claim a divorce—for instance, upon the ordinary grounds, confesses to his own disgrace, and his own lack of true manliness of character; so in regard to property, and many crimes even, where it may be said we suffer the penalties of a state of things which we had no voice in creating, and ought of right to be exempt from, and there is an intrinsic meanness in exposing us to the conditions. There is a certain conventional code, often unjust and oppressive, which women recognize in their intercourse with each

---

1   Dram, a small quantity.
2   From *Areopagitica; A Speech of Mr. John Milton for the Liberty of Unlicenc'd Printing, to the Parliament of England* (1644), by the English poet John Milton (1608–74). Written in opposition to the Licensing Order of 1643, Milton's political tract argues against prepublication licensing and censorship by the government.

other, and the tenacity with which they insist upon its observance argues a strong ability in them to keep all laws which they may be instrumental in making.

There is something in the spirit of the age inviting to action, not thinking merely—and often do we hear women say, "I feel a desire to do something beyond my present sphere—to act—I am tired of endurance merely." To such we would say solemnly, tenderly—Up and do—it is the voice of God, it may be calling you to a divine work. She that feels a latent power within her calling her to action, is culpable for her neglect to obey the voice. Mistakes, failures, must and will ensue—what then? it is something to have attempted great things—if the motive be pure, it is godlike, and good will come of it. Vanity, pretension, soon find their level, but the great and holy aim is in God's keeping, and must go onward conquering and to conquer. I care not that a woman sometimes fails in her attempts, as thousands of the other sex do,—it will not injure her, provided there is any magnitude in her nature: but I reverence the sentiment in her soul that dictated the movement. I feel there must have been deep need within her which she was bound to recognize, and that the mantle that perhaps slipped from her too delicate shoulders may be broadcast upon others more nobly proportioned.

We have passed the era of civilization when a woman was condemned solely to the productive and laborious part of the domestic arrangement. True, in England she may yet be harnessed to a cart for the conveyance of coal, and she may be in many parts of the world burdened and tasked beyond measure—but these are evils growing out of the general enormities of society, through which the race must work its emancipation: they are evils aside from the general object of these articles.

The woman of the Chivalrous Ages would not content the woman of the Nineteenth Century. Modern mechanism has superseded the necessity of her cares of embroidery, and the breaking up of old forms has made her duty of distributing alms, and ordering her band of retainers, unnecessary—nor would she be content to lean from her balcony watching the first gleam of her lover's plume returning from his seven years' warfare; or to sit in solemn state the Queen of Beauty and homage; or to listen to the songs of bearded Troubadour. The day for the worship of beauty, solely, is long since passed, and the woman of Thought usurps her place. These foregone types were but the preludes to this—beautiful in their day—or tolerated as the best the world afforded. Something more noble, more full, is required now. Now the true full woman must be more enlarged—more reflective, contemplative, and more loving even. Her tenderness has a broader field, even as her thoughts have; she is capable of more; she feels the stirring of more within herself, and feels a stirring to action too—for all power is vital, and wherever it may be lodged, it will out at some time.

Such being the case, it is useless to talk of restricting women in the action of their faculties. In our age, unless the women of intellect—(for the type is maturing itself to that development which is highest and most beautiful)—unless she is allowed the free exercise of her talents, is far more lonely and wretched than her poor sister of a bygone age, who toiled because her soul as well as body was in bondage, or the handsome Dame, who moved the Queen of Beauty, listening with proud grace to the songs of her admirers. These were content, for the day-star of better things had not risen upon them; but the woman of our day is not content, because she sees a newer and better light, and she reads the handwriting upon the wall, which says: "Thou art weighed in the balance and found wanting,"[1] and therefore she is ready to cast her whole being, her thought, her aspiration, all into the scale of public good, and in being true to herself, become true to the world's destinies.

1 Daniel 5:27.

Appendix B: Tecumseh, Captivity Narratives, and Indian-White Romance

1. From John Dunn Hunter, *Memoirs of a Captivity among the Indians of North America, from Childhood to the Age of Nineteen: With Anecdotes Descriptive of Their Manners and Customs*, 3rd ed. (London: Longman, Hurst, Rees, Orme, Brown, and Green, 1823), 42–48

[John Dunn Hunter's *Manners and Customs of Several Indian Tribes Located West of the Mississippi; Including Some Account of the Soil, Climate, and Vegetable Productions, and the Indian Materia Medica: to Which Is Prefixed the History of the Author's Life During a Residence of Several Years among Them* was published in 1823 in Philadelphia by J. Maxwell and then reprinted the same year in London with a new title emphasizing Hunter's captivity. Two more English editions would appear with added materials, notably Hunter's "Reflections on the Different States and Conditions of Society; With the Outlines of a Plan to Ameliorate the Circumstances of the Indians of North America," which explicitly criticize US Indian policies. In 1826 Lewis Cass, an American military officer and politician who participated in the Battle of the Thames in which Tecumseh died and who worked to formulate and implement Andrew Jackson's Indian removal policy, published a review contesting the facts of Hunter's *Memoirs* and denouncing him as a fraud.[1] This attack cast suspicion upon Hunter but also generated scrutiny of Cass's own argument, with defenders who pointed out weaknesses in his case. A subject of this controversy is Hunter's portrayal of Tecumseh and his speech, which was widely cited and has contributed to the Shawnee leader's popular legacy.]

---

1   "Indians of North America," *The North American Review* (January 1828): 53–119.

[...] We remained among the Grand Osages,[1] till early in the next fall. During our stay, I saw a number of white people, who, from different motives, resorted to this nation: among them, was a clergyman, who preached several times to the Indians through an interpreter. He was the first Christian preacher that I had ever heard or seen. The Indians treated him with great respect, and listened to his discourses with profound attention; but could not, as I heard them observe, comprehend the doctrines he wished to inculcate. It may be appropriately mentioned here, that the Indians are accustomed, in their own debates, never to speak but one at a time; while all others, constituting the audience, invariably listen with patience and attention till their turn to speak arrives. This respect is still more particularly observed towards strangers; and the slightest deviation from it would be regarded by them as rude, indecorous, and highly offensive. It is this trait in the Indian character which many of the missionaries mistake for a *serious* impression made on their minds; and which has led to many exaggerated accounts of their conversion to Christianity.

Some of the white people whom I met, as before noticed, among the Osages, were traders, and others were reputed to be runners from their Great Father beyond the Great Waters, to invite the Indians to take up the tomahawk against the settlers. They made many long talks, and distributed many valuable presents; but without being able to shake the resolution which the Osages had formed, to preserve peace with their Great Father, the President. Their determinations were, however, to undergo a more severe trial: Te-cumseh, the celebrated Shawanee warrior and chief, in company with Francis the prophet,[2] now made their appearance among them.

He addressed them in long, eloquent, and pathetic strains; and an assembly more numerous than had ever been witnessed on any former occasion listened to him with an intensely agitated, though profoundly respectful interest and attention. In fact, so great was the effect produced by Te-cum-seh's eloquence, that the chiefs adjourned the council, shortly after he had closed his harangue; nor did they finally come to a decision on the great question in debate for several days afterwards.

I wish it was in my power to do justice to the eloquence of this

---

1   A band of the Osage known as the Great Osage or Pahatsi.
2   Hildis Hadjo or Josiah Francis, the Creek Prophet.

distinguished man; but it is utterly impossible. The richest colours, shaded with a master's pencil, would fall infinitely short of the glowing finish of the original. The occasion and subject were peculiarly adapted to call into action all the powers of genuine patriotism; and such language, such gestures, and such feelings and fulness of soul contending for utterance, were exhibited by this untutored native of the forest in the central wilds of America, as no audience, I am persuaded, either in ancient or modern times, ever before witnessed.

My readers may think some qualification due to this opinion; but none is necessary. The unlettered Te-cum-seh gave extemporaneous utterance only to what he felt; it was a simple, but vehement narration of the wrongs imposed by the white people on the Indians, and an exhortation for the latter to resist them. The whole addressed to an audience composed of individuals who had been educated to prefer almost any sacrifice to that of personal liberty, and even death to the degradation of their nation; and who, on this occasion, felt the portraiture of Te-cum-seh but too strikingly identified with their own condition, wrongs, and sufferings.

This discourse made an impression on my mind, which, I think, will last as long as I live. I cannot repeat it *verbatim*, though if I could, it would be a mere skeleton, without the rounding finish of its integuments:[1] it would only be the shadow of the substance; because the gestures, and the interest and feelings excited by the occasion, and which constitute the essentials of its character, would be altogether wanting. Nevertheless, I shall, as far as my recollection serves, make the attempt, and trust to the indulgence of my readers for an apology for the presumptuous digression.

When the Osages and distinguished strangers had assembled, Te-cum-seh arose; and after a pause of some minutes, in which he surveyed his audience in a very dignified, though respectfully complaisant and sympathizing manner, he commenced as follows:

"*Brothers.*—We all belong to one family; we are all children of the Great Spirit; we walk in the same path; slake our thirst at the same spring; and now affairs of the greatest concern lead us to smoke the pipe around the same council fire!

"*Brothers.*—We are friends; we must assist each other to bear our burdens. The blood of many of our fathers and brothers has run like water on the ground, to satisfy the avarice of the white men. We,

---

1   Natural coverings, as in skin, membrane, hair, etc.

ourselves, are threatened with a great evil; nothing will pacify them but the destruction of all the red men.

"*Brothers.*—When the white men first set foot on our grounds, they were hungry; they had no place on which to spread their blankets, or to kindle their fires. They were feeble; they could do nothing for themselves. Our fathers commiserated their distress, and shared freely with them whatever the Great Spirit had given his red children. They gave them food when hungry, medicine when sick, spread skins for them to sleep on, and gave them grounds, that they might hunt and raise corn.—Brothers, the white people are like poisonous serpents: when chilled, they are feeble and harmless; but invigorate them with warmth, and they sting their benefactors to death.

"The white people came among us feeble; and now we have made them strong, they wish to kill us, or drive us back, as they would wolves and panthers.

"*Brothers.*—The white men are not friends to the Indians: at first, they only asked for land sufficient for a wigwam; now, nothing will satisfy them but the whole of our hunting grounds, from the rising to the setting sun.

"*Brothers.*—The white men want more than our hunting grounds; they wish to kill our warriors; they would even kill our old men, women, and little ones.

"*Brothers.*—Many winters ago, there was no land; the sun did not rise and set: all was darkness. The Great Spirit made all things. He gave the white people a home beyond the great waters. He supplied these grounds with game, and gave them to his red children; and he gave them strength and courage to defend them.

"*Brothers.*—My people wish for peace; the red men all wish for peace: but where the white people are, there is no peace for them, except it be on the bosom of our mother.

"*Brothers.*—The white men despise and cheat the Indians; they abuse and insult them; they do not think the red men sufficiently good to live.

"The red men have borne many and great injuries; they ought to suffer them no longer. My people will not; they are determined on vengeance; they have taken up the tomahawk; they will make it fat with blood; they will drink the blood of the white people.

"*Brothers.*—My people are brave and numerous; but the white people are too strong for them alone. I wish you to take up the toma-hawk with them. If we all unite, we will cause the rivers to stain the great waters with their blood.

"*Brothers.*—If you do not unite with us, they will first destroy us, and then you will fall an easy prey to them. They have destroyed many nations of red men because they were not united, because they were not friends to each other.

"*Brothers.*—The white people send runners amongst us; they wish to make us enemies, that they may sweep over and desolate our hunting grounds, like devastating winds, or rushing waters.

"*Brothers.*—Our Great Father, over the great waters, is angry with the white people, our enemies. He will send his brave warriors against them; he will send us rifles, and whatever else we want—he is our friend, and we are his children.

"*Brothers.*—Who are the white people that we should fear them? They cannot run fast, and are good marks to shoot at: they are only men; our fathers have killed many of them: we are not squaws, and we will stain the earth red with their blood.

"*Brothers.*—The Great Spirit is angry with our enemies; he speaks in thunder, and the earth swallows up villages, and drinks up the Mississippi. The great waters will cover their lowlands; their corn cannot grow; and the Great Spirit will sweep those who escape to the hills from the earth with his terrible breath.

"*Brothers.*—We must be united; we must smoke the same pipe; we must fight each other's battles; and more than all, we must love the Great Spirit: he is for us; he will destroy our enemies, and make all his red children happy."

On the following day, Francis the prophet addressed the Osages in council; and although he repeated almost precisely the language of Te-cum-seh, and enlarged considerably more on the power and disposition of the Great Spirit; yet his discourse produced compara-tively little effect on his audience. He was not a favourite among the Indians; and I am of opinion, that he did more injury than benefit to the cause he undertook to espouse.

After they had concluded, I looked upon war as inevitable; and in its consequences contemplated the destruction of our enemies, and the restoration of the Indians to their primitive rights, power, and happiness. There was nothing I then so ardently desired as that of being a warrior, and I even envied those who were to achieve these important objects the fame and glory that would redound as a neces-

sary result. In a short time afterwards, however, the Osages rejected
Te-cum-seh's proposals, and all these brilliant prospects vanished.

2. From James E. Seaver [and Mary Jemison], *A Narrative of the Life of Mrs. Mary Jemison, Who Was Taken by the Indians, in the Year 1775, When Only about Twelve Years of Age, and Has Continued to Reside amongst Them to the Present Time* (Canandaigua, NY: J.D. Bemis & Co., 1824), 44–48

[Mary Jemison (1743–1833) was taken captive on the frontier in
Pennsylvania during the Seven Years' War, when a French and
Shawnee party attacked and killed her parents and siblings. Jemison's Shawnee captors gave her to two Seneca women who adopted
her into their family; she then married, raised children, and lived
her life among the Seneca in the Genesee Valley of Western New
York. In her late years, Jemison related her story to Seaver, whose
version of the narrative would undergo further revisions and addi-
tions in subsequent editions.]

Sheninjee was a noble man; large in stature; elegant in his appearance; generous in his conduct; courageous in war; a friend to
peace, and a great lover of justice. He supported a degree of dignity far above his rank, and merited and received the confidence
and friendship of all the tribes with whom he was acquainted.
Yet, Sheninjee was an Indian. The idea of spending my days with
him, at first seemed perfectly irreconcilable to my feelings: but
his good nature, generosity, tenderness, and friendship towards
me, soon gained my affection; and, strange as it may seem, I loved
him!—To me he was ever kind in sickness, and always treated
me with gentleness; in fact, he was an agreeable husband, and a
comfortable companion. We lived happily together till the time
of our final separation, which happened two or three years after
our marriage [...]

I had then been with the Indians four summers and four winters, and had become so far accustomed to their mode of living,
habits and dispositions, that my anxiety to get away, to be set
at liberty, and leave them, had almost subsided. With them was
my home; my family was there, and there I had many friends to

whom I was warmly attached in consideration of the favors, affection and friendship with which they had uniformly treated me, from the time of my adoption. Our labor was not severe; and that of one year was exactly similar, in almost every respect, to that of the others, without that endless variety that is to be observed in the common labor of the white people. Notwithstanding the Indian women have all the fuel and bread to procure, and the cooking to perform, their task is probably not harder than that of white women, who have those articles provided for them; and their cares certainly are not half as numerous, nor as great. In the summer season, we planted, tended and harvested our corn, and generally had all our children with us; but had no master to oversee or drive us, so that we could work as leisurely as we pleased. We had no ploughs on the Ohio; but performed the whole process of planting and hoeing with a small tool that resembled, in some respects, a hoe with a very short handle.

Our cooking consisted in pounding our corn into samp or hommany, boiling the hommany, making now and then a cake and baking it in the ashes, and in boiling or roasting our venison. As our cooking and eating utensils consisted of a hommany block and pestle, a small kettle, a knife or two, and a few vessels of bark or wood, it required but little time to keep them in order for use.

Spinning, weaving, sewing, stocking knitting, and the like, are arts which have never been practised in the Indian tribes generally. After the revolutionary war, I learned to sew, so that I could make my own clothing after a poor fashion; but the other domestic arts I have been wholly ignorant of the application of, since my captivity. In the season of hunting, it was our business, in addition to our cooking, to bring home the game that was taken by the Indians, dress it, and carefully preserve the eatable meat, and prepare or dress the skins. Our clothing was fastened together with strings of deer skin, and tied on with the same.

In that manner we lived, without any of those jealousies, quarrels, and revengeful battles between families and individuals, which have been common in the Indian tribes since the introduction of ardent spirits[1] amongst them.

---

1   Liquors such as brandy or whiskey.

3. From John Tanner and Edwin James, *A Narrative of the Captivity and Adventures of John Tanner, (U.S. Interpreter at the Saut de Ste. Marie,) during Thirty Years Residence among the Indians in the Interior of North America* (New York: G. & C. & H. Carvill, 1830), 155–58

[John Tanner (c. 1780–c. 1846) was kidnapped by the Shawnee at age nine from his family's frontier home along the Ohio River and then sold to an Ottawa woman, with whom he moved to Michigan and Manitoba. He grew to adulthood, married, and raised children among the Ojibwe and other Native peoples in the Great Lakes and Red River Valley regions, and he heard the Shawnee Prophet's message as it travelled by an emissary from Prophetstown, Indiana. Tanner reentered white society with great difficulty, given his thorough acculturation to Indian life and the prejudices his Indian family confronted. He was employed by Henry Rowe Schoolcraft in the 1820s after moving to Sault Ste. Marie (where Edwin James recorded Tanner's narrative), and his mysterious disappearance when Henry's brother, James Schoolcraft, was murdered caused allegations that he committed the crime.]

It was while I was living here at Great Wood River, that news came of a great man among the Shawneese, who had been favoured by a revelation of the mind and will of the Great Spirit. I was hunting in the prairie, at a great distance from my lodge, when I saw a stranger approaching; at first, I was apprehensive of an enemy, but, as he drew nearer, his dress showed him to be an Ojibbeway; but when he came up, there was something very strange and peculiar in his manner. He signified to me, that I must go home, but gave no explanation of the cause. He refused to look at me, or enter into any kind of conversation. I thought he must be crazy, but nevertheless accompanied him to my lodge. When we had smoked, he remained a long time silent, but, at last, began to tell me he had come with a message from the prophet of the Shawneese. "Henceforth," said he, "the fire must never be suffered to go out in your lodge. Summer and winter, day and night, in the storm, or when it is calm, you must remember that the life in your body, and the fire in your lodge, are the same, and of the same date. If you suffer your fire to be extinguished, at that moment your life will be at its end. You must not suffer a dog to live; you must never strike either a man, a woman, a child, or a dog. The prophet himself is coming to shake hands with you; but I have come before, that you may know what is the will of the Great Spirit communicated to us by him, and to inform you that the preservation of your life, for a single moment, depends on your entire obedience. From this time forward, we are neither to be drunk, to steal, to lie, or to go against our enemies. While we yield an entire obedience to these commands of the Great Spirit, the Sioux, even if they come to our country, will not be able to see us: we shall be protected and made happy." I listened to all he had to say, but told him, in answer, that I could not believe we should all die, in case our fire went out; in many instances, also, it would be difficult to avoid punishing our children; our dogs were useful in aiding us to hunt and take animals, so that I could not believe the Great Spirit had any wish to take them from us. He continued talking to us until late at night; then he lay down to sleep in my lodge. I happened to wake first in the morning, and perceiving the fire had gone out, I called him to get up, and see how many of us were living, and how many dead. He was prepared for the ridicule I attempted to throw upon his doctrine, and told me that I had not yet shaken hands with the prophet. His visit had been to prepare me for this important event, and to make me aware of the obligations and risks I should incur, by entering into the engagement implied in taking in my hand the message of the prophet. I did not rest entirely easy in my unbelief. The Indians, generally, received the doctrine of this man with great humility and fear. Distress and anxiety was visible in every countenance. Many killed their dogs, and endeavoured to practice obedience to all the commands of this new preacher, who still remained among us. But, as was usual with me, in any emergency of this kind, I went to the traders, firmly believing, that if the Deity had any communications to make to men, they would be given, in the first instance, to white men. The traders ridiculed and despised the idea of a new revelation of the Divine will, and the thought that it should be given to a poor Shawnee. Thus was I confirmed in my infidelity. Nevertheless, I did not openly avow my unbelief to the Indians, only I refused to kill my dogs, and showed no great degree of anxiety to comply with his other requirements. As long as I remained among the Indians, I made it my business to conform, as far as appeared consistent with my immediate convenience and comfort, with all their customs. Many of their ideas I have adopted; but I always found among them opinions which I could not hold. The Ojibbeway whom I have mentioned, remained some time among the Indians, in my neighbourhood, and gained the attention of the principal men so effectually, that a time was appointed, and a lodge prepared, for the solemn and public espousing of the doctrines of the prophet. When the people, and I among them, were brought into the long lodge, prepared for this solemnity, we saw something carefully concealed under a blanket, in figure and dimensions bearing some resemblance to the form of a man. This was accompanied by two young men, who, it was understood, attended constantly upon it, made its bed at night, as for a man, and slept near it. But while we remained, no one went near it, or raised the blanket which was spread over its unknown contents. Four strings of mouldy and discoloured beans, were all the remaining visible insignia of this important mission. After a long harangue, in which the prominent features of the new revelation were stated and urged upon the attention of all, the four strings of beans, which we were told were made of the flesh itself of the prophet, were carried, with much solemnity, to each man in the lodge, and he was expected to take hold of each string at the top, and draw them gently through his hand. This was called shaking hands with the prophet, and was considered as solemnly engaging to obey his injunctions, and accept his mission as from the Supreme. All the Indians who touched the beans, had previously killed their dogs; they gave up their medicine bags, and showed a disposition to comply with all that should be required of them.

We had now been for some time assembled in considerable numbers; much agitation and terror had prevailed among us, and now famine began to be felt. The faces of men wore an aspect of unusual gloominess; the active became indolent, and the spirits of the bravest seemed to be subdued. I started to hunt with my dogs, which I had constantly refused to kill, or suffer to be killed. By their assistance, I found and killed a bear. On returning home, I said to some of the Indians, "Has not the Great Spirit given us our dogs to aid us in procuring what is needful for the support of our life, and can you believe he wishes now to deprive us of their services? The prophet, we are told, has forbid us to suffer our fire to be extinguished in our lodges, and when we travel or hunt, he will not allow us to use a flint and steel, and we are told he requires that no man should give fire to another. Can it please the Great Spirit that we should lie in our hunting camps without fire; or is it more agreeable to him that we should make fire by rubbing together two sticks, than with a flint and a piece of steel?" But they would not listen to me, and the serious enthusiasm which prevailed among them so far affected me, that I threw away my flint and steel, laid aside my medicine bag, and, in many particulars complied with the new doctrines; but I would not kill my dogs. I soon learned to kindle a fire by rubbing some dry cedar, which I was careful to carry always about me; but the discontinuance of the use of flint and steel subjected many of the Indians to much inconvenience and suffering. The influence of the Shawnee prophet was very sensibly and painfully felt by the remotest Ojibbeways of whom I had any knowledge; but it was not the common impression among them, that his doctrines had any tendency to unite them in the accomplishment of any human purpose. For two or three years drunkenness was much less frequent than formerly; war was less thought of, and the entire aspect of affairs among them, was somewhat changed by the influence of one man. But gradually the impression was obliterated, medicine bags, flints, and steels, were resumed; dogs were raised, women and children were beaten as before, and the Shawnee prophet was despised. At this day he is looked upon by the Indians as an impostor and a bad man.

4. From R.S. Dills, *History of Greene County, Together with Historic Notes on the Northwest, and the State of Ohio* (Dayton, OH: Odell & Mayer, 1881), 269–70

[While historians agree that the story is improbable, the legend of Tecumseh's love for a white woman made its way into print in this history and was perpetuated by the Galloway family.]

In 1813, probably, George Galloway (usually designated Pennsylvania George) and Rebecca Galloway, oldest daughter of James Galloway, sen., were married. Miss Galloway had had a former suitor, which she had rejected, who was no less a personage than the distinguished

Himself. He had been a frequent visitor in the family, and took a wonderful liking to the white girl; and, according to the Indian custom, made his advances to the father, who referred the case to the daughter. The undaunted chief appeals to the girl herself, offering her fifty broaches of silver. She told him she didn't want to be a wild woman, and work like the Indian women. He told her she need not work. Notwithstanding the rejection of his suit, he ever after remained friendly with the family, though he was sometimes found to be rather a tough customer.

General Harrison and Tecumseh (1810?). William Ridgway (engraver), after John Reuben Chapin (artist). Picture Collection, the New York Public Library, Astor, Lenox, and Tilden Foundations.

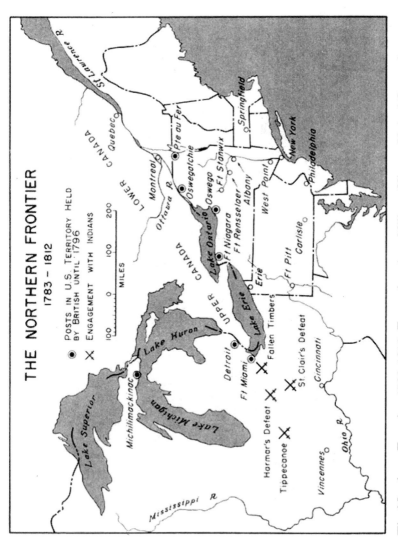

The Northern Frontier, 1783-1812. From *American Military History*, United States Army Center of Military History (1989). Courtesy of the University of Texas Libraries, the University of Texas at Austin.

Appendix C: Stories of Harrison and the Shawnee in Campaign Biographies

1. From James Hall, *A Memoir of the Public Services of William Henry Harrison, of Ohio* (Philadelphia: Key & Biddle, 1836), 111–19

[Stories and speeches of Tecumseh and the Shawnee Prophet circulated in campaign biographies promoting Harrison during his two runs for president in 1836 and 1840 (see Introduction, pp. 22–25). Hall's biography makes an argument for Harrison's heroism in dealings with the Shawnee while explicitly challenging Tecumseh's reputation as a noble, eloquent leader.]   *political agenda*

Intrigues of Tecumthe[1]—Council at Vincennes.

Up to the year 1811, Tecumthe and his brother were engaged, as we have seen, in constant intrigues against the United States. They had disturbed all the councils that were held, and endeavoured to prevent every treaty that was made. Surrounded by a lawless band, composed of desperate renegadoes from various tribes, by the young and hot, the dissolute and dishonest, they scarcely practised even the Punic[2] faith of the Indian code. They asserted that all the lands inhabited by Indians belonged to the tribes indiscriminately—that no tribe had a right to transfer any soil to the whites without the assent of all—and that, consequently, all the treaties that had been made were invalid.

In 1808, the prophet established his principal place of rendezvous on the Wabash, near the mouth of the Tippecanoe—a spot which soon became known as the Prophet's Town. Here a thousand young warriors, such as we have described, rallied around him; sallying forth in greater or smaller parties, to commit the most atrocious

---

1   Variant of Tecumseh.
2   Treacherous; having the treacherous character attributed to the Carthaginians by the Romans.

deeds of depredation and murder, along the whole frontier of Indiana. Vincennes, the seat of government,[1] was often threatened; and the governor's house was scarcely considered safe from the intrusion of the maddened savages. But the prophet, while he exercised his priestly function in such a manner as to excite the superstition of his motley crew of followers, was indolent, sensual, and cowardly; and his mal-administration soon reduced the number of his followers to less than three hundred. Even these were so much impoverished by their excesses and improvidence, that on one occasion they must have starved, had not the benevolence of Governor Harrison induced him to send them a supply of provisions. The return of Tecumthe, who had been absent on a visit to the distant tribes, restored order.

In 1809, Governor Harrison purchased from the Delawares, Miamis, and Potawatamies, a large tract of country on both sides of the Wabash, and extending up that river about sixty miles above Vincennes. Tecumthe was absent, and his brother, not feeling himself interested, made no opposition to the treaty; but the former, on his return, expressed great dissatisfaction, and threatened some of the chiefs with death, who had made the treaty. Governor Harrison, hearing of his displeasure, dispatched a messenger to invite him to come to Vincennes, and to assure him, "that any claims he might have to the lands which had been ceded, were not affected by the treaty; that he might come to Vincennes and exhibit his pretensions, and if they were found to be valid, the land would either be given up, or an ample compensation made for it."

Having no confidence in the faith of Tecumthe, the governor directed that he should not bring with him more than thirty warriors; but he came with four hundred, completely armed. The people of Vincennes were in great alarm, nor was the governor without apprehension that treachery was intended. This suspicion was not diminished by the conduct of the chief, who, on the morning after his arrival, refused to hold the council at the place appointed, under an affected belief that treachery was intended on our side.

A large portico in front of the governor's house had been prepared for the purpose with seats, as well for the Indians, as for the citizens who were expected to attend. When Tecumthe came from his camp, with about forty of his warriors, he stood off, and

---

1   The capital of the Indiana Territory, of which Harrison was governor.

on being invited by the governor, through an interpreter, to take his seat, refused, observing that he wished the council to be held under the shade of some trees in front of the house. When it was objected that it would be troublesome to remove the seats, he replied, "that it would only be necessary to remove those intended for the whites—that the red men were accustomed to sit upon the earth, which was their mother, and that they were always happy to recline upon her bosom."

At this council, held on the 12th of August, 1810, Tecumthe delivered a speech, of which we find the following report, containing the sentiments uttered, but in a language very different from that of the Indian orator:—

"I have made myself what I am; and I would that I could make the red people as great as the conceptions of my mind, when I think of the Great Spirit, that rules over all. I would not then come to Governor Harrison to ask him to tear the treaty; but I would say to him, Brother, you have liberty to return to your own country. Once there was no white man in all this country: then it belonged to red men, children of the same parents, placed on it by the Great Spirit to keep it, to travel over it, to eat its fruits, and fill it with the same race—once a happy race, but now made miserable by the white people, who are never contented, but always encroaching. They have driven us from the great salt water, forced us over the mountains, and would shortly push us into the lakes—but we are determined to go no further. The only way to stop this evil, is for all the red men to unite in claiming a common and equal right in the land, as it was at first, and should be now—for it never was divided, but belongs to all. No tribe has a right to sell, even to each other, much less to strangers, who demand all, and will take no less. The white people have no right to take the land from the Indians who had it first—it is theirs. They may sell, but all must join. Any sale not made by all, is not good. The late sale is bad—it was made by a part only. Part do not know how to sell. It requires all to make a bargain for all."

Governor Harrison, in his reply, said, "that the white people, when they arrived upon this continent, had found the Miamis in the occupation of all the country of the Wabash; and at that time the Shawanese were residents of Georgia, from which they were driven by the Creeks. That the lands had been purchased from the Miamis, who were the true and original owners of it. That it was ridiculous to assert that all the Indians were one nation; for if such had been the intention of the Great Spirit, he would not have put six different tongues into their heads, but would have taught them all to speak one language. That the Miamis had found it for their interest to sell a part of their lands, and receive for them a further annuity, in addition to what they had long enjoyed, and the benefit of which they had experienced, from the punctuality with which the *seventeen fires*[1] complied with their engagements; and that the Shawanese had no right to come from a distant country, to control the Miamis in the disposal of their own property."

The interpreter had scarcely finished the explanation of these remarks, when Tecumthe fiercely exclaimed, "It is false!" and giving a signal to his warriors, they sprang upon their feet, from the green grass on which they were sitting, and seized their war-clubs. The governor, and the small train that surrounded him, were now in imminent danger. He was attended by a few citizens, who were unarmed. A military guard of twelve men, who had been stationed near him, and whose presence was considered rather as an honorary than a defensive measure,—being exposed, as it was thought unnecessarily, to the heat of the sun in a sultry August day, had been humanely directed by the governor to remove to a shaded spot at some distance. But the governor, retaining his presence of mind, rose and placed his hand upon his sword, at the same time directing those of his friends and suite who were about him, to stand upon their guard. Tecumthe addressed the Indians in a passionate tone, and with violent gesticulations. Major G.R.C. Floyd, of the U.S. army, who stood near the governor, drew his dirk: Winnemak, a friendly chief, cocked his pistol, and Mr. Winans, a Methodist preacher, ran to the governor's house, seized a gun, and placed himself in the door to defend the family. For a few moments all expected a bloody rencounter. The guard was ordered up, and would instantly have fired upon the Indians, had it not been for the coolness of Governor Harrison, who restrained them. He then calmly, but authoritatively, told Tecumthe, that "he was a bad man—that he would have no further talk with him—that he must return now to his camp, and take his departure from the settlements immediately."

---

1   The 17 states at that time forming the United States.

The next morning, Tecumthe having reflected on the impropriety of his conduct, and finding that he had to deal with a man as bold and vigilant as himself, who was not to be daunted by his audacious turbulence, nor circumvented by his specious manoeuvres, apologized for the affront he had offered, and begged that the council might be renewed. To this the governor consented, suppressing any feeling of resentment which he might naturally have felt, and determined to leave no exertion untried, to carry into effect the pacific views of the government. It was agreed that each party should have the same attendance as on the previous day; but the governor took the precaution to place himself in an attitude to command respect, and to protect the inhabitants of Vincennes from violence, by ordering two companies of militia to be placed on duty within the village.

Tecumthe presented himself with the same undaunted bearing which always marked him as a superior man; but he was now dignified and collected, and showed no disposition to resume his former insolent deportment. He disclaimed having entertained any intention of attacking the governor, but said he had been advised by white men to do as he had done. Two white men—British emissaries undoubtedly—had visited him at his place of residence, had told him that half the white people were opposed to the governor, and willing to relinquish the land, and urged him to advise the tribes not to receive pay for it, alleging that the governor would soon be recalled, and a good man put in his place, who would give up the land to the Indians. The governor inquired whether he would forcibly oppose the survey of the purchase. He replied, that he was determined to adhere to the *old boundary*. Then arose a Wyandot, a Kickapoo, a Potawatamie, an Ottawa, and a Winnebago chief, each declaring his determination to stand by Tecumthe. The governor then said that the words of Tecumthe should be reported to the President, who would take measures to enforce the treaty; and the council ended.

The governor, still anxious to conciliate the haughty savage, paid him a visit next day at his own camp. He was received with kindness and attention,—his uniform courtesy, and inflexible firmness, having won the respect of the rude warriors of the forest. They conversed for some time, but Tecumthe obstinately adhered to all his former positions; and when Governor Harrison told him, that he was sure the President would not yield to his pretensions, the chief replied, "Well, as the great chief is to determine the matter, I hope the Great Spirit will put sense enough into his head to induce him to direct you to give up this land. It is true, he is so far off, he will not be injured by the war. He may sit still in his town, and drink his wine, while you and I will have to fight it out."

This is an accurate account of an interesting council, the proceedings of which have been much misrepresented. A love for the romantic and the marvellous has induced speeches to be written for Tecumthe, which were never delivered. His conduct was distinguished on this occasion by violence, not by eloquence; his art was displayed in attempts to intimidate the Americans, and to create an affray, by stirring up the vindictive feelings of his followers, and not by any display of argument.

2. From Samuel Jones Burr, *The Life and Times of William Henry Harrison* (New York: L.W. Ransom, 1840), 107–10

[Burr's biography includes a "translation" of Shawnee tradition in a speech delivered to Harrison by an old chief, portraying the Prophet as a politically savvy figure who blended new and old spiritual doctrines to his advantage.]

For some years the success of the Prophet was quite doubtful, and his converts were few. His brother was, of course, the first to embrace the new fangled doctrine, and shortly after some of his relations and intimate friends embraced the tenets. He now gained a great influence over his own tribe, and flattered the pride of the SHAWANEES by renewing an old tradition which made them the wisest, most intelligent, and respectable people in the world. This we give in the language of an old Shawanee chief, who spoke at the council at Fort Wayne, upon the subject, in 1803. Much of this speech was addressed directly to Governor HARRISON. With much native dignity, the venerable savage thus delivered himself:—

"The Master of Life who was himself an Indian, made the Shawanees before any others of the human race, and *they* sprang from his brain.[1] The Master of Life gave them all the knowledge which

---

1   [Burr's note:] There is a strong resemblance here to the mythological account of the creation of Minerva.

he himself possessed. He placed them upon the great island,[1] and all the other red people are descended from the Shawanees, he made the French and English out of his breast. The Dutch he made out of his feet. As for your Long Knives[2] kind, he made them out of his hands. All those inferior races of men he made white, and placed them beyond the great lake.[3]

"The Shawanees were masters of the continent for many ages, using the knowledge which they had received from the Great Spirit, in such a manner as to be pleasing to him, and to secure their own happiness. In a great length of time however they became corrupt and the Master of Life told them he would take away from them the knowledge they possessed and give it to the white people; to be restored when, by a return to good principles, they would deserve it.

"Many years after that, they saw something white approaching their shores. At first they took it for a great bird, but they soon found it to be a monstrous canoe, filled with the very people who had got the knowledge which belonged to the Shawanees, but they usurped their lands also. They pretended, indeed, to have purchased their lands, but the very goods which they gave for them were more the property of the Indians than of the white people, because the knowledge which enabled them to manufacture these goods actually belonged to the Shawanees.

"But these things will now have an end. The Master of Life is about to restore to the Shawanees both their knowledge and their rights, and he will trample the Long Knives under his feet."

The old chief who delivered the above was supposed to be in the British interest, and that his object was to prevent all negotiations. The Prophet used the tradition, and by it brought over thousands to his way of thinking. The subject was a good one, and he turned it at once to his own purpose.

---

1   [Burr's note:] The Continent of America.
2   [Burr's note:] The Americans, though at first the term was applied by the Indians to the Virginians and Kentuckians.
3   [Burr's note:] The Atlantic Ocean.

Appendix D: Oakes Smith and the Schoolcrafts

1. Leelinau (Jane Johnston Schoolcraft), "Moowis, The Indian Coquette. A Chippewa Legend." From the manuscript magazine *The Muz-ze-ni-e-gun, or Literary Voyager* 4 (12 January 1827). Henry Rowe Schoolcraft Papers, Manuscript Division, Library of Congress, Washington, DC. Container 65. Microfilm

[Jane Johnston (Bamewawagezhikaquay) met and married Henry Rowe Schoolcraft while he was working as an Indian agent in Sault Ste. Marie, Michigan, where they worked together as writers and ethnologists on projects including handwritten, manuscript magazines that circulated among a select audience. Versions of Jane's "Moowis" later appeared under Henry's name in *The Columbian Lady's and Gentleman's Magazine* (1844) and in *Oneóta, or The Red Race of America* (1845), the miscellany in which Oakes Smith's "Machinito" appears. His retelling includes a prefatory note explaining that the tale "addresses itself plainly to girls; to whom it teaches the danger of what we denominate coquetry. It would seem from this, that beauty, and its concomitant, a passion for dress, among the red daughters of Adam and Eve, has the same tendency to create pride, and nourish self-conceit, and self-esteem, and assume a *tyranny over the human heart*, which writers tell us, these qualities have among their white-skinned, auburn-haired, and blue-eyed progeny the world over." Jane's treatment of courting and marriage in this telling of "Moowis" is more ambiguous in its moral lesson and purpose.]

There was a village full of Indians, and a noted belle or *muh muh daw go qua* was living there. A noted beau or *muh muh daw go nin nie* was there also. He and another young man went to court this young woman, and laid down beside her, when she scratched the face of the handsome beau. He went home and would not rise till the family prepared to depart, and he would not then arise. They then left him, as he felt ashamed to be seen even by his own relations. It was winter, and the young man, his rival, who was his cousin, tried all he could to persuade him to go with the family, for it was now winter, but to no purpose, till the whole village had decamped and had gone away. He then rose and gathered all the bits of clothing, and ornaments of beads and other things, that had been left. He then made a coat and leggins of the same, nicely trimmed with the beads, and the suit was fine and complete. After making a pair of moccasins, nicely trimmed, he also made a bow and arrows. He then collected the dirt of the village, and filled the garments he had made, so as to appear as a man, and put the bow and arrows in its hands, and it came to life. He then desired the dirt image to follow him to the camp of those who had left him, who thinking him dead by this time, were surprized to see him. One of the neighbors took in the dirt-man and entertained him. The belle saw them come and immediately fell in love with him. The family that took him in made a large fire to warm him, as it was winter. The image said to one of the children, "sit between me and the fire, it is too hot," and the child did so, but all smelt the dirt. Some said, "some one has trod on, and brought in dirt." The master of the family said to the child sitting in front of the guest, "get away from before our guest, you keep the heat from him." The boy answered saying, "he told me to sit between him and the fire." In the meantime, the belle wished the stranger would visit her. The image went to his master, and they went out to different lodges, the image going as directed to the belle's. Towards morning, the image said to the young woman (as he had succeeded) "I must now go away," but she said, "I will go with you." He said "it is too far." She answered, "it is not so far but that I can go with you." He first went to the lodge where he was entertained, and then to his master, and told him of all that had happened, and that he was going off with her. The young man thought it a pity she had treated him so, and how sadly she would be punished. They went off, she following behind. He left her a great way behind, but she continued to follow him. When the sun rose high, she found one of his mittens and picked it up, but to her astonishment, found it full of dirt. She, however took it and wiped it, and going on further, she found the other mitten in the same condition. She thought, "fie!! why does he do so," thinking he dirtied in them. She kept finding different articles of his dress, on the way all day, in the same condition. He kept ahead of her till towards evening, when the snow was like water, having melted by the heat of the day. No signs of her husband appearing, after having collected all the cloths that held him together, she began to cry, not knowing where to go, as their track was lost, on account of the snow's melting. She kept crying *Moowis*[1] has led me astray, and she kept singing and crying Moowis nin ge won e win ig, ne won e win ig.[2]

2. Elizabeth Oakes Smith, Letter to Jane L. [Johnston] Schoolcraft, 25 April 1842. Henry Rowe Schoolcraft Papers, Manuscript Division, Library of Congress, Washington, DC. Container 46. Microfilm

[Oakes Smith sent this letter to Dundas, Canada West (now Ontario), where Schoolcraft was visiting her sister and died unexpectedly on 22 May 1842 at the age of 42. The "L." in the salutation refers to "Leelinau," a name used by Schoolcraft.]

To Mrs. Jane L. Schoolcraft,

I need not say, my dear Madam, that your very kind note gave me the greatest pleasure, nor that it will be preserved amongst my most treasured memorials; for you, who are so full of womanly affection, can well understand how gratifying must be this proof of interest and regard from one of her own sex, to one who has ever been emulous to merit them. I will not with affected modesty disclaim the tribute you have awarded me, but rather make it an incentive to be more deserving, convinced as I am that it is the earnest and affectionate language of a warm and generous heart, self-styled a 'child of the woods'; of one, who has not lost amid the seductions of society, her primitive simplicity and truthfulness of character.

Allow me, My dear Madam, to present you a few lines suggested by your kind letter, which I am sure will be read with indulgence.

With sentiments of sincere regard and esteem, I remain yours.

E.O. Smith

---

1   Translated in Henry's prefatory note as a term that is "one of the most derogative and offensive possible," derived from the Ojibwe noun "mo, filth, or excrement" (*Oneóta* 381).

2   Translated in Henry's version: "Moowis, you have led me astray—you are leading me astray" (*Oneóta* 384).

To Mrs. J.L. Schoolcraft

Yes, Lady, thou hast read a heart,
That passive hears the voice of fame—
That could not feel its life-blood start,
Though glory echoed forth its name—

But even in its secret bower,
It listeth to that still small voice
Where love is telling every hour,
That even here we many rejoice—

That even here, where love must bring
Its many hopes, its many fears,
There is a balm beneath its wing,
That gives a blessedness to tears.

New York 25ᵗʰ April 1842

3. From Henry Rowe Schoolcraft [with Elizabeth Oakes Smith], "Nursery and Cradle Songs of the Forest," in Schoolcraft's *Oneóta, or Characteristics of the Red Race of America* (New York & London: Wiley & Putnam, 1845), 212–15

[Schoolcraft's comments on the translation of these Ojibwe songs reveal his collaboration with Oakes Smith as a writer whom he trusted and respected with this material. His partnership with his own wife, who possessed both poetic skills and fluency in the Ojibwe language, ended with her premature death in 1842.]

The Indian child, in truth, takes its first lesson in the *art of endurance*, in the cradle. When it cries it need not be unbound to nurse it. If the mother be young, she must put it to sleep herself. If she have younger sisters or daughters they share this care with her. If the lodge be roomy and high, as lodges sometimes are, the cradle is suspended to the top poles to be swung. If not, or the weather be fine, it is tied to the limb of a tree, with small cords made from the inner bark of the linden, and a vibratory motion given to it from head to foot by the mother or some attendant. The motion thus communicated, is that of the pendulum or common swing, and may be supposed to be the easiest and most agreeable possible to the child. It is from this motion that the leading idea of the cradle song is taken.

I have often seen the red mother, or perhaps a sister of the child, leisurely swinging a pretty ornamented cradle to and fro in this way, in order to put the child to sleep, or simply to amuse it. The following specimens of these wild-wood chaunts, or wigwam lullabys, are taken from my notes upon this subject, during many years of familiar intercourse with the aboriginals. If they are neither numerous nor attractive, placed side by side with the rich nursery stores of more refined life, it is yet a pleasant fact to have found such things even existing at all amongst a people supposed to possess so few of the amenities of life, and to have so little versatility of character.

Meagre as these specimens seem, they yet involve no small degree of philological diligence, as nothing can be more delicate than the inflexions of these pretty chaunts, and the Indian woman, like her white sister, gives a delicacy of intonation to the roughest words of her language. The term wa-wa often introduced denotes a *wave* of the air, or the circle described by the motion of an object through it, as we say, swing, swing, a term never applied to a wave of water. The latter is called tegoo, or if it be crowned with foam, beta.

In introducing the subjoined specimens of these simple see saws of the lodge and forest chaunts, the writer felt, that they were almost too frail of structure to be trusted, without a gentle hand, amidst his rougher materials. He is permitted to say, in regard to them, that they have been exhibited to Mrs. Elizabeth Oakes Smith, herself a refined enthusiast of the woods, and that the versions from the original given, are from her chaste and truthful pen.

In the following arch little song, the reader has only to imagine a playful girl trying to put a restless child to sleep, who pokes its little head, with black hair and keen eyes over the side of the cradle, and the girl sings, imitating its own piping tones.

Ah wa nain?	(Who is this?)
Ah wa nain?	(Who is this?)
Wa yau was sa—	(Giving light—meaning the light of the eye)
Ko pwasod.	(On the top of my lodge.)

Who is this? who is this? eye-light bringing
    To the roof of the lodge?

And then she assumes the tone of the little screech owl, and answers—

Kob kob kob   (It is I—the little owl)
Nim be e zhau   (Coming,)
Kob kob kob   (It is I—the little owl)
Nim be e zhau   (Coming,)
Kit che—kit che.   (Down! down!)
   It is I, it is I, hither swinging,   (wa wa)
      Dodge, dodge, baby dodge;

And she springs towards it and down goes the little head. This is repeated with the utmost merriment upon both sides.

Who is this, who is this eye-light bringing
    To the roof of my lodge?
It is I, it is I, hither swinging,
    Dodge, dodge, baby dodge.

Here is another, slower and monotonous, but indicating the utmost maternal content:

Swinging, swinging, lul la by,
   Sleep, little daughter sleep,
'Tis your mother watching by.
   Swinging, swinging she will keep,
Little daughter lul la by.

'Tis your mother loves you dearest,
   Sleep, sleep, daughter sleep,
Swinging, swinging, ever nearest.
   Baby, baby, do not weep;
Little daughter, lul la by.

Swinging, swinging, lul la by,
   Sleep, sleep, little one,

And thy mother will be nigh—
Swing, swing, not alone—
Little daughter, lul la by.

This of course is exceedingly simple, but be it remembered these chaunts are always so in the most refined life. The ideas are the same, that of tenderness and protective care only, the ideas being few, the language is in accordance. To my mind it has been a matter of extreme interest to observe how almost identical are the expressions of affection in all states of society, as though these primitive elements admit of no progress, but are perfect in themselves. The e-we-yea of the Indian woman is entirely analogous to the lul la by of our language, and will be seen to be exceedingly pretty in itself.

2. The original words of this,[1] with their literal import, are also added, to preserve the identity.

(a.)

Wa wa—wa wa—wa we yea, (Swinging, twice, lullaby.)
Nebaun—nebaun—nebaun, (Sleep thou, thrice.)
Nedaunis-ais, e we yea, (Little daughter, lullaby.)
Wa wa—wa wa—wa wa, (Swinging, thrice.)
Nedaunis-ais, e we yea, (Little daughter lullaby.)

(b.)

Keguh, ke gun ah wain e ma, (Your mother cares for you.)
Nebaun—nebaun—nebaun, e we yea, (Sleep, thrice, lullaby.)
Kago, saigizze-kain, nedaunis-ais, (Do not fear, my little daughter.)
Nebaun—nebaun—nebaun, (Sleep, thrice.)
Kago, saigizze-kain, wa wa, e we yea, (third line repeated.)

(c.)

Wa wa—wa wa—wa we yea, (Swinging, twice, lullaby.)
Kaween neezheka kediausee, (Not alone art thou.)
Ke kan nau wai, no me go, suhween, (Your mother is caring for you.)
Nebaun—nebaun—nedaunis-ais, (Sleep, sleep, my little daughter.)

---

1 The above lullaby, presumably penned by Oakes Smith, the "first" before this second version.

Wa wa—wa wa—wa we yea, (Swinging, &c. lullaby.)
Nebaun—nebaun—nebaun, (Sleep! sleep! sleep.[1])

4. Henry Rowe Schoolcraft, "Idea of an American Literature Based on Indian Mythology" ["A Prospective American Literature; Superinduced from Indian Mythology"], *Oneóta, or Characteristics of the Red Race of America* (New York & London: Wiley & Putnam, 1845), 246–48

[In this critical appraisal of the representation of Indians in American literature, Schoolcraft compares Oakes Smith to other popular writers and gives her high praise. His opinion held great weight, as evident in critic and anthologist Rufus W. Griswold's assertions in *The Prose Writers of America* (1847) that Schoolcraft's "ethnological writings are among the most important contributions that have been made to the literature of this country" (300), and that Oakes Smith is the American writer "who has succeeded, perhaps better than any other person, in appreciating and developing the fitness of aboriginal tradition and mythology for the purposes of romantic fiction" (34).]

In bringing forward his collection of the historical and imaginative traditions of the Indian tribes, the writer has been aware, that he might, herein, be at the same time the medium of presenting the germs of a future mythology, which, in the hands of our poets, and novelists, and fictitious writers, might admit of being formed and moulded to the purposes, of a purely vernacular, literature. So far

---

1 [Schoolcraft's note:] These translations are entirely literal—the verbs to "sleep" and to "fear," requiring the imperative mood, second person, present tense, throughout. In rendering the term "wa-wa" in the participial form some doubt may exist, but this has been terminated by the idea of the *existing* motion, which is clearly implied, although the word is not marked by the usual form of the participle in *ing*. The phrase lul-la-by, is the only one in our language, which conveys the evident meaning of the choral term e-we-yea. The substantive verb is wanting, in the first line of b. and the third of c. in the two forms of the verb, to care, or take care of a person; but it is present in the phrase "kediausee" in the second line of c. These facts are stated, not that they are of the slightest interest to the common reader, but that they may be examined by philologists, or persons curious in the Indian grammar.

as his reading of popular literature extends, the tendency of public taste, to avail itself of such a mythology, (notwithstanding those who turn up their nose at it, and affect vast dislike for the "nasty Indians,") and to seize upon it as a basis for the exhibition of new and peculiar lines of fictitious creations, is distinctly perceptible. This is shown in various ways, but takes its most formal shape perhaps, if not its exact era, in a series of legends, which first appeared, a few years ago, in London, under the title of "Wild Scenes in the Prairies and Forest," a volume not as well known as it deserves to be, on this side of the water. This volume is subsequently known to have come from the pen of the author of "Greyslaer," and a "Winter in the West." Mr. Hoffman[1] has looked with the eye of an artist, and the taste of a connoisseur, on the scenes spread before him, in the wide prairies, the towering peaks, the deep matted forests, and the wide winding lakes of the western world. Wherever his view was directed, in that wild theatre of western life, or at the Alpine sources of his native stream, the Hudson, he has seen the footprints of the red man, and felt rising in his mind, the strong associations which the sonorous aboriginal names of streams and places have awakened. It is under such views of western scenery that he has, in his "Vigil of Faith," invested with flesh and blood, an aboriginal theory of a future state, and it is in the same spirit that he has cast his tales and legends, and drawn out his geographical descriptions.

There are also frequent evidences in the diurnal and magazine press of the country, of late years, in a kind of mixed historical legends, of a growing taste on this subject. Writers seem, at intervals, at least, to be more aware of the eminent difficulty of getting laurels by following the old track of Grecian mythology, beaten as that track was by Greece herself, and smoothed and polished as it has subsequently been by Roman and English and Continental authors. Germany, has to a great extent, reinvigorated ancient literature, and made it national and peculiar, by an appeal to her own myths and popular legends, while our writers, for the most part, are yet endeavoring to re-do, re-enact, and re-produce, what the bards

---

1   Charles Fenno Hoffman (1806–84), author of *Wild Scenes in the Forest and Prairie: With Sketches of American Life* (1840), *Greyslaer: A Romance of the Mohawk* (1840), *A Winter in the West* (1835), and *The Vigil of Faith, and Other Poems* (1842).

and essayists of England alone have forever settled, and rendered it hopeless to eclipse. Originality of literature, if it can be produced in the West, as the critics of Europe leave us room to think, must rely on the scenes, associations, and institutions of the West. Nor will American literature, we apprehend, ever command the attention and receive the sealing approbation of the old world, while it is either built with the materials or dressed out and adorned with the cast off literary decorations of her own authors.

These remarks refer exclusively to an imaginative literature, and have no relation to subjects of science. The defects which have been noticed, in the wide and scattered range of American magazines, and other periodicals, in city and country, east and west, exist in verbosity and redundant description, false sentiment, and erroneous manners. Most of the attempts noticed, at the same time exhibit vigour, and some talent, but they fail strikingly in those essentials of mental *costume*. They are, to characterize them by a stroke, English figures, drest[1] in moccasins, and holding a bow and arrows.

To render an Indian tale successful, Indian manners, and sentiments, and opinions must be accurately copied. Above all, the Indian mythology and superstitions, as shown in their religious rites and ceremonies, must be observed. It is this mythology that furnishes the poetic *machinery* of the native fictions. It does more. It furnishes the true theory of their mental philosophy, and lies at the foundation of their often strange and unaccountable acts and policy. It is by the power of Indian *manitoes*[2] and the Indian JEESUKAWIN,[3] that all their wonders and impossibilities are performed.

The chief points of failure, in the mere literary execution of attempted Indian legends, consist in want of simplicity, conciseness and brevity. Nothing can exceed the doric[4] simplicity of an aboriginal tale. It admits of scarcely any adjectives, and no ornaments. A figure of speech, or a symbol is employed, in cases where comparisons and illustrations, would be used in English composition, or where the native language falls short in words. But ordinary scenes and desires, are expressed in ordinary words. The closest attention, indeed, is required, in listening to, and taking notes of an original

---

1   Dressed.
2   Spirit beings.
3   Art of prophecy.
4   Rustic.

legend, to find language simple and child-like enough to narrate what is said, and to give it, *as said*, word by word, and sentence by sentence. A school boy, who is not yet smitten with the ambition of style, but adheres to the natural method, of putting down no more words than are just necessary to express the precise ideas, would do it best. And when this has been done, and the original preserved in the words of the Indian story teller, it is often but a tissue of common events which would possess very little interest, were it not for the mystery or melodramic effect, of their singular mythology. To imitate such a tale successfully, is to demand of the writer an accurate knowledge of Indian manners and customs, often his history and traditions, and always his religion and opinions, with some gleams of the language.

In the introduction of the following legend of the origin of the Evil Spirit,[1] it is only justice to it to say, that the false theory and defects alluded to, as marking the popular effort of writers, have been avoided both in manner and matter, to a degree which surpasses any thing of the kind, which has fallen under our notice. It is in fact, completely successful, and furnishes a model for things of the kind. It is true to the Indian myths—it possesses the appropriate simplicity of thought. It proceeds by the true modus operandi of the natives of telling the story. Its reasonings are not a white man's reasonings. It depicts the Great Spirit, as being characterized not by christian attributes, but by the reasons and caprices of a man. He makes things to please himself, not knowing exactly what they will be, and when they do not strike his fancy, he casts them aside and makes others. He never sees the end from the beginning. He is always trying and trying and "making and making." He is the impersonation in mind, of a perfect Indian philosopher, who only sees and hears, and tastes and desires, like any other Indian. He pitches a lump of clay in the water, and it becomes an island. He casts an old woman against the moon, and there she sticks to this day. (Vide[2] Wyandot Traditions of Good and Evil, No. 3.) He does not reveal any traits—any high moralities—anything approaching to the innate holiness of the immaculate Alohim.[3] He is the veritable Indian master of life—the

---

1   Oakes Smith's "Machinito, The Evil Spirit," included in this volume, pp. 215–21.
2   See; consult (Latin).
3   Elohim; a Hebrew name for God.

great Wäzheaud or maker; and the idea which Mrs. Smith has eliminated, that Machineto, or the God of Evil, was accidentally created out of the leavings and cast away things of the Creator, helped out with the ravenous and venomous creatures of the sea and land, is a poetical conception worthy the pencil of Salvator Rosa,[1] or the pen of Dante.[2] We commend it to the pencil of Chapman.[3]

5. Elizabeth Oakes Smith, "Mrs. Henry R. Schoolcraft," *Baldwin's Monthly* 8.3 (March 1874): 2

[Oakes Smith's sketch of Jane Johnston Schoolcraft provides a glimpse of both her personal and professional interactions with the Schoolcrafts (see Introduction, p. 27–35).]

Among the celebrities of New York, twenty years ago, was the Schoolcraft family. Every one familiar with American literature is aware how much our writers of Indian legends are indebted to Henry R. Schoolcraft for the material of their works. He had passed thirty years upon the frontier, living with the Western tribes in the most familiar manner, as United States Agent. He had studied, as no one else in the country has done, their habits, their mental characteristics, their language and mythology. His Indian vocabulary is a mine of suggestive thought, and his *Algic Researches*[4] one of the most interesting books of the kind ever written. In the production of this work he was largely indebted to his wife, whose Indian blood, and wild wood imagination revelled in the poetic side of the Indian character.

Mr. Schoolcraft was born in Guilderlead,[5] Albany Country, N.Y., March 28, 1793. He must have been a precocious youth, having entered college at fifteen. When I knew him he was a large, heavy man, fond of talking upon his frontier experiences, and re-

---

1 Salvator Rosa (1615–73), an Italian painter, printmaker, poet, and satirist.
2 Dante Alighieri (1265–1321), a major Italian poet.
3 American artist John Gadsby Chapman (1808–89), whose *Baptism of Pocahontas* (1840) in the US Capitol rotunda is among his works depicting Native Americans.
4 *Algic Researches, Comprising Inquiries Respecting the Mental Characteristics of the North American Indians.* 2 vols. (New York: Harper & Brothers, 1839).
5 The correct name of the town is Guilderland.

lating Indian legends. I had read with delight the *Algic Researches*, and the first stanzas of my poem, "The Acorn," embodied the idea of the Puckwudjies, or Little Vanishers, as gathered from his work. In a note also, I had enlarged upon the idea, tracing the word Puck, supposed to be Shakespearean, to the Algonquin language. Julian C. Verplank, in the notes to his edition of Shakespeare,[1] so unfortunately lost in the great fire which subsequently destroyed the printing-house of the Harpers, had been so struck with this view that he had embodied it into his notes of "The Midsummer Night's Dream." It was thus, from a certain sympathy of thought, some kind friends brought Mr. Schoolcraft to see me. He had published several numbers of a magazine, illustrative of Indian thought and life, and desired me to furnish him an article. I did so, writing "A Legend of Ronkonkomon Lake, Long Island; or, The Origin of Evil."[2] This attracted some considerable notice at the time, and Mr. Schoolcraft declared it "truly Indian," with much more, in an appreciative vein; but what was much to me, it brought me the acquaintance and friendship of that remarkable woman, his wife.

Henry R. Schoolcraft and his brother George had married two sisters,[3] granddaughters of Sir William Johnston, the grandmother being Molly Brant, the sister of Thayendenegea,[4] so celebrated in the annals of our war for Independence. I had the impression that these two sisters were daughters of Sir William and Molly Brant, but I am told in this I must be mistaken. Mrs. Schoolcraft always spoke of her mother as a Mohawk Queen, and spoke of her with admiration. The sisters were educated in France, and were quite accomplished. Mrs. Henry R. spoke the Algonquin, French and

---

1 Gulian C. Verplanck (1786–1870) created the first fully illustrated edition in America, *Shakespeare's Plays: With His Life*, published in three volumes by Harper & Brothers in New York between 1844 and 1847.
2 See "Machinito, The Evil Spirit" and Appendix D4.
3 Anna Maria Johnston Schoolcraft or Omiskabugoqyay (1814–56) married James Schoolcraft (c. 1807–46), not "George."
4 Thayendanegea (also spelled Tyendinaga) or Joseph Brant (c. 1742–1807), a Mohawk war chief and British ally. Oakes Smith is mistaken in linking the Johnston sisters, whose father John Johnston was born in Ireland, to Sir William Johnston. Their mother, Susan Johnston or Ozhaguscodaywayquay, was the daughter of the Ojibwe chief Waubojeeg, and thus an important figure but not a "Mohawk Queen."

English languages fluently, and read Latin, Greek and Hebrew. Both played the piano, and conversed with vivacity and taste. They dressed much in the prevailing fashion, varied with admirable skill, just enough to present a *soupçon* of the Indian wild wood, if by nothing more than a belt of wampum. Their complexions were a clear olive, with a slight touch of color, only when animated. The hair was purple black, very abundant and very straight, growing quite low upon a broad, smooth forehead. Mrs. Henry was rather above ordinary height, straight and slender, with a graceful, easy motion, and, like her people, with very small feet and hands. Her mouth was flexible, of a good width, and very soft and sweet in expression, and with white even teeth when she smiled, was a most attractive feature. I have observed the softness of the mouth is characteristic of the aborigines of our country as described, or rather hinted at, by Halleck in "Red Jacket:"[1]

"Who will believe that, with a smile whose blessing
  Would, like the Patriarch's, soothe a dying hour,
With voice as low, as gentle and careening,
  As e'er was maiden's lip in moonlit bower;

With look, like patient Job's, eschewing evil;
  With motions graceful as a bird's in air;
Thou art, in sober truth, the veriest devil,
  That e'er clenched fingers in a captive's hair."

It would not be possible to rightly describe Mrs. Schoolcraft's eyes. They were deep-set, of a dark gray, deepening in emotion to black, the lid large and clear; but there was, when at rest, a look of intense sadness, and when she broke the silence after this expression, her voice was a musical sigh, a something like an echo dying out, which was very touching. I have noticed this cadence in more than one Indian; but never in the negro, whatever his status.

Speaking of the beautiful softness of the mouth pertaining to the Indian, reminds me that it is exactly that which art has given

---

1   Fitz-Greene Halleck (1790–1867). Red Jacket, born Otetiani and renamed Sagoyewatha (c. 1758–1830), a Seneca chief and renowned orator.

to the Apollo, and the general contour must be such, as is evident from the exclamation of the artist West on first seeing the Apollo Belvedere,[1] he being quite moved out of his Quaker propriety by uttering, "My God! how like a Mohawk Chief." No amount of culture takes this away, or imparts that anxious compression of the lips that follows civilization. I noticed this in Dr. Wilson, an educated Indian of Cattaraugus,[2] and I noticed too, that these men and women, like persons of genius, who go back in a way to the aboriginal, delight in whatever carries them home to the Indian life.

There was a group of disinterested persons at my house one evening, among whom was Dr. Wilson, the Schoolcrafts, and others; all of whom talked with animation, but I observed the Doctor seemed ill at ease in our ordinary drawing-room chairs, his bulky figure quite protruding over them, and testing their strength fearfully. One of the guests queried whether cigars would be objectionable. Of course not, but the Doctor was provided with a pipe, which I begged him to consider a calumet, and smoke with an eye to comfort. He at once settled his head down into his collar, much as Horace Greeley[3] used to do preparatory to a sleep in church, and began to pour out volumes of smoke. I am sure he thought me a very obliging white "Squaw," for indulging him in his native luxury. We had some recitations after this, and I called upon the Doctor for a war-whoop. Our guests seconded the call, and the Doctor's eyes flashed an old primeval fire, such as had inspired the tribes to battle for long centuries. He implied that it was too much, that it would frighten us all, but I had heard it in a large hall from Catlin,[4] who was as lithe and springy as a leopard, and had hardly calculated upon its effect from a heavier physique. He threw back his shoulders,

---

1   The painter Benjamin West (1738–1820) encountering the renowned Roman sculpture known as the *Apollo Belvedere*.

2   Dr. Peter Wilson (d. 1871), a Cayuga who worked for a time on the Cattaraugus reservation.

3   Horace Greeley (1811–72), founder and editor of the *New York Tribune*, the newspaper in which Oakes Smith first published *Woman and Her Needs* (see Appendix A2).

4   George Catlin (1796–1872), American artist who specialized in portraits of American Indians.

sprang forward, and beginning low, rose to a fearful yell—so deep that it made me think of a lion's roar—so intense that the windows rattled. These Indians are apt to go back to their original wildness, and I could not but suspect, that a few repetitions of the war-whoop might suggest to him the propriety of taking our scalps.

Some twenty years ago a young English girl fell desperately in love with one of these handsome, educated savages, and married him; but he eventually developed a playful fancy of seizing her by the scalp-lock and waking her from a sound sleep with a war-whoop, which so preyed upon her nerves that she escaped from him and made her way back to her friends. These marriages of different races rarely ever prove fortunate.

At the time Lord Morpeth (Earl of Carlisle) was traveling in this country[1] Mrs. Schoolcraft came one morning to invite me to join the party on the western tour. How grave, and yet how breezy and earnest were her importunities, so unlike our hackneyed conventionality!

"Go with us," she said, "and you shall be paddled down the Saut St. Marie,[2] in the handsomest canoe, and by the handsomest Indian of the West;" and again she reiterated, "You have an Indian soul, all that an Indian exults in would speak to your mind, you should go to the sources of the Mississippi, which my husband was the first to discover, and we would talk over those rare old mythologies, so little known and appreciated by white people. You will delight to hear the language of the Indian spoken in the midst of the waterfalls and mountains; listen:" she raised her eyes and with wonderful pathos, and solemn depth of intonation, uttered what caused cold chills to run down my back and my breath to stop with awe.

"What was it?" I whispered.

"Our Lord's Prayer in Algonquin."

How handsome—how inspired she looked! How much would

---

1   Lord Morpeth, George Willliam Frederick Howard, seventh Earl of Carlisle (1802–64), was a British politician, writer, and orator who traveled in the US and Canada in 1841–42.

2   Sault Sainte Marie, the rapids of the Saint Marys River, where the river leaves Lake Superior and forms the Canada-United States border between the twin cities of Sault Ste. Marie, Ontario, and Sault Ste. Marie, Michigan.

women gain could they so far forget civilized training as to be thoroughly true and in earnest.

Mrs. Schoolcraft delighted to recite the legends of her people, and would playfully, sometimes, when her listener was fully absorbed, go off into Algonquin, which had a most musical sound. She was, unquestionably, nearly, if not quite, the author of the *Algic Researches.*

Works Cited and Select Bibliography

Primary Texts

Anonymous (Winkfield, Unca Eliza [pseud.]). *The Female American*. 1767. Ed. Michelle Burnham. 2nd ed. Peterborough, ON: Broadview P, 2014.

Child, Lydia Maria. *An Appeal for the Indians*. New York: William P. Tomlinson, 1868.

——. *The First Settlers of New-England: or, Conquest of the Pequods, Narragansets and Pokanokets. As Related by a Mother to Her Children*. Boston: Munroe and Francis, 1829.

——. *Hobomok, A Tale of Early Times*. Boston: Cummings, Hilliard, & Co., 1824.

——. *Hobomok and Other Writings on Indians*. Ed. Carolyn L. Karcher. New Brunswick, NJ; Rutgers UP, 1986.

Cooper, James Fenimore. *The Leatherstocking Tales, Vol. 1: The Pioneers (1823), The Last of the Mohicans (1826), The Prairie (1827)*. New York: Library of America, 1985.

——. *The Leatherstocking Tales, Vol. 2: The Pathfinder (1840), The Deerslayer (1841)*. New York: Library of America, 1985.

——. *The Wept of Wish-ton-Wish: A Tale*. Philadelphia: Carey, Lea & Carey, 1829.

Derounian-Stodola, Kathryn Zabelle, ed. *Women's Indian Captivity Narratives*. New York: Penguin, 1998.

Dumont, Julia Louisa. *"Tecumseh" and Other Stories of the Ohio River Valley*. Ed. Sandra Parker. Bowling Green, OH: Bowling Green U Popular P, 2000.

Frost, John. *Thrilling Adventures Among the Indians: Comprising the Most Remarkable Personal Narratives of Events in the Early Indian Wars, as Well as of Incidents in the Recent Indian Hostilities in Mexico and Texas*. Philadelphia: J.W. Bradley, 1849.

Fuller, S. Margaret. *The Essential Margaret Fuller*. Ed. Jeffrey Steele. Rutgers: Rutgers UP, 1992.

——. "The Great Lawsuit. Man versus Men. Woman versus Women." *The Dial* 4 (July 1843): 1–47.

——. *Summer on the Lakes, in 1843*. Boston: Little and Brown; New York: Charles S. Francis & Co., 1844.

——. *Woman in the Nineteenth Century*. New York: Greeley & McElrath, 1845.

Haefeli, Evan and Kevin Sweeney. *Captive Histories: English, French, and Native Narratives of the 1704 Deerfield Raid*. Amherst and Boston: U of Massachusetts P, 2006.

Hall, James. "The Indian Hater." In *The Western Souvenir: A Christmas and New Year's Gift for 1829*. Ed. James Hall. Cincinnati: N. and G. Guilford, 1828. 256–72.

——. "The Pioneer." In *Tales of the Border*. Philadelphia: Harrison Hall, 1835. 13–101.

Hoffman, Charles Fenno. *Greyslaer; a Romance of the Mohawk*. 2 vols. New York: Harper & Brothers, 1840.

——. *The Vigil of Faith, and Other Poems*. New York: S. Colman, 1842.

——. *Wild Scenes in Forest and Prairie*. 2 vols. London: Richard Bentley, 1839. New York: William H. Colyer, 1843.

——. *A Winter in the West*. 2 vols. New York: Harper & Brothers, 1835.

Hunter, John Dunn. *Memoirs of a Captivity among the Indians of North America, from Childhood to the Age of Nineteen: With Anecdotes Descriptive of Their Manners and Customs*. 3rd ed. London: Longman, Hurst, Rees, Orme, Brown, and Green, 1823.

Jackson, Helen Hunt. *A Century of Dishonor: A Sketch of the United States Government's Dealings with Some of the Indian Tribes*. New York: Harper & Brothers, 1881.

——. *Ramona*. 1884. Ed. Siobhan Senier. Peterborough, ON: Broadview P, 2008.

Longfellow, Henry Wadsworth. *The Song of Hiawatha*. Boston: Ticknor and Fields, 1855.

Rowson, Susanna. *Reuben and Rachel; or, Tales of Old Times*. 1798. Ed. Joseph F. Bartolomeo. Peterborough, ON: Broadview P, 2009.

Schoolcraft, Henry Rowe. *Algic Researches, Comprising Inquiries Respecting the Mental Characteristics of the North American Indians*. 2 vols. New York: Harper & Brothers, 1839.

——. *The American Indians, Their Condition, History, and Prospects. From Original Notes and Manuscripts*. Buffalo: George H. Derby & Co., 1851.

——. *The Indian in His Wigwam, or Characteristics of the Red Race of America. From Original Notes and Manuscripts.* New York: Dewitt & Davenport, 1848.

——. *Oneóta, or Characteristics of the Red Race of America. From Original Notes and Manuscripts.* New York and London: Wiley and Putnam, 1845.

——. *Travels in the Central Portions of the Mississippi Valley: Comprising Observations on Its Mineral Geography, Internal Resources, and Aboriginal Population.* New York: Collins and Hannay, 1825.

Schoolcraft, Jane Johnston (Leelinau). "Moowis, The Indian Coquette. A Chippewa Legend." From the manuscript magazine *The Muz-ze-ni-e-gun, or Literary Voyager* 4 (12 January 1827). Henry Rowe Schoolcraft Papers, Manuscript Division, Library of Congress, Washington, DC. Container 65. Microfilm.

——. *The Sound the Stars Make Rushing Through the Sky: The Writings of Jane Johnston Schoolcraft.* Ed. Robert Dale Parker. Philadelphia: U of Pennsylvania P, 2007.

Seaver, James E. *A Narrative of the Life of Mrs. Mary Jemison.* Canandaigua, NY: J.D. Bemis, 1824.

Sedgwick, Catharine Maria. *Hope Leslie, or Early Times in the Massachusetts.* New York: White, Gallaher, and White, 1827.

Sigourney, Lydia. "The Bell of St. Regis." *Poems.* Philadelphia: Key & Biddle, 1834. 150–51.

——. *Lydia Sigourney: Selected Poetry and Prose.* Ed. Gary Kelly. Peterborough, ON: Broadview P, 2008.

——. *Pocahontas, and Other Poems.* New York: Harper & Brothers, 1841.

——. *Traits of the Aborigines of America: A Poem.* Cambridge: Hilliard & Metcalf, 1822.

Smith, Elizabeth Oakes. "The Acorn." *Dew-drops of the Nineteenth Century: Gathered and Preserved in Their Brightness and Purity.* Ed. Seba Smith. New York: J.K. Wellman, 1846. 146–55.

——. *Bald Eagle, or the Last of the Ramapaughs: A Romance of Revolutionary Times.* New York: Beadle & Adams, 1867.

——. "Beloved of the Evening Star." *The Opal for 1847: A Pure Gift for the Holydays.* Ed. John Keese. New York: J.C. Riker, 1847. 45–59.

——. *Bertha and Lily, Or, the Parsonage of Beech Glen: A Romance.* New York: J.C. Derby, 1854.

——. "Correspondence of the Advertiser" [Route to Katahdin]. *Portland Daily Advertiser* 19 (12, 15, 26 September; 8 October 1849): 2.

——. "The Crusade of the Bell." *Potter's American Monthly* 4.43 (July 1875): 518–20.

——. *The Dandelion.* Boston: Saxon and Kelt, 1846.

——. *Hints on Dress and Beauty.* New York: Fowler & Wells, 1852.

——. "Hobomok: A Legend of Maine." *The Rover* 2.2 (1843): 175–76.

——. *A Human Life: Being the Autobiography of Elizabeth Oakes Smith.* N.d. (c. 1885). MS. Elizabeth Oakes Prince Smith Papers, c. 1834–1893. New York Public Library, Manuscripts and Archives Division.

——. "'A Human Life: Being the Autobiography of Elizabeth Oakes Smith': A Critical Edition and Introduction." Ed. Leigh Kirkland. Diss. Georgia State U, 1994.

——. "Indian Traits: The Story of Niskagah." *The Ladies' Companion* 13 (July 1840): 141–44.

——. *The Keepsake: A Wreath of Poems and Sonnets.* New York: Leavitt, 1845.

——. "Kinneho: A Legend of Moosehead Lake." *Godey's Magazine and Lady's Book* 42 (1851): 175–79.

——. Letter to Jane L. [Johnston] Schoolcraft, 25 April 1842. Henry Rowe Schoolcraft Papers, Manuscript Division, Library of Congress, Washington, DC. Container 46. Microfilm.

——. "Machinito, The Evil Spirit; From the Legends of Iagou." In *Oneóta, or Characteristics of the Red Race of America. From Original Notes and Manuscripts,* by Henry Schoolcraft. New York and London: Wiley and Putnam, 1845. 248–53.

——, ed. *The Mayflower for MDCCCXLVII.* Boston: Saxon and Kelt, 1847.

——, ed. *The Mayflower for MDCCCXLVIII.* Boston: Saxon and Kelt, 1848.

——. *The Moss Cup.* Boston: Saxon and Kelt, 1846.

——. "Mrs. Henry R. Schoolcraft," *Baldwin's Monthly* 8.3 (March 1874): 2.

——. *The Newsboy.* New York: J.C. Derby; Boston: Phillips, Sampson & Co., 1854.

——. *Old New York: or, Democracy in 1689; a Tragedy, in Five Acts.* New York: Stringer & Townsend, 1853.

——. *The Poetical Writings of Elizabeth Oakes Smith.* New York: J.S. Redfield, 1845.

———. *Riches Without Wings; or, the Cleveland Family.* Boston: George W. Light, 1838.

———. *The Sagamore of Saco.* New York: Beadle & Adams, 1868.

———. "The Sagamore of Saco: A Legend of Maine" *Graham's Magazine* 33 (July 1848): 47–52.

———. *The Salamander: A Legend for Christmas. Found Amongst the Papers of the Late Ernest Helfenstein* [pseud.]. New York and London: Putnam, 1848. Republished as *Mary and Hugo: or, The Lost Angel: A Christmas Legend.* New York: Derby and Jackson; Cincinnati: H.W. Derby, 1857.

———. *Sanctity of Marriage.* Syracuse: Lathrop's Print, 1852.

———. *Shadow Land; or, The Seer.* New York: Fowler and Wells, 1852.

———. "The Sinless Child: A Poem, in Seven Parts." *Southern Literary Messenger* 8.1–2 (January–February 1842): 86–89, 121–29.

———. *The Sinless Child, and Other Poems.* Ed. John Keese. New York: Wiley & Putnam; Boston: Ticknor, 1843.

———. *Stories for Good Children* [*The Dandelion, The Moss Cup, and The Rose Bud, or the True Child*]. Buffalo, NY: George H. Derby, 1851.

———. *The True Child.* Boston: Saxon and Kelt, 1845.

———. *The Western Captive; or, The Times of Tecumseh. The New World* 2.3–4 (October 1842; Extra Series, nos. 27–28): 1–39.

———. *Woman and Her Needs.* New York: Fowler and Wells, 1851.

Smith, Seba. *Powhatan; A Metrical Romance, in Seven Cantos.* New York: Harper & Brothers, 1841.

———. "Squando, the Indian Sachem." *Dew-drops of the Nineteenth Century: Gathered and Preserved in Their Brightness and Purity.* Ed. Seba Smith. New York: J.K. Wellman, 1846. 156–70.

Stanton, Elizabeth Cady, and Susan B. Anthony. *The Selected Papers of Elizabeth Cady Stanton & Susan B. Anthony. Vol. 1: In the School of Antislavery, 1840–1866.* Ed. Ann D. Gordon. New Brunswick, NJ: Rutgers UP, 1997.

Stephens, Ann S. *Ahmo's Plot; or, The Governor's Indian Child.* New York: Beadle and Adams, 1863.

———. *The Indian Queen.* New York: Beadle and Adams, 1864.

———. *Mahaska, the Indian Princess: A Tale of the Six Nations.* New York: Beadle, 1863.

———. *Malaeska, the Indian Wife of the White Hunter.* New York: Beadle, 1860.

——. *Mary Derwent*. Philadelphia: T.B. Peterson, 1858.

Tanner, John. *A Narrative of the Captivity and Adventures of John Tanner, (U.S. Interpreter at the Saut de Ste. Marie,) During Thirty Years' Residence Among the Indians in the Interior of North America*. London: Baldwin & Cradock, 1830.

Thoreau, Henry David. *The Maine Woods*. Boston: Ticknor and Fields, 1864.

——. *Walden; or, Life in the Woods*. Boston: Ticknor and Fields, 1854.

Whittier, John Greenleaf. *Mogg Megone: A Poem*. Boston: Light & Stearns, 1836.

Wyman, Mary Alice [and Elizabeth Oakes Smith]. *Selections from the Autobiography of Elizabeth Oakes Smith*. Lewiston, ME: Lewiston Journal Company, 1924.

Zitkala-Sa [Gertrude Bonnin]. *American Indian Stories*. 1921. *American Indian Stories, Legends, and Other Writings*. Ed. Cathy N. Davidson and Ada Norris. New York: Penguin, 2003.

Secondary Sources: History and Biography

Berkhofer, Robert F., Jr. *The White Man's Indian: Images of the American Indian from Columbus to the Present*. New York: Knopf, 1978.

Burr, Samuel Jones. *The Life and Times of William Henry Harrison*. New York: L.W. Ransom, 1840.

Dawson, Moses. *A Historical Narrative of the Civil and Military Services of Major-General William H. Harrison, and a Vindication of His Character and Conduct as a Statesman, a Citizen, and a Soldier. With a Detail of His Negotiations and Wars with the Indians, until the Final Overthrow of the Celebrated Chief Tecumseh, and His Brother the Prophet*. Cincinnati: M. Dawson, 1824.

Demos, John. *The Unredeemed Captive: A Family Story from Early America*. New York: Knopf, 1994.

Dills, R.S. *History of Greene County, Together with Historic Notes on the Northwest, and the State of Ohio*. Dayton, OH: Odell & Mayer, 1881.

Dowd, Gregory Evans. *A Spirited Resistance: The North American Indian Struggle for Unity, 1745–1815*. Baltimore: Johns Hopkins UP, 1992.

Drake, Benjamin. *Life of Tecumseh, and of His Brother the Prophet; With a Historical Sketch of the Shawanoe Indians*. Cincinnati: E. Morgan, 1841.

Drinnon, Richard. *Facing West: The Metaphysics of Indian-Hating and Empire-Building*. Minneapolis: U of Minnesota P, 1980.

——. *White Savage: The Case of John Hunter*. New York: Schocken Books, 1972.

Edmunds, R. David. *The Shawnee Prophet*. Lincoln: U of Nebraska P, 1983.

——. *Tecumseh and the Quest for Indian Leadership*. Boston: Little, Brown, and Company, 1984.

Folsom, George. *History of Saco and Biddleford, with Notices of Other Early Settlements, in Maine, Including the Provinces of New Somersetshire and Lygonia*. Saco, ME: Alex C. Putnam, 1830.

Foxe, John. *Fox's Original and Complete Book of Martyrs; or, An Universal History of Martyrdom. Actes and Monuments of these Latter and Perillous Days, Touching Matters of the Church, 1563*. London: Alexander Hogg, 1795.

Hall, James. *A Memoir of the Public Services of William Henry Harrison, of Ohio*. Philadelphia: Key & Biddle, 1836.

Klinck, Carl F. *Tecumseh: Fact and Fiction in Early Records*. Englewood Cliffs, NJ: Prentice Hall, 1961.

Martin, Joel W. *Sacred Revolt: The Muskogees' Struggle for a New World*. Boston: Beacon Press, 1991.

McAfee, Robert B. *History of the Late War in the Western Country, Comprising a Full Account of All the Transaction in That Quarter, from the Commencement of Hostilities at Tippecanoe, to the Termination of the Contest at New Orleans on the Return of Peace*. Lexington: Worsley and Smith, 1816.

McKenney, Thomas L. *History of the Indian Tribes of North America*. Vol. I. Philadelphia: D. Rice, 1836.

——. "Petalesharro." *History of the Indian Tribes of North America*. 143–52.

——. "Tenskwautawaw." *History of the Indian Tribes of North America*. 47–67.

Namias, June. *White Captives: Gender and Ethnicity on the American Frontier*. Chapel Hill: U of North Carolina P, 1993.

Oaksmith, Appleton. Letter to Ulysses S. Grant, 25 September 1869. In Ulysses S. Grant, *The Papers of Ulysses S. Grant. Volume 19: July 1 1868–October 31, 1869*. Ed. John Y. Simon. Carbondale: Southern Illinois UP, 1994. 538–40.

Rugeley, Terry. "Savage and Statesman: Changing Historical Interpretations of Tecumseh." *Indiana Magazine of History* 85.4 (December 1989): 289–311.

Stanton, Elizabeth Cady, Susan B. Anthony, and Matilda Joslyn Gage. *History of Woman Suffrage.* 3 vols. Vol. 1: 1848–1861. New York: Fowler and Wells, 1881. Vol. 2: 1861–1876. New York: Fowler and Wells, 1882. Vol. 3: 1876–1885. Rochester, NY: Susan B. Anthony, 1886.

Stevens, Kenneth R. *William Henry Harrison: A Bibliography.* Westport, CT: Greenwood P, 1998.

Sugden, John. *Tecumseh, A Life.* New York: Henry Holt, 1997.

———. *Tecumseh's Last Stand.* Norman: U of Oklahoma P, 1985.

TePaske, John J. "Appleton Oaksmith, Filibuster Agent." *North Carolina Historical Review* 35.4 (October 1958): 427–47.

Thatcher, Benjamin Bussey. *Indian Biography: or, An historical account of those individuals who have been distinguished among the North American natives as orators, warriors, statesmen, and other remarkable characters.* 2 vols. New York: J. and J. Harper, 1832.

Tucker, Glenn. *Tecumseh: Vision of Glory.* Indianapolis: Bobbs-Merrill, 1956.

Turner, Frederick Jackson. "The Significance of the Frontier in American History." 1893. Rpt. in *The Frontier in American History.* New York: Henry Holt, 1921. 1–38.

White, Richard. *The Middle Ground: Indians, Empires, and Republics in the Great Lakes Region, 1650–1815.* Cambridge and New York: Cambridge UP, 1991.

Secondary Sources: Literary Criticism

"American Opinions." Review of *Uncle Tom's Cabin* by Harriet Beecher Stowe and *Hints on Dress and Beauty* by Mrs. E. Oakes Smith. *Sharpe's London Magazine of Entertainment and Instruction for General Reading.* Ed. Anna Maria Hall. Vol. 1, New Series. London: Virtue, Hall and Virtue, 1852. 250–54.

Baym, Nina. "Melodramas of Beset Manhood: How Theories of American Fiction Exclude Women Authors." *American Quarterly* 33 (1981): 123–39.

———. *Woman's Fiction: A Guide to Novels by and about Women in America, 1820–1870.* Ithaca, NY: Cornell UP, 1978.

Beam, Dorri. *Style, Gender, and Fantasy in Nineteenth-Century American Women's Writing.* New York: Cambridge UP, 2010.

Castiglia, Christopher. *Bound and Determined: Captivity, Culture-Crossing, and White Womanhood from Mary Rowlandson to Patty Hearst*. Chicago: U of Chicago P, 1996.

Derounian-Stodola, Kathryn Zabelle, ed. Introduction. *Women's Indian Captivity Narratives*. New York: Penguin, 1998. xi–xxviii.

Dickinson, Susan E. "Women Writers. A Chapter on Their Ephemeral Reputations. Hopes and Ambitions That Have Faded in Sad Disappointments." 9 July 1885. Handwritten in margin: *Evening Leader*, Wilkes-Barre, 13 July 1885. N.p. Elizabeth Oakes Prince Smith Papers, c. 1834–1893, New York Public Library, Manuscripts and Archives Division. Loose Clippings in Box 3.

Griswold, Rufus W. *The Prose Writers of America. With a Survey of the History, Condition, and Prospects of American Literature*. 1846. Philadelphia: Carey and Hart, 1847.

Harris, Susan K. *19th-Century American Women's Novels: Interpretive Strategies*. Cambridge: Cambridge UP, 1990.

Hegeman, Susan K. "Native American 'Texts' and the Problem of Authenticity." *American Quarterly* 41.2 (June 1989): 265–83.

Jaroff, Rebecca. "'I Almost Danced Over My Freedom': Elizabeth Oakes Smith's Liberation from the Literary Marketplace." *Popular Nineteenth-Century American Women Writers and the Literary Marketplace*. Ed. Earl Yarington and Mary De Jong. Newcastle upon Tyne, UK: Cambridge Scholars, 2007. 172–88.

Karcher, Carolyn. Introduction. *Hobomok and Other Writings on Indians*. New Brunswick, NJ: Rutgers UP, 1986. ix-xxxviii.

Kelley, Mary. Introduction. *Hope Leslie, or Early Times in the Massachusetts*. New Brunswick, NJ: Rutgers UP, 1987. ix-xxxvii.

Kete, Mary Louise. "Gender Valences of Transcendentalism: The Pursuit of Idealism in Elizabeth Oakes-Smith's 'The Sinless Child.'" *Separate Spheres No More: Gender Convergence in American Literature, 1830–1930*. Ed. Monika M. Elbert. Tuscaloosa, AL: U of Alabama P, 2000. 245–60.

Kirkland, Leigh. "Being an Introduction to *A Human Life: Being the Autobiography of Elizabeth Oakes Smith*." "'A Human Life: Being the Autobiography of Elizabeth Oakes Smith': A Critical Edition and Introduction." Diss. Georgia State University, 1994. 1–67.

———. "Elizabeth Oakes Smith (1806–1893)." *Nineteenth-Century American Women Writers: A Bio-Bibliographical Critical Source-*

book. Ed. Denise D. Knight. Westport, CT: Greenwood, 1997. 324–30.

Kolodny, Annette. "Dancing through the Minefield: Some Observations on the Theory, Practice and Politics of a Feminist Literary Criticism." *Feminist Studies* 6.1 (Spring 1980): 1–25.

———. *The Land Before Her: Fantasy and Experience of the American Frontiers, 1630–1860*. Chapel Hill: U of North Carolina P, 1984.

———. *The Lay of the Land: Metaphor as Experience and History in American Life and Letters*. Chapel Hill: U of North Carolina P, 1975.

Konkle, Maureen. *Writing Indian Nations: Native Intellectuals and the Politics of Historiography, 1827–1863*. Chapel Hill, NC: U of North Carolina P, 2004.

Ljungquist, Kent, and Cameron Nickels. "Elizabeth Oakes Smith on Poe: A Chapter in the Recovery of His Nineteenth-Century Reputation." In *Poe and His Times: The Artist in His Milieu*. Ed. Benjamin F. Fischer. Baltimore: Edgar Allan Poe Society, 1990. 235–46.

Margrave, Veronica. "Elizabeth Oakes Smith (1806–1893)." *Writers of the American Renaissance: An A-Z Guide*. Ed. Denise D. Knight. Westport, CT: Greenwood P, 2003. 277–81.

Namias, June. "Editor's Introduction." *A Narrative of the Life of Mrs. Mary Jemison*. By James E. Seaver. 1824. Norman, OK: U of Oklahoma P, 1992. 3–45.

Nickels, Cameron, and Timothy H. Scherman. "Elizabeth Oakes Smith: The Puritan Feminist." *Femmes de Conscience: Aspects du féminisme américain (1848–1875)*. Ed. Susan Goodman and Daniel Royot. Paris: Presses de la Sorbonne Nouvelle, 1994. 109–26.

Parker, Robert Dale, ed. "Introduction: The World and Writings of Jane Johnston Schoolcraft." *The Sound the Stars Make Rushing Through the Sky: The Writings of Jane Johnston Schoolcraft*. Philadelphia: U of Pennsylvania P, 2007. 1–84.

Poe, Edgar Allan. Review of *The Poetical Writings of Elizabeth Oakes Smith*. *The Broadway Journal* 2.7 (23 August 1845): 103.

———. Review of *The Poetical Writings of Elizabeth Oakes Smith*. *Godey's Lady's Book* 31.6 (December 1845): 261–65. Rpt. in *Edgar Allan Poe: Essays and Reviews*. Ed. G.R. Thompson. New York: Library of America, 1984. 906–17.

Pratt, Mary Louise. "Arts of the Contact Zone." *Profession* (1991): 33–40.

Ray, Angela G. *The Lyceum and Public Culture in the Nineteenth-Century United States.* East Lansing: Michigan State UP, 2005.

———. "Performing Womanhood: The Lyceum Lectures of Elizabeth Oakes Smith." *Society for the Study of American Women Writers Conference,* Philadelphia. 2006. Web.

Read, Thomas Buchanan. *The Female Poets of America: With Portraits, Biographical Notices, and Specimens of Their Writings.* 1848. Philadelphia: E.H. Butler & Co., 1849.

Richards, Eliza. "Elizabeth Oakes Smith's 'unspeakable eloquence.'" *Gender and the Poetics of Reception in Poe's Circle.* Cambridge: Cambridge UP, 2004. 149–90.

Rose, Jane E. "Expanding Woman's Sphere, Dismantling Class, and Building Community: The Feminism of Elizabeth Oakes Smith." *CLA Journal* 45.2 (December 2001): 207–30.

Sayre, Gordon. *The Indian Chief as Tragic Hero: Native Resistance and the Literatures of America, from Moctezuma to Tecumseh.* Chapel Hill: U of North Carolina P, 2005.

Scherman, Timothy H. "Elizabeth Oakes Smith." *Dictionary of Literary Biography (vol. 239): American Women Prose Writers, 1820–1870.* Ed. Amy Hudock and Katharine Rodier. Detroit: Gale Research, 2000. 222–30.

Stickney, Charles. "Two Howitts of America: Two Forgotten Geniuses Once Famous in the World of Letters." *Boston Evening Transcript* 26 May 1894: 7.

Tompkins, Jane. *Sensational Designs: The Cultural Work of American Fiction, 1790–1860.* New York and Oxford: Oxford UP, 1985.

Treuer, David. *Native American Fiction: A User's Manual.* Saint Paul, MN: Graywolf, 2006.

Walker, Cheryl. *The Nightingale's Burden: Women Poets and American Culture before 1900.* Bloomington: Indiana UP, 1982.

Wayne, Tiffany K. *Woman Thinking: Feminism and Transcendentalism in Nineteenth-Century America.* Lanham, MD: Lexington Books, 2005.

Wiltenburg, Joy. "Excerpts from the Diary of Elizabeth Oakes Smith." *Signs* 9.3 (1984): 534–48.

Woidat, Caroline M. "Puritan Daughters and 'Wild' Indians: Elizabeth Oakes Smith's Narratives of Domestic Captivity." *Legacy: A Journal of American Women Writers* 18.1 (2001): 21–34.

Womack, Craig S. *Red on Red: Native American Literary Separatism.* Minneapolis: U of Minnesota P, 1999.

Woodward, Robert H. "Bryant and Elizabeth Oakes Smith: An Unpublished Bryant Letter." *Colby Library Quarterly* 5.4 (December 1959): 69–74.

Wyman, Mary Alice. *Two American Pioneers: Seba Smith and Elizabeth Oakes Smith.* New York: Columbia UP, 1927.

Yagelski, Robert. "A Rhetoric of Contact: Tecumseh and the Native American Confederacy." *Rhetoric Review* 14.1 (Autumn 1995): 64–77.

From the Publisher

A name never says it all, but the word "Broadview" expresses a good deal of the philosophy behind our company. We are open to a broad range of academic approaches and political viewpoints. We pay attention to the broad impact book publishing and book printing has in the wider world; we began using recycled stock more than a decade ago, and for some years now we have used 100% recycled paper for most titles. Our publishing program is internationally oriented and broad-ranging. Our individual titles often appeal to a broad readership too; many are of interest as much to general readers as to academics and students.

Founded in 1985, Broadview remains a fully independent company owned by its shareholders—not an imprint or subsidiary of a larger multinational.

For the most accurate information on our books (including information on pricing, editions, and formats) please visit our website at www.broadviewpress.com. Our print books and ebooks are also available for sale on our site.

On the Broadview website we also offer several goods that are not books—among them the Broadview coffee mug, the Broadview beer stein (inscribed with a line from Geoffrey Chaucer's *Canterbury Tales*), the Broadview fridge magnets (your choice of philosophical or literary), and a range of T-shirts (made from combinations of hemp, bamboo, and/or high-quality pima cotton, with no child labor, sweatshop labor, or environmental degradation involved in their manufacture).

All these goods are available through the "merchandise" section of the Broadview website. When you buy Broadview goods you can support other goods too.

broadview press
www.broadviewpress.com

The interior of this book is printed on 100% recycled paper.